I0831276

The Content of Things Undone

Herina Ayot

Published by Reewrite Publishing Group

Cover Design: Lindsay Trezza of Juneberry Creative

First Printing: 2016

ISBN: 978-0-578-18728-0

Reewrite Publishing Group
152 Randolph Avenue
Jersey City, NJ 07305

www.herinaayot.com

For the ones who taught me how to love

"The search is the meaning, the search for beauty, love, kindness and restoration in this difficult, wired and often alien modern world. The miracle is that we are here, that no matter how undone we've been the night before, we wake up every morning and are still here. It is phenomenal just to be"

~Excerpt From: Lamott, Anne. "Stitches." Penguin Group, USA, 2013-09-23. iBooks.

Prologue

1967

The screams had ceased and now there was only the sound of leather against flesh signaling either extraordinary strength or death. There was no way to be sure which. The girl sat motionless against her headboard and counted the seconds on the pocketwatch Luther had given her summer before last.

Eight hundred eighty two. Eight hundred eighty three. The beatings never lasted this many seconds. The walls vibrated with each stroke of love disguised as hate, the struggle on the other side splintering wood and busting seams. The wallpaper, a pale shade of pink was peeling at its edges. Worn and tattered. It had seen many days, many beatings, the weight of agony bearing down on its fabric.

Eight hundred ninety one. Ninety two. Ninety three. The watch really was beautiful, 14 carat solid gold all the way through, a regal pattern embroidered around its rim. Peering into its face was like seeing through time, a make believe world that boasted of chocolate candy, boys who played nice, and terribly sad movies with happy endings.

The reason was never a good one as if there could be a good reason to beat the boy so viciously. She had watched the man sit back in his chair, puff on his pipe as he normally did, and ask the boy for the tool. He said the socket wrench was in the basement in a black metal tool box beside the water heater. It wasn't the question that invoked tension for tension was a constant when Luther was home. But, the girl would be leaving soon just weeks from her high school graduation. She wished the summer to be a swift one and yet a slow one at once. *What about the younger ones. What about Momma?*

When the boy disappeared beneath the basement steps and reappeared nearly twenty minutes later empty handed, the girl's heart sped. Momma had gone to Bible study down at the church and had taken the other girls with her and there was no one there for the boy.

"What took so long?" The man boomed. Luther sounded like God spewing out his wrath when he searched for Adam and the woman in the Garden after the great big fall. They hid themselves and covered up with leaves and branches to hide their nakedness. But they couldn't hide from God. And Luther knew the answer before he asked the question.

The boy had stood with his hands at his side, eyes glued to his father's, his breath caught in his belly. He admitted defeat. "I can't find it, Daddy."

The girl had jumped from her seat at the kitchen table. "I'll help you. Let's look again."

"Sit down," Luther thundered. Then he got up, fixed his red suspenders on his shoulders, cursed the boy with his eyes, sauntered past him and stomped down the stairs.

The boy's mouth contorted, his eyes frozen in terror, his cheeks a blood red. The girl, sat motionless, searching her mind for some solution. She hoped for a distraction, a telephone call, a knock on the door, the second coming of Christ.

When the man emerged seconds later, bearing with him the infamous socket wrench, he held it to the boy's head and said, "I should beat you with this." Instead he opted for the leather belt kept above the refrigerator, and ordered the girl out with a single word. "Leave."

She would grab the cast iron skillet atop the stove and swing it mercilessly at his head. Or run out the door to Mrs. Jameson's place across the street. "He's gone kill him," she'd say. Or she would run down to the basement behind the bookshelf and pull out Daddy's hunting rifle that she knew he kept there secretly and shoot him dead like he was nothing more than the deer he hunts. All of these thoughts entered her mind that day but the girl simply stood up, walked to her bedroom in the back and shut the door tight.

Nine hundred. She lay down on her side facing the window that faced a tan house, with red trim. Slightly faded, siding beginning to fall away. At dusk, as it was, only the silhouette of the house shown, the red more of a dark shadow. The sky was cloudy, the outline of the trees like something out of a spook film. She could still hear him, the man not the boy, but the grunts were drowned out or blurred together like she was underwater falling deeper into oblivion. She didn't fight it, the drowning. It was almost better to accept it. It felt easier. Her eyes welled with fluid, and then a tear flowed over the bridge of her nose, her fat cheek, and moistened the pillow. Without hope. Without reprieve. With no chance of amelioration. The boy's life would be given to the abyss. She wondered if his strength would be enough to sustain him. When she reached Nine hundred and sixety six, it was finished. She heard his boots clunk through the hallway and rest on the inside of his bedroom door. The beating lasted sixteen minutes and six seconds.

The boy was barely seven years old.

The girl got up, peaked out of the slit in her door to see him lying in a ball in the middle of the kitchen floor. She went to him and stroked the side of his cheek, by now a bright pink.

"Are you ok?" she whispered.

Four long seconds later. "I'm ok Gracie. I'm okay."

PART I

Chapter One

I read a news story about a woman who intended to kill her children and then herself, but something went wrong. She poisoned her children and they died a terribly painful death. Then, she poisoned herself, but she survived. Now she's a convicted felon on death row. What scares me is that I understand her predicament.

Summer 2008

"Kericho."

"Kericho."

"Kericho, are you happy here?"

Mrs. Blaney pronounced my name wrong. She stressed the second syllable like the "e" in "reach" instead of like the "i" in "lick". She caught me dosing off in my corner cubicle, my head resting on my fist, black hair hung in my face, and my other hand pressed on my keyboard. I opened my eyes on the second "Kericho", but didn't budge, focusing on the continuous stream of "t's" trailing across my computer screen.

Mrs. Blaney and I were not the same. I went into this industry because I cared about people and feelings and emotions, and I believed there was a place in the world for everyone. Even the head maintenance worker in the North Tower who was a recovering heroin addict trying to stay clean when he lost his life in the 9/11 Attacks. Even him. And his wife who was left to care for 3 children by herself and didn't get any money, or accolades, or even sympathy from the media since they only seemed to care about the higher ups, the CEO's, the CFO's and Managing Directors that perished in The Attacks. Even she mattered in my book.

Death is a very mysterious thing. I was 4 years old when my mother told me the uncle I never met shot himself through the mouth in his parents' basement. She said he couldn't bear the evils of this world. I only saw a handful of pictures and never heard his voice so the only memories I could have of my mother's baby brother were the ones I made up in my own head. There were the facts. He was 19 when he died, the middle of seven children, born to a religious mother and an abusive father. My Auntie Deena was the one who found him on a Sunday afternoon sprawled on the wooden basement floor in a pool of blood, the side of his face blown off with a sawed off shot gun, scattered brain fragments on the walls. Her screams must have enveloped the whole neighborhood.

My grandmother knew it was Jamie when she heard Auntie Deena scream. She said God told her early that morning that a life would be taken. Normally when she got dressed, she stepped into her dresses from the bottom up, but that day, for some reason, she decided to pull her dress over her head. When she closed her eyes, she saw the Kingdom of God, heaven and its pearly gates. And then she knew. First she thought her own life would be taken that day but she prayed to God to spare her reminding Him that of her 7 children, she still had two that were yet growing and needed a mother to guide them along the way. Maybe God considered her prayer and took Jamie instead, or maybe Jamie was the one God had in mind all along. Either way, Jamie was gone and all my mother had to show me were a few withered pictures from his late teenage years.

He was a tall fella. Slender like Denzel Washington in Malcolm X. Skin brown like baked apple pie when you leave it in the oven too long.

Fine.

Yeah that's what I think when I look at the photos now. He was AWOL from the Navy when he died. They must have taught him to stand the way he did. Rock hard body, back straight, posture precise, solemn face, confident, yet something in his eyes said he was holding back. Maybe fear I suppose. His hands reminded me of Zeus, king of the gods. Big and muscular, fingers spread out like he could hold the whole world in his palm. I wonder what he could do with his hands. Where he would choose to put them on my body if we had met in some other life. I imagine him grabbing my bare bottom like a watermelon, pushing himself deep inside me in the midst of our lovemaking. In some other life, he could have been my knight. But not in this one, because if he had lived, he would be 25 years my senior and my blood uncle. So instead, I'll just imagine him as he is in the picture. Young, good looking, and distant.

Jamie was the one I thought of first when Daddy got sick. I thought of how Grace must have felt losing her brother, then years later, her father, even if he was the devil, and now the threat of losing her husband, three men anyone would argue are the most important in a woman's life. But it was a fleeting thought since the idea of Daddy dying was never real to me. Ever since I was, he was.

I have more pictures of Daddy than we do Jamie. Pictures of him carrying me and Sunday home from the hospital. Pictures of us playing in our backyard. Pictures of him kissing Grace in happier times. I don't have any pictures of Daddy crying. I don't know if he ever did cry or if he was even capable. He always said as long as we had a roof over our heads and food to eat, there was never a good reason to cry. And even if we didn't, everything happens for a reason and God works out our misfortune for good. Daddy was an optimist. Grace always imagined the worst. The what ifs that worried her half to death usually never happened. So maybe the two of them complimented each other, a kind of balance that attracts two people together.

Grace said she never cried when Jamie died. Some people might think it's because she is so strong, but I see it instead as a sign of weakness. A fear of feeling. I cried for Jamie even though I've never met him. His life was like a film that doesn't get good until an hour in and he left before it was over. I have a habit of falling asleep in the middle of boring movies. I'd wake up when the credits were rolling and my sister would look over and shake her head. "You missed the best part Baby Girl. The plane crash was a dream, he gets the girl in the end and turns out the stalker he thought was trying to kill him was really his guardian angel. You should've stayed up Baby Girl. You should've stayed."

I have never seen anyone die, but I have seen people broken. I imagined them like an old Chinese vase my grandmother kept on her kitchen table. I used to trace my finger along its hairline cracks and chipped crevices. Broken but never shattered. Dying but never dead. When I was old enough to wonder, I asked myself which was worse--dying or being dead. But since the dead don't live to tell of their experience, I guess I'll never know until I am.

The Memorial Project. I got a job in fundraising and development to put my persuasive writing skills to work raising money to support families of lost souls who were victims in The Attacks. Every year, we had a gala benefit at New York's Cipriani's to honor those hardworking board members that dedicated their time and energy to our mission. Carol Blaney was the Development Director there and she made 4 times my salary. I could tell by the designer bags she carried, the cashmere sweaters, the private cars, and I always secretly thought she had some cosmetic work done. Something in the pout of her lip. She wasn't a very tall woman but her attitude would never let you know it. She was serious about her work, and organized a team under her to deliver properly. Business breakfasts started promptly, gala invitations perfectly streamlined, always with a live stamp that I personally had the honor of placing on over 1000 envelopes. The menu at each gala, impeccable. And she always looked amazing. Donna Karan suits hung snug but not too snug over her forty-something frame. Golden brown hair draped her shoulders. Diamonds in all the right places. Any young lawyer in Manhattan wanted to be her. Money, power, and working hands on with the Mayor of New York to "rebuild lower Manhattan." Must be nice.

What bothered me about Mrs. Blaney, however, was her over attention to achievement and lack of real passion about people. Her galas made her look good and when she raised three times more money than the Wildlife Conservation Society, it made her feel all mushy inside. She constructed a Board of Directors made up of Manhattan's elite, people who ordered private cars to drive them 4 blocks, vacationed in the Hamptons, and wanted their name on a board, any board, because it looks good on fancy letterhead.

Last week, the development team went out to lunch to "discuss work" and I ordered a gourmet cheeseburger that cost 20 dollars. We drank wine and had dessert on the company card and when the bill came, I thought about our donors, regular folk who get our "Support our Charity" mailings with return address labels enclosed embossed with a picture of the American flag. I'm sure there was some old woman in Idaho who took 20 dollars of her social security payment to give to a "good cause." I wonder what she'd think about paying for my 20 dollar cheeseburger.

"Kericho," Mrs. Blaney continued coming closer and rubbing her hand on my shoulder. "You've been here eight months and I love having you on board as part of the team, but I need to know if you're fulfilled. Do you like it here?"

"I love it here. I love my job, Carol. Just exhausted this week." I lied. This job was not at all what I had hoped or imagined it would be, but when the babies came I needed to survive for them. This life was bad but still preferred to staying in a dead end relationship where every morning, a gunshot wound to the head sounded better than getting out of bed.

I don't like children. But when I felt the baby move inside me, I fell in love, and when the doctor said I was having twins, I like to think God blessed me twice for good behavior. Church folk say He never puts more on you than you can bear, so I didn't understand why my monthly bills exceeded my monthly income and the daycare was constantly threatening to discontinue my children's attendance if I couldn't keep up with the weekly payments. This job was a must have and I wouldn't let Carol think of it any other way.

"I had a long night. Couldn't get much sleep, but I finished the grant proposal. You can review it."

"If you're that tired, maybe you should take the rest of the day off. We all have our days. Come back tomorrow refreshed and ready to work."

I was running late for my appointment with Dr. Hannah for the second time this month, and beginning to think, I didn't even need these therapy sessions anymore. I continued to write Dr. Hannah ten dollar checks to cover the copay, but she wasn't cashing them, out of pity. The extra expense was only causing more stress and I could barely even fit the 45 minutes into my schedule Monday evenings after work before I got the twins from daycare. My physician suggested I go since I lost 20 pounds in the last few months, now down to a scrawny 98 pounds, and my clothes hung on my bone thin frame like I was a little girl playing dress up in my mother's closet.

"It's the stress," I had told the physician 2 months before, after she commented on my rapid weight loss. "I'm not starving myself, I promise. I just can't find time to eat with work, chasing two toddlers around, keeping the house clean, and when I do have a moment to breathe, I don't have an appetite."

"How's your home life?" Dr. Elizabeth Kelly wasn't listening. Yes, she was standing there, her glasses balancing on the bridge of her nose, her age showing through her blotchy skin and graying roots with her white coat on, files in hand ready to write down her observations of me, and my life, but she wasn't listening. Because if she had been listening, she would have heard me tell her just a moment before that my home life consisted of me waking up at 6am, getting my two year olds ready for school, feeding them breakfast, and running out the door just in time to make the 7:30 train to work. Then, listening to Mrs. Blaney bark orders all day about the kind of mustard she wanted catered at the next corporate lunch, coming home to microwave dinner, draw a bath for the children, and on some nights, if I'm lucky, masturbate to reach orgasm once before falling asleep in my still-not-paid for rent-to-own bed. Then, after 5 or 6 hours, I'd wake up and do it all over again.

"My home life?" I repeated unsure of what she meant.

"Sometimes emotions can get in the way of living a productive life. Are you very social? Do you have support from family, friends, co workers?

"I think therapy might do me some good. I'm feeling very drained lately and I'm not opposed to getting help with managing my time better." So it was me who suggested the therapy. Yes, I remember now. I was a psychology major in college so I'm an advocate of all things mental. It starts in the head. I'm not one of those people too proud to admit they need help. I wanted to talk. I needed to talk to someone to find out what I was missing. Why did my life feel like I had waded too far out into the ocean, lost my grip in the sand, closed my eyes and started swimming back to shore, only to realize after so long that I hadn't moved at all, and wasn't any closer to the shore than when I first begun?

"Therapy is a good idea. Call your insurance to get a list of providers in the network. I'll write up a referral."

I started therapy two weeks later. I found Dr. Stephanie Hannah on the African American Psychologists Association website. Her picture looked friendly. Genuine. She was a young woman, early thirties. Or mid-thirties with good genes. She had short neat ropes of hair in her picture. The first time I went to see her, surprisingly, I wasn't nervous. I was so excited to be able to get some things off my chest, things that had been brewing for months. She was the Wizard of Oz and once I was on her couch, everything would be all better. But here I was, 6 sessions later, and everything wasn't better. I was still treading water, miles away from the shore.

Today when I walked in, 20 minutes late, the receptionist looked at me and then the clock.

"I'm sorry I'm late. I was stuck on the train. It won't happen again."

"You can go on in. Dr. Hannah is waiting for you."

I nodded and opened the door to Dr. Hannah's office cautiously. She had a desk but wasn't sitting there. She was in the corner by the window in her oversized doctor's chair, looking down at something in her lap. When she looked up, she motioned for me to join her on the couch across from where she sat. I liked it here. The old Brownstone was cozy with its hardwood floors and exposed brick walls.

Home.

There was a huge rug that covered the floor and couches made for lounging and cuddling. It lacked a fireplace, but not much else.

"I'm sorry I'm late," I apologized again.

"Not a huge problem. Our session will just have to be cut in half. Have you been keeping a notebook of your thoughts like I suggested?"

I saw the flash of light first and then I heard the cackling sound of thunder. "It's raining. I forgot my umbrella." She was silent. "Yes. I started to. I just feel silly writing down all of the things I think about. It makes me seem crazier than I actually am when I read it out loud." A shy smile.

"How has the week been for you?"

"Man told me yesterday he plans on filing for a modification. Can you believe that? I'm barely making ends meet now and he wants a modification. I wrote in my journal after that conversation."

"And?" Dr. Hannah uncrossed and recrossed her legs in the opposite direction.

I dug through my bag and pulled out my mini notebook. Took a deep breath before I started to read.

> *"What am I here for? This struggle, this one here, makes no time to really live because I'm always trying to find a way to survive the day. I wind back my clock but time only moves forward, the past a memory etched in stone. This is not me. I make fun of girls like this. The ones with beauty but no brains, ending up old and lonely with half a life left...that won't be me. I still have plans. Hope, I finally learned is food and water. I need it to survive. So why do I still feel like this? Probably because I keep waiting for a break that never comes."*

I closed the book and looked up at Dr. Hannah. The rain started in a soft pitter patter against the bay window.

"That's good. And what are you waiting for? What kind of break?" she asked me.

"More money. So I can breathe. I'm breathing a lot easier since I left, but I'm not exhaling like I need to."

"You're waiting to exhale?" She smiled.

"Yep. That's exactly it. I want to enjoy my two year olds. I mean really enjoy them. I love them but it hurts me that I can't give them the whole world. I wanted so bad to do this right. I wanted to be the perfect mom."

"Kericho, no one is perfect."

"I know. I know that. But I don't want my children to suffer through my bullshit." I pulled at the skin around my cuticle. "They're so innocent. So malleable. They bend to their environment so I don't want to mess that up for them. I just need a raise. A thousand dollars more a month would put me in a good place."

"So, is money really the issue?" The rain grew heavier, now a stampede of horses. Another flash of lightening.

"Yes. It is. I know they say money is not the key to happiness, but for me, it would cure my insecurities. I'd look better. I'd be better, I'd feel better. I haven't been able to get my hair done in months. My wardrobe is old and worn and I bet that's the reason I can't get a man. But even if I could, I don't have money for a babysitter so he would never be able to take me out. We'd be relegated to the couch and a Saturday night movie."

Dr. Hannah looked at me in silence for a few moments. She smirked and then we both keeled over in laughter.

"Kericho, you're way too hard on yourself. You look good. You look happy." She shifted in her chair. "Let me ask you something. What is it that you want people to think of you? How do you want them to see you?"

"I don't know. I guess we all want people to see the best in us."

"I don't know what we all want and frankly I'm not concerned. What do you want? Let me rephrase. How do you believe they see you now?"

"Who is they?"

"The world. Your circle. Your coworkers. Your friends. Your family."

I sighed. "I think everyone used to see me as someone who had it all together. Someone who always looked good and smelled good and had the best things. They didn't know how I did it either. It was my secret. It was supposed to look easy but really wasn't."

"And now?"

"Now? Now I'm having trouble keeping up. I'm tired." I sat back in my chair and took a deep breath. Remembering was always physical pain. My stomach tightened and I closed my eyes for a few brief moments before I spoke again. "I remember having a fight with Man. The babies had just been born. 3 months. Maybe 4 months old. I had my strength back. Grace and I were speaking again. She started sending me money. A hundred dollars here and there. I made a hair appointment for a Saturday. Left the babies with Man for a few hours. When I came home, he was upset. Said I spent too much money on my hair and we had unpaid bills. I told him I didn't spend any more than I normally do and it had been months before the babies since I had last gotten my hair done. I wanted to do something for me. I needed to do something for me. But he...he didn't understand. He said I was screwing another man. Called me a child. It turned into a yelling match. You know how the Bible says your words have power. Maybe Leonard was summoned by the gods. We didn't speak for days after that, me and Man. That was the beginning of the end."

"So what do you think about that now?"

"I think—" the cackling split the sky and shook me. "I think it was stupid. I really just wanted him to tell me I was pretty. I'd probably heard it a dozen times on my way home from the salon from street guys, but I couldn't get him to say it."

"Was that an argument about money or an argument about selfishness?"

"You tell me doctor. I thought you get paid for this."

"I want to know what you think. I wasn't there."

"I think...I think it was an argument about control. He controlled everything. He controlled the money since he was the one making the money. When things were good, it was our money. It was our house. When things were bad, it was *his money* and *'get out of my house.'* Now I know, he didn't have it easy. I know he was fresh out of college himself trying to make a way to pay rent and buy groceries and everything else we needed. I know that. But I just wanted to be included. I wanted to be a part of the decision making. I was never the girl who wanted to be a housewife and cater to her husband hand and foot. I don't how to be that. I had my own life and my own desires that were put on hold. Damn near reversed and if he couldn't see that getting my hair done was important to me even if it was trivial to him, I couldn't help that."

"And why is it so important to you?"

"Dr. Hannah, you ask too many questions." I snapped.

"I think there's more here. More than you're allowing yourself to see."

"Why does anyone go to a hair salon? I went for the same reason. To feel good. To regain my self-esteem. To get that old thing back. Aside from the physical stress the babies had put on me, I had lost contact with all of my friends. My family was distant. I stopped working so I didn't have any money. I was dependent on Man for everything, and I hated it. It was like I was a child asking him for an allowance. I felt worthless. And that was never how I envisioned my life to be. I was always somebody. I was the girl all the guys liked. I was the girl they chased. I was the one with the power. So this new thing felt foreign. This wasn't me. I was ready to live again. The way I remembered."

"You sound like you were trying to keep up a persona."

"So what's wrong with that?"

"I didn't say anything was wrong with it."

"So why say it? It's as if you're implying I should have let myself go. I was losing me. And it didn't feel good."

"Kericho. I don't have the answers. I just know how to ask the questions so you can find the answers."

I hated when Dr. Hannah played with my head like that. That "search within yourself" bit was played out. The thunder subsided but the rain was steady against the window. I returned my attention to my cuticle.

"I don't know if I can come here anymore." She stared blankly but didn't say a word. Just twiddled her pen between her fingers. "I'm....ya know I'm strapped financially. And maybe you've given me all the help you can."

"I really don't think you should stop coming. If it's about the money, I'll waive the copay. You've let me in tremendously over the past weeks and I don't want to lose you. This is therapy. It's supposed to hurt a little bit. It's supposed to be uncomfortable at times. Just like a good workout. That's how you know you're making progress."

"I just don't know what my goal is anymore. I don't know when I'm ever going to feel whole again. I've come undone."

I stumbled up the steps to my walk up apartment on the third floor holding the boy in my left arm, and a stack of mail in my right, the other boy following close behind holding my pants leg. My cell phone vibrated in my purse as I put the key in the door. I rushed in, put the boy down on the couch, and grappled for my phone, pulling it out a second too late.

Luke.

Luke was like candy. He tasted good but never filled me up. I knew Luke before the babies came. Before Man. Before all that, in the beginning, there was Luke. The first time we made love, it felt like melting butter. Warm and moist. And inviting. I'd follow that scent anywhere. But Luke wasn't mine. Luke wouldn't belong to anybody. He was a wandering soul, free spirited and whimsical. Luke made his own rules. Still, my heart skipped a beat whenever he called.

No voicemail this time.

We had spaghetti for dinner, the boys and I. I warmed up the leftovers from the night before. A bath. A story. They were in bed by 9:00. I swept the kitchen floor, set the dirty dishes in the sink and double checked the bolt lock on the door. Now it was my turn. I always liked my bathwater extra hot. Lots of bubbles and scented candles. It was my release at the end of the day. And it was just me. My way. I settled in and let the bubbles rise to my chin.

Luke and I used to take bubble baths together at his place. It was a while before I was comfortable enough to do that. A long time after we had sex. The sex was easy. I would close my eyes and let him kiss me. Then he would take my clothes off and I would pretend I was outside myself looking in. The feeling was euphoric.

But a bath? A bath was intimate, much more intimate than sex. Men don't bathe with hookers. They fuck them. A bath is personal. Luke knew how to make a girl feel special.

One day, 3 years ago, I had just finished finals for the semester. It was Christmastime. Luke and I had drinks in the city to celebrate and got back to his place late. I was wearing the black dress that hugged my waist and fell at my thighs. He took me by the hand and led me to his bedroom door, but before we went inside, he stopped and held my face between his hands and kissed me. A sensual kiss, full of passion and fervor.

"Let's take a bath,"' he said.

I chuckled a little. "What? Are you trying to tell me something?"

"No. It's not that. You smell wonderful. But I want to admire your body. Naked. I want to relax with you and take my time. Let me massage your shoulders. I know you had a rough semester."

I obliged. He drew the bath water and put on a Kem CD. The perfect mix of jazz and R&B. I had bought him some candles that smelled like chocolate for his housewarming party a few months before that he never used. They were stashed away in a closet. We got those out and turned the room into our own hotel suite. It was beautiful. But I was tense when he pulled my dress over my head to expose my nudity. The lights were still on and he could see everything. Luke has strong hands. They complement his frame, shoulders like a football running back, in direct contrast to my small frame. He said I reminded him of a baby doll. 5'4" on a good day but no one would know it since I always wear 4 inch heels. When I slipped them off, I was at Luke's shoulder and he had to bend down to kiss me. He pulled my hair into a knot on the top of my head.

"Let's get in," he said.

The water was warm but not as hot as I would have preferred. I nestled between his legs and he massaged my back and shoulders, the smell of chocolate opening my senses.

"Luke," I said. "Can I ask you something?"

"What's that?"

"How come it's been over a year since we've met, and we never turned into anything more than what we are right now?"

"What do you mean?"

"Do I have to spell it out for you? You know what I'm talking about. I don't want this to be just sex."

"It's not just sex. Is that how you see it?"

"I know sex is not all we do, but sometimes I wonder if we would do anything else, if we didn't know sex would follow."

"I'm confused."

"I'm not saying I want more. I'm still in school. You just finished. I don't know what I want. I just know I'm not happy with this."

He kept me waiting. "Kericho, you wanna know why? You wanna know why it was never more?"

"Why is that?"

"Because when we first met, you told me you weren't looking for a relationship."

He was right. I did say that. I met him at a college football game. He wasn't playing that day because of his shoulder injury. Just before halftime I snuck up behind him on the bench and told him the game was lacking his skills on the field and I hoped his shoulder was better before the playoffs. When I saw him a few days later on campus, we exchanged numbers. But we were both holding back in our initial conversation. I didn't want to seem needy. I was a freshman in college, barely 18 years old. I was exploring the world, testing the waters, so I told him up front that I wasn't looking for anything serious and he shouldn't get his hopes up. In hindsight, maybe he should have been the one saying that to me.

"Luke, you're right," I answered. He stopped rubbing me and let me relax against his chest. "I didn't want to give what we have a title. But right now, this is not enough."

"Why do you think so much? You're young. I'm young. We have forever to be 'more'. Right now, just live in the moment."

That night ended with sex in the bed at 4 in the morning, and it was almost two years before I would see him again. Now here I am, at 24, sitting in a bathtub watching my fingers get all pruny, still "living in the moment", still waiting for Luke to want me like I do him.

Chapter Two

This time I was on the highway driving fast. Cruise Control doing at least 100 over the bridge. Kiefer and Kye were in the backseat, seatbelts unbuckled. I turned the music up to drown out their tiny voices yelling "Mommy, too fast." Chaka Khan was screaming "I'm Every Woman." The pills and vodka made it easier. I couldn't feel anymore. It was best that way.

I woke up to the sound of my cell phone ringing. Chaka Khan had made her way into my dreams. I answered just before it went to voicemail.

"Babygirl, wake up. I have news," said the voice on the other end.

"Morning to you too," I answered.

"Morning? It's 11:30. You have some nerve to still be in bed. I'm on my way to you now."

I sat up and cleared my throat. The sheets fell below my bare breasts and I smelled the kiwi in the air. The clock read 11:35. "It's Saturday," I answered. "One of only two in the month that the children are with their Daddy and I get to sleep in. One of only two days in the month that I get to sleep at all. And girl, I'm tired."

"Mmmhmmm. Well lest you forget. I'm a mother too. I know your woes. But this is too beautiful a day to sleep it all away."

The sky outside my window told a different story. For 6 days now, the sky had not let up. Dark clouds blocked any hint of the sun and thick droplets of rain splashed against the glass. "It's raining," I said.

"So what? You scared of a little rain?

I had to pee and sighed taking Sunday in the bathroom with me. "What's your news anyway?"

"Are you sitting down?"

"I'm peeing."

"Babygirl. I have a date tonight. Out near you. Nigel has a work thing so he's driving into the city from Connecticut. He wants to meet me for drinks after."

"That's exciting. Your 5-year crush is finally showing some interest."

"Shut up. I'm coming over. You have to help me shop for something cute to wear. And we can have lunch. I'll pay."

After we hung up, I scanned the room for my robe. Sleeping in the nude was something I had gotten accustomed to since Man. The cool sheets against my skin felt good too. I'd lay diagonal in my bed and sink into my pillow top mattress on loan to me from Aaron's Rent to Buy. The only time I covered up was when Sunday spent the night. She'd sleep next to me in bed and it kind of felt like old times when we were young and shared a bedroom. We would talk each other to sleep not even remembering the last thing we said.

My mother named my older sister Sunday because that's the day she was born. She only weighed two pounds four ounces and came out 3 months early but the doctors said they couldn't keep her in any longer. She was a chocolate baby with a full head of hair and a belly button that looked just like a rose. The wrinkles and folds were the petals and the skin was tinted a pale pink.

Sunday.

In the old days, we called her Sunday Rose e'en though that wasn't her name on paper. A miracle baby, she was born premature, but now, she's the tallest girl in our family. Thick too, with curves for days, a plump, round booty and breasts that came straight from Africa. The boys liked Sunday better than me. In high school, they stopped me after school.

"Hey Kericho," they'd say and motion me over. Then I'd get all excited because the football jocks wanted to talk to me. At first, I had to act uninterested because it would look desperate, but I always came over.

"Yes."

"Why don't you pass this note to that fine sista of yours? Miss Sunday, always lookin just like Sunday mornin'. I hear she's got a rose for a belly button. Gee, I'd love to lick on that."

"You want me to give her a note?" I turned my nose up.

"Or you could just give me her digits. That would be a nice thing to do."

Then I'd huff, fold my arms, and say, "Ask her yourself. I'm not a messenger."

I didn't have a voluptuous body to brag about but I was a pretty face. The boys always said, "When you get just a little older and a little thicker, you won't be able to keep the freaks off you."

But despite all that, folks used to ask if Sunday and I were twins, because we were so close. I used to believe it too. Grace dressed us alike when we were kids. We always wore opaque white stockings with our dresses and patent leather shoes for church. She pressed our hair out real straight with a hot comb and tied it back in matching pig tails. Later, we dismissed my mother's idea of what a lady is, and the both of us became rebels. When I was old enough to make decisions, I threw out the white stockings and decided my hair suited me better when it was sprayed all over my head in fluffy curls.

Sunday found her stride making men drool all over themselves at school, in church, just about anywhere she went. Daddy caught her with a boy in her room when she was in the tenth grade and that boy jumped out the second floor window to get away.

"I don't want to die by no machete. You fuck with Sunday, you got to be ready to get your balls cut off by that daddy of hers."

"What daddy?"

"You know her daddy come from Africa. They slice you up real good over there and feed your private parts to the pigs."

No matter the rumors, the boys took their chances and kept on coming anyway. That kiwi of hers had a hold on em, and the boys had a hold on her. She went for the tall light skinned ones with pretty hair.

When I was 14 and she was 16, she got into an argument with our mother and locked herself in her room with a bottle of Tylenol. My mother had found out she skipped school that day and went joy riding in her new Honda, which was a gift for good grades and getting her learner's permit. The birth control pills Grace found in Sunday's nightstand drawer confirmed for my mother that Sunday was sexually active and that was way too much for my mother to handle. She demanded the car keys, which Sunday gave up but not without a fight.

"Adolescents often go through a rebellious stage when their disobedience is really just a cry for attention," I overheard the doctor say to my parents that night in the hospital. Sunday was going to be okay. Her swallowing the pills was just a cry for attention because she was an adolescent. I once heard a television evangelist say that the word "adolescent" is only used in the English language. In all other languages there is no proper translation. You are either a boy, or a man. A child or an adult. There is no in between. You are one or the other. But in the English language you are allowed to be older than a child, but not yet an adult. It gives you the freedom to lack common sense and make stupid decisions because you are not an adult, and you can mouth off to your parents and disregard rules because you are no longer a child.

A month later it happened again. The doctors pumped over twelve grams of acetaminophen out of Sunday's stomach. It was more than three times the daily limit for someone her size. They siphoned liquid from her stomach through a tube passed through her nose and deep into her body. I cried for her wondering if the process was less painful than whatever caused her to overdose in the first place.

Percocet was her drug of choice, and since the drug was more serious this time, the doctors called in a psychotherapist for an evaluation just in case it was more than a cry for attention. They sentenced her to ninety days hard labor at The Lightfoot Wellness Center. It was a therapeutic residence for teens struggling with behavioral problems, family conflict, and low self-esteem, or in my own words, an asylum for crazy folk.

For a month, I went to Sunday's teachers at school and collected work for the week so she wouldn't get behind in her studies. The first time I went with Daddy to visit her, he argued with Grace for an hour at home before we left without her. My mother was a woman raised on traditional roles of parent and child. "I'm not giving her the attention she wants. I'm not feeding into her games," she said to my father with her hands on her bone thin hips. Relentless, I've never known that woman to apologize for anything. My father pleaded with her that day, but she was certain that going to see her oldest daughter at the crazy house would only make matters worse. I sat on the steps by the front door half listening until my father came over, keys in hand. "Let's go," was all he said.

Sunday was losing weight. We brought her a Big Mac from McDonalds and french fries to supplement the awful food they served in there. She shared a room with a Puerto Rican girl with blond hair.

"She's suicidal," Sunday said to me when the girl left the room. "And a drug addict. She does Meth."

"And what are you?" I said half joking.

"I'm not like the rest of these people. There's a cute doctor here. Dr. Bellapianté. He meets with us individually to talk about our progress. I might be crazy but I kind of feel like he knows I don't belong here. He knows I'm really not crazy like everyone else.

He talks to me like a regular person."

A knock at the door. It was a staff server with a tray of milkshakes topped with whipped cream. "Compliments of the chef!" He announced. "Would you like one?"

"Don't mind if I do." Sunday reached for a shake. "Pedro, this is my sister visiting. "Can she have one too?"

"Sure thing sweetheart. Apple pie milkshakes."

"Sounds too good to pass up." My first sip was ecstasy. "Yum..."

"It's good right." Sunday said after Pedro left. "Forgot to mention these are the best."

I took another sip. "Never heard of an apple pie milkshake."

"I don't know how he makes them or what's in it."

"Who cares. This thing is creamy crack."

She laughed. "Guess this place has its perks." We sat drinking our shakes, moaning with pleasure. I sat back against her pillow. Her head on my chest, heaven on our tongues and everything else faded.

"Get well soon Sunday. I miss you at home."

"You know I don't really want to die. I just want to, you know, disappear for a while. So I don't have to feel."

"What about me?"

"You were always a lot stronger than me. You will be fine."

"Sunday, don't talk like that. I need you. Me and Daddy need you." My father was talking to the doctors about Sunday. But they are only allowed to give out limited information. They have a confidentiality agreement with the patients, that says even though they are minors, they have a right to privacy. It stimulates openness with the patients, they explained.

We didn't stay long. Daddy came back into the room and we said our goodbyes and gave each other bear hugs.

"I love you, Babygirl," said Sunday on our way out. "Tell Mommy, I love her too."

Sunday was released for good behavior after 45 days. I know

my mother was happy to have her home even if she never said it. I could tell by the extra time she spent on dinner each night the first week Sunday came home and I once overheard her on the phone talking about Sunday's good grades at school. Maybe she should've said it to Sunday because my sister still found her applause in a much more sinister place.

One time a few months later she snuck in late through the back door and tip toed up the steps to find me sitting up in her bed in the dark.

"Where you been, Sunday? I was worried," I asked her.

"Sshh! You gon wake Mommy."

"I'm sorry. Geez. I almost started to tell her you went missing."

Sunday slipped out of her mini shorts and tank and climbed in bed next to me.

"Baby girl, tonight was real special. Reggie took me out to the shore in his truck." She closed her eyes. "He laid me down, pulled my shorts off and he went real slow."

"In his truck?"

"No girl. We laid on the sand, just the moonlight guiding him to all my secret places. It felt like a little piece of heaven."

"Sunday I'm worried about you. Do those boys love you?"

"Love will come," she shrugged. "I can make them love me."

A year later, Sunday was pregnant with her first baby at 18. She was right about making them love her 'cus Reggie married my sister in a little chapel down the street from our house. If it wasn't real love, maybe fake love was just as good. She had the dress that just covered her baby bump, the flowers, the kisses from family.

"Is that daughter of yours going away to school," the church ladies would ask Grace.

"No," she smiled. "She's happy being married."

And Grace was happy too. It smoothed things over just fine.

Her marriage to Reggie was over by the summer of '05 after the birth of her second daughter. She came back from Guam, alone with the girls, a frown pasted on her face. I met her at Mommy's house with open arms.

"I was wrong Babygirl. I can't make him love me."

Today, Sunday arrived in a sundress. It was cool for late September and the dress was inappropriate for the dreary day, but one could always count on Sunday to lend a little light where there was none.

"Are you going to sleep with him?" I asked her once we sat down for lunch. Seafood was our cuisine of choice and there was something in those cheddar biscuits that kept us coming back here.

"Of course not. It's just drinks. And some conversation. Some long overdue conversation. I want him to know I'm ready to be exclusive. I want to work on building a relationship." She enunciated that last word like it was new vocabulary and smoothed her brown hair down and behind her ear.

"You don't think that's a bit presumptuous? I mean he called you, what, this morning?

"Last night."

"Ok, last night. But how long has he known he was going to be in town this weekend? How do you know you're not his plan B after plan A decided she was busy?"

"You think I'm his backup plan?"

"I don't know. I just don't want you to expect too much, that's all." I poked at my salad.

She squinted. Chewed. Swallowed. "Could this, in any way, be related to you and Luke?"

"Not at all." She sucked her teeth and cut her eyes at me. "No, this is not about him," I repeated. She didn't let up. "Sunday, what's wrong with being practical? I don't want you to spend your life putting all of your eggs in Nigel's basket when he's only playing with your emotions. You're way too good for that anyway."

"No, Babygirl. You're way too good for Luke."

"I'm over Luke. We're more occasional friends now than anything else."

"There is no such thing as an occasional friend. He's either your friend or not. And if he is, you wouldn't let him come by when he only wants to sleep with you." She stuffed a forkful in her mouth.

"How do you know it's not me letting him come by when I'm the one that wants to sleep with him?"

"I could believe that if I didn't already know you went and got your heart involved. Face it, Babygirl. I don't know of any woman who can sleep with a man over and over again and not get her feelings involved. Lots of us say we can, but we can't. It never works out that way. Believe me. I'm one to know."

My lettuce reminded me of the grass Luke and I almost made love in. It was late one night a long time ago. There was a field of weeds and a small creek behind one of the college dorms. We went back there to talk. When the intimacy deepened, he unzipped my sweater and started feeling in taboo places. His neck kisses were moist like Snapple Apple and made from the best stuff on earth. "Ya know, Luke and I almost made love in grass," I said. "How can you not fall in love with a man willing to get naked in a field of weeds with you?"

"Almost? What stopped you?"

"Police sirens in the distance. And maybe God."

She smiled and shook her head. "Whatever it was, you better be glad. Your skin is too delicate to be scarred up by rotten grass."

We laughed. Sunday had that effect on us. Even when Reggie joined the Marines and she moved with her baby girl and the other one all the way to Guam, she was still close in my heart.

But I got busy pursuing my own goals and dreams and so I couldn't expect her not to pursue her dream family. She was a new mother and back then, I couldn't even begin to understand such a responsibility. We talked less but wrote often. My senior year of college, I went abroad to study in Africa and we were indeed on opposite sides of the globe. Her in Guam. Me, in Ghana. Somehow, I still felt connected to her, if only by the brief moments on the phone with a bad connection accompanied by static. I was still Babygirl and she was my ice cream Sunday. A few months ago, I found a letter she had written me from that time, 3 years ago. When I read it over with fresh eyes, it was like her words could see into the future. She was speaking about life now as if she knew what it would hold then. They were living words, like the Living Bible, true then and true now.

There is a certain rule inherent in a family that can never be broken, try as you might. What is is what is and will always be. DNA says a hell of a lot more about a bloodline than anyone could ever fabricate. A family is set in place by God and no other, and if I had it all to do over again, I'd beg God to allot me this position in this family, and most importantly, to appoint Sunday as my sister. Sometimes, I wish everyone could feel like I do when it comes to loving each other because you know, if you think about it, this is our story...our lives...everything we do and say, every hug, every kiss, every argument is a line in the story of us.

I do believe that it is an art to love, a skill really. I don't think there are different kinds of love like a mother-child love, a husband-wife love, a brother-sister love. I just believe in love. A feeling that can't readily be qualified.

By the time I returned from Africa, our worlds had been turned upside down. Sunday was divorcing and moving back home with my parents and by then I had met my own demise, one on each breast, wrapped in swaddling cloth.

She picked a satin forest green dress for tonight with spaghetti straps. It was long enough to prove she's a lady but short enough to show she's a woman.

"Come out with us," she said to me. We were back at my apartment. She was powdering her face. I was sprawled on my bed browsing the latest issue of Essence.

"Threes a crowd," I answered without looking up.

"We're going to a wine bar. Be social. You'll meet someone."

"Every guy I've ever met at a bar has never had anything in common with me. I don't want to tag along. I'll be fine here."

"That sounds good in theory. Except you won't be. As soon as I walk out the door, you're going to pop popcorn and put on another romance movie that reminds you of everything you don't have."

"Correction. Everything we don't have. Just because you have a date tonight, don't get carried away. He's going to turn around and go back to Connecticut after tonight. It'll be six months before you see him again."

"Why so negative? What if it wasn't six months? What if I saw him again next weekend? And the weekend after that?"

"If it turned into something great, I would be happy for you."

She turned and blew me a kiss. "You better be."

"Have you forgotten about our agreement?"

"How could I, Kericho, I came up with it. Whoever finds a man first is obligated to find the other one a man next."

"And if we turn 40 and still aren't married, we marry each other."

She turned abruptly. "Uh uh, who said that?!"

"I added that part just now. You don't like it?"

"Baby Girl, that's incest and you know I don't even get down that way."

"Me too, I was just playing."

"And I'll be damned if I turn 40 and I'm still buying dresses last minute and dating like some school girl." She smoothed the lipstick on her lips and pressed them together.

"I feel you, but don't tell me you're waiting to find a man to begin living your life. I'm tired of hearing women plan to find a man and build around that like men are magic in a 3-piece suit. What if it doesn't happen? I don't mean to be cynical, but I don't want to spend my life being incomplete just because my knight in shining armor never came."

"He will."

"No, no, no. I'm serious," I sat up. "I know it's not easy but let's start living our lives as if we already have everything we wanted. Let's go on vacations. Let's buy that house. Let's take those motorcycle lessons."

"Ok, Miss I-have-all-this-money. I'm with you if you find a way to pay for it."

"You know what I mean. If we don't have the money, let's get the money. Let's stop making excuses and depending on the rest of the world to tell us when it's okay to be happy. If they can define happiness for you, then you also give them permission to tell you when you're supposed to be sad. And when that time comes, you end up swallowing a bottle of aspirin and then sitting in a "sharing" circle in a home for troubled teens."

Sunday put the lipstick down, rested her hands on her hips and smiled one of those thoughtful half smiles. "That was a long time ago," she said. "And let's not think about that because tonight, I have a date with Nigel Johnson, and I must be going to hell because it's got to be a sin to look this good." She stepped into her sling back stilettos and grabbed her purse from the bed. "I'm off. He wants me to meet him in midtown. If you change your mind about coming out, call me. Otherwise, I'll be back tonight. Late, so don't wait up."

"Will do," I said waving goodbye as she shimmied out the door.

I got up and locked the front door behind her. Tonight I was in the mood for a gritty drama. I popped a bag of popcorn, extra butter, and sat down to browse TV channels.

My eyelids grew heavy and the room faded. I heard a key in the door. Could it be Luke coming over unannounced? He was known to "stop by." No, he didn't have a key anymore. I had given him a key to my house a few months before as a signal that I wanted to move our relationship forward. But, when I realized the relationship only really existed in my head, I asked for it back and he obliged.

The key in the door wiggled and then the devil came in, wearing the same dark suit and bearing framed photographs of times past and future. I gave him one swift look and knew what was coming. I clenched my fists and braced myself for the blow.

Chapter Three

A gun would be messy. I'd save that for myself. I thought about that Yates woman who drowned her children in the bathtub. That's a miserable way to die.

The devil often visited me in my dreams to remind me of my sins. I was used to him by now and prepared well.

Luke always used a condom. That's how I knew the baby couldn't be his. The truth of the matter is that I'm happy I went to Ghana because Kiefer and Kye may not be here if I didn't go. I had read about it in the glossy pamphlet I found in the academic office on campus.

"At Study Abroad in Ghana, you'll have an exciting opportunity to experience firsthand the diversity and complexity of West Africa."

The year was 2005. I was a senior in college still waiting for life to get interesting. When would I have an opportunity like this again? I called my mother on that evening 3 years ago when I knew she would be settled for the night, glass of wine in hand. She answered on the third ring.

"Mommy, how are you?" I said.

"Kericho. I'm fine. Just reading in bed. How are things at school?"

Grace's tone was always uncomfortable. Her inquiries hardly seemed genuine but instead like she was making small talk at a cocktail party where she had arrived alone and was attempting to mingle.

"They're good. Things are good." I decided to get right to the point. With Grace, it was better that way. The longer I took, the more pressing in her mind the question of what exactly I called for. She was the sacrificing kind, quick to give up her own desires for the good of the group, not because she really wanted to but because she felt it was her duty.

When I'd call and ask for money, she'd sigh softly and hammer out a reluctant "how much do you need?" Those new shoes she planned on buying for herself would have to wait. When I turned sixteen and got my license, I begged her for two weeks straight to buy me a brand new Civic that really was a good deal for being never used, never driven, and under full warranty. She pushed back but soon gave in.

But Grace was no push over. No instead she was quite the opposite. Grace wore pearls, long skirts or dresses always with pantyhose but underneath all that, she wore the pants in our family. I asked Grace for permission to go to the movies with Hanif Jones when I was 15. It would be my first outing with a boy and even though he was 18 and had his own car, Grace reluctantly obliged. When I needed help with schoolwork, or needed a parent to sign my field trip permission slips, it was Grace I went to, not Daddy. Daddy was for lighter things like walks in the park, and late night stories. When Daddy did something he wasn't supposed to, it was

Grace that would set things straight.

Sophomore year in college, I flunked right out of Physics. It was one of those mandatory classes I needed to take and needed to pass to get all my credits for the year. But the tests were only a few questions long. So short that if I just got two or three wrong, I was already down to a D-. The year came to an end and I cried to Grace to let me stay in New York for the summer. It was half because I didn't want to spend my summer back in New Jersey, and half because I wanted to take that silly class over again and graduate on time.

She said no. She couldn't afford to pay all that money for me to stay in New York and pay for the extra summer class. It was just too much of a burden. I cried. Still she said no. I suggested we sell the Civic and use whatever we got for it to cover the expense. That's when she knew how much it meant to me. She said she would sleep on it and think on it. A week later, she withdrew $5,000 from her pension to pay my way through summer school. I was elated. Mommy had come through for me, again.

That's why this particular day when I called I figured I get right to the point. "I have a request."

"Okay?" she said, her listening ears on.

"I want to go to Ghana. And before you say anything, I've done all the research. I can take all of my required classes there and tuition won't cost you anything more than what you already pay. All of my scholarships and loans will transfer. All I need is money for a plane ticket."

"Africa?" She said the name of the continent like it was some foreign object she had only heard bad things about, odd considering my parents honeymooned there in the early eighties after five years of courting and a cheap wedding. But the continent must have left a sour taste in my mother's mouth because she rarely spoke of it and now, her words were full of disdain. "You want to go that far? Africa is far away, and very...different. It's fine if you want to go, but I don't know. When I was growing up, things were done a certain way. You go to college, you work hard, you graduate and get a job. This talk about traveling and going from country to country is strange to me."

"Mommy, I never heard of anyone saying that seeing the world is a bad thing. When will I ever be able to see the world like this again? I mean sure, I can wait until after school, and go on a vacation and stay in a resort for 5 days, but that's not experiencing Ghana for real. I get to live there for a year. I get to mingle with the natives and grocery shop and party and work with the children. When you were in school, you didn't have these kinds of opportunities. But now I do."

"You sound excited."

"I am. I applied to the program two weeks ago. I got my acceptance letter today. So I am excited. A little afraid. Nervous about what the future might hold, but still excited. Please say yes."

"I think you should talk to your father, first." Grace was never the kind who got too excited over anything in particular. She remained for the most part in a medium that never swayed too far one way or the other. She was a routine kind of woman each day mimicking the one behind it. Any suggestion of a deviation was met with disfavor, an inconvenience in her plans of having no plans.

She taught English literature at a rundown school in the neighboring community. She got home at 4:30 every day and started dinner for the family, just herself and my father now in her empty nest days. When he suggested they go out to eat, she complained she was too tired, the restaurant would be crowded, she had papers to grade, or all of the above.

I saw glimpses of something else in my mother but never a full picture, sneak peeks of a woman with a heart. Once on my seventh birthday, my mother took Sunday, my cousin Lizzy, and me to the dollar theatre in Cinnaminson to see “Problem Child”. When we got back home, I slumped on the couch next to her while Sunday and Lizzy argued over the best parts of the movie.

"Did you enjoy your birthday," she asked me in secret.

"Well. The movie was nice, but I don't know. Just doesn't feel like my very own special day."

"Hmm...I have an idea. Come on." She motioned for me to follow her while she grabbed her purse and we snuck out to McDonalds just the two of us, leaving Sunday and Lizzy to their shenanigans. We shared a meal of cheeseburgers, french fries, and milkshakes under a setting sun just like in the commercials.

I thought Grace might say no to Africa. Sunday quit college after her freshman year and opted for married life instead. Now she was two babies in and living halfway across the world in a place called Guam that no one really knew how to find on a map. I was an hour away from my parents in New York but moving to Africa for a year would mean leaving my parents to themselves.

Mommy didn't much enjoy Daddy anymore. I don't know if she ever enjoyed him. She tolerated him. Mommy was a graduate student at Antioch in 1978 when she met Daddy. Her professor in Comparative Literature extended an invitation to his class to a special symposium where he was the guest speaker.

"When your professor tells you he is speaking somewhere and invites you to go, you go," I remember Grace telling me years later when she recounted the story. She must have been one of two students with any wisdom because when she showed up dressed in a cotton blouse and pleated skirt, the room was full of other professors and old scholars with white hair and white skin...and then there was Daddy. After the talk, the professor introduced the two over a glass of red wine and a plate of cheese and crackers. She wrote down her phone number on a fancy napkin and Daddy took her for coffee at a diner the next afternoon.

I imagined the two of them sitting down in a corner booth, the smell of bacon and strong coffee in the air. "Grace," Daddy must have opened that day. He rolled his 'r's and it would sound more like he was saying grits. "That is a nice name. Simple. It is a simple name."

"My mother got it from the Bible. She says God always gives

us enough grace for the day. We run into problems when we try to use today's grace for tomorrow." Grace would sit nervously, both hands wrapped around her mug.

Daddy didn't understand but he smiled anyway. "And mine too. My name is Lemuel Blu. King Lemuel was spoken of only wonce in the Buk of Proverbs. That ees my Christian name. It means towards God. But I have many names. In my country, you don't give just one name. You give many."

Grace sits, her hands, now neatly folded, leave her lap only to lift her mug to her thin pursed lips and then return.

"In my country, they would treat you as a queen. We treat all women as queens. But you are something special."

Grace adjusts her glasses, blue cat eye frames she had since her high school days.

"Where are you frum?" Daddy asks.

"I'm from Detroit, Michigan."

"What brings you all the way to Pheeladelphia?" He pronounces each syllable with precision.

"I'm here on a teaching fellowship. Professor Maddow says you studied in England before coming here?"

"Yes. Yes, I studied fine arts and literature in England. I'm doing a Masters in African studies. The diaspora. Do you know much about the African diaspora?"

Grace fidgets in her seat. Adjusts her long hair over one shoulder. Adds cream to her coffee.

"I believe I must take you back to my country. You will love it so much you will not want to leave. The people you will love. They will treat you as gold. Pure gold."

Daddy proposed to my mother after 5 years of courting and a stolen virginity one night in his shabby apartment. This part I learned from Daddy.

"I would like for you to be my wife," he said. No ring. No knee. Just a request like he had calculated the pros and cons and came to a decision.

"Well I don't know. I'm not sure yet. Let me think about it," said Grace. For six long weeks she mulled it over. She even brought Daddy to Detroit with her for Thanksgiving and introduced him to her parents, Mr. And Mrs. Crawford as Daddy referred to them. That night when the men were having beers on the front porch, Mommy sat with Bea, my grandmother, at the kitchen table eating shortbread and talking about Daddy.

"I just don't know Mama."

"Is he what you want?" Granny said.

"I don't know if he's what I want. I never much thought about it. I wanted to finish school and be a teacher. I did that. After that, I never thought about any other plans. Never thought about what kind of wife I would be."

"Marry him Grace. He's a good man. He's a churchgoing man. Marry him and give him some babies." The decision to marry or not to marry was simple then. You find a man in church who dresses nice and pays his tithes, and well, that was enough. It wasn't like the way things are now. I learned that the hard way from Man.

"I guess so. I guess he is a good man. I guess I might as well marry him," she said it as if she had lost a bet and decided to concede.

So they got married on New Year's Eve on my grandparents sun porch with the Reverend Doctor George Jenkins officiating. All the family was there except Mommy's oldest sister Mildred. Auntie Robin witnessed the marriage certificate. Jamie, Deena, and the twins were there dressed in their Sunday best. Daddy didn't have much family stateside, so after the wedding, he took Mommy to Kenya. I don't know if they treated her like gold or not, but she vowed to never go back again for the rest of her life.

"I'm going to retire there," was Daddy's constant proclamation. He planned to buy a big house on big property and grow old in the place he remembered as home. Sunday and I always wanted to go but kept pushing back the date for a lack of money or time, or both. Ghana isn't Kenya, and Kenya isn't Ghana. The two countries are on opposite sides of the second largest continent in the world. The people have different customs and traditions, speak different languages, and even differ in physical features, but Ghana was a small step closer to a part of me that I never knew.

I knew Daddy would say yes and when he did I booked a flight for early January. I would spend the year in Ghana and live with 30 other students in a housing complex in the capital city of Accra. I moved out of my dorm the day after I took a bath with Luke and made love until dawn.

It was just the three of us that Christmas. Mommy, Daddy, and me. They bought me luggage for my trip. I was going to one of the poorest countries in the world, in style.

Chapter Four

This world is a funny kind of thing. There's no way out alive.

It was Monday again. Dr. Hannah was sitting in her swivel chair that hugged her wide hips and posed her question.

"What happened in 2006? Africa. What was that all about?"

It was a loaded question that required a thorough answer if I so chose to give that to her. The devil had conveniently reminded me of things I'd hoped to forget so the memories were fresh.

The three weeks that made up winter break 2005 were three weeks that changed my life forever. There were not enough hours in the days to do everything that needed to be done before I left the country. Cholera, Yellow fever, Malaria. Just some of the infectious diseases that I could and probably would contract if I didn't take all of the required precautions. I made two appointments for vaccine injections and got a prescription for weekly malaria pills. I shopped to have the proper attire for both the rainy season and the dry season. I had my hair professionally washed and straightened and packed all the essentials to maintain my hair myself over the next year. Who knew what services or products I'd be able to find in the foreign desert I was headed to. Two days before my flight, I was finished. I was ready to go and now all I needed to do was wait.

My phone rang Saturday afternoon. I was dosing off on my bed.

Manfred's voice was heavy. I mean his breathing was heavy, his voice was...deep. Now that I think of it, what he actually said is not clear. But the conversation ended in his invitation to come over. Manfred was one of those men you call when you have nothing better to do. He was a preacher's kid, a hundred and fifty pounds overweight, and a good listener. The kind women talk to about other men. Always the friend, never the lover. He was the kind of man a pretty woman walks into the room with and everyone wonders what's in his bank account to draw women like her. Only Man didn't have much in his bank account. He was just out of college, working a government job, living in the cheapest apartment he could find. He invited me over for a party, just us two. A going away party, he called it, to wish me luck in Ghana.

Man was my friend if the definition of friend is associate. He was just there. A space filler, the guy I talked to every now and then. I wasn't doing anything else. Sunday was playing wife in a distant land. Luke was too far away to care and for him, too far wasn't far at all.

In those days I admit I was the selfish kind. Always wanting what I wanted when precisely I wanted it. But learning to be selfless is an art form, a process that takes one many years to cultivate. When we're born aren't we the most selfish of all? Unable to see past our own needs and wants. When the twins were born, I laid them sometimes side by side, or even sat them up, propped by pillows to face each other, to acknowledge each other and coo or smile. But even in these instances they didn't seem to care. It was almost as if they looked past each other. They cared only about themselves. Their food, their water, their comfort. Even if my nipples were tender and sore, my body rest deprived, and my head aching with the pains of stress, they didn't care about me or anyone else.

And as they grew they became, I suppose, a bit less selfish. And it must have been so even with me. I called upon Man when he satisfied some need of mine. An ear to listen, company for dinner, something to do in the days before I left for Ghana. I never really gave much thought to his needs, unable to see past my own. So when he invited me over two days before my flight, when the clock was moving so slowly, it could have been moving backwards, I was so restless that I obliged.

"I'll come by at 8," I said, but I arrived at 7:55.

Chapter Five

I heard a young woman on Oprah say if you sit in scorching hot bath water, you can kill your unborn fetus. A sort of homemade abortion. It wasn't true though.

In Africa, the sun sets a little more beautifully than it does anywhere else. The air smells different too. I noticed that first when I stepped off the plane greeted by baggage handlers smiling ear to ear with teeth as white as cotton. It smells of a cultural mix of food, history, and home. This felt good. For the first time in my life, I was in a place where brown was the majority and not the minority.

Orientation lasted 6 hours the day of my arrival. We were told to avoid long walks at night for fear of rapists, and to avoid carrying a bag for fear of muggers, and to avoid drinking tap water for fear of cholera, and to avoid mosquitoes for fear of malaria. "Symptoms of malaria include but are not limited to nausea, headache, loss of appetite, and vomiting," Dr. Akosua Perbi told us. If we experience any of these symptoms we should alert a doctor right away.

Soon the fears subsided and the living began. The housing complex was beautiful. It was surrounded on all sides by a barbed wire gate guarded by a 24-hour security guard. The brick cobblestones inside were something out of the Wizard of Oz and each of the four homes were two stories of brand new furnishings, a stainless steel kitchen, and a balcony. Every day was summertime here inside the gate, but outside the gate were rundown homes, dirt roads, and children the color of beauty running and playing in sandals like they never knew what it was to be poor or have plenty. They only knew how to laugh.

I lived with the boys and Bella. A house full of 6 men...and two ladies. Gerald Asare was a CRA. Community Resident Assistant. He was 26 years old, a native of Ghana, and an employee of the university. They put him in the house to guide us students along. A native of the land who could show us the ropes and answer the millions of questions we had living in a foreign nation, like how to guard against being cheated out of our money, and how much a taxi should cost.

I started with four classes and I loved all of them. The History of Africa was a bit presumptuous in name but interesting nonetheless. We only glazed the surface of a rich history reaching back thousands of years and spanning a continent that covers more than 20 percent of the earth's total land area. I learned all of the countries of Africa in alphabetical order from Algeria to Zimbabwe and memorized each colonial power and date of independence. Africa was a country beaten and prodded, imprisoned and starved. They had both their legs broken and never learned to walk again.

Prostitution was rampant, young girls selling their bodies and their souls for change I keep in my car.

We were making student films for a class in communications. I sat in Dr. Diawara's class and explained my choice in topic to the professor and a room full of socially conscious 20-year-olds.

"Prostitution says much more about the conditions young girls are brought up in and desperation than it does moral values. I want to highlight the humanness of it all," I had said.

"This will be a tough topic," said the professor.

"How so?"

"First, you will need to find women in the business who will be willing to talk to you," he said in his accent, thick and bold like the man that he was.

"I understand that but I'd like to think I can handle that. I just need two or three willing to speak on camera. I really want to investigate their home lives and their childhoods to find the reasons they choose this lifestyle over the next. Reasons that may not be so obvious."

"Kericho, I admire your vision. If given the time, you would make a great film out of this, but be realistic. You have 15 minutes to develop a story that offers your audience something new."

"I think I can do more than that. I can teach them something and I can teach myself. I find a wealth of knowledge in every experience. Let me try and if it doesn't work, fail me for the class."

"Is that a bet?"

"I'm scheduled to graduate soon. I can't afford a failing grade at this point. Call it confidence."

I breathed in Ghana like cigarette smoke those first few weeks. Time passed much slower than it did in New York. The air was lighter, the roads were softer. When I wasn't in class, I walked the streets, stopping at "corner stores", wooden tables set at intersections where you could buy fresh fruit, magazines, and have your shoes repaired all at once. On lazy days, I stayed at home, watching whatever came on the two channels we got. They showed the movie Roots every day. Sometimes I ordered delivery from the food court downtown. They sold fried chicken, tacos, cheeseburgers, and pizza, comfort food born across the Atlantic.

It took me some time to warm up to Bella. She was a free spirit and I admired that. The tattoos, her eccentric dress. I watched her pair polka dot leggings with a floral sundress. It suited her well. Just fine for a Korean girl who spoke three languages fluently. English, Korean, and Bitch. I heard her on the phone each night, I presumed talking to the same boy. She often sounded like she was arguing but the conversation always ended in

"I love you."

The others in the house were full of personality. Justin, who insisted we call him Justice was a new age Black Panther revolutionist. Matt was from Maine and had never been anywhere south of Maryland before. His pale skin brightened like a Christmas light the first week in, effects of an African sun. Later when his skin darkened to a nice sunbaked tan, we all agreed a little sunshine never hurt anyone. Harvey was awkward. Bowlegged and four eyed. Jun was a modern day Confucious. And Idris, he was the loner.

Gerald, however, was my favorite. I watched Gerald a lot. The uneasy way he sauntered around. He'd come in, find me planted on the couch watching a movie and eating plantain. He would say hello, stop for a moment mid-stride and watch with me, then continue to his room, a private door in the back. Sometimes the discourse was longer. "I've seen this one. It's good." Or, "I went to the market. Do you like mangos?" His goatee was thick, and covered even thicker lips. Once, I got close enough to get a good look at them. He sat next to me on a van ride to campus and I peered over pretending I was looking out the window. They looked soft, like soup coolers. That's what we called lips back home. The kind that were made for cooling soup and looked delicious enough to kiss. I wanted to know him. I wanted to talk to him but he was quiet. Just a few words here and there. One night just a few days in, I told him I was hungry and asked where a good place to get a burger would be. The Green, he said was a restaurant downtown. They deliver for a small fee. "Thanks, would you like anything," I had asked him. "No, I don't like to eat too late," was all he said.

I had a habit of boiling tap water to purify it and then refrigerating it for later. I was doing that in the kitchen this particular afternoon when Gerald came in eating a banana.

"Hey," he said

I turned, startled. "Hi Gerald."

"It has bin a month. You enjoying your time here?" Despite his accent, he spoke slowly by nature and I could understand every word. He always walked upright like he had been trained in posture and just under his shirt I could see the imprint of pectoralis muscles. *He must work out*, I thought. I turned around to face him and rested my back on the counter.

"I'm having a lot of fun. Ghana is much different than what I'm used to at home, but I can adjust to anything."

"Is it really so different?"

"Yes. Yes it is. At home, I don't have to boil water in order to drink it and taxis come with a meter so the price is the same for everyone going the same distance."

"Why did you decide to come here?" His movements were subtle. He walked slowly, chewing his banana in between sentences.

"Well. I've wanted to visit Africa for a long time. You know my father's from Africa. Born and raised."

"Really? He has an accent?"

"He does. He's from Kenya. Someday I hope to make it there."

"And your mudder?" He leaned against a small table tossing the peel.

"Born and raised in the United States. She's black."

"Interesting way to look at it. I thought the politically correct term was African-American." He was showing off.

"I prefer black. It was never explained to me why every other race and nationality has to have a pre-qualifier in front of the term American except for white people. So I refuse to use it."

Gerald smiled. "So your fudder...he never tuk you to Kenya?" Six, maybe seven steps between us. I wanted him to come closer. I wanted to get another look at his lips, but maybe distance was good. I folded my arms.

"No. Unfortunately not yet. But I want to see much more of Africa. Not just Kenya and Ghana. South Africa, and Egypt, and

Ethiopia. All places I want to visit. I like to think I have time."

"Sure you have your whole life."

"And what about you? Have you been to the U.S.?"

"No. "

"You've never been to America? You're kidding." He shook his head. "Wow," I said. "You have to go. You have to see what it's like."

"I want to go soon. The United States is a difficult place to get into. But I work for an American University now, so my chances of getting a visa are high."

"Right. So what's your story? What brings you here to work with these spoiled American kids?"

"I was in graduate school at The University of Ghana. I saw the advertisement for the position. The pay is good, free room and board. And I like the idea of meeting new people with a different view of the world."

“So that’s it. Just like that?”

“Not just like that. There was a long interview process.”

"Well congratulations on getting the job. It’s a big deal moving in here with us. Is this your first group?"

"No no. I started last semester. That would make this my second group."

"Oh ok. What were they like, the last group? Do you remember them?"

"Of course. Why wouldn't I remember them?" A nervous laugh.

"I don't know. We come. We go. Seems like we may all kinda blend together in your memory at some point."

"No I remember. I remember very well." Gerald had a shyness to him. I could tell he was making an intentional attempt at conversation. I could tell that he thought I was pretty. It was in the careful way he lingered between sentences. His gaze met mine for just a moment as he begun to talk and then he looked away, down, at the trash can where the banana peel sat.

"So, what do you do for fun around here? Tomorrow is Friday and I can't let another weekend go by without seeing what nightlife in Accra is all about."

"I can definitely show you around. Afrodisiac is a nightclub not far from here. Lots of locals. You can party the true Ghanaian way."

I smiled big. "It's a date!" I said.

He returned the smile and turned to leave. "Don't let your water boil over."

I wore a white halter dress that night that made my breasts look two cup sizes bigger than they actually were. Gerald's jaw dropped when I came out of my bedroom. "I'm ready," I said spinning around to give him a good look.

"Wow," was all he managed.

It was a fifteen minute cab ride to Afrodisiac and I saw a huddle of scantily clad women at the front door. Once inside, we took a seat at the bar. Gerald was a gentleman.

"Wat can I get you to drink?"

"How about a vodka cranberry? Not too strong."

The music was a mix of hip hop and R&B with a Caribbean flavor. The reggae coupled with the liquor relaxed me. Gerald had a beer.

"Are you sure you're supposed to be drinking with me? Does it violate a code of rules from the university," I asked him over the music.

He laughed. It was a kind of signature laugh. "It's ok," he explained. "We are just two friends hanging out tonight. Nothing wrong with having a beer." We finished our drinks and ordered a second round.

"Do you go out often?" I asked him.

"I don't come to clubs that much. I don't think I'm that gud of a dansa."

I peered at the crowd through the dark haze and strobe lights, the music reverberated on my insides.

"Well let's find out." I stood up. "May I have this dance?"

We maneuvered through the crowd and took our drinks to the floor-- kept our distance at first, swaying and rocking to the music. It's been so long since I've felt like this. Free. Calm. Loose. Luke never danced. We would go out. He'd pick me up back in New York and we'd head to the trendiest new bar. Then I'd sit, he would buy me a drink, and then he'd make his round of hellos to all the bartenders, acquaintances, and homeboys he knew. I was arm candy at best. His show and tell toy for the night.

But this was different. Gerald was there with me. He was interested in me, not in the appearance. The mood intensified and the alcohol settled in so we moved closer. Relinquishing my empty glass, I wrapped my arms around his neck and let him guide my hips to the beat.

The music was tropical, the tempo was strong. I felt sexy, provocative. Wayne Wonder's "No Letting Go" was playing, a fusion of handclapping, drums, a melody that anyone could fall in love to.

"You're not so bad," I said.

"This is just an exceptional night fa mi. You make mi poot my best foot fowad."

His accent was intriguing. I've never dated a foreigner before. I wondered just for a moment what the love making would sound like.

Gerald was gentle and I could feel the warmth of his chest against my bare skin. I turned around and grazed his crotch with my butt. No stiffness yet. Something about giving a man a hard on always made me feel like I had accomplished something, that I could be powerful enough to bring on such a reaction. But Gerald was, in a way, my superior at five years older than me. He was a chaperone of sorts and so this encounter with him felt naughty.

Five songs later, he suggested another drink. This time we sat on the chaise against the wall.

"Your boyfriend back home must miss your moves," he said getting comfortable.

"I'm sure he would if I had one."

"Pritty gal like you doesn't have anyone chasing her tail? I don't believe it."

"I didn't say that. They're chasing, but they can't catch me." I laughed and rolled my eyes playfully.

"Rightfully so. Your head should be in your buks. What are you studying?"

"Right now, I'm kind of taking a break from my normal studies to learn about this country I know so little about. But I'm majoring in psychology, minor in journalism."

"So, you're reading my mind right now so you can write about it later?"

I blushed. "I like that. But no. It's not that simple. In fact, I think the human mind is one of the most complicated things in life. If you think about, who we are, what we do, how we think and operate has all been shaped by our experiences since birth, everything we've seen and witnessed."

"So you're an advocate of nurture over nature?" He sipped his beer awaiting my response.

"Not completely. Some things we are born with, yes, but the reason babies are so precious, is because they come equipped with everything they need to live a normal life. They are unscathed, unscarred, new, fresh out the box. They have ears to hear, eyes to see, a mouth to speak, a heart to love. They are so malleable, so innocent, because they have little control over what they hear, or see, and later, how they speak or their readiness to love. Each experience is a chipping away of the full equipment they were born with. Babies from all over the world are born ready to speak any language and make any sound they become accustomed to. I was only exposed to English daily, and now I can't easily learn a new language or make sounds with my tongue I've never made. It's the same with life. Every experience, good and bad becomes an unraveling of the complete person that was present at birth. A kind of undoing of what was already set in place by God from the point of conception."

"So?" He was curious.

"So...the result? Who I am right now...my beliefs, my fears, my abilities, my personality, my hindrances, it is all as a result of everything that came apart over the course of my life. I am the content of things undone."

He squinted, sipped his beer. "Does that mean we all have to accept the idea that we are incomplete?"

"Well it's difficult to put back together a shattered vase, but not impossible. With the right amount of glue in the right places, done by the right craftsman, it could be as good as new."

"Well said. You gave me something to think about. Tell me--"

"No, no, no. The nightclub is no place for thinking. Enough talk about philosophy. We'll finish some other time," I said standing up. "Right now, to the dance floor sir. I'm ready for round two."

He followed my lead. I danced closer this time, my back nestled in his chest, his arms wrapped tight around my waste. This time he rose to the occasion. The stiffness in his pants got the best of my imagination.

Chapter Six

Life hurts a lot more than death

"It could be alcohol poisoning, or it could be malaria."

I loved that Bella had a sense of humor. First, I thought I would have little in common with a tattooed Korean girl who wore a lot of makeup and painted her nails black. But I can only charge that to a narrow mind on my part. Bella grew on me like an ugly sweater you get for Christmas and only wear to spare feelings until one day you realize it's not so ugly after all and in fact goes well with your favorite earrings.

She was really a pretty girl, edgy, and smart. The day we met, I got to our room first and started unpacking. She came in, threw her things on the other bed, and then threw herself down next to them.

"Hi. Bella right?" I opened.

"That's me. Exhausted from the flight. I just wanna sleep a few. Would you wake me when it's time for dinner?"

I did but when we filed in the van and rode over to a nearby restaurant, one that would have a special buffet laid out for us students nightly, Bella didn't sit with me. She opted instead for a table across the room with some of the boys. In fact our bond first began over a boy. It was a couple of weeks in, after one of those long distance calls with her late night lover. She was arguing about him being out too late, not returning her calls in an acceptable amount of time and lying about... a girl. I lay on my back in the dark room, my bed encased in a mosquito net, staring up at the ceiling. I was half listening to Bella, who had no shame in broadcasting her personal" conversation, and half reminding myself to see a doctor as soon as I got back to the States. *I gotta get on birth control. I've been reckless and Gods grace will soon run out on me.*

This time I didn't notice Bella's perfunctory "I love you" before she hung up the phone. At this point she had a habit of turning over to go to sleep but that day, instead she sighed heavily and said "so what's your story?"

I was unsure if the question was directed to me. "Huh, what? My... my story?"

"Boys suck. They really do you know. I've been with the same kid for like 3 years now. He's in China, and I get that that's far, and we can't be together all the time, but damnit don't lie about who you're with and for how long, and what you did. That's disrespectful. I can't stand that shit.

"I'm sorry to hear."

"What about you? You have someone?"

"Nah. I mean I date. But no real relationship. I haven't found that person yet. I doubt I'm that person yet."

"Yeah. That may be best. I don't know, I've just always been the relationship kind. This boy, Hubert, I thought we were going to get married. I'm not so sure now. I want to. I love him. I'm comfortable with him but he's, I don't know, he's difficult."

"Hmm, how'd you meet?"

"I was in China. I went to a boarding school in China before coming to New York for college. He stayed back there. We visit every couple of months. But now you know with me being here I won't see him for a while and he must be getting... antsy. You know how boys get. They need their penis played with, sucked, kissed, or it's like they can't control themselves."

She was forward. I gave the common "uh huh." I let her talk. I let her tell me and then we went to sleep. I liked that she was open, and a couple of days later, I told her about Luke. The sex, the baths, the way I wanted more but I wasn't sure he did.

"What are black guys like in bed?" She had asked."

I shrugged. "I've never been with anyone else to compare."

"Me neither. I mean not black guys but Asians. Maybe I should date outside the box. I just feel like they get me ya know. Our crazy customs. They understand."

Today it is Saturday and we are sitting in the kitchen having breakfast. Since last night's fun at Afrodisiac, I haven't been feeling well. "I think it's just a stomachache," I said.

Bella made pancakes for me and Gerald and Justice. Justice was reminiscent of the militant Black Panthers from the seventies who walked around in leather jackets stirring up a revolution. Only Justice didn't wear a leather jacket since Africa was 100 degrees on a cool day, so he opted for white tank tops and black bandanas wrapped neatly around his head. He was passion personified. Lots of students here were passionate about the same kinds of things. Human rights, rebuilding communities, finding art in uncommon places. Africa was like that.

The alcohol was still settled in my stomach from the night before, when I danced against Gerald's moon for the second half of the night. The pancakes looked and smelled amazing but my stomach rolled with the smallest bite. "It just takes time. I've been here before."

"Get better fast so you can do it all over again tonight," Bella said.

"Tonight, I'll just stick to Coke. Gerald, where we goin?" I asked. The mission tonight would be to charm a few prostitutes into talking to me for my documentary.

Gerald was quick. "We'll go where the prostitutes are. None other than California," he said with a wink. We all looked at him confused.

"California?" I repeated. "That's a few miles away, wouldn't you say."

"Let me guess, it's the name of a bar?" Justice chimed in.

Gerald smiled. "Yes. This guy knows Ghana."

"Not really," said Justice. "I just know they steal everything from the States."

"Doesn't everyone?" I said.

"It's true," said Justice. "Locals here refer to Labone as L.A. Downtown as D.C. They know all the popular cities in America."

"And here I just found out about Ghana last year," Bella joked. "Figured it would be a cool place to visit. I go where the wind takes me." We all looked at her and smiled. Only Gerald thought she was serious. She swallowed the last of her milk and stood. "Tonight," she proclaimed. "We find the hoes."

Everyone is beautiful in California. The air tonight was dry. Warm, but it felt good. The moon was full and high in the sky. The same moon Sunday had seen millions of miles away just a few hours ago in Guam. I saw it's brightness against the nighttime sky and was in awe of God's work. God's brilliance shines its best when it's dark outside. That moon, the same moon I followed across the sky driving along the eastern shore of New Jersey was here above me now in a remote corner of the world. "He doesn't withhold his glory even from the poorest of the poor, or the richest of the rich. We all partake but few really see." I read that in a devotional once.

This. Is. Life. It's not merely living or existing, but I stepped out of the taxi cab onto a bustling street in the center of Accra and swallowed the air whole. It tasted like newness, though it felt very ancient. African Mahogany trees danced against the breeze and a drummer played in the distance. The atmosphere oozed with a certain ease and carefree ambition. I never felt quite like this before. I wore a black dress that clung to my petite frame and accented the few curves I had, but inside California was the epitome of sex that forced me to fade into the background. It was a small bar with no walls and speakers that amplified the highlife band playing on stage, songs of happiness and freedom from worries and those nights that feel like they might last forever. The singer sang like he believed it, like he lived it morning til night and he made me believe it too. Positive thinking makes the world go round. His dreadlocks stretched below his waist. He had bare bones for fingers and used them to string his guitar to accompany his melodic voice that we floated on. I followed Gerald's lead, Bella on Justice's arm close behind us, and we settled at a table near the wall.

Cigar smoke was thick here and I could smell the brown liquors that cluttered each table. The women were calm, cool, and in the mood, by far the most interesting accessory in California. The waitress came over clad in black shorts that could barely contain her backside and a spaghetti strap halter. My party's choice in liquor was Guinness beer, that dark beer that awakened the senses. I was never a beer drinker until I came here to Africa. Beer seemed to compliment the scenery well. It wasn't fancy like fine wine but gritty and earthy like the terrain.

Justice took a long sip from his glass and breathed a heavy sigh. "That's a good beer," he said.

"Is this place really anything like California?" I asked him, yelling over the music.

"I'm from California, and if you mean that everyone here puts on a façade, then yes," He yelled back.

"What do you mean a façade?" asked Gerald.

"People are not the person they portray themselves to be. In Los Angeles, everyone is an actor or a model or singer. Everyone. Even the men. They go to clubs at the end of a week and buy a few hundred dollar bottles of hard liquor to show everyone what they can afford when in reality they just spent every last dollar of their paycheck that they just got, in an effort to show off. Not who they say they are. Every woman in here is a prostitute. Nearly everyone. But to an outsider, they wouldn't know it. They wouldn't know these women are compromising their bodies and their lives out of desperation for a way out. Morals have lost its value here." Justice looked much older than 21 with a beard that almost mimicked Abe Lincoln's. But he had a stronger build, muscles that were made for construction work and fair skin that hinted his Daddy wasn't a black man.

"But California is much more than Los Angeles," interrupted Bella. "Northern California is the best place to go."

"I agree," said Justice. It's a little bit of quiet in a world full of thunder there."

"How do you know so much about Ghana," I asked Justice.

"I read. I travel. I was here two years ago with a program that told stories through art. I'm a photographer in training. You know how they say a picture says a thousand words?"

"Yeah," I said.

"Mine say much more than that. I can tell you all day about baby rape that goes down all over this country and you would listen for a few minutes but if I show you a picture of a one year old baby girl having her vagina sewn back together, you'd probably throw up."

We all were silent at the thought.

Gerald chimed in. "So what draws you to Africa?" he asked him.

“Hmmm...the women," he said and licked his lips.

"The women?" Gerald and I repeated together asking for clarification.

"When I see them it reminds me of Christmas morning when I was 5 years old waking up to a room full of toys. I couldn't contain myself. That's how the women here make me feel. Fine from head to toe. Their form is truly a creation from God. Breasts that make grown men cry just to imagine nipples erect beneath their clothes. Asses so big, they don't make pants to fit them, and waists so petite I can almost wrap my hands completely around them. The women keep me coming back here."

Bella looked up from her beer. "That almost makes me love them too."

Justice looked around and set his eyes upon a damsel 3 tables over. "Take this woman. In the red dress. Her neckline is low enough to make you look there. Makes me want to lick the crease in between her breasts like ice cream."

"Justice, you talk about the women like they're a prize in one sentence and reduce them to sexual objects in the next. Are they good for nothing more?" Bella said.

"I'm a man. At the end of the day, I'm still a man. I'm going to love everything on a woman that I don't have. It's something about her delicateness that gets to me every time."

Gerald laughed. "He knows what I'm talking about," said Justice. "Our capacity to reason weakens when our senses are stimulated with the sensuality of a woman. You women have it so easy. You can have us under your spell as soon as you take your clothes off." He motioned to the red dress woman. "Men here, white men with money, will pay her more than what seems reasonable for one night to feel her up and she knows it. That's why she has so much power."

Justice was right about one thing for sure. There was no denying her beauty. Her skin was the color of coffee, with a little bit of milk. Her hair, a mane of tight curls that framed a face with delicate features and full lips painted red. I watched her where she sat with two other women. One of them said something funny and she laughed, her lips parting showing pearls for teeth and...dimples. She has dimples.

"How do you know she's working," I asked Justice.

"They all are," he said. I looked at Gerald for confirmation and he nodded in agreement. Justice continued, "She's with two other women, and none of them have a drink in front of them."

"They're waiting for a man to buy them a drink?" I asked.

"Sure," he said.

"So a group of women can't have girl's night out here without being hookers?" Bella asked.

"Sure they can. But they generally don't," said Gerald.

I sipped my beer and sat back with a sigh. "She's beautiful. I'm sure she could find a man to love her for free. I mean really love her and take care of her."

"Since when is sex the same thing as love?" Justice was picking my brain.

I was silent for a moment and remembered my high school years when I often interchanged the two. I lost my virginity in my school's cafeteria late one night after a basketball game to a guy who told me he was in love and didn't call the next day. "For these women, maybe there is no difference."

"So how should we lure her over?" Bella was anxious.

"I don't want to be too pushy. Let's take it slow. I definitely don't want to scare her away or make her suspicious," I said. The waitress came back with our second round of beers and I motioned for her to lean in close. "That woman in the red dress. Offer her a drink of whatever she wants. Tell her it's on me. I admire her beauty." The waitress smiled and I watched her walk over to the woman with red lips.

"I like your style, Kericho," said Gerald.

"I do too," I said. "I learned it from all the charming men I've encountered."

"So what are you going to do after she accepts the drink," Bella asked me.

"I don't know yet. I'm making it up as I go along."

The waitress bent down to talk to Beauty and gestured briefly in my direction. I smiled slightly when she looked up. A head nod and a brief interchange of words before the waitress scurried away.

"I wonder what she ordered," I said aloud.

"Probably something very strong," said Justice. A few moments later, the waitress, brought over a tall glass with a pinkish liquid and set it down before Beauty.

"It's something fruity." I said.

"She's being modest," Justice retorted.

"What do you think she is thinking about me? About us?" I asked.

Bella chuckled. "We're a table full of foreigners. She is most likely wondering what the hell we want from her."

"So much for being subtle." I said.

"Foreigners in this country are synonymous with money. She likely doesn't care what you want with her as long as you're willing to pay," said Gerald.

"And what if we're wrong. What if she doesn't have sex for money and we all just underestimated her?" I asked.

Gerald sighed. Justice looked over at Beauty who had returned to her own private conversation. "Nah," he said sipping his drink. "We won't be wrong. If anything, she's a high class hoe. The kind that wants more than a simple exchange of money for sex. She's looking for a lifestyle."

"Aren't we all," Bella inquired rhetorically. "As women, we always feel a little better about ourselves sleeping with a man after he's wined and dined us and not before. Does that mean there is a little hoe in all of us, or is wanting a man with some financial stability a crime?"

"You have a point, Bella," I said. "I knew a girl once that slept with a man over and over again. She didn't like him or the sex, but she was in love with all of the gifts he showered her with. It's hard to give up a lifestyle once you have it."

"Now, that's a whore if I've ever seen one," said Justice.

"I'm sure you only sleep with women for love?" Bella inquired.

"No, I've never been in love," answered Justice. "I said women were beautiful, but they're also conniving."

"So cynical." Bella was offended. "If you feel that way, why give them your soul?"

"My soul?" he asked.

"Yes, your soul. When two people have sex, they become one, even if it is just for a few brief moments."

"It's much longer than that," he retorted.

"I'm sure," Bella said. Her sarcasm made me chuckle. "So answer the question. Why give them any part of you if they're really the conniving bitches you claim they are?"

"I like the way they feel. Nothing is as incredible as the grip of a vagina dripping with fruit juice around my dick. Nothing."

"Point taken. And that doesn't make you a whore?"

"I'm a man, so that's not possible by definition."

She sucked her teeth. I laughed. Gerald smiled. Then Beauty walked over. She stood before our table and I could see the width of her hips. Curves like a coca cola bottle. The red dress hugged her thighs for Gerald and Justice's viewing pleasure.

"Hi," I said to her. "Have a seat."

She did. When she started to speak, I noticed the sound of her voice complimented her beauty. It was soft, her accent was thick, but she spoke with a delicateness that said *I'm a woman so be kind to me.* "It's a beautiful night tonight. Thank you for the drink."

"You're very welcome," I said. "You're very beautiful. I hope you don't take my kindness inappropriately but I like to compliment where compliments are due. I'm Kericho," I extended my hand.

"As in Kericho, Kenya?" she asked shaking it.

I laughed. "You know your African cities well. Please meet my friends. This is Gerald, Justice, and Bella." Everyone nodded cordially. Justice took her hand, looked her deep in the eyes and then kissed it. *The sensual bastard.*

"My nem is Esi," she said.

"Esi. What does that mean?" I asked.

She smiled shyly. Then Gerald interceded. "Esi is a common

name here. It means she was born on Sunday."

"I have a sister who was born on Sunday. We call her Sunday."

"That's a fitting name." She said. "What brings you all here to Ghana?"

"Gerald is a native here. I'm sure you can tell. The three of us are students who also love the vibe of the country. Or perhaps you can say we love the vibe of the country and also happen to be students."

Beauty played with her glass. It was just ice now. "Can I get you another?" I asked her.

"Sure."

I waved the waitress over and she ordered a guava juice mix with top shelf vodka. "What brings you to California, tonight," Justice asked her.

"Oh you know...it's a nice place for hanging out. I like the music. I like the men."

"And I like the women," he continued. "Especially you." This made Beauty smile, her dimples protruding inward.

"Esi, what else is there to do for fun around here," I interrupted their fiasco. "Best to hear it from a girl who looks like she has fun."

"I love open bars like thez one. Live museec, nice people. There is another place like this on the rooftop of The Nile Hotel. Many people like you there."

"Like me?"

"Americans. I am sorry. Lots of Americans and visitors from other countries. An eclectic mix of cultures. Also the beach is very nice. It's always warm here and there are many many concerts on the beach. Good restaurants. They can be expensive, but the food is delicious."

"I've heard so much about the beaches. I'm sure I will get there soon. " I glanced over and saw that Beauty's friends had been joined by two men. One was black. The other was white.

"Did you want to ask your friends to join us? They are welcome?"

Beauty looked at them and then looked at me. "No they are just fine. We often split up when we go out together. It's our way of mingling."

"You know, this place is getting kinda tired anyway," Justice said stretching in his seat. "What do you say, we hit the beach tonight?"

"I'm for it," said Bella.

"Tonight?" asked Gerald. It's already late. I thought this was going to be an easy night."

"I'll go if Esi leads the way," I said. "Gerald, you have absolutely nothing to do tomorrow. What does it matter if we dance the night away barefoot in a sea of sand?"

The beach was serene. The water was calm but the people were not. Both the women and the men were all sweating bullets shaking their tail feathers to the heavy beats in the speakers. There were five to ten musicians on stage strumming guitars, banging drums, and belting out lyrics full of energy and charisma. A couple hundred people gyrated hips barefoot in the sand and the women left their drinks at the bar for freedom to do whatever they wanted with their hands.

Esi kicked her shoes off too along with myself and we danced like no one was watching. Justice left us to enjoy his share of the women while Gerald hung back at the makeshift bar with Bella. They were more reserved partygoers, lookers and not doers. But Esi was having fun. She loved to smile and I loved to watch her do it. Her dimples drew me in, so deep they looked like they could carry water. Her curls bounced around while she danced, occasionally slowing down to pull down the hem of her red dress. I followed her lead, laughing and giggling like a school girl. My attempt to spin my hips in circles was a failure and she noticed. She held me on both sides and guided my hips. "Like this," she said.

At that, I was ecstatic. "Esi, you're too much," I said, yelling over the music. "I love the way you move. It's like each part of your body has a mind of its own. Your hips move like they are separate from the rest of you. Your butt jiggles like it's not connected. Your legs. Your hands. Your itty bitty waist. Very sexy."

"Oh, it comes naturally. And you will get the hang of it too in time."

"I hope so. Because right now, I can't keep up. Everyone is so sensuous. They move effortlessly. Even the men. They move like this is what they were born to do."

"It is. Well it is a part of the story."

"Everyone is watching you. That man there, dancing with his girlfriend. He keeps glancing over. He likes you."

"How do you know it is not you he is watching?"

"Because I don't move like you. And I don't look like you."

"But you are very beautiful."

"You think so? What is the going rate for beauty these days?" It was time.

"It is priceless."

"That may be so. But what do you charge?" I asked the question like I was asking for a piece of jewelry.

Esi's smile dwindled and her hips slowed.

I continued my line of questioning. "The men who find you irresistible. How much do you charge them?"

"Who are you really?" Now she stopped dancing completely and her smile turned to a look of disdain. I stopped dancing too and put my hands on my hips to catch my breath.

"Kericho. A student from the United States."

"What are yu? A reporter of sum kind?"

"I'm not a reporter. I'm a student. And I want to learn about you. I want to write about you."

"Write about what?" She was quick.

"Let's go have another drink. Maybe water this time." I motioned to the bar. She followed reluctantly and we sat at a bar stool. "Two waters," I called to the bartender.

"Esi." I said carefully turning my attention to her. "I'm investigating prostitution in Accra. I just want to talk to you and if you feel comfortable I'd like to get your side of your story for a short film."

"I'm not a prostitute."

"Then what are you?"

"A woman who likes nice things and I work hard to get them."

"Do you sleep with men for money?"

"Sometimes. That doesn't make me a prostitute."

"I see you have a problem with that word. I won't use it. Esi. I think you're beautiful. The fact that you like nice things does not make you less beautiful. All of us want nice things. All of us indulge in luxury. But all of us don't exchange sex for money. We don't all compromise our bodies. I want to know why you do."

Esi was quiet for a moment. She looked down at her glass and then out at the dancers on the sand. Like she was in thought, contemplating how much of her world she should share. "You know it's a way of life," she finally said. "We have to work much harder for the things you have naturally. We are not afforded the same opportunities."

"Esi, I wasn't born with a silver spoon in my mouth. But I understand, you face many obstacles here."

"My mother never had much of anything. My father was a drifter. Here some days. Gone the next. He was with many women and they gave him their bodies and got nothing in return. Not even love. I think if love is not possible...if love is not a reality, why not get something just as good if not better."

"Money?"

"A lifestyle."

"Why do you say that is better than love?"

"Love is fleeting. Here one day. Gone the next. Love does not stay. It is like a dream. A figment of our imagination."

Chapter Seven

Three things we require in life. Something to do. Someone to love. And something to look forward to. Losing all three makes life hard to fathom.

"I don't think that you have malaria. A common stomach virus can explain the nausea. You can wait it out. I'm sure it will go away." The nurse on campus sat behind her desk, her glasses pushed down on her nose. Her wig needed adjusting and all I could do was stare at the simulated part too far off to the side of her head. She came to the campus twice a week on Mondays and Wednesdays. When Wednesday came and my stomach pains hadn't subsided, I took a walk to her office. She asked me some questions about the symptoms I had been having and concluded I was reading too far into it. "If you would like, we can go to the community hospital and have your blood drawn for testing. Then, we will know for sure."

I wasn't in pain. It was more so discomfort. Like the feeling you get when you eat too much at Thanksgiving, and while the food was good, all you can do is sit still and wait for it to digest so that you can move about again. Like vomiting would give some relief and while you may need to wipe down the toilet seat after, it's worth it to feel like normal. That is how I felt, and I was not satisfied with waiting out a stomach virus, because what if it was something much worse? Something deadly that could have been cured if it was treated properly in the right window of time. I've heard news stories about people dying of cancer that wasn't caught soon enough and I know those people wish they could turn back the hands of time, so why should I "wait it out" if the clock was ticking. I had time and opted to take advantage of it.

The taxi ride to the hospital was bumpy. Each time the car stopped, peddlers crowded the windows selling American magazines, fruit, cigarettes, Coca-Colas. Women with small children held their hands out for money. The smells in the air were strong. Almost too strong to be bearable and I thought I wanted the windows up, until I had to choose between the smells or the heat. No air conditioner and the 100 degree weather forced me to choose the former.

Once inside the hospital, the nurse and I took a number and a seat. I felt much more like I was waiting in a deli line than in a hospital. It was crowded that day, ailing men and women piled in the waiting room and I stood in line at least thirty minutes for the bathroom so I could pee in a cup to confirm what was already lurking in the corner of my mind. I waited another two hours for the lab to test my urine and when finally I stood before the doctor in his cramped office that smelled like old couch cushions that had just been washed, he said looking down at a white piece of paper,

"You've tested positive for pregnancy."

Chapter Eight

Instead of fishes, I dreamt of a sea of blood. A lot of blood. Like the Red Sea. Only God wasn't around to part it.

Man did the unthinkable the night before I left for Ghana. He took my panties off and my soul went with them. My life dissolved with the wetness of his tongue, only I didn't know it until now.

That night he invited me over, I was prompt in arriving at his house. Standing at his front door, I looked at the time on my cell. 7:55pm. He greeted me without touching me and invited me in. Two menus for takeout were on the couch. Chinese or pizza. I opted for pizza and mozzarella sticks. It would go well with the bottle of wine I brought over.

His apartment was nearly vacant, or maybe just without a woman's touch. He had the bare essentials. A couch, lopsided coffee table, and a small tv on a broken stand furnished his carpeted livingroom. He had just two plates, two glasses, and two sets of utensils. Just enough for the two of us to enjoy the food.

No pictures on the wall except for the infamous image of the 1968 Olympics medalists Tommie Smith and John Carlos with black-gloved, clenched-fists gesturing "Black Power" during an awards ceremony.

We watched something funny on TV. What it was, I don't remember, but I laughed…that innocent and slightly uncomfortable laugh you do when you're in the company of someone you don't know well, and the elephant in the room is taking up more space than the two of you. Man was attracted to me. I knew it and could tell by the way he bit his bottom lip nervously. But he was a nice guy. Not the kind I would normally go for. I wanted a bad guy "on top of the world". I liked men who took control. The kind that walked with confidence and didn't wait for me to spread my legs because they did it for me. The kind that drank hard liquor but never got drunk or didn't let it show at least. They always kept their cool and made me feel protected well enough to drive me home after a late night drinking at The Corner Social. The kind I felt secure with, almost like he was God or something.

But Man was nothing like that. Man was insecure and overweight. Man was more in love with the idea of being with a pretty girl than he could ever be with a real person. I was too good for him and much too far out of his league. He suffered from narcolepsy or sleep apnea or something like that and would fall asleep at any given moment. In the middle of a conversation. While driving. While eating. He sweated profusely and the fat pockets under his arms carried a pungent stench that couldn't be washed away with soap and water.

I loathed him, yet here I was on his couch, a quarter to midnight, my stomach full off pizza and wine, my eyelids heavy with sleep. He suggested we get in the bed. I obliged. An oversized Nets t-shirt and Victoria's Secret panties was all I wore. The bedroom was warm. In temperature and in mood. He was lacking shades on the windows and I noticed it was a full moon tonight. I cracked the window to let in the cool breeze. Once I was in bed, he climbed in next to me and laid flat on his back, his hands clasped over his chest. His stomach was protruding outwards. It reminded me of a mountain or a small hill and I was completely hidden on one side. I dozed off easily within ten minutes.

I hadn't been sleeping long when I awoke to something tugging at my leg. It was dragging me sideways across the bed. Then I felt hands on my torso, creeping up my side. I opened my eyes just enough to see him kneeling on the side of the bed, a praying position, my body positioned horizontally across the bed, my pelvis just under his chin. This was a side of Man I had never seen before.

"What are you doing," I whispered, my voice cracking under the guise of sleep.

He didn't answer me. Instead, he grabbed my panties and pulled them down just enough to slip his head underneath. His tongue felt cool on the sweetness between my legs. He grabbed my thighs and pushed my knees high up in the air. I had him pinned there, his head between my opening and my panties. Just his thick black hair was visible from my view. For a moment I squirmed and tried to get away, but I didn't try very hard and then I stopped trying at all. I let him lick me and suck the juice right out of my body. I did it because it felt good and even though Man was not remotely attractive, right here in this moment, I imagined he was Luke. Nearly a month without sex had left me wanting. I was a sexual being and my hormones were at their peak. I needed to be filled up with only that thing that a man has to offer. I wanted Luke here right now. To fill every crevice, every corner, ever space inside me from wall to wall. But Luke was not here. Only Man, and in the moment, it didn't matter so much that Man was not Luke and Luke was not Man because all tongues feel the same in the dark and right now, he was making me feel good. Oohwee good. Lock the door and make me scream good. I wanted him inside me bad.

Man was good at what he was doing to me. I was moist and he drew my juices forth like the moon draws the tide. Then he stopped. He stopped and he climbed back in bed, lay on his back and invited me to climb on top. I hesitated, but needed to be filled right here in this moment. Even if it was just for a second or a few seconds, I wanted to feel his hardness inside of me. So I sat up and draped one leg over the width of his thighs and pushed myself down on him.

"We shouldn't do this," I said. "We don't have a condom." Man didn't keep condoms because he didn't use them because he didn't have sex. The last time he had a girlfriend was never and so the times he did have sex were few and far between. I moved up and down on his hardness once. Twice. Three times and then I eased him out of me and fell into the pillow beside him. "I don't want to do this," I said. He was silent. It was a bad idea.

The next morning I hated myself for being so reckless, so haphazard in allowing something like that to happen. I made an agreement with myself to see a doctor for some prescription birth control pills immediately when I was back from Africa. But those thoughts came a day too late since conception had taken place that night Man was on his back and my thighs were spread open on top of him.

The initial shock of pregnancy gripped me like the sudden death of a beloved friend. I was held captive there in that moment the Ghanaian doctor read my test results aloud. *You've tested positive for pregnancy.* I was silent for a moment trying to remember another definition for positive in a situation such as this, because my defenses would not allow me to believe the possibility of having a baby right now, when having a baby right now was not an option. I thought I had malaria, that infectious disease born from parasitic mosquitoes, and infiltrates blood cells resulting in death, but here,

I learned the only parasite was a bundle growing inside me that pro-life activists called a blessing from God. I wondered if contracting malaria would have been better.

I was numb for the taxi ride home. No not numb, because I could feel. It was a culmination of a thousand feelings all at once. My face, expressionless had not yet regained the ability to cry. The nurse was silent. I was reluctant to tell her. "You were right. I don't have malaria," was all I could muster when I emerged from the doctor's office, my body cold with shock. It was sunny out. A beautiful day free of clouds or rain. Children gathered around the car each time we slowed and held their fingers to their mouths to indicate hunger. "The children are not hungry, They are fed well," I remembered Dr. Perbi had told us at orientation. "If you feel you must give them something, give them a pencil. Stimulate reading and writing. Pencils are a treasure here."

A pencil would be nice right now. I would erase my present and rewrite history. I would scrub hard until the pink eraser was near gone and spread into tiny pink particles all over the paper. Then I would take a deep breath and scatter them like dust into the air and rewrite my life as I once knew it or would have known it in the absence of today. In the absence of the day Man released his legacy into my crevices and filled me with regret and in the absence of all the days in between that day and today, I would be made whole again. I would erase the events that led up to now. Blot them out like Jesus blotted out our transgressions that day on Calvary. I would get rid of them and remember them no more. But I didn't have a pencil. So I couldn't.

Instead, I remembered to breathe and I watched the trees as their branches danced in the wind and I was reminded that the universe bends to forces I cannot see, but can only feel.

The car pulled up to my housing complex and I remembered to thank the nurse for her time before running past the security guard and inside the barbed wire gate to my front door that was left ajar to let the breeze in. The TV was on, blaring news about a hurricane in New Orleans and the superdome but none of my housemates were around to hear it. So I went to the back of the house, to Gerald's room and knocked hard in anticipation. I wanted to get this burden off of my chest or out of my belly and felt relief would only come at the ears of a confidant. Not a judge, but a friend.

I needed release so I knocked and when Gerald opened the door, I was speechless. He was nearly nude. Plaid shorts and shirtless, I forgot Luke there in that moment, because Gerald became my Luke. A perfect chest made for laying my head and arms built to hold me. For just a brief second I forgot the life growing inside me and Man and that awful doctor at the hospital that delivered the terrible news. I envied Gerald's future wife.

"What happened at the hospital? Do you have malaria?" he smiled sarcastically.

"Ma--laria? No. I'm pregnant. The doctor said I'm pregnant." With that I hurried away, my face in my palm and settled on the living room couch in front of the TV and that woman still talking about a hurricane she was calling Katrina. He followed me, unable to speak whole sentences.

"Wha...," was all he blurted.

"Yes. I know. It's a shock to me too."

"When did this happen?"

"Before I came here. In the States. Before I left."

Gerald sat on the opposite couch, facing me. Still shirtless in plaid shorts. He sat and clasped his hands in front of him leaning forward in concern.

"What should I do?" I asked him.

"Who is the fudder?"

"It doesn't matter. We aren't together. We weren't a couple. Just friends that had an accident one night."

"An accident?"

"Yep. An accident. This wasn't supposed to happen. I went to my friend's house one night and we had sex. We imitated sex, but it was just enough of the real thing to get me pregnant. For all of this, it wasn't even worth it."

"Have you told him? Does he know?"

"When was I going to tell him, Gerald?" I asked rhetorically. "He's thousands of miles away and here I just found out myself moments ago. So in answer to your question, no, I haven't told him."

"I think you should." Gerald was calm.

"I just found out. Not even one hour ago. I think I need to figure out what I want before I involve him. For me, I just need to sort this thing out."

"This is really surprising. Wow. Pregnant." Gerald still had shock on his face. I could tell he wasn't sure whether to hug me and offer his condolences or slap me high five and celebrate. So he just sat there as if deep in thought with his hands clasped together and I sat across from him, my knees drawn to my chest, still unable to cry, but heartbroken with disbelief. The room fell silent except for the hum of the TV and the woman still fussing about Katrina.

The coming days were filled with anxiety I had never witnessed before. Anxiety greeted me each morning, watched me brush my teeth, then stopped by to say hello midday. Anxiety was waiting at my doorstep each time I came home and waiting for me in bed at night. The nausea was constant but subsided with the pills the doctor gave me. In exchange I slept for hours, sometimes all day.

When I did tell Man, he froze and was silent for an eternity there on the phone. After the initial shock, the idea of a baby settled in for the both of us. I wanted to abort. Man didn't.

Once in class, I felt the sudden urge to vomit and hurried away from my desk to find the bathroom. I locked myself in the stall and keeled over the toilet just in time. There in those few moments, coughing up my insides, I wondered if I could throw up so much that the embryo came with it. I wondered if I coughed hard and loud enough, the tiny fetus growing in my belly would be forced to come up too. Because I had dreams bigger than I had hands to hold and here I was, a senior in college, set to graduate at the end of the year. Then what? Then, graduate school for a Masters and a Ph.D and then a job, and my own house. I would do research and counseling in clinical psychology and change the face of the prison system here in America. I would write a book one day and maybe produce a documentary film for HBO on the compromising conditions inner city children grow up in and the effects it has on the mind.

I would get married. To a man just as ambitious as I, excelling in his field and complimenting me well. We would have two children. Maybe three, or maybe six, once I could find the time. Our children would grow up in a loving environment, with parents who gave each other everything we had. We would be a family built on God, and love, and trust.

But there in that stall, kneeling in front of a toilet, saliva dripping from my mouth, I saw each dream tossed into the toilet with my morning meal. I coughed and watched my college degree dissolve. Then I hacked and saw my hope of graduate school slip into the toilet with it. I felt like my stomach was being pumped and with each pump, I saw the book, the feature film, the husband I had yet to meet walk away from me without even a wave goodbye. My stomach was pumped until there was nothing left except the tiny fetus growing into a baby. That's what I was left with. So I flushed the toilet, sat back on my bottom, rested my head on the wall behind me, and then I cried.

I cried for the first time since I heard the news and I cried for a long time to get it all out. All the emotions that I had been holding were pouring from my eyes there in that stall and I wept like Jesus wept for Lazarus. I wept like a new born baby when it first sees the light of day. I held my chest to keep my heart from bursting forward and cried until I could no more. My lips quivered and my face was soaked in my own tears. I was broken and falling apart without a soul to put me together again. No Sunday. No Luke. No Man. Just me, and the baby inside my womb who refused to let go of my inside walls and be flushed with the rest of me. He was busy being shaped and formed by the hands of God. He was being put together piece by piece, organ by organ, cell by cell. His veins were being knit and his lungs developing. He was being finished but I was coming undone.

Chapter Nine

Asphyxiation is the term given to blocking the airway, preventing someone to breathe and ultimately causing death. The hard part is letting them watch you watch them die.

Another Monday. I was in the hot seat once again. I heard Dr. Hannah ask me why I kept my baby. But now, nearly three years had passed since the conception and the reason or reasons were moot. Sometimes I wondered if Dr. Hannah and I did these sessions for her own weekly dose of entertainment or if this was in fact *my* therapy. Today it was raining. Rain always put me in a sorrowful mood.

"Kericho," she called to me. She always said my name the right way pronouncing it like Jericho, the Israeli city near the Jordan River.

"My father was always against abortions. My mother killed two of his children and he never forgave her." I paused.

"Kericho, do you not want to talk about this?" Dr. Hannah asked me after a full minute of silence. I sat on her couch trying to think of the best way to answer her question.

"You know...when I was little, my family used to pray before we all went to bed. We would kneel down in our living room with our faces in the couch cushions and my father would say a prayer to keep us all protected in the nighttime hours. One time he prayed for all the babies that never had a chance to see the light of day because their lives had been snuffed out while they were still in the womb. My mother got up mid prayer and walked out."

Dr. Hannah nodded slowly. "She was upset at his prayer," she said intently.

"I never really knew why she walked out at the time. I must have been 7 or 8 years old. Now I often wonder if she walked out because she didn't agree with his prayer or because she couldn't bear the reminder."

Chapter Ten

"The tragedy of life is not death but what we let die inside of us while we still live."

In those days, I decided to keep my baby partly because I couldn't find a clinic in Africa willing to give me an abortion and partly because I did not want to have any regrets thinking on what could have been. I told Man I didn't want to get married. Maybe some time in the future if things went in that direction, but we had yet to even date each other, and I didn't want anyone putting a ring on my finger because of what was growing inside me. I would finish school even if I had to take my last finals while I was in labor and if I needed to move in with him for a little while, that's all it would be. A little while.

Gerald helped me find a doctor to care for me. His name was Dr. Doe and I thought what an unfortunate name. When I finally wound the courage to tell Sunday, she called my bluff and demanded my doctor's name as proof of my story's truth.

"Dr. Doe," I said.

"Really?" She laughed "Dr. Doe? As in John Doe?"

I laughed too at the thought.

Now I sat at a window table in the back at The Blue Lagoon,

waiting for Esi to appear. She agreed to meet me for lunch. I wanted to get some ideas for my film.

She came in wearing a blue polk –a-dot dress that nearly dragged the floor. The spaghetti straps and plunging neckline showed off her bulging breasts beneath the thin material. Her hair was pinned up this time, just a few curls hung in her face covered heavily in make-up. Red lipstick, eye shadow, blush, mascara. She spotted me when I raised my hand and took a seat at the table.

"Sorry, I'm a bit late," she started.

"Not a problem. Thank you for meeting me, Esi."

"I must admit, I still am not sure what you hope to accomplish. I already told you, I'm not a prostitute."

"I just want to talk about your life, then. It will be a conversation about you and your relationship with sex."

The waiter came over and brought us two waters. I ordered the Spaghetti Carbonara. Beauty got a Chicken Caesar salad.

"If I didn't know better, I'd think you were watching your figure," I said to her after the waiter left.

She smiled. "I'm not really that hungry. I had a big breakfast at Coco Beach."

"Is that that gorgeous hotel with the golden pillars in front?"

She nodded

"It looks like a palace. What were you doing there?"

"I had a date with a Russian. He's here on business and wanted to show me his hotel."

"Wow. How did you two meet?" I sipped my water.

"Axim was having drinks at a bar downtown and I happened to run into him."

"How often do you meet Russians at downtown bars?"

She smiled. "I meet a lot of men at a lot of places."

"What type do you usually go for? Me, I love Ghanaian men. So big and strong. And their accents are insatiable."

"For me, you are the one with the accent. The men you find attractive, are the ones I grew up detesting."

"Why is that? Why hate your own?"

"These are the men taught to control their women. They were raised to be selfish and often only look out for pleasing their own desires. But I have desires too."

"Sure. Me too. "

"I go for men who want to please their women. Men who welcome beauty with open arms and lavish gifts upon us in thanks for just being beautiful. I want to be taken care of, to want for nothing. I enjoy nice things and it wasn't until I started dating foreign men that I was able to see the inside of a hotel more beautiful than a king's palace."

"Tell me more about your home life. What was your relationship with your mother growing up."

"My mother was both weak and strong. Weak because her husband had many lovers, never faithful, never reliable, yet she depended on him for her well being. Too worried that she could not be independent. Strong because she endured all the pain he brought to her and managed to get on with life."

"Are you independent, Esi?"

"I live my life on my own terms. You may not agree with all of my decisions, but I don't need your approval to be satisfied with myself."

The waiter brought our lunch over. Esi took a big bite of chicken and romaine lettuce.

"That looks delicious."

"It is," she said her mouth full.

I looked down at my spaghetti and the sauce reminded me of blood. When I lost my virginity in my high school cafeteria kitchen, I left behind puddles of blood on the stainless steel counter. The pain was intolerable but the joy in doing something meant for grownups felt good.

"How many sexual partners have you had?" I asked her.

She swallowed and then looked up at me. "How many have you had?"

"I'm not sure. A few."

"A few to you may be many to another. I stopped counting a while back."

"Is it because counting makes it real? When you count, it's like looking yourself in the mirror and seeing the truth for what it is."

"Do you keep count of the number of times you've eaten ice cream? It's not important."

"I beg to differ. You can't contract a virus from eating ice cream."

"You can if it's been sitting in the humidity too long and the bugs have gotten to it."

"What is your point Esi?"

She put her fork down. "My point, sweetheart, is that you can contract an STD from having just one sexual partner if that one is the wrong one. The number of times you have sex has little to do with it."

I half smiled. "I guess you're right. Point taken." I twirled my fork in my spaghetti and stuffed a heap full into my mouth.

"You know, you and I we are not all that different" Esi continued. "You come with your Versace sunglasses and your straightened hair and you think you are somehow different. We bleed the same."

"I never took money for sex?"

"Why not?"

"Why not? It's not right. Our bodies are worth more than that. The gods say our bodies are sacred."

"Hmm... Then why do you not wait until you marry. Why not save your sacred woman parts?"

"I wanted to. At one time I wanted to." I remembered the baby growing in my womb and wished I had. I debated telling Esi. How will she react? What will she say of me? "Esi?"

She finished her mouthful and gave me her attention.

"Esi, have you ever been pregnant?" She was taken back at

first, then held up three fingers.

"Three times. My first child was born when I was 14 years old. He was a healthy baby boy with so much hair. I was still a child so the baby was given up for adoption. The second time was by my husband."

"You're married?"

"I was. My husband ran off after I miscarried. He said I was damaged."

"And the third?"

"The third time was another kind of miscarriage. One by my own hands. I'm not fit to be a mother."

"Don't say that Esi. You're a woman, surely you were made to be a mother."

"You have all the answers, don't you girl? Just cus God gave you a kiwi, don't mean you were made to have babies. Maybe you were made to give men pleasure. So much pleasure they keep coming right back for more. The kind that makes them leave their wives at home, spend days or weeks with you. The kind they pay top dollar for. Maybe that's what your kiwi is for."

"Esi I used to think that. Maybe in some ways I still do. But if that's the case, why am I always left feeling worse after than I did before?"

"Because you make it a struggle. You tell yourself there is wrong in it. I tell myself it is right. You say I'm a prostitute. I say I'm a woman. In her truest form." She finished off her glass of water and sat back in her chair. I rubbed my hardened stomach, despair in the air.

Chapter Eleven

Life asked Death, "Why do people love me but hate you?" Death responded, "Because you are a beautiful lie and I am a painful truth."

The Nyaho Medical Centre in Accra was like an outdoor restaurant, only the waitresses wore nurse uniforms and the chefs looked just like doctors. The lobby had only three walls. Just an open building, letting in cool breezes and smells of fried plantains and guava juice from up the street.

Now, three months pregnant, I had a seat alone in the doctor's waiting room. It was calm here. A perfectly square room with chairs lining the white brick walls and a table in the middle for reading materials, but I didn't feel like reading. I laid my head back against the wall behind me and thought of what my mother would say when she found out about my "blessing from God."

I was fifteen when I got my first taste on the kitchen counter in my high school's cafeteria, but I had dabbled with the forbidden fruit well before that. Kissing, fondling, touching. All things that were fun to do before I could garner the courage to go all the way. I was lying in bed one night, on the phone, listening to sweet words of adoration from Justin Hopewell, a boy two years older than me and the quarterback of the Junior Varsity football team. He was skinny for a quarterback and wore cornrows that hung to his shoulders, but the coach liked him and so did half the girls in high school. Justin liked me too.

"So how come you always playin' hard to get?" he said that night on the phone.

"You know...you have all the girls chasing you. I don't run with the crowd."

"Oh, you like to be different? I like that. I really like that. I got a lot of girls chasing me, but the one I really do want won't give me the time of day."

"I'm talking to you right now, ain't I?"

"It's about time. But you know I'm not satisfied."

"Is that right?"

"That's right. I want to see you in person."

"It's midnight. And we have school tomorrow."

"So what does that mean? Baby, I want to look you in your eyes and tell you how fine you are. I want to see your pretty face. I want to kiss you if you'll let me."

I was quiet for a moment contemplating the decision of the hour. My parents were asleep downstairs, as was Sunday in her room across the hall, and even if she wasn't she would be my help.

I swallowed hard. Justin was the boy I was crushing on for a long time now, and even though I had never had sex, I wanted to. I wanted to know what he would feel like inside me. Sunday's monologues on her sexcapades always had me in awe. I wanted to stay up late eating caramel popcorn and tell *her* what I did with Justin.

"Girl, we went to the beach and he took my shoes off at the edge of the shore. Then he kissed my feet and told me I was beautiful. Just feeling the muscles in his hands slide up my thigh was like waiting at heaven's gates. I opened wide and he slid inside me. It hurt at first, but I could handle it because he made me feel safe. Then the pain went away and all I felt was ecstasy. He grabbed my breasts like he was palming a basketball and squeezed. Girl he squeezed and devoured me with his mouth like he couldn't wait to taste my goodness. He moved in and out like the tide and then I felt a burst of joy like the waves that crash against the seashore. It was dope."

I wonder if Justin can really make me feel like that...

"Justin, I like you. I really do," I said into the phone.

"Show me."

"How do we do this?"

Justin lived with his parents about a mile away from my house. We agreed to meet by foot halfway and he would walk me back to his house. I got up and pulled on a pair of jeans and a sweatshirt. I tiptoed down the stairs and out the sliding back door, leaving it slightly ajar for my easy return. The night air was brisk. It was cool but not too cold. The moon was high in the sky, a perfect sickle, no stars in sight. I walked fast and made good time. I could see him in the distance when I got much closer. The collar was turned up on his blue leather jacket.

"Hey Sweety," he said to me when we were face to face. I smiled and he kissed me on my cheek. Back at his house, we tiptoed up the steps and settled on his twin size bed. He moved real close to me and this time he kissed me on my lips.

"I've been waiting a long time to get you here. You're beautiful." He caressed the side of my face and kissed me some more. "I got a walk in closet," he said. "Why don't you go in there and take your clothes off. I'll be right back." I sat quiet as he got up and dimmed the lights before he left the room.

Why the closet? I didn't want my first time to be like this. It seemed so rushed. So insincere. I imagined it would feel different. I took my sneakers off and looked around the room. He had a full length mirror on the closet facing me where I sat. The room was dark but I could still see a faded and blurred version of me. *I really am beautiful.*

Justin Hopewell came back in wearing just a white t-shirt and a condom over his erect penis. He looked surprised to see me still dressed on his bed. "I thought you were going to get in the closet," he said. "That way if my parents wake up, they won't see us."

"Why? Just close the door. We'll be fine on the bed."

"I guess you're right." He came over and unbuttoned my jeans. I laid back and let him pull them off. Then he tugged at my sweatshirt and pulled that over my head. Then my panties. He tried to undo my bra but gave up quickly. He spread my legs and just when I felt his hardness against me, I sat up.

"Stop," I blurted. "I don't want to."

"You don't want to what?"

"This. I don't want to do this. Please let me get up."

He backed off of me without a fight and I got dressed.

"You mean you came all this way for nothing," he said.

I paused for a moment before answering. "I guess I did." I walked down his stairs, this time not tip toeing and out his front door without looking back. He didn't care enough to follow or call to make sure I made it home safe at 3am.

My mother found out. I don't know how she knew for sure, but a week later, I spent an hour on my mother's computer writing an email to my best girlfriend detailing my rendezvous. I must have saved it on the hard drive by accident.

Driving home from a high school basketball game, Grace pulled over and turned to me in the passenger seat. She was small, like me, but had a stare that could kill. Today, her look was cold and cutting.

"It hurts me that my daughter is becoming a slut."

I felt like somebody beat me up with those words. Like I just got punched by Muhammad Ali when I wasn't looking. My breathe was somewhere stuck in my throat and I couldn't swallow.

"Don't ever think you're smarter than me," she continued. "I really do hope you start using your brain and if you ever bring a boy into my house, you might as well leave with him and never come back."

I didn't say anything. Just watched her shove her pointer finger in my face and managed to hold back the tears until I was at home in my room alone. I was still a virgin, but she didn't know that or care to ask.

"Kericho Blu."

I looked up and my memories were cut short.

"The doctor will see you now," said the nurse.

As soon as I stood, my head felt light. I started walking towards the door anyway, and the room went blurry. Just a small circle of light from the outside shown in and my peripheral vision was all dark.

"Ms. Blu...Ms. Blu."

I didn't feel the hardness of the fall, but I did open my eyes at the bottom. Dr. Doe and his nurse kneeled above me.

"Ms. Blu, are you alright," said the African doctor. "It seems you have fainted."

I sat up slowly with their help. Dr. Doe held my arm and helped me to my feet. "I'm ok now," I said. "I just felt dizzy for a moment. The room was spinning and everything suddenly went dark."

I moved into the examination room and sat on the table. The nurse waited quietly by the bedside.

"You look gaunt, Kericho," the doctor continued. "Are you eating at all?"

"I can't keep it down. Every time I try to eat, it all comes back up."

"You've got to eat something. You've got to try."

I was silent while Dr. Doe felt the top of my head.

"That was a terrible tumble you took. How does your head feel? I don't see anything abnormal. No bruising. Yet. I want to admit you. I am hoping it will just be for a night or two."

"No doctor, I really don't think that will be necessary. I'm fine really."

"I'm sure you will be. But we want to take the necessary precautions. We will give you an IV with some water and nutrients. You are severely dehydrated. It seems you may be suffering from Hyperemesis Gravidarum."

"What?"

"It is a big word, but do not let that scare you. It is caused by vomiting and severe nausea. Your body is adjusting to the new life inside you at your expense."

"Dr. Doe. I'm in school. It is very important to me to finish my classes this semester. If I don't finish now, when will I ever be able to go back with a baby to care for? I don't want to be admitted. I have class and school work. I'm working on a documentary."

Dr. Doe listened for a moment to my hysterics. Then he rubbed my back. "You just have to ask yourself, what is the cost? Is it worth finishing school right on time but giving birth to an unhealthy baby, or much worse, a corpse? There will be time for school. Right now, let us tend to the child."

I was quiet for a moment, unsure of my feelings.

Dr. Doe took a breath. "So," he said matter of factly. "Get undressed. Your gown is here on the bed. It is time to see her up close and personal."

After the doctor and his nurse left the room, gently closing the door behind them, I cried a little bit, but there were no tears. This was a tearless cry. The kind that happens only on the inside. My soul was crying but my eyes were dry. The reality of a permanent stain on my life was unbearable and I shuddered at the thought of what my life would be next year, two years, three years from now.

I closed my eyes and said in a whisper, "God, be with me." Then I undressed and covered myself with the gown just like the doctor ordered.

By dusk, I was settled into a hospital bed in a small room to myself. It was about the only thing I had left for me, since the baby had already taken over my life and he was yet the size of a baseball.

A big woman called Nurse Atieno came in to insert the needle into the tiny vein in my hand. She was quick and forceful. I started to jerk away but she held my arm tight. "You must be still." I obeyed and winced at the pain.

After she left, I reclined my bed and closed my eyes, blocking out the fluorescent lights. The smell of medicine, rubber gloves, and fresh linen filled my nose. The sheets were cool against my skin. There was silence.

Just moments later, the door opened again. *Oh no, what now? Another needle? A pill? More orders?* I opened my eyes to see. This time it was Gerald, all smiles, holding a white teddy bear, a bow tie wrapped around its neck.

"Gerald!" I smiled back.

He laughed that signature laugh and came to my bedside. "I came as soon as I heard. I stopped to buy one of these. I hear you Americans like things like this."

I hugged him hard. "We do. Thank you."

Gerald settled in the folding chair next to the bed, tucking the bear in beside me. "How are you?" he said concerned.

"I'm ok. Really. Trying to be optimistic. I'm three months pregnant now and the doctor says the hard part is almost over."

"I thought the hard part came in the end when it's time for the baby to come out."

"Babies," I said. Gerald looked confused. I smiled. "Dr. Doe told me today I will be having twins." It was true. The sonogram Dr. Doe had done showed two heads.

"Twins?"

"Yes. Either that, or I'm having a two headed baby."

"That is a blessing."

"No, I was reading somewhere it was a curse. A long time

ago, multiple babies were killed at birth. Animals have multiples, not humans. They were some kind of freak of nature. I heard."

"Well I think it's a blessing, and you have to admit, that lends a little something special to your pregnancy." He smoothed his mustache down around his lips.

"It does make me feel better. Like somehow God saw it fit to give me two babies instead of one. He must think I'm pretty responsible."

"So I say again. The hard part is yet to come. Pushing two babies out must be double the pain."

"Oh, that's a long way off. I'm just trying to get through the week. Really the hardest part of this whole thing is in telling my mother I'm going to have a baby."

His eyes widened. "You haven't told her yet? Kericho."

"I haven't felt the need to. My mother was never the comforting kind. Maybe when I was small. When I'd fall off my bike and scrape my knee, she always rescued me like a mother should. Then it was easy."

"Easy to do what?"

"Easy to show affection, I guess. A child's mind can only comprehend the small things. A kiss is just that, a kiss. No more. No less. But I grew up and the 'I love you's' came few and far between." I looked away, up into the fluorescent lights as if there were answers there, an explanation for Grace. "Now it seems she only says it in letters or emails. I miss hearing the words, you know. Maybe she's waited so long to say it that now she's afraid to say it. Afraid of what I might think of her. Afraid of the astonishment that would bring silence, the kind of awkward silence that pervades a room when a man first utters those three words to his lady. His vulnerability leaves him open to her scrutiny, her judgment, her unwillingness to return the sentiment."

"Oh, but Kericho, there are many love languages. Your mother's unique way of expressing love does not mean it is not there."

"My mother is quite the conventional kind. She has rules and sticks to them. Wood is wood no matter how you look at it." I distorted my voice to resemble my mother's scolding tone. "'I'm not raising anymore babies,' she would tell us growing up. 'If you're old enough to make one, you're old enough to move out and live on your own. And I won't call to check in on you. I'm the mother. You're the daughter. Don't even think about a baby shower, or a mother's day card. I won't celebrate the pregnancy.' She was cold and distant during my sister Sunday's pregnancy. When Sunday got married, it was like Grace couldn't wait to tell the women at her church. Like the marriage made it all better. Took the shame away or something. I don't doubt my mother loves us. She brought us up with a good education and gave us a lot of opportunities. She told me once that she prays for me and Sunday every night. But I'm afraid she doesn't know the difference."

"The difference in what?"

I met his gaze. "The difference between raising a child, and loving one."

Gerald lowered his eyes for a moment and then looked back at me. He took my hands in his. "She's your mum. She will come around. Give her time. And I'm sure she will grow to love your babies just as she has loved you. Tell her. Soon. She may surprise you. What if you fall sick? You're not well now, and your mother should know you are in a hospital bed thousands of miles away from her."

I noticed how big Gerald's eyes were. It was as if they were peering deep inside me, boring into my soul, reading my thoughts. My heart fluttered. A blind man could see the chemistry. Maybe in some former life, I was Gerald's wife, and he was my twins' father. I remembered the hardness in his pants that night at Club Afrodisiac. So I lingered here in this moment just to hold on to the satisfaction of wishing we could be when I knew the truth is we could never be. I lingered here to imagine the possibility of letting Gerald inside my world, both figuratively and literally. The space in between my thighs lubricated itself with the expectation of his own engorged penis. But making love was a lifetime away and I would never have the courage to catch up.

"I will tell her. I promise."

Gerald left me and I fell asleep quickly. I dreamt of me when I was a little girl. My Daddy used to tell me stories. My mother would tuck Sunday and me in for bed at night and we'd say, "Tell Daddy to come upstairs." This night, when he did, he knelt down at the head of the bed and told us stories about Africa. The room was dark except for the golden glow of our night lite and Sunday and I huddled close in bed, our ears inclined to my father to hear his fairytales about life in that faraway place. He told us about the elephants and the hyenas. We listened with eagerness to his story about the time he fought the lion barehanded when he was only a boy and our mouths formed a perfect "O" in awe. Then we listened to him sing songs in Luo and even though we didn't know what he was saying, the next morning, we still remembered the words.

I woke up to a full bladder and a full moon. The clock on the wall read 2:09am. Still just early evening at my mother's house, several time zones away. I climbed out of bed and dragged the metal pole attached to my IV to the toilet, peed, and then settled back in bed. I only looked at my cellular phone for half a minute before I dialed Grace.

"Hello." She answered on the second ring and her voice was sweet.

"Hi Mommy."

"Hi Kericho. It must be late there. What are you doing up?"

I breathed deeply knowing the best way to get through this was to spit it out. *Spit it out Kericho. Who cares what she says. Who cares how she feels. This is about me now. Me and God. Me and the twins. That's all there is left.*

"Mommy, I really just called because I wanted to let you know that I'm pregnant. Man knows. It's his and I'm keeping it. I'm here in the hospital now because I got very sick. And well, I just thought I should let you know." Then I closed my eyes and held my breath.

She said, "Okay." It was a matter-of-fact "okay" as if I had told her I was making her least favorite dish for dinner. The lack of emotion in her voice made me cold and the chills froze my insides.

"Okay?" I repeated.

"Okay." I heard the click in the phone on her end, but couldn't remove the earpiece from my own ear. My lip quivered, and my still closed eyes swelled with tears. I was reluctant to open them, afraid of the wetness my tears would leave on my cheek. But I did open them, and my face became the rushing waters spilling out into a mighty waterfall. I dropped the phone and covered my mouth to shield my cry. I told myself it didn't matter and that I didn't care if she cared. But I wanted her to care. I wanted her to ask me how I was doing and if I was scared. I wanted her to tell me she loved me and everything was going to be okay. I wanted her to be the mother she was so many years ago when I would fall off my bike and scrape my knee. I wanted her to rescue me like a mother should.

Chapter Twelve

I had the same dream five nights in a row. A masked man crept into my home in the middle of the night wielding a knife. My first instinct was to protect the children. When I couldn't anymore, I told them to run. Run away as fast as you can.

Luke's shoulders were made for two things. They were for me to grab when he was on top of me and for filling out a suit. He always wore a suit well, fitted in all the right places, tailored to his form, and made for the cover of GQ Magazine. He was the color of chocolate milk. Tall. Fine. And poised. I never saw Luke get too excited about anything. He always surprisingly remained composed under any form of pressure and that got to me, in a good and bad way. Depends which day you asked me.

It was September 2008. The Memorial Project would be holding its annual gala in one week and I needed a date. Dr. Hanna told me to do things that made me feel good. She wanted me to come out of my shell and live.

"I thought of taking the twins," I told Luke over the phone

tonight. "But at two, they're just a few years too young. Would you do me the honor?"

"I'm flattered. Are you sure you can trust me at a work event?" Whenever Luke spoke, it was like heaven's gates opened and God himself had the microphone. His voice was deep and manly, and he spoke with such assurance, such confidence, like he knew he had the world's attention.

"Would that be a mistake?"

"I hope not. Let me check my schedule. I'll get back to you.

"Well don't take too long. It's next week. I don't want to be left in the cold."

"I'll make sure I give you a prompt response."

Three days later I hadn't heard from him. Luke was flighty like that. He lived in the moment. Sunday told me once that men don't lie. They mean exactly what they say at the time that they say it. If they tell you they love you, if they tell you you're the most beautiful woman in the world, at that moment they believe what they are saying is true. And if they say the same thing to another woman the next day, just means they had a change of heart.

Luke never deliberately lied. He was just forgetful and had an attention span that lasted just a few minutes. When we were together, I was his world, but the moment we parted, I left not only his world, but also his mind. I get that now.

After the dissolve of my relationship with Man, I had looked him up. Luke wasn't living far. I was surprised our paths hadn't crossed. He was in the same apartment we bathed in almost two years earlier, the one we made love in, our skin still moist.

"I'm sure they're adorable," he said when I told him I was now a mother of twin boys.

Kiefer had a fever tonight. I gave him a cool bath and put him to bed early with a spoonful of medicine.

"Brother sick," the younger twin said pointing to Kiefer as I laid him down.

"He is sick. He needs to get lots of rest. You come with

mommy. We'll make cookies."

I enjoyed the rare moments I had with just one of my babies. I tried to get back what I lost in having twins. That is the bonding moments that would be plentiful if I only had one to bond with. My life had become three's company, always a trio, never a twosome. I breastfed two babies, sometimes both at one time, and rocked two babies to sleep, one in each arm. But sometimes...times like tonight, I could hold the gaze of just one toddler and pay special attention to the size of his hands and how his fingernails looked when they were covered in cookie dough. I listened to his laugh and found the distinctions from his brother in the way he said "mommy." Kye's voice was just a little softer and he held the first syllable a little bit longer.

We sat at the kitchen table, baby Kye in his booster seat eating chocolate chip cookies and milk. His warm. Mine cold. He was a happy baby who looked just like Man. Two years old, walking and talking, laughing and playing like any baby should. I rested in my chair, tasting the sweetness of the chocolate, listening to my son laugh at the mess he made on his hands.

We finished the plate and I got up to do the dishes, turned around and just like that, he was sleeping, his head slumped to one side, just a little twitch in his eye. *I wonder what babies dream about.*

I laid him down and returned to the kitchen to clean up. And then my phone rang.

Luke. I waited ten seconds to answer.

"Kericho. Bad time?"

"No, not at all. I was just putting the babies down."

"I've yet to meet those little men of yours. I'm wondering if all this time you've been making them up."

"Oh you know…precious things you have to keep hidden."

"I was calling because uh...because I was wondering what I should wear to this benefit you invited me to. Is the offer still on the table?"

"It is. But what if it wasn't? You waited a while to get back to me."

"I did. And I'm sorry. It slipped my mind until now."

I hated when he did that. Treated me like I was an unimportant add on to his life. A detail he often overlooked.

"Can I come over?" he asked.

"I don't know. I have an early morning." I was already imagining his hands on my waist, his kisses on my neck.

"Kericho, it's not even 9 o'clock. Plus I have that new Denzel flick on dvd and I can pick up a couple of slices of that red velvet cake you like so much."

"Well...I did just put the babies down. I suppose there is no harm."

"I'll be there in a half hour."

I changed into a purple negligee.

A half hour later, I opened my door to the black stallion that was Luke. He had on a pea coat and a Yankees cap turned backwards. He held up a bottle of wine and smiled.

"Surprise," he said.

"If I didn't know better, I'd think it was Friday night instead of Wednesday."

"Every day is Friday where I come from."

"And where's that."

"A place where we all party when we feel like it. Are you gonna let me in or are we cracking open this bottle of wine in your doorway?"

I opened the door wider and stepped back to let him inside. He hugged me. And then he kissed me.

"You taste like you've been drinking already," I said once he was settled on the couch.

"Do I?"

"You do."

He pulled me on top of him and planted more kisses on my face. My neck. My lips.

"I missed you," he said eagerly.

"Luke it hasn't been that long. A couple of weeks. Sunday was here last weekend. She had a date with a friend of hers from Connecticut. She asked about you."

"Really? How is that thick and juicy sister of yours?"

"Thick and juicy?"

"She always did have meat on her bones. The good kind. Not too much. Just enough to make men imagine squeezing her ass in the middle of the night. She reminds me of a steak. Thick and juicy. You don't want to just look at her. You want to eat her." He laughed.

"I'm offended," I said half kidding. "That's my sister you're objectifying. Plus, I thought you only had eyes for me."

"I'm a man sweetheart. I have eyes for all things beautiful. And you should take it as a compliment. Beauty runs in your family. I'd be worried if I was your Daddy."

"Why is that?"

"Having to think about men running after his daughters all the time. Using your pictures to masturbate. That can drive a man crazy. That's why I always say I want boys. And if I happen to have a girl, she better be ugly. "

I laughed. "You're silly."

"Kiss me."

"Luke, didn't you come over to watch a movie?"

"Why watch a movie when we can make a movie?"

"I think you're just drunk."

"I think I am too. So what? I know you didn't put on that sexy slip just to tease me."

I reached in Luke's coat pocket for the dvd. "I saw this already. Movie date with a guy I met a few months ago. The movie was good, but the date wasn't. I never did like going to the movies on a first date. I like conversation. A first date is all about getting to know someone. Kind of hard to do that during the movie."

"So you're dating other men now and telling me about it.

What am I? Your gay friend?"

"No. It's not like that. I'm just mentioning that I saw this movie already. Don't act like I'm the only woman you're seeing."

"When I'm with you, I'm with you."

I climbed off of Luke's lap and sat down next to him. "What made you decide to go to the gala with me?"

"Ummm...you asked me and I didn't want to let you down. Plus I know there is going to be a lot of old money in the building and I never pass up an opportunity to network."

"There are definitely going to be some people you'll want to keep in your rolodex."

"See, exactly. And we haven't been out anywhere in a while. I want to show you we can have fun together outside of the bedroom."

Luke got up to open the bottle of wine and I got two glasses from the kitchen. In this moment, I felt like we were a team. Like our lives belonged inside each other's. We sat down with the wine. "This is smooth," I said taking a sip and nestling close to him. I draped my legs over his. "You did well."

"I'm glad I'm good for something."

Luke made me feel sexy. The wine, the kisses. It all felt so right. Like I belonged with him.

"Luke, you ever want to get married?"

"Are you trying to ask me something?"

"No. I mean I'm not saying do you want to marry me? I'm just asking, you know, if marriage is something you want to do."

"I think maybe one day. I'm not sure. I hear marriage is hard work. I'm too selfish to work that hard when I don't have to."

"Did you ever think about me when I was in Africa?"

"Of course I did. Here and there. But I don't dwell too much on things like that. I didn't know if you were coming back or when you were coming back or if you would ever want to see me again. I can't waste time on things I can't change."

I'm a Cancer in the zodiac and that means I'm emotionally

needy and quite independent at the same time. I don't need somebody to take care of me. I just need somebody to want to. I need Luke to think of me when I'm near or far. I want him to try to win my love even if my love is hard to win.

"I suppose," I said.

The night of the gala Luke swung by my house in a cab to pick me up. I wore a knee length satin deep grey dress that exposed one of my shoulders. It was on sale at a boutique shop in Soho. The twins were spending the weekend with Man so tonight, I belonged to Luke. Tonight my arms belonged to him. My legs belonged to him. My heart belonged to him. My head belonged to him. From my updo down to my red-wine-red painted toe nails, I was a one-man woman.

The ballroom at Cipriani's was gorgeous, but gorgeous is what Carol Blaney did best. Dimly lit. Pressed white tablecloths covered a hundred round tables, each with a glass centerpiece, a replica of the twin towers. In the back of the vast room, a sprawling wall was covered with "notes of hope" as Mrs. Blaney aptly titled them. They were notecards people had written detailing their memories of 9/11, where they were, how they felt, what they thought upon hearing the news.

The fanfare was glamorous. Cameras emanated flashes all over the room, somebody was playing the piano, I heard drums but they were soft. The crowd was dressed to impress. I even spotted Bobby De Niro in the crowd, Mr. New York City himself.

Luke and I, two of a handful of black faces in the crowd sauntered over to the bar and got us a couple of chardonnays. We scanned the room and mingled. Luke fit in well. He walked like he belonged and for just a moment I imagined him as my husband, me as his wife. The picture was pretty and we belonged on some sort of fortune 500 magazine cover, a humble philanthropist and a New York financier painting the town with good looks and even better hearts...in love raising two and a half children. And a dog. The American Dream was us if not for the speck that was Keifer and Kye who were lovely to look at but were the seed of another man, a reminder of a past that shouldn't have been, and wouldn't have been if it weren't for that clumsy night with a whole lot of wine and no condom.

It's amazing the difference a day makes. The love that is born from an awkward night and bad sex is unexplainable. Keifer and Kye I loved, but that speck was a stain I could never get out even with the best detergent or the expensive dry cleaners I used in the West Village. That speck was there to stay.

Luke, let's hatch a plan. I know a guy who knows a guy that can get rid of Man forever. Then we can get married, you can adopt Keifer and Kye and we'll live happily ever after.

My thoughts stayed in the back of my head and were never allowed to reach my lips. Three days earlier Luke and I fucked like rabbits on my couch, my lips stained with the red wine he brought, his dick deep inside me, penetrating my innermost parts, bringing forth moans that would wake the children and the neighbors if he didn't muffle them with his hands clasped tightly over my mouth.

I was in love. In that moment on the couch and in this one in my satin dress watching Luke schmooze the crowd, sipping wine like a natural. I. am. in. love. Because this is what I yearned for and wanted more than I wanted air to breathe. I wanted...I wanted. I wanted Luke. To want me as much as I needed him. I wanted him to crave me like a pregnant woman craves ice chips. No, more than that. Like Sunday wanted a toilet that night we ate bad Mexican and got stuck in traffic on the way back home. Yeah, like that.

So I watched him. I stood there in my satin dress and I scanned his profile, dissected his lips with my eyes and studied the way they moved. I looked at his brow bone and noticed how deep his eyes were set. I photographed his tongue in my mind and, the very glimpses I got in between his words were enough to drive me insane wondering how it would feel if that tongue was mine. If I owned it and knew it and all of him belonged to me and not another. *He is beautiful. Utterly, majestically, beautiful.*

We ate steak for dinner. Medium rare. Thick and juicy just like Sunday. We sat at a table of ten with Joanna Borelli, the widow of Ed Borelli, casualty in The Attacks. She was a small woman with a bony frame, and dark thin hair.

"I can't imagine what that must have been like for you, ya know hearing about your husband and all with three small kids to raise," I said to her cutting my steak.

"Of course, it was difficult," she said. She had a New York Italian accent and talked with a slight nervousness. "I was on the treadmill, it was what I did every morning after Eddie went off to work and I sent the kids off to school. I turned on the news, grabbed a bottle of water and did my daily run in front of the television." She cut her steak and took a bite. Then as she chewed, "the plane hit the first tower. It was the south tower and everyone thought it was an accident. My TV screen was covered in flames and smoke and I got worried. I called Eddie on his cellular. See, Eddie was in the North Tower. That's where he worked, there on the 92nd floor." She swallowed her steak and sipped from her water glass.

Then she continued. "Eddie answered and he said honey, I don't know what's going on. A plane crashed into the south tower. People are panicking, but everyone is telling us to be calm. We're okay in here."

"They should have evacuated," I said. "Had they evacuated right away, your husband and a lot of others would still be alive."

"Hindsight is 20/20. But you have to understand there was falling debris everywhere from the first plane crash. They weren't letting anyone out of the North Tower. People on the ground had shards of glass in their head."

"Better to have glass in your head and live, than to die."

"My husband didn't think he was going to die. When I saw the plane hit the second tower, I called Eddie again. He answered and I could hear the fear in his voice. There was a lot of noise. A lot of commotion. But I did hear him say I love you. I heard him say that. And then the phone went dead. I never saw my husband again."

I closed my eyes and imagined the scene. "I can't imagine what horror that must have been. People were jumping. What horror it must have been inside that building, where jumping from the 92nd floor was the better option. They never found your husband's body. Have you found closure?"

"It was difficult at first. But yes. Eddie said his goodbyes. We did not have a perfect marriage. Anyone who says they do is lying. But we had love. And I know Eddie would want me to move on."

"My prayers are with your family."

After dinner, there was a keynote speaker, dessert, awards, and a performance by an Asian pianist who looked like Lucy Liu. She was excellent. We were both exhausted on the cab ride home. Luke had loosened his tie. He was sitting next to me holding my hand, his head slumped on the headrest, eyes half closed.

"Luke," I called.

He said nothing. Either he didn't hear me or he didn't care to answer. So I said his name again.

"Luke."

"Hmmm"

"Do you believe in God?"

"What?"

"Do you believe in God?"

He opened his eyes. "Yeah. Sure I believe in God."

"You think Eddie Borelli believed in God?"

"Who?"

"Joanna's husband. The North Tower."

"Oh. I hope so."

"I should have asked her."

"Asked her what?"

"At dinner, I should have asked Joanna Borelli if she believes in God. If she saw his hand in all of this..."

"Kericho, it's late. Much too late to be thinking of such things. Relax."

"I am relaxed, I just think I should have asked her."

The cab stopped outside my apartment and after Luke paid the driver, I got out and led Luke up the stairs to my third floor walkup.

Once inside, I went to the bedroom and changed into a pair of oversized sweatpants and a black tank top. Luke took his shoes off, threw his jacket on the chair by my bed and sat down to watch me dress.

"It feels so good to finally get out of those heels," I said to him stretching out on the bed in front of him.

He motioned for me to lay face down across the bed and he lifted my shirt a little and rubbed my back. It felt good. A midnight backrub is just what I need.

"You look like you can use a backrub." *He read my mind.* "Kericho, thank you for inviting me out tonight. I had a nice time, despite the memories of 9/11."

"I had a nice time too. I'm happy you came. I can't wait to do more of this."

"More?"

"Yeah sure. What, you don't want to come to anymore corporate events with me?"

"I'd love to. You know that."

"I don't know. Sometimes, I'm not so sure what you want."

"I want you."

"You want me? Or you want me right now?"

"I can't speak for the future. All that is certain is right now and right now, I want you bad."

"And what about tomorrow?"

"Let's talk about tomorrow when tomorrow comes."

The massage was lulling me to sleep. His hands were so big and muscular, strong, firm, but yet so gentle. I closed my eyes and focused on the deep tissue he was kneading. The house was quiet and I thought some music might be nice, but no. This was better. Silence was golden.

"You know, Kericho, every time we go out, I come to pick you up and I sit in the car and watch you walk over and I get excited. You do that to me. You're gorgeous, but I've seen gorgeous before. I can talk to you. I can listen to you, and it's not a task. I think about you when I don't want to. I think about you when I got other shit to think about."

Sounded good. His voice, his words were so calming. I was slipping away and he knew it. He pulled my oversized sweats down just under my butt and I let him. My blue lace thong exposed. Now he was working my gluteus maximus, palming my cheeks and kneading like two balls of dough. Slow. I laid there, eyes closed, breathing deeply, still conscious but on the verge of slipping. Now he was quiet, Just the still in the air and the quiet sound of his hands on my skin.

He kissed me on the hill rising above the backs of my thighs. He bent down and kissed me on my butt. His lips were soft to the touch and I wanted more. He must have read my mind because he obliged. More kisses and I started to moisten. He pulled my pants down some more. Just enough for him to spread my legs a little and move the blue lace to the side. I couldn't help but let out a moan, almost like a purr when I felt his tongue on my sweetness. He licked. Slow at first and then a little faster. He sucked. Soft at first. And then a little harder. And I let him. Partly because I was exhausted and didn't have the strength to say no, stop, or wait. Mostly because I didn't want him to stop or wait. I wanted him to keep going because I liked it. I anticipated his next move and let him control me like a babydoll.

Last time, we fucked hard. This was different. He was being gentle tonight. Now my pants were on the floor. I turned my head to the other side and he didn't hesitate getting on all fours in a crouching tiger position. He curled one of my legs up and bent down to slurp like the fruit juice was too good to let a drop go to waste. He paused and sat up out of frustration. The blue lace was in the way so he started sliding my panties down when I stopped him, turned over and asked what he was doing.

"Let me put you to bed," he offered.

I didn't say anything. Just watched him stand, his pants already unbuckled. He took me by the hands and pulled me off the bed to stand facing him. Then he pulled my shirt over my head exposing all my goodness, firm and erect. He slid his hand up my side and stared at my breasts, cupping them with both hands. He turned to sit on the edge of bed and pulled me close, me naked, just my blue lace thong covering my kiwi. Then he took my nipple in his mouth, massaged the brown with his tongue. Sucked like a baby's bottle. I wanted him inside me.

I reached under his shirt and felt his hard body. I undressed him like he did me, inviting the sex. I was juicy and couldn't hide it once he slid my panties down and let them fall to the floor, a trickle of fruit juice easing down my inner thigh. He licked his fingers and touched my wet spot. Moved them back and forth across my place and then inserted two inside me. He pulled me closer and I watched the bulge in his pants grow bigger. His mouth moving from one breast to the other. One hand grazing my backside, the other deep inside me. He stood up and forced me on the bed, got rid of his pants, his boxer briefs, and climbed on top. Spread my legs open wide, and gave me all of him.

He listened to me sing the rest of the night. Thrusting in and out. I moaned for him like it was the first time. Told him it was good and begged him not to stop. He gave all of me attention. Kissed my breasts the whole way through. Grabbed my bottom and went in deep. Kissed my lips and gave me his tongue. My neck. My ear. No part of me was left out.

I climaxed twice before he came, and then we both fell fast

asleep.

Chapter Thirteen

The road to hell is paved with good intentions

With Luke, the sex was drunk. Even if we weren't intoxicated, that is how it always felt. It was sex with my senses partially obscured, my mind under the influence of loneliness, despair, self pity or all three. With Gerald it was different. Gerald had opened my senses and made me come alive.

Two years prior, the summer of 2006, I made love to Gerald, five months pregnant with Man's twin boys.

Of course it wasn't a planned thing. Even the thought of it now makes me cringe. There was no denying the chemistry between us. He was my rock when there was no one else. The days after I was released from the hospital for hyperemesis gravidarum, I took things easy. I traveled to class and then back home, ate simple foods like soups and stews, and prayed to keep it down. The smells in Accra bothered me the most. Spices and potpourris and incense burning throughout the markets filtered into our living room whenever the windows and doors were left open. I'd walk into the house, find it teeming with potent smells, and hurry to shut and lock all the windows. Once Gerald found me in a frenzy, rushing from window to window.

"What's your problem?" he asked me. "It's warm and muggy in here. We should air the place out. Catch a breeze."

"I can't. The smells outside are so strong!"

I stayed indoors a lot. I wrote to Sunday, studied the countries of Africa in alphabetical order, and talked to God. At 4 months, I started to feel the babies moving around. Butterflies here and there, a hard kick every now and then. I could even see the movement and I started to feel something for the little guys. I don't know what it was, but my heart bent a little in their favor.

Man was happy I decided to keep the babies. He called when he got the chance to add money to his international calling card but our conversations were always short. I told him we were having twins. He said that he couldn't believe it. He promised to make a home for us and to always take care of us and never to leave us even to the end of time. His promises were eerily similar to the promises of Jesus just before he was caught up into heaven to sit at the right hand of God.

I kept the babies a secret for as long as I could but I was beginning to show and my overnight stays in the hospital were becoming harder and harder to explain to the rest of the students.

"You're going to be a mama!" was Bella's first reaction when she heard the news. "I knew it! I knew you were pregnant!"

"Just know, I'm here for you. Whatever you need, I'm here," Justice had said when he heard the news through the grapevine.

The school organized a weekend trip to the northern region at my five month mark.

"We think that it is best for you and your unborn baby if you stay. It gets to be over one hundred degrees where we are going and we wouldn't want any illness to befall you while we are there." The campus nurse managed to make her orders sound like a request but I knew better. So I acquiesced and stayed behind with Gerald as we watched the crew pile into two vans and head due north for a long weekend.

"You don't have to babysit me," I had said to Gerald. "You

should have gone with them."

"I'm not here to babysit you. I have been where they are going many times. I'd rather stay behind. I don't feel up to the trip."

So he went out and picked up some dinner. Chicken and rice. We ate in a quiet dining room, just Gerald's humming in between bites.

"How's your chicken?" He asked me.

"It's alright I guess."

"Mine is quite dry."

"Sorry to hear."

He finished his last bite and threw his napkin down. "How are things with the baby?"

"Better. I'm starting to feel better. I'm in my second trimester now so I'm not so sick. I still feel weak and tired a lot." I contemplated telling him about Grace. "My mom hasn't said much of anything to me. I told her. I told her what is going on and she's mad, I can tell. Disappointed probably."

"And your fudder?"

"Huh. Oh I don't know. I don't know if he knows. I don't think she would tell him. I certainly haven't told him."

"Why not?"

"My dad was never the kind you talk to about things like this. He's just not. I don't know. He'll find out sooner or later. You know my sister Sunday was in a situation similar to mine a few years ago with her first daughter. In college, pregnant, not married. It seems my parents grew to love her children."

"And they will love yours too. You're doing the right thing."

"I don't know. I don't know if I am. Some days it feels right. Like I'll talk to Man and it feels like everything is going to be okay."

"Man?"

"Huh? Oh Manfred." I dropped my fork. "That's… you know he's… he's the father."

"Ah..Is he supportive?"

"He is. I think he's a man of his word. I'm just scared." I sighed.

"Well you really need to take your mind off the bad." Gerald got up from his chair. "Stay here."

"Where are you going?"

"Let me run to my room. I think I have something you will enjoy." He hurried down the corridor. I pushed my plate away and leaned back in my chair, my hands on my stomach. A minute later, Gerald returned carrying a box. It was a game. A boardgame.

"What's that?" I inquired.

"Oware. Have you played?"

"I can't say I have."

He smiled and bared his pristine white teeth. "Let's move to the couch. You should be comfortable."

I followed him into the livingroom and we settled on the couch. I propped a pillow behind me. He opened the box and brought out a wooden board with cups or pits carved into it along with a small bag of pebbles.

"These are called seeds," he explained. "The object is to capture the most seeds. It is a game about sowing and reaping." He placed the board between us on the couch and distributed the pebbles evenly in the pits. "We take turns moving the seeds around. Let me show you."

I brushed my hair behind my ears to concentrate. Gerald removed all of the pebbles from one of the pits and then redistributed them one by one in each of the remaining pits. When he reached the last pebble and the last pit, he removed all of those too and hid them behind him.

"Ah," I felt a hard movement in my stomach.

"What happened?" Gerald asked.

"Baby A moved. I felt it."

"Baby A?"

"Yes, that's how Dr. Doe refers to the babies. Baby A and

Baby B." I lifted my sheer shirt to expose my bulging belly. "Do you want to feel? Maybe he'll do it again."

Gerald extended his hand and placed his fingers around my stomach. "Here, press in," I said. He was being gentle. "A little harder. You won't hurt me."

He pressed. We waited. If I were being honest, the invitation to Gerald was an excuse to find some human touch, whether it be on the life within my abdomen or elsewhere. His caress felt good. Then it happened again. "Did you feel that?"

Gerald jerked his hand back. "Wow. That was a hard kick. What does that feel like?"

I wanted him to touch me again. "Hmm, strange. It feels strange. Do you want to feel again? Maybe we can feel them both move at the same time." *Was it obvious I enjoyed his touch? Could he tell I only wanted to feel his hands once more on my skin, the tenderness in his fingertips, the warmth of his palm?* He hesitated but then moved his hand back towards my side. His skin, so rich and deep reminded me of a touch I missed so much. Luke. Man. There were many from my past, but Gerald was something new, a mystery I yearned to uncover. Gerald represented the unknown. I covered his hand with both of mine. He wasn't getting away this time. The babies were still. I felt his gaze upon me. When I looked up, our eyes caught each other. After a beat, the discomfort pushed me to look away. "Maybe over here. Give me your other hand."

He inched closer, and extended his other hand, now clasping my belly on both sides. We sat in stillness. My heart beating faster, his hands growing warmer. *Was this wrong? Why were my heart and all of my senses inclined in Gerald's direction? Why did I want him this much right now? Why had we been left alone tonight?* "I think they stopped. Yes th—they stopped m—moving." I looked back up at Gerald to see his eyes had not left my face.

"You're so beautiful Kericho. Don't let anybody ever tell you that you're not."

Now it was me that scooted away. I inched backwards and he

followed. "G—Gerald." It was just a whisper. The hum of the still air, the distant crickets, and our breathing was our music.

"Can I kiss you?" he asked me.

I tried to inch further away, but my back was against the arm rest. Another whisper. "Please G-Gerald." *Please what? What was I asking him for? Please kiss me? Please stop? Please remove your fingers from my body? Please go on? Please make me feel good tonight? What was it that I wanted from him? Did I want him to stop or did I want him to go? Or could it be that I wanted both of these things equally and simultaneously?*

No. Not equally. There was one I wanted just a little more. He leaned in and enveloped my lips in his. He sucked, moving his right hand from my belly to the back of my head, pushing my mouth into his. He tugged at my shorts, removing them swiftly. When he entered, I hung my head back in both agony and ecstasy. I prayed for an orgasm and forgiveness at the same time. This wretched man that I am. Father, deliver me.

Chapter Fourteen

"I'm not afraid of death. I just don't want to be there when it happens."

It was August 3rd, 2006. I had the babies after seven months when my water broke in the middle of the night and Gerald rode with me in a taxi cab to the hospital. Dr. Doe came in to perform an emergency C-section. I cried like a baby.

Maybe it was because I didn't want to be alone. Maybe I wanted Man here with me or Sunday. Yes, Sunday should be here. Maybe it was because I envisioned giving birth to my first child with my husband by my side and a perfectly prepared baby nursery at home. Maybe I was crying because I didn't want to have a baby in Africa in the first place. *The doctors here don't know what they're doing.* Medical technology was not advanced enough and I don't want my babies coming out speaking a language I can't understand.

I cried when the doctors delivered the anesthesia and they all thought it was because I was afraid of needles.

"It won't hurt honey. You won't feel a thing. And everything will be alright."

But the truth was I was afraid the anesthesia wouldn't work and I would feel Dr. Doe slice me open with his scalpel. I would feel him rip my babies out of me and I would feel my insides being moved around. I would feel everything but the pain would be so great that I wouldn't be able to open my mouth. I wouldn't be able to talk, or scream, or tell them to stop. I was afraid the doctor would slice away and chop my stomach into mincemeat without a care. I was afraid I would become a statistic. One of those mothers who dies in childbirth and leaves her legacy to grow up without ever hearing her voice.

I was crying because I was afraid of becoming a mother. Babies come out after nine months, not seven. That means God still owes me two months to prepare and if I screw up now, it's his fault. Not mine.

I was crying because I hadn't spoken to my mother in nearly four months and that grueling phone call was still weighing heavy on my mind. "Okay," she had said. *Okay? Okay!? That's all you have to say? Your youngest daughter just told you she's going to have a baby. Your baby is having a baby and all you can think to muster is "okay?" Well, fuck you too!*

Grace wrote me a letter after that conversation as a way to get some things off of her chest. When you mail a letter to Africa, it reaches the recipient in two weeks, two months, or never. I got Grace's letter six weeks ago. I read it on my porch on a day when it was raining.

Dear Kericho,

I feel regret that you have decided for your life to take this direction. This is not what I would have wished for you. I was hoping you knew what you were doing. I thought you were smarter than that. I thought your older sister getting pregnant while she was still in school would have taught you something.

Have you made up your mind yet about where your life goes from here? Have you worked things out with Man? And if you work things out without him, make sure you know what you're doing.

What are you planning to do about your education? You cannot work and go to school, and how will you do either unless you have money for childcare? Your father may be willing to be a babysitter, but I don't intend to go back to help raising kids. I've looked forward to the day when I wouldn't have children in my house. I don't intend to turn back time because of stupidity.

The main thing now is to get things settled for this child. Besides yourself, you now have a responsibility for the next 18 years. Just to begin with, your baby will need a crib, a car seat, blankets, diapers, baby supplies, and food. There is also medical care. In these situations, it's usually the woman who pays the price.

Kericho, remember that I love you and I hope and pray that you make for yourself a good life.

Love,
Mommy.

I imagined tearing that letter up and throwing it in the garbage on my way inside, but instead I folded it and tucked it away in a drawer by my bed. Now here I was in labor, crying because Grace only saw the bad, and never the good.

I was crying because Man would make a terrible father. His fat genes don't belong in my family. I don't want my babies to be fat. Luke should be the twins' father. Or Gerald. Or Dr. Doe. Anyone but Man. And his fat ass couldn't even be here with me now at the time I need him most. I was crying because I couldn't figure out why I was the only one having these babies when I damn sure wasn't the only one making them.

I cried until my eyes were dry and then I took a deep breath. My abdomen went numb and so did the rest of me. When Dr. Doe pulled the first baby from my stomach, I heard him say "Your son looks great." And then a tiny cry that sounded more like a cat than a human child. The second baby was quiet for the first few seconds, and then a cry just like the first baby. Dr. Doe's team wrapped the babies in swaddling cloth like baby Jesus in the manger and held them side by side in front of me. Then something burst.

A blood vessel. Or the seam where they sewed me up. But it wasn't painful. Instead it was the overwhelming sensation of...emotion. No emotion I had ever experienced and all of them at the same time. My heart was bursting at the seams at the sight of my two sons, identical, and equally lovely.

I often wondered if when you fall in love, your heart stops. Just for a moment –the moment when you fall. It seems like it might because you hit the ground below so hard, your heart won't be able to withstand the fall. In that moment, that split second, I think it is possible for the heart to stop and then resume again at a different pace and in a different direction than it originally beat.

Dr. Doe and his team rushed my babies away and put me back together again. Physically they redid what was undone to remove the life inside me, but mentally I would never be the same. I fell into a deep sleep, a side effect of the anesthesia.

In my dream I was walking in a desert, a vast open space, brown and dusty. I held the twins in my arms, wrapped tight. My long white gown was tattered and torn at the edges where it dragged the dirt. I was tired and thirsty. The journey had been long.

Where was I coming from? Where was I going? Why was I alone? I walked until I stood before a wide river that spanned the length of the dessert. We have to cross over. A basket, like the one baby Moses laid in was before me. I knelt and placed the twins inside. One baby began to moan. And then the other let out a cry. "Shhh..." I quieted. "It won't be long now."

I turned to stand and gather my dress around my thighs. "I'll swim and hold on to the basket. We'll make it to the other side." But when I set the basket in the water, it began to float away. I climbed in after it but couldn't catch up. It was floating way too fast. The water was deep. I dove under and kicked my legs. The basket was far out of reach. The babies cried. I kicked and paddled. It was moving faster. The current was driving the babies away. "Stop!" I screamed. My voice echoed. "God no." I swam faster. Faster. I fought the water. We were at battle. The basket just a speck in the distance now. "Help me. God help me!" Tears escaped my eyes and blended with the water already soaking my face. I kicked harder. Swam faster. But the basket was nowhere in sight."

When I woke up, Gerald was with me. He was watching the news on the hospital television. He didn't notice I was awake.

"You never fail to amaze me," I said to him, still groggy.

He turned quickly. "What did you say?"

I tried to sit up, but the pain in my abdomen stopped me. "How long was I sleeping?"

"A few hours. It's noon. Your twin boys were officially born on the third of August."

"Sounds like a good day. All this time you've been sitting here with me? If I didn't know any better, I'd think you were the dad."

He laughed. "If I didn't stay, who would be here to greet sleeping beauty when she awoke?"

"How sweet of you. I really do appreciate it, Gerald."

"Did you call your husband back home?"

"My husband?"

"You know who I mean."

"Ohhh. You mean Man. Yes, I called him last night before they cut me open. He says he wishes he could be here and he can't wait to see me."

"He should come. Africa is just a plane ride away."

"I know, but it's expensive and he works. And the truth is, I'm not so sure I want him here right now. I'm enjoying you too much."

Gerald smiled and folded his hands in his lap. "He is a lucky man to have you. You shud build with him. He must love you."

"I'm not so sure it's me he loves. He loves the idea of me. The idea of having a family. But me? He couldn't possibly love Kericho."

Gerald looked at me intently. I wanted him more and more

after that intimate night on the couch, him inside me, me fighting off the devil. He made love to me and then rocked me to sleep.

The next morning we had both agreed that couldn't happen again. He apologized. I wasn't sure what to feel. I had violated the babies growing in my belly. Man was oblivious. It was a secret I would have to take to my grave.

Sometimes Gerald and I stole a look, when the group was at dinner, or on a van ride to town, or at our weekly house meetings. It was always a brief look, and even now I wonder if it wasn't all just in my head. Did he want me like I did him? Did our love session somehow make him the Daddy of my twins?

We never spoke about that night again. Gerald continued on as if it didn't happen. We talked. He comforted me but never so much as a kiss. I longed for his lips, his caress. In my deepest meditations, I discovered I wanted his heart.

But what would become of us? I would soon be returning to another part of the world. He would stay behind. Would our paths ever cross again? Was he capable of giving me his heart? Could he love me? Could he? These are the things I pondered in my alone time, but the questions never escaped my lips, not to Bella, not to Justice, certainly not to Gerald.

I changed the subject. "Have you seen the babies?

"They wouldn't let me. The intensive care unit is for immediate family only."

"I just encountered a pivotal moment in my life. A transition from selfish single woman to mother. I just underwent surgery and here I am in a hospital bed with bandages wrapped around my midsection and you are the only one here with me. If that doesn't qualify you as family, I don't know what does."

"So what's next?"

I took a deep breath. "Next...next I keep reading to find out what the next chapter of my life is all about. I'm still figuring it out. Just two classes shy of my degree. I didn't come all this way to give up now. "

"So what will you do."

"Medical leave of absence. That's what the university calls it. So I take a few months off and I go back home. Man says I'm welcome to stay with him as long as I need to or want to. Then when I get my strength back, I finish my last credits in New York and then put on a cap and gown. I really did want to graduate at the end of this year, but I asked myself if in the scheme of things, getting a degree six months later in life really makes much of a difference. It doesn't."

"I enjoy your optimism. When is the wedding?" I can't say his eagerness to let me go didn't sting a little.

"Gerald, I'm a sucker for love. Unadulterated, pure love. If or when I get married, I want it to be because someone saw something in me that made them want to spend the rest of their life with me. Not because I got pregnant before either of us was ready to be a parent, and not because my mother won't want to speak to me in public. Not because we want to make it work for the children. I want to get married because I want to make it work for us. No wedding bells anytime soon. Not that I can see."

The door opened slowly and Gerald and I both turned. Bella poked her head in.

"Someone's being nosy," I said when I saw it was her.

She smiled and flung the door open wide sauntering in to give me a bear hug.

"Kericho," she said. "You're officially a mommy. Congratulations doll!"

Justice followed behind her. He was carrying a single flower. A yellow daffodil, I think it was. "I got you something sweetheart," he said coming over to my bedside and presenting me with the flower.

"What's that?" I asked.

"What do you mean, what's that? Don't you see it's a flower?"

"I didn't take you as the flower type."

"Really? I picked it on the way over. It caught my eye because it's almost, but not quite as beautiful as you."

I took the flower and smiled. "I'm flattered. Have a seat. Have a seat. Stay a while."

Justice pulled up a folding chair from the corner and Bella settled on the edge of my bed.

"Has Gerald been good company? I hear he's been here all night. I love you baby, but I couldn't be doing all that," she said.

"Gerald is a real friend. I know that now."

She grimaced.

"When do we get to see the little fellas?" Justice chimed in.

"If someone could help me into this here wheelchair, we can all go down to the NICU together."

My firstborn was smaller, but alert, and I named him Kiefer after Kiefer Sutherland. His name would always be a conversation starter much like my own. Kye was the baby, a fat baby considering his gestational age, and sleepy. He slept the entire month he stayed in the neonatal intensive care unit at Nyaho Medical Centre and was fed through a tube inserted in his nose down to his stomach.

At four weeks old, they were both discharged and a week after that I was catching a flight back to the States. The hardest part in leaving was saying goodbye to Gerald. It ended outside the airport with a hug and a kiss on the cheek.

I said to Gerald over the murmer of the planes and the requests from baggage handlers in Twi. "If you see Esi, tell her that I'm sorry we never made that film. I'll have to take a raincheck. Next time."

"I'm sure she will understand. You have more important things to tend to." He motioned to my newborns swaddled in their carriers.

I looked at Gerald long and hard. I peered into his soul and he met my gaze. It was an unspoken conversation that said we both knew we may never see each other again.

"I had fun," I said.

"Make sure he is sweet to you."

I smiled. It was the same smile I wore on the inside when I first noticed Gerald's build under his shirt that day in the kitchen. This time the smile was on the outside, heavy on my face. Then I turned and walked off in the direction of my gate, my babies in tow.

It was a four hour flight to London and another eight hours from there to New York. My babies didn't cry for longer than a minute at a time. They were good babies. I didn't like breast feeding but I did it anyway. The sucking aroused me a little. It made me think of the men I desired. Luke on one breast and Gerald on the other. The thought of either of them taking my breast out of its cup and playing with my nipple made me feel like a woman.

I drifted in and out of sleep, but I never slept too deeply. I had a lot of surface dreams. Half reality, half made up in my own mind. I dreamt of my mother, Grace, and Sunday, and my Daddy. What would he say when he saw my babies? What would he think about me and my husbandless life?

My father, Dr. Lemuel Blu was a doctor of philosophy, not of medicine, and I loved him more than I had room or time to express. Daddy said he would pick me up from the airport in New York. I bought a woven bracelet for him as a gift. In my dream, I was about 10 and I was crying in my driveway. I had on a pretty dress and my mother had done my hair in Shirley Temple curls. I was holding my violin in its box. Yes, I had a recital tonight. Daddy couldn't come and Grace was inside yelling at him. I could hear her through the screen door. He had some very important business to tend to tonight and it made me upset.

Grace told him he was upsetting me and I should be more important to him than work.

I leaned on the car. It was a station wagon, baby blue with chipped paint and wood paneling on the side. My mother came out in a hurry, letting the screen door slam behind her. "Lemuel, you do what you want to do! I'm the only one who has sacrificed for our children anyway!"

My mother helped me in the backseat and then got in up front. She started the engine but we didn't move. She didn't back up or even put the car in gear. She just sat there and closed her eyes as if to slow her breath or her heart rate. A few moments later, she turned on the radio and smiled in the rearview. "You ready?" she said.

I nodded.

Then as she began to reverse, Daddy came out of the house, locking the door behind him with one hand and securing his cap on his head with the other. It was an old baseball cap he must have gotten in a garage sale. But it suited him well. Grace stopped the car and Daddy climbed in the passenger side. They were silent the whole way to my school but I smiled like it was my birthday.

When my plane landed, I gathered my babies and my luggage and headed outside. My heart was beating fast and I stopped at every water fountain to try and slow it down. I saw Daddy there just before the revolving doors. He looked older than I'd remembered him before I left for Africa. He was always a thin man, but now he looked thinner. His button down shirt hung loosely over his frame and he was wearing his baseball cap and his glasses. Glasses he only needed for reading but often wore them just to make him look distinguished. They went well with his face, skin the color of dark chocolate, and small eyes that always seemed as if they were looking through you and not at you.

When Sunday and I were small, Daddy would come home every day after work and we would hear his keys in the door. We ran past our mother usually cooking dinner in the kitchen to greet him as he stepped inside. Daddy would pick me up first because I was the baby.

"I want to touch the ceiling, Daddy," I would say.

"Okay. Okay. Reach," he would tell me and then he'd lift me high over his head. Touching the ceiling then felt like I was touching heaven. He would do the same with Sunday, and right here, right now, in this airport, I was hoping he would treat me like that little girl I used to be and pick me up to touch the sky.

I was walking slowly. So slowly, I could have been walking backwards, yet I was getting closer and with each step towards my father, the knot in my chest got tighter.

He was standing with his hands in his khaki pants, not looking at anything in particular. Daddy was never easy to read. He did well at keeping his thoughts under wraps. Some days that was a good thing. Not today. I felt like one of those girls in the movies. Everything and everyone in the airport faded away. The sounds were like faint muffles, not easily understood, and not important to make out for the scene. The focus was on me. Me and Daddy and he was all I saw, but was afraid to face.

I wondered if it would have been better if Man made the drive to get me from the airport. Man was a part of the disaster that was my life now and so there would be no judgment on his part. I could avoid the discomfort of facing Daddy or Mommy or anyone that might look at me sideways because I left for Africa childless, and came back a mother. But I heard Lauryn Hill once say that that our first instinct at any sign of discomfort is to retreat...to run away, when in fact confrontation is the only real way to resolve anything.

Whether I did it now or later, I was going to have to talk to my father once again. I was going to have to have the dreaded conversation in which he tells me how much I let him down, the conversation that confirms for me that he knows I've been having sex. But Daddy was gentle. Grace was harsh. Daddy's words were filled with love. Grace's words were filled with something else and

I never knew quite what to call it. Perhaps hers were words of love too but her love language was one I didn't speak nor understand. I never picked up foreign languages easily.

Just a few more steps and I would be standing in front of my dad. He didn't see me. The airport really was crowded, but for me, I didn't see anyone else. I approached, pushing my stroller with one hand and lugging my suitcase on wheels with the other.

"Daddy," I said. It was a statement and a question. It was an announcement of my arrival and an inquiry into his state of mind, an ascertainment of his mood. In that word, it was as if I was asking one hundred questions at once. *Do you know? Are you mad? Do you still love me? Can we be friends again?*

He turned to regard me and my offspring and then the world came tumbling down.

PART II

Chapter Fifteen

In the summer of 2008, a mother and her three children were found dead after their home went up in flames. The smallest children had their throats cut. Reports said the oldest boy was responsible for the murders and his own suicide. I always thought it was the mother.

"Daddy knew how to answer a question without answering a question. Sunday and I got bits and pieces of the puzzle but never put it all together. Daddy came to America in his early adulthood. Then Daddy got married to extend his visa. Then Daddy met Mommy and lied about his previous marriage and Mommy didn't find out until years later. Or no. Daddy came to America. Daddy had a child with a woman he barely knew. Then Daddy met Mommy and lied about the child and Mommy didn't find out until years later. Wait a minute. Daddy came to America. Daddy married Mommy. But Daddy was not accustomed to monogamy and Daddy slept with many other women and Mommy didn't find out until years later.

"Maybe the truth was none of these versions of the story. And maybe it was all of them. But the common thread was that mommy was duped into marrying Daddy and regretted it for most of her life."

My eyes always lit up a little when I talked about Daddy. Dr. Hannah called me on it. She smiled this Monday night, settled back in her chair, and said "Tell me more. What are your fondest memories of your Dad growing up?"

"I stayed up late one Friday night when I was 16 watching a horror flick and eating ice cream sandwiches. Daddy came in the room just as the movie was ending to find me sitting in the dark at 2am.

"Are you still up," he said to me squinting. Everyone said Daddy had a typical African accent. But to me it sounded different. Maybe it was because I was his daughter and grew up hearing him speak from the time I was born. Maybe it was because he was my Daddy and my Daddy didn't sound like anyone else. Yet still his voice was not as deep as most men's and he was often mistaken for a masculine woman on the phone.

"I'm watching TV. It's Friday. What are you doing up?"

"Oh I just got up to make some tea." He sighed heavy. "Your mother is hard to please."

"I thought I heard you two arguing earlier. What was it about this time?"

"What is it ever about? Everything and nothing at all." He came over with his mug and sat down next to me on the couch.

"You two are so different Daddy. Sometimes I wonder how you ever got together."

"I knew how to take gud care of your mother."

"Really? Something about her tells me she didn't need to be taken care of."

"Every woman needs to be taken care of. Even those that don't know it or want to admit it. I met your mother when she was still in school. I had a good job, and apartment and a bright future."

"What more could she ask for, huh?" I said smiling.

"Of course I was a gud catch. I could provide for a family. I would be a gud husband and a gud fudda."

"Did you love her?"

"Yes I love her."

"Did she know that? Does she know that?"

"Oh love. Americans put so much weight in love. Love is not important. Love will come."

I watched Daddy sip his hot tea and smiled faintly for a lack of words.

"Love is important Daddy. Do you want me to grow up to marry a man who doesn't love me?"

"I want only the best for you girls. So what if he loves you and he cannot pay the mortgage or give you food to eat or clothes to wear. What good is love when it is not enough to survive?"

"Sometimes I think it is enough to survive. The other necessities will come."

That day my Daddy looked at me there standing in flight arrivals, his eyes were both happy and sad. Happy to see me. Sad to see what I had become. I felt for a moment like the prodigal son in Jesus' parable. I was arriving home after a long time away, after realizing home was what I needed most and the glamour of the world wasn't so glamorous. Only Daddy didn't have a ring and golden slippers or a purple robe fit for a queen to lay on my shoulders. Just his solemn stare met my gaze and although he didn't smile with his mouth, he indeed warmed my heart.

My world as I knew it stopped for a moment and the part of me that questioned my father's approval stood still. I waited. Yet nothing. The distinguished Dr. Lemuel Blu parted his lips and then he said my name. "Kericho Blu."

Kericho. A city largely desert, hot, and dry, reminiscent of the time of year I was born. Summertime. Like the city, I was a whole lot of nothing, but beautiful nonetheless. Serene and sentimental, but at my core I was alive and I was ready and willing to show you my best parts if you took the time to get there.

Blu. My granddaddy's first name became my father's last name as was the custom in his time. "Where are you from?" people would ask me upon hearing my name. "African? You're too pretty to be African," was the response I got when I was in grade school, the ignorance of the masses. "African? That makes sense. You're too pretty to be anything but..." was the response I got these days from the cultured.

In the sixth grade, I told my first boyfriend, Calvin Lundy, "I'm not changing my last name when I get married. I'm African and folk should know it."

"So you're going to use the hyphen, huh?" he said. "That's stupid."

"I think so too. That's why I'm not using the hyphen. I'm just not changing it. I'm going to be Kericho Blu until the day I die. It's my identity so it's only right."

"Well I can't marry a girl unless she takes my last name. Even the Bible says a man and woman become one when they marry. You have to be Kericho Lundy if you want to be my wife. "

"Guess I don't want to be your wife that bad."

Daddy never said it but I always knew he was upset that he never had any boys to carry on his name. I imagine he wonders if the babies Grace aborted would have turned out to be boys. Maybe somehow he's comforted in believing that they were. Sunday had two girls and I think Daddy gave up the idea of teaching boys how to be men.

"Their names are Kiefer and Kye Blu. Twin boys," I finally said without a motion to the stroller. I was hesitant because I was still unsure where I stood with my dad.

"Oh wow. Your sister told me. This is a beeg surprise. I was not happy when I got the news, but the best thing now is to be a gud mudda. What matters is that you are home, you are safe and you and the babies are healthy." Daddy bent down to get a closer look at my newborns, sleeping soundly in their stroller.

"Do you want to hold them Daddy?"

"Uhhh...no. Let's go home. There will be plenty of time for that at home."

My breath quickened and my eyes filled with water. I let go of my grip on the stroller and reached for Daddy. He hugged me back and with my chin resting on his shoulder, I let the first tear fall.

"I love you Daddy."

He patted my back. "And you too." Daddy was trying. *I love you* was never something a father said to his children. But Daddy was trying.

At home, Sunday baked a cake for me. It was chocolate with a buttercream frosting and it was good.

It was as if Africa never happened. The smells, the sounds. Gerald, Bella, Justice.... Even Esi. Home was familiar. It was back to reality, back to the basics, back to Grace Blu and the harsh strains of life pulling on my muscles from the inside out. Sunday had returned from Guam, now a single lady. Her girls had grown so much, now almost unrecognizable. Just 8 months I was away, and the world was so different and yet very much the same. The house in New Jersey smelled like a worn couch and an often used kitchen. It was broke in and had years of conversations around the dinner table, soup stains on the carpet, and peeling wallpaper to prove it. Just a day removed from Africa, and it was already so far behind me.

"We'll just have to plan a belated baby shower," Sunday said sitting down holding one of my twins watching me eat cake. "I can put everything together in, let's say, two weeks."

"I don't want a haphazard baby shower. You know I like to do everything in style," I said. "I'm thinking a black and white affair. Let's choose a nice restaurant, with white linen tablecloths and good food. No silly baby games."

"You got it Babygirl."

I ate a forkful of cake. Then with a mouthful, "You think Mommy will come?"

"Have you talked to her since you've been home?"

"She said hello. Not much else."

"Give her time. She'll come around."

"What does she think about your divorce? What happened to you and Reggie?"

Sunday adjusted baby Kye in her arms. "Uhhh...sometimes I think she regrets telling me to get married. Other times I think she just wishes I stayed married. Reggie and I were very young. We still are and somehow we both decided we were tired of trying to fit our own idea of a married life into each other's."

"Do you miss him?"

"I do. We were doing a whole lot of fighting, but now sometimes I think I miss having someone to fight with."

"How are the kids holding up?" Sunday had a 1 year old and a three year old. Two little girls, light and bright and almost white. They both looked just like their Daddy.

"At first, Priscilla cried a lot. You know Reggie's still in Guam, so it's hard for her having to go without seeing him. Pansy is easy. She wonders about him but not for too long."

"You think you'll get married again?"

"Isn't growing old with someone what we all want? I want to find the right man, settle down and all. But this time I want to do it right, Babygirl. No half steppin'. What 'bout you and Man? Can you see yourself marryin' him?"

I finished the last of my cake, and said with a mouthful, "No. I don't know. I'm a fan of love. I love love. I don't want to marry Man because I had his babies. People say I have to think about the children and giving them a good home, a mother and a father, but I am thinking about the children when I say I would be miserable.

That's no way to raise children. Try as I might, I can't pretend to be happy when every day I wish I was never born. That's the way it would be if I stayed with Man. We have no connection. No chemistry. No common interests. He's a sperm donor."

"Don't be silly. Don't jump to conclusions so fast. I'm sure you and Man have more in common than you know. Take your time to uncover those things."

"I can't shut him out of my life. I won't shut him out of my life. I am considering the possibilities, wondering where life may take me." I set my plate down.

"You like?" asked Sunday gesturing to the plate.

"Always."

Man came over that night after he got off work. He sat down with my mother and father to talk about our future plans. I was against it. I'm grown. I'm not some sixteen year old teenager having a baby when she's a baby. I'm an adult, and I'm quite old enough to take responsibility for my own decisions. The thought of sitting down with Grace, listening to her decades old diatribe about how kids these days have no common sense made me want to vomit like I was in my first trimester all over again. I never did do well with judgment because most of the time anything anyone could say to me about the mistakes I made, I had long ago said to myself. Grace would be offering no new information, nothing I agreed with anyway. She had a track record for dwelling in the past, the coulda, shoulda, woulda's, instead of the here and now.

But we obliged my parents, Man and I, by sitting down in the living room to talk about the future. I was only half listening, half pretending to be interested.

"I always thought Kericho and I had a great relationship," Grace said. "But I stopped lending my opinion to her life when she stopped listening." *Yaddayaddayadda.* "So what are you two going to do?" *Blah blah blah* "Getting an apartment together? What about insurance for the babies?" ....."I do hope you know what you're doing."

Man was the son of a preacher man. His father was Pastor Jonathan Wright of New Birth Missionary Baptist Church. My mother was a member.

Preacher's kids are a lot like normal people, only they're watched a lot closer so they have to be careful. Sunday and Man put their money together to throw me a baby shower at Capitale Restaurant and Grill. We got an intimate private room for 20 and invited our closest family and friends. I had custom made invitations drawn up, so beautiful, you'd think they were for a wedding, but I never passed up an opportunity to do something fancy.

The night of the shower, Sunday asked my mother if she was coming. I was in my room putting on a chiffon black dress, tight around my bust, and low cut to show off the growth my milk had brought me. Sunday came in smiling.

"Zip me up, will you?" I said.

"Mommy said she's not coming."

"I figured as much." I held back the tears. The time to cry had passed. I couldn't spend my life waiting for my mother to love me the way I needed to be loved. Sometimes we have to do that for ourselves. Disappointment comes in expectation. If you don't expect anything, you can't be hurt, your heart escapes unscathed and it feels so much better.

"I told her it's not right," Sunday continued. Whether she agrees with the pregnancy or not, this is her baby daughter's baby shower and she may never have another. Then I told her Pastor Jon will be there. She seemed surprised. 'Oh really,' was her response. Guess it's hard for her to fathom some folk just aren't as cynical as she. Witch."

I let out a slight giggle. "Help me grab the babies; we're going to be late for my own thing."

Man met us at the restaurant. Everyone was there. Highschool friends, some church folk, Man's Daddy, the pastor, and his stepmom. Just before the food arrived, Grace walked in with Daddy. *Guess she decided to come.* She sat at the opposite end of a long table the restaurant prepared for us. I glanced at Pastor Jon, and then back at Grace. Then I knew.

My mother had a lot of secrets. I asked her how come her baby brother killed himself, and she told me it was because he had a real big heart, but a weak body and his body just couldn't bear the size of his heart anymore. The world's atrocities got to him. But I knew better. People just don't off themselves because of world hunger, or street crime. They do it because something in their own private world beats them up every night. But Mommy couldn't tell me or anyone else about Luther, the man who hated his own children more than anything else, and bruised them with his own hands and any other household item he could find, and her mother who could do nothing but stick around to watch. But the darkest bruises came from his mouth. He piled words of scorn and disdain upon curse words that stunk like skunk shit. He never told his children he loved them, probably because he didn't. My mother couldn't tell anyone her childhood secrets any more than she could tell them that she inherited her father's callous ways, unable to feel, accustomed to indifference and thinking there was nothing wrong with that. "That's just the way I am," she'd say.

To Grace, she was nothing like her father, Luther Joe. She was a survivor, a woman strengthened by her past and not a product of it. To me, she was the content of a broken life, a shattered mind, and a wounded soul. Grace found her solace in other's thoughts of her. "When you get as old as me, you stop caring what other's think of you," she said to me one day. Oh but I beg to differ. Grace cared only what other's thought of her. Or maybe it was what she thought of herself. She knew Pastor Jon would be at my shower. Her pastor of eleven years, the same pastor, she would see time and again each Sunday she sat in the church pew. It's easier to get dressed and come to a baby shower than to explain to a pastor why you didn't.

Chapter Sixteen

Ernest Hemmingway said, "Every man's life ends the same way. It is only the details of how he lived and how he died that distinguish one man from another."

Christmas 2006 was bittersweet. The apartment we moved into was not much to look at but still more than Man could afford. We got a place in Brooklyn close to the city so I could take the classes I needed to get my degree. Tan carpet, three bedrooms, a master and two smaller ones. A newly renovated kitchen and windows that looked out into the courtyard.

Man was the perfect gentleman. He adored the twins, replicas of himself in many ways. They had the same nose as he, and lips that curved upward naturally, even before they knew how to smile. Man took some time off of work to help us all get settled into our new home. We bought two cribs, and with a cash advance from a credit card, I got me a rocking chair and a playpen and a whole lot of baby clothes. Man cooked for me often and sometimes we ordered in. Pizza and cheesesteaks. My favorite was Popeye's Chicken.

We stayed up late staring at our sleeping babies, watching old movies and some new ones. One day we tried to have sex, but after the baby weight came off, I was down to 105 pounds and Man weighed three times that. His stomach protruded over his boxer shorts, the fat hanging below his undershirt. Stretch marks covered his arms and shoulders. I closed my eyes tight and thought of Luke. By this time, it had been a year since I last saw him or spoke to him and I wondered if he was only an imaginary character, like an imaginary number in algebra, invented so that every quadratic equation would have a solution. Luke was my solution since without the image of his hands on my thighs, I wouldn't be able to lubricate myself in expectation of Man.

But it still didn't work. The awkwardness of him on top forced us to try other positions and by the time we figured out what we had to do, the mood had long ago left us. Man would fall asleep and snore loudly like he had animals in his throat and after he found me one morning on the living room sofa, unable to bear the sounds, he agreed to spend his nights there instead of me. So we went on sharing a home and children, but not a bed. Our days were warm but our nights were cold.

By Christmas, my mother and I were speaking again. She warmed up to Kiefer and Kye just like Gerald said she would. Man and I spent half of Christmas Day at Pastor Jon's house and the other half with my parents, Sunday, and the girls. He bought me a necklace. I got him a pair of football tickets with a loan from Sunday.

Dr. Doe warned me about the hormones. He said that my body would be going through many changes and that sometimes I may not feel like myself but I should remind my loved ones that it was physical and not personal. I cried often those first few months after the babies came, my face almost permanently wet with tears. My eyes would water at the smallest slight or insensitive comment from another, or my inability to find a clean pot in which to make oatmeal, or Kye's crying because his bath water was too warm or too cold, or my clumsiness with the babies' diapers. I cried when it rained just because it seemed like the right time to cry and I cried whenever Man saw a pretty girl on television.

Man comforted me the best way he knew how but it wasn't enough to calm the storm raging inside me. Some days I thought I was an unfit mother, unworthy of Kiefer and Kye. I had no money, and was just a child myself. How could a person so small depend on me for a proper upbringing I couldn't deliver? I wanted out. But a mother who leaves her children often goes down in history books as the worst mother of all. What the history books often failed to see that I now could was that it's not that the mother who walks away does not love her children, but rather, that she loves them more than her heart or mind can handle. She loves them so much that she can't see herself sticking around to ruin their lives.

After the New Year, the problems worsened. I woke up one morning to a pain in my abdomen, the place where I was sewn back together after the surgery. Man had already left for work and I could barely move. When I did get to my phone, I called Man and he hurried home to take me to the emergency room. The doctors there said my incision had become infected, but with a little antibiotics and fresh stitches, I would be alright.

Within days, the pain subsided with the help of prescription Percocet. *Take as needed for pain not to exceed 1 tablet every 6 hours.* I kept the pills in our kitchen drawer, more than half the bottle left the day I decided I no longer needed them.

Soon after, Man started bringing up marriage and I became less and less interested in such a commitment. He bought me a bridal magazine one day at the grocery store and said he thought I might want to start brainstorming. I thought about it. Marrying Man and living life with him as my husband. Some days it didn't seem so bad. No man would ever love and care for the twins as much as he and something about being with the father of my children was romantic. I could learn to love him. I could learn to adore him. Perhaps. But other days...most days I cringed at the thought of being relegated to sleeping with a plus size man for the rest of my life and becoming the First Lady of a church Man came to pastor. I would have to invest in longer dresses and put my potty mouth to bed. No more memorable nights that I could barely remember dancing so hard to 90's hits in the club and finishing whole bottles of wine on Friday nights just because it's Friday. I would be a different kind of woman, reserved, and responsible in the kind of way that my mother wished I was. The kind of woman who doesn't swear. Ever. And only always has sex in the missionary position. Only with Man, that wasn't possible so with him I would have to give up my love of sex and replace it with a love for the Lord, the conventional kind of love that did everything the way the books said. It wasn't me and never would be. Marrying Man would mean losing myself.

Maybe he thought I just needed to see a ring and my thoughts of him would change. Maybe he thought I would magically fall in love with him the second he proposed. But that was wishful thinking. He put an engagement ring on layaway and one day hid it in a Popeye's Chicken box wrapped in a napkin. I was holding Kiefer on my lap, now six months old, stuffing french fries in my mouth when I saw it. Man got on one knee and gave me a speech that said how much he loved me and couldn't bear life without me and the boys.

I froze there for a few minutes trying to think of what to say. Why did he have to go and ruin such a peaceful day with this nonsense? *You love me? You love me? You don't even know me. You think you know me? Well, what's my favorite color? And what do I love to do? What's my favorite place in the whole world and why? How come I'm so pretty?*

My favorite color is black because it goes with anything. I love to write because a picture says a thousand words, but a thousand words can paint the prettiest picture. My favorite place? The beach, it's what God looks like. And I'm so pretty because my Daddy's from Africa, where the most beautiful children in the world are made.

Man would know all that if he cared to know, but his mind could only comprehend one thing and that was his own vision of what his life should be. A wife, two kids, and Webster's definition of love.

"Sure, I'll marry you," I said to keep the peace, but I wasn't happy and those words were quickly taken back days later when Man found me sobbing on the couch one Sunday after church. I told him I couldn't go through with it. Not now. I don't know if I ever could but only time would tell if I had a change of heart.

He was angry. He wanted answers. Why was I playing house with him and living off of his money and was I planning to move out after I finished my classes. Was I merely using him? But, I was the kind of girl that determined my life from day to day and if I couldn't even decide what I wanted to eat for lunch, how could I possibly know what I wanted from him in the long run. I knew what I didn't want. I didn't want a man who enjoyed the idea of me more than he did me. I didn't want a man who aimed to please his daddy, and his mama, and his church family more than he cared about being genuine. I didn't want fake hugs and kisses and tiptoeing around each other to avoid conflict. I didn't want a life of solitude because even though I was with him, I still felt so alone.

Yet I needed Man for my own survival, both emotional and physical. I was 12 weeks away from obtaining my college degree and Man enabled me to be at home with my children during the day and go to class in the evenings. Without him, I'd have to get a job, and put the children in daycare, or move back in with Grace, the woman who still despised me even though she said it a lot less now and as much as I hated living with Man, living with my mother would be an admission of defeat, a plea for help from someone who's daily mantra was "I told you so." Moving back home with two babies was not an option. It was not an option because the emotional strain would be enough to kill me, either by psychological stress or my own hands much like Jamie and the sawed off shotgun.

I needed Man because he provided a home for me in the meantime. The time between me setting up a life for myself and the life being established. The interim, he was my crutch, my help in my time of need, my salvation from the emotional unraveling I would experience at home. But the kind of shelter he provided was not, in my own mind, a permanent structure because I wanted more than Man could ever give me. I wanted the home in the city, the career, the husband who was just like me at the core, shared my nontraditional ways of operation, my sense of ambition, my carefree attitude, my love of all things beautiful.

Just a few more months. When I finish school, I'll get a job. A good job. And my own place, and the kids will be a year old then. I can put them in daycare. "Babies need at least a year to bond. Mothers should raise children, not facilities." I read that in a pregnancy magazine once. It made sense to me.

I'm not a homemaker. I don't wear long skirts or dresses and I don't know how to sew. I'm learning to cook but right now I'm best at boiling hot dogs and dialing out for Chinese. I prefer long dinners at fancy restaurants and business suits with low cut blouses that show off my legs and breasts. I want to make my own money because women who depend on their husbands for their livelihood make me vomit a little, and I won't give up my wants, my desires, my passions for a life of raising children and being a good wife. I like babies. I love babies. But life for me didn't stop the moment I gave birth and it's okay to still have girl's night out and curse after the children are in bed. It's ok to have sex on the washing machine and on the livingroom couch, and in the shower. It's okay to be a mother and take trips to the Caribbean without the kids, and bake brownies with a little reefer inside just for fun.

That was the life that attracted me to me and if getting there meant sharing a home with a man that didn't share my sense of joy for just a little while, I would suck it up and do it, because how else was I supposed to get through the meantime.

One Friday, Man came home from work and found me on the bedroom floor flipping through photographs from Africa. By now, Gerald, and Justice, and Bella seemed so long ago and so far away. I remembered Esi, the woman I named Beauty that stole a room just by her walk, and thought on the things I missed so much. Bar California and the sandy beach. Afrodisiac and Gerald's hands on my waist.

Man stopped in the doorway and I looked up.

"Let's go out tonight," I said easily.

Man never wanted to go out and while I was usually content with staying home and watching reruns of The Cosby Show, I missed sparkly dresses and 5 inch heels and wearing makeup. I missed getting dolled up for a reason and having something to look forward to.

But Man was frugal and made no attempt to disguise it. He noted that the babies had no sitter and getting one would mean double the money. Money for a babysitter and money to go out and it was all money we didn't have.

"It's worth it," I said. "To me, I think it's worth it."

But Man didn't share my point of view even it was just once in five months, just once that we spent the extra hundred dollars and spent an evening away from home, with a waiter and dinner, followed by dessert and a movie in a theatre and not our living room. Man didn't see the value even it meant making me smile after weeks of tears, aches and pains both physical and emotional. Man didn't think it would be smart, so we stayed home that night. He made baked chicken thighs and brown rice and we watched an old episode of the Family Feud.

The next night we argued in the bedroom. I cried and said I didn't know if I could ever marry him because the thought of sharing a bed with him made me a little sick. He yelled. And then he went out to the front room, sat on the couch, and I'm not sure, but I think he cried. I didn't know what to say to him so I lay down and soon I went to sleep. The next morning I found a finished bottle of rum and my empty bottle of Percocet on the kitchen counter. I looked over at Man snoring on the couch. He slept the whole day but at least he was still alive.

Man and I usually went to the A & P grocery store together. We would all go on a Saturday afternoon or a Sunday after church. I would carry Kye in a harness around my waist and we always put Kiefer in his baby seat in the cart. Today when we went to the checkout line, I watched Man pull out his debit card, swipe it through the card reader and then put it neatly away in his wallet. That's when I knew Man was controlling even if no one else could see it.

"No he doesn't hit me," I said to Sunday that night on the phone. I was in the bathroom with the door closed which was the only way I could talk on the phone without Man hearing me or interrupting. "But he's passive aggressive about it. I don't know. He's always saying how he wants us to be a real family, to blend our lives together. But he hasn't even offered to add me to his bank account or let me use his debit card to grocery shop without him. I told him I wanted to get a part time job to help with expenses but he was against it. He doesn't want me to work. He doesn't want me to have my own money."

"Baby girl, I know you're the last one to ever let someone control you. Put your foot down. Tell him the way it's going to be."

"I just feel so powerless right now. So...at his fingertips, to be pushed and pulled around. I'm depending on him and that's the one thing I never wanted to do."

"I'm sure you're overreacting. Just tell him how you feel. He doesn't realize what he's doing or what you think he is doing. Tell him. See what he says."

I took Sunday's advice. After I was in my pajamas, just before

I got in the bed I told Man what was on my mind. "I want to be added to the bank account. I really think it's unfair that we share children and yet you don't trust me with the finances."

He gave me an odd look, one of hesitation and uncertainty. He went back and forth saying he didn't know if we were ready to take that step. "I can't feel like I'm in this if you keep shutting me out," I complained. "You know you're gone all day, every day at work and I'm here stuck in the house. What if I want to go for ice cream with the babies, or get some gas in the car and run errands, the dry cleaners, the grocery store, the library? I need to have a life too. You want me to marry you but how can I possibly agree to sign up for a lifetime of this."

He caved. I don't know if it's because he agreed with me or because he wanted to avoid the argument. *Many people avoid conflict to the detriment of themselves and their relationships.* I read that in a self-help book once that described the pitfalls of avoiding conflict. The Behavior Theory says that the fear of conflict is a result of negative reinforcement where the individual most likely experienced rejection, abandonment, or the "silent treatment." Therefore, fear and avoidance of conflict is a learned and conditioned response. The bottom line is fear. In fact, many people see conflict as a big scary monster, like Freddy Krueger. When approached with the right skills, conflict can be more like Elmo; a benign monster that can actually operate as a great impetus for growth and learning.

The next day we made a trip to the bank and I got a shiny new debit card and checks with my name printed neatly in script.

A week later, I carried the babies with me to the A & P alone when Man was working. The ease with which I pushed the cart down the aisle was daunting and my confidence was different. I walked taller and even when other customers asked if they could help me in the checkout line since I had my hands full with the twins, I said no. "I can handle it. But thank you."

A week after that, I went back to the store to get a couple of steaks for a special dinner. I went straight to the butcher and ordered two New York Strips. "I made sure I got you a good cut, pretty eyes," he said handing me the steaks wrapped up neatly. I thanked him and went home to marinate the steaks a bit before Man got home.

That night, we ate good. A home cooked meal that was restaurant quality. Parmesan encrusted steak, sautéed spinach, and sweet mashed potatoes. I didn't even know I could cook like that but a new sense of freedom can do that to you. Man said that he didn't know what it was, but he was happy that I was happy and that just warmed my heart. I let him lay with me in the bedroom that night, and just as I began to slip away, he kissed me on my neck and then pulled off my panties just like he did that night it all began. He pulled me to the edge of the bed and knelt on the floor and I felt his tongue on my wet spot and I didn't stop him. I let him kiss and suck and for a moment it felt right. I closed my eyes and imagined...I imagined....I imagined Man loving me and not Gerald, and not Luke. After I came, he got off his knees, kissed me one last time, and then took his pillow to the living room couch.

The next day I got a greeting card in the mail. It was from my mother and enclosed were two fifty dollar bills. Inside the card, she printed the words:

Every woman needs a little something on
the side for herself. I love you. –Mommy

She always did things like that. Hurt me to my core and then turned around only to make me cry tears because I knew she really loved me. A few days later, I went back to the bank and opened my own account with the hundred dollars she gave me. I planned on saving a little bit at a time but when I saw the slingbacks in the window at the mall for 30% off, marked way down from their original price, I had to buy them. I kept them hidden in a corner of the closet for a whole week until one Sunday, I put them on for church. Man saw the brand new box and asked me where I got the money for new shoes.

"It's not your money, Man. Don't worry." But he was adamant so I told him. "My mother, she gives me money every now and then, so you know, I wanted something nice and saw these shoes and they were on sale so I bought them." He wasn't happy still, but he let it go. We went to church in silence, sat through a long winded sermon that didn't say much of anything I hadn't heard before. *Trials will come, God will bring you through. Just hold on. Joy comes in the morning. Have faith. Be steadfast in the Lord.*

Kye fussed a little and I took him to the nursery to feed him. When service was over, we rode home in silence. I knew something was still bothering Man, but I wasn't sure if it was the new shoes or my lack of enthusiasm to marry him or something else, and I decided in the car that I didn't much care either way. Asking him would begin an argument that would never be resolved so I kept my silence. It lasted well into the night and invaded the next morning.

Monday, I was up early on the computer trying to finish a class paper before the babies' first feeding. Man walked by the doorway and shot me a cold look before grabbing his coat on his way to work.

"Is something wrong?" I called. He peeked in the doorway. Just a solemn look on his face. No response. "Do you...do you not like me...or something?" I asked.

I must have hit a nerve because right then and there, Man could have written a tell-all book. He opened up and poured into me all that had been on his mind, that morning, that past weekend, those past few weeks, or months. He told me sometimes he didn't like me, and what he really wanted was for me to love him and even though he knew school was important to me, far too often I made him feel like graduating was more important than him or our family. He hated that I preferred a degree to spending my life with him... and the shoes...the shoes were just confirmation that I was still much too superficial and materialistic to give a damn about anyone else. He said he was struggling to pay the rent, and buy groceries, and keep gas in the cars, and diapers in the nursery, and if I get a little bit of money, the very least I can do is throw it in the pot. He told me I was a spoiled brat that was using him and if I didn't want to marry him now, then when? He said I'd better make a decision because he couldn't stand for too much more of this living in limbo, seeing what the day brings, waiting for a love that may never come.

And the whole time he flailed his arms delivering his diatribe, I sat at the computer desk and watched the way his stomach hung over his belt and the way his tie barely reached the middle of his shirt, and the sweat stains growing under his arms. Normally, I loved a man in control, a man who knew how to dominate a situation. Aggressive men were sexy to me, but not this man. This man was pathetic.

He finished by offering me an ultimatum, I had to decide if I was going to marry him or not and if not, then there was no reason to continue playing house. Sometimes I wondered why people who give ultimatums of marriage would even want to marry someone under such force. Me, I choose to love someone who voluntarily loves me back, who stays because they want to and enjoy more my company than our legal status. I didn't mean to say it so indifferently, but the words came out before I could catch them in my throat. "I have three months left of school. After that, we'll be out of your hair."

Chapter Seventeen

Death is only the end if you assume the story is about you.

The days dragged on. Man wanted me gone, but I refused to leave reminding him of our conversations when I was pregnant in Africa and he convinced me that sharing our lives wouldn't be so bad, and even if marriage wasn't in our forecast, he would forever love me and the children we made. He didn't remember those conversations or acknowledge their existence and I fell further away from him day by day. My daytime was filled with TV time with the babies, breastfeeding, and trips to the grocery store. Mondays and Wednesdays I went to class in the evenings when Man returned from work, and on the nights we both stayed home, I spent my time on the computer mostly working, sometimes websurfing and chatting with old acquaintances, but mostly working. Sunday called some nights and my mother kept sending money. On the weekends, Man would often go to visit his father, the pastor, and I had the house to myself after the babies were asleep. They started sleeping through the night early. They were good babies.

Leonard Forde, the butcher at the grocery store knew me by name. I noticed him smiling when he saw me walk up to the counter today. I thought he was kinda cute, muscles like a wide receiver shown under his white coat, dreads that he wore tied back under a net, cleanly shaved face, skin like coffee with a whole lot of milk.

"Ms. Kericho, right?" He said.

I nodded, adjusting Kye in his pouch.

"What can I get for you today?"

"What might you suggest?"

"Our special today is the filet in a special beer steak marinade. It's a little sweet."

"I hope not too sweet."

"I'm sure it's not as sweet as you."

That drew a smile. "What's with the Billy D.?"

"Just giving you a compliment. I won't go too far. You have a baby in your arms. And another in your cart. You probably have a husband too."

"That's cute, but no."

"No husband? Pretty as you are, I know you have men falling all over you."

"I'm so single right now." It just came out and there in that moment, it felt a bit like I was outside myself looking in, watching the scene take place as if in a movie. Then I laughed. "That wasn't....an invitation...I'm just you know...telling you."

He stared at me a few seconds and then, "So...can I get you the steak?"

"Sure, I'll try it. Two please. I'll eat one tonight and save the other for another day."

"Or you could invite me over for dinner."

"I could."

He pulled two filets from the window and began wrapping them. "I work in the city at night. Paid for studio time to work on this music thing I'm doing. You should come with me one day."

"So cutting meat is just a day job?"

He laughed. "As much as I love the smell of fresh beef, this is just a way to pay the bills. I plan on being a pretty big deal one day. A super producer."

"That's great. Are you any good?"

"I like to think I have a whole lot of untapped talent."

"I'd love to hear some of your work. What genre?"

"I do a lot of everything. R&B, hip hop, a little pop. My Daddy was a jazz player so you can even hear some of his influence in my stuff."

"I love music. I don't know a whole lot about it. What goes into it, I mean. I played a couple of instruments a long time ago but I was never any good. I'm more of a listener. There's a tune for every mood. I like to close my eyes and lay in it."

He handed me the meat wrapped in cellophane with two stickers on it. One with the price, the other with his phone number handwritten in ink. I looked at it. He said, "Will you call?"

"I might."

"If you don't, I may be upset the next time I see you in here."

"I said I might."

"We could just cut out all the suspense right now if you give me your number."

"I don't know if that's a very good idea."

"You said you're single right? Sounds like a great idea to me."

Being bad sometimes felt good. So I wrote my number on an old receipt I found in my purse and slid it across the counter.

Three days went by. The first time Leonard called, I was lying in bed in the middle of the day. Nude. The twins were asleep and I had just finished bringing myself to orgasm with a glass of ice water and the tips of my fingers. I stared at my cellphone listening to the ringer play an old Jodeci tune. I had programmed his number in my phone under "Leonard the butcher."

"Hello," I said melodically. I tried to sound unmoved but

really, I was happy to see him calling. It was something new in an otherwise uneventful life.

"Kericho, like Jericho."

"What?"

"I am calling Kericho right? I was trying to reach Kericho."

"Yeah. This...this is me."

"Hey girl, it's Lee."

"Leonard the Butcher, right?"

"You got it. You're not busy are you? You sound like you were asleep. I mean if this is a bad time, I can call you back."

"No. It's not a bad time. I was laying down. Not sleeping."

"I guess your little ones can wear you out in the middle of the day."

"They can...sometimes."

"What do you do? If you don't mind me asking...for a living. What do you do for a living?"

"I work from home," the lie rolled off my tongue like hot butter. I rolled over on my bed and propped myself up on my elbows. "I stuff envelopes and send them in."

"Really? How is that working out for you?"

"You can make a lot of money that way. You know if you stay busy. I have the babies so this way I can stay home with them. And I'm finishing school."

"Sounds good. Listen, when I said I wanted you to come to the studio with me, I meant it. I'll be there tonight. Can you get away?"

"Tonight? I don't know. It's short notice."

"I want to learn about you. We can grab some takeout, head back to the studio and I'll show you how everything works."

"I might be able to swing it."

"Tell me where you live. I'll come by and get you around 8."

"I'll meet you. Just let me know where."

"You sure? I can get you. It's no problem."

"It's fine. Really, I can manage."

When I think about it, I don't know if there was just one reason I did it. It could have been to regain some of the thrill of my youth. It could have been because I thought I needed sex. It could have been because I was looking for a release from the depression that hovered over me day and night, even if the release was only temporary. Or maybe I needed to push Man away for him to believe me when I tried to convince him we would never work. I needed to rebel to feel peace. I wanted to feel sexy one more time. Yes I think it was all of these things and more.

When I told Man I was going to the campus library to study with friends, I did it because the truth no longer mattered. Not even a little bit. I put on my stepping out jeans, knee high boots, and a blue button down sweater that hugged the curve of my breasts and accentuated my hips. I fed the babies and put them down and told Man not to wait up. "I have a lot of studying to do. Just haven't been able to really get anything done here."

These days it seemed we never said more than a few words to each other. We said what needed to be said to carry out the day's operations and not a word more. Man had stopped reaching for embraces or puckering his lips for a kiss after he realized I never really wanted any of that. But tonight he said I love you. He looked at me with eyes that said he needed to cry but didn't know if it was safe. They were eyes that had given up. Eyes that said what will be, will be. He assured me he wouldn't wait up and then he said that he loved me. And I said, "I'm late okay, so I gotta go."

I met Lee at Blue 9 Burger in the city. He wasn't the kind of sexy that got my blood flowing or my heart racing, but he was a little bit fine. Seeing him tonight as Lee and not Leonard the Butcher changed the dynamics of things. He was in a pair of jeans and a grey V neck sweater, his dreadlocks pulled back in a messy bun.

"You clean up nice," I said upon my arrival. Lee got up from his seat by the wall, held my hand and brought it to his lips.

"Thank you." He looked me over. "You look beautiful as

always." I smiled. It was a sheepish smile that said I was both flattered and a little nervous. "We should get some burgers. How do you like yours?"

On our walk to the studio, 3 blocks over, fast food in tow, He wrapped his arm around my shoulders and leaned in close. "You and your kids' daddy? What's that about?" The air was warm for late February in New York City, but brisk enough to encourage me to lean back into him.

"Well you know, we just couldn't make it work. We shared a place, but we were fighting all the time and life is just too short to be unhappy."

"I hear you. That must be a little tough though. Twins huh?"

"It was tough. It is tough. But I adjust well. I think I do alright."

"I think you do more than alright. You know I see you every week in the grocery store and you make it look easy. I know it's not though. My moms was a single mother for a long time. She remarried and had a couple more kids but I remember her always being tired. I'd want to play and she'd want to take a nap. Stress from bill collectors and work, and not enough hours in the day got to her."

"Where was your father? Was he ever around?"

"Pops was a rollin' stone. He was a traveling musician so I saw him every once in a while. Every few years for a few hours. We just started getting closer recently…within the last year or so. He stays here in the city with his fiancé and sometimes I stay with him when I'm working late, or just need to crash in the city. We have an understanding. He's a lot more like a friend than a Daddy. I don't know if he ever learned how to be a Daddy, and if he did it was too little too late."

Manhattan was easy at night. The sky was dark but the city lights kept the streets awake. This felt good. This felt right and I let myself forget about Man and for the time being Kiefer and Kye. "So I have to admit, I'm a little surprised you wanted to date me seeing the babies and all," I said.

"Sexy is sexy. I have eyes and to be honest, the fact that you have children kind of turns me on. It tells me you're not all in the streets...That you're responsible, and you know how to cook." We laughed at that. Then we stopped in front of a black door between two store fronts and Lee took out a silver key.

"Is this it?"

"We have arrived," he said turning the key in the door and leading me up a dimly lit staircase.

"It's hidden. No sign out front to let you know where you are."

"That's the idea." When we got to the second floor, we walked down a short hallway and into a doorway on the left. Inside the cozy room was a red leather couch, and in front of the couch, a stool and a kind of operation table with a thousand buttons and keys. In front of that, a clear glass window into another little room with a microphone.

"So this is where you make beats?"

"Yes ma'am. He pulled up a chair from the corner and gestured for me to have a seat in front of the keyboard. 'Let's get to these burgers before they get cold."

We were quiet for the first few moments while we ate, savoring the first few bites of a Blue 9 Burger. Then, "I brought you here to show you my work. I think you might like this last track I just wrapped up." He started up his laptop and played a song that sounded like something ol' school with a twist.

"Kinda reminds me of Marvin Gaye's Sexual Healing, but the bass line is way heavier. That's dope. You did that?"

"I did that," he smiled in between swallows. "I like the sound of seventies and eighties music but the grimy feel of present day hip hop. When I found out how to put them together, I made magic. Right now I'm looking for an artist to put words to this. Something sexy. I call this song, Night Sweat. You know when you wanna work out, you put on something energetic, something to get your blood flowing and keep you on your toes so you can break a sweat. Well this song is all of that, only you're not working out in a gym, you're working out in the bedroom, puttin' in work to satisfy your man or your lady."

"I like that. "

"You got any singers in mind?"

"Why are you looking at me funny? I'm no singer."

"I was kind of hoping you were."

"So you workin' on a whole album?"

"I'm putting a few songs together, something solid to showcase my work."

"I'm glad you have a dream. I'm a strong advocate of going after what you want. You seem talented. You seem driven. I think you'll be successful. If anyone tries to shut you down, fuck 'em."

Lee showed me the keys, the bass, the tambourine, the acoustic guitar. "I never knew so many sounds could come together so well." We finished our burgers and our fries and our sodas over small talk and minimal touching. He rubbed my thigh, my shoulder, held my hand in between talks of his Daddy and my Daddy, and the funny things he witnesses at the butcher counter like the old lady who always orders the finest meat and then complains about the price. We talked about his locs and why he can't work a corporate job because he won't cut his hair. We talked about relationships and why he's never had a serious one.

"Relationships are hard. I know I can't be everything to one woman right now and to pretend would be largely disrespectful so I often don't even try," he said. I hear men say things like that and like to think I have the power to change their position. I like to think they've never met a woman quite like me. I like to think so.

Lee was a subtle aggressor. His moves were calculated, or maybe they just seemed that way. He wasn't shy. He wasn't nervous. He showed me he was interested but said he was no one woman man. He was charming, but not overly tender. He was all man, but gentle in his approach. The night advanced, the two of us stuffed from the food, we moved to the couch and listened to the sounds of MelkySedeck.

"I love this album," I said with my eyes closed. "It's because nobody sounds like this. One of a kind."

"We have similar taste in music. I'm glad. It's not every day you meet someone so in sync with you." I rested my head on Lee's shoulder and let him brush my knee with his fingertips. He was right. We vibed like we knew each other in some past life. If only I had met him before I met Man, life would be different for me now. "It's such a shame, you're taken." He read my mind.

I paused a moment and swallowed before opening my eyes. "What?"

"Kericho, sweetheart, you don't have to lie to me. I know." I sat up. What did he know? He knew I was still with the father of my children. Living in the same house physically but emotionally removed to the point of no return. He knew I lied to another man to be with him tonight and although what I was doing was wrong, I didn't want to be right. "You always have way too much food in your cart to just be feeding you. I know the babies are too small to eat steak and you always buy them in pairs. You lick stamps for a living? Funny. Me too." Sarcasm always sounded threatening to me. "You wouldn't let me pick you up. And that's cool, but I'm wondering why you felt like you couldn't tell me."

I had never been caught in a lie before. Not like this. I wasn't used to being so easily read so it offended me a little. I licked my lips and prepared an explanation. "I told you I was single because right now, that's how I feel. He and I, we live together out of convenience. Neither of us really want to be there."

"So why are you here with me tonight?"

"You asked me to come."

He nodded slowly. "Will you do anything I ask you to do?"

"I don't know. It depends on what you ask?"

"Come home with me tonight." He didn't miss a beat.

"That didn't sound like a question."

"That's because it wasn't. I want...you to come home with me tonight."

"Yes."

Leonard the Butcher, Lee, the light skinned man with the dreads was an escape and even though I knew nothing would come of our union, and a job cutting meat at the local grocery store could hardly take care of me and the boys, I still needed to be in his arms tonight. I still was curious to see what would come of this night and I wasn't expecting anything at all and everything one could imagine altogether at the same time. If we laid there in his bed with our clothes on and talked some more about whatever we damn well pleased, well, that would be fine. And if we undressed each other just to see what we looked like naked and what it felt like to feel the warmth of his skin on mine, well, that would be okay. If we went a step further, and made our bodies one, his love stick nestled deep inside the space between my thighs, I suppose that would be fine as well. I imagined strawberries, and roses, and chocolates and all of the things a romance novel is made of.

So I let him take me by the hand, and together we walked back to his car, and then drove to the Financial District to his Daddy's place. The high rise condo was beautiful. I walked into a quiet room with cherry hardwood floors, a spiral staircase and a bay window that overlooked the Brooklyn Bridge. He led me to a bedroom in the back. "My father isn't here. He's traveling this weekend. You can relax. I use this spare bedroom whenever I need it."

I was quiet on the ride over, unsure of what to say, and I kept my peace now, as I slipped my boots off and sat on the bed. It started with a kiss. Lee sat down next to me, grabbed my chin in his hand and kissed me long and hard. His tongue was new, like nothing I ever tasted before and the part of my heart that had long ago froze, began to melt. Then my insides dripped like ice cream left out on the counter too long and I was ready for a physical interaction. It started with a kiss and it ended with Leonard the Butcher penetrating not only my body, but every other facet of my life, and he did it all with his undershirt still on.

Chapter Eighteen

I thought the phase was over, but then I found myself laying in bed and counting the number of ways to kill instead of sheep.

"My mother is an advocate of the death penalty, but I always thought killing to deter killing didn't make much sense. 'Only if they have no remorse,' she would say. 'If they show remorse for what they've done, execution is not necessary. The lesson has already been learned.' But after I saw Primal Fear with Richard Gere and Edward Norton, I knew anyone can be an actor when their life is at stake.

The question of Life or Death depends largely on the state in which the crime is committed and who the victim is. In some states, capital punishment is only given in cases where a federal official or an officer of the law is killed. So because they chose a career in law enforcement and got a legal pass to shoot guns, their life is worth way more than mine. Sounds like bullshit to me.

Hundreds of death row inmates attempt suicide while in prison only to be saved from their own hands and handed to the state for full control over their last breath. *You die when we say you die.* "

I was here recounting my past life to Dr. Hannah, memories still vivid. She was confused. "Kericho, what are you talking about?"

"If my life were on the line today, according to my mother's logic, I'd be walking the green mile to the death chamber because I had just killed the only morsel of hope Man had in me and I didn't even feel bad. I didn't feel good. But I didn't feel bad. I thought I might go home that morning and hang my head in despair. I thought I might feel a sense of urgency to confess and repent. To Man. To God. I thought I might paint a red A on my chest for adulterer and tear my clothes and sully my hair."

But I didn't. Leonard the Butcher, drove me to my car the next morning, kissed me innocently on my cheek and watched me drive away. I drove in silence for a few minutes thinking of the night's affair and what had just transpired between me and Leonard, and Man and the twins because even though there were only two of us in the room, our sexual act could possibly affect the five of us in ways we had yet to imagine. If there were anything still holding Man and me together, it was now severed completely because I cheated. The deed was done, making it so much easier for it to happen again. And again. Or maybe, I just needed one night to feel something I hadn't felt in a long time.

So I would go home and make up a lie about pulling an all-nighter in the library and then crashing at a friend's place. Then I would shower to cleanse my nipples from the scent of Lee's tongue, kiss the babies and give them my milk as usual.

When I walked in, Man, who had been sleeping on the couch, baby Kye in his arms, didn't even ask where I had been. But I offered an explanation as not to seem thoughtless. It was then that I didn't imagine Man would ever touch me again the way he once did, the way Lee did the previous night, or the way any man might show affection to his lady. Man would never show that to me again. Not because he was withholding his demonstration of love, but rather because it was no longer there.

It was some kind of life I had built for myself living in the seconds between taking my final breath and my heart ceasing to beat. I was dying a temporary death in that house, holding on to the hope of living again just as soon as I made my own way out. I was willing to embrace death for the moment to have life in the ever after, like Jesus and his agony on the cross. So I counted the days. And I browsed internet classifieds for apartments in the city, preparing for life after my own resurrection.

I often lay in bed at night, Man asleep in the next room, imagining life on the other side of death. After receiving my college degree, I would quickly get a job and excel in my field. My apartment would overlook the Hudson River and soon Luke and I would pick up our romance where we left off. He would fall in love with me and the babies that were not his own and we would be together. All of us. And if not Luke, some other man, even better than Luke, fine in all the right places, like Jamie, my uncle from so many years ago. Together, we would learn a new life, an unconventional one, a blended family, and in due time, we would add to the litter. Another boy. Or maybe a girl.

I thought on these things when I fed the babies from my breasts, my milk beginning to dissipate. When I watched them laugh at the tiniest things I hardly found funny, like a dancing Elmo, or the TV remote falling to the floor, I thought of the babies' future and I yearned to laugh with them. I bathed them in the tub and put on an old Chaka Khan cd hoping to conjure a bit of the peace I felt in her music.

Weeks went by and I didn't hear a word from Leonard the Butcher. Most of me wasn't expecting him to call, but my heart needed him to. I avoided the grocery store and the butcher counter for fear of reliving that night at the studio, the cheeseburgers, the kisses, the sex in his father's condo. Seeing Lee again would force me to admit that the night was real, and he didn't call after, and I was what men termed a loose woman who didn't guard the diamonds in her secret place. It was a word that rhymed with sore which was the condition Lee left me in when we parted ways. But I kept it to myself.

I harbored a place within my own head to store away memories of this sort. I busied myself with college class work and job prospects, and finding joy in hard to find places. And then one day he packed his bags.

It was late in the day. 7, maybe 8pm. I sat on the couch in the front room eating potato chips and watching TV. Man walked towards the door, a duffel bag on his shoulder and keys in his hand. Said he was leaving. And just like that...he was gone.

I saw a family move in across the hall. A middle aged woman and her teenage children. I didn't see a Daddy but that doesn't mean they didn't have one. I sat by my window and watched the woman go back and forth to the U-Haul truck and pull out boxes, chairs, pieces of furniture. I didn't offer to help. I just watched and talked to the babies like they were my friends.

"We're getting new neighbors," I told them. "They look nice. I'm sure they're nice. Though not as nice as a man would have been. Daddy's gone now, so we'll have to get you a new Daddy."

When Man left, I had $34.56 in my savings account. He closed our joint account and took out all the funds. The rent was a week past due, and my gas tank was on E. If I didn't find a new source of money, in a week I would starve to death.

The first stop was The Office of Social Services. I found the address in the phone book and left early Monday morning with the babies and their diaper bag in tow. It was a big building, with 4 or 5 floors, and a lot of different offices and signs with arrows directing people where to go. To the left for Food Stamps, to the right for General Assistance, Medicaid, Childcare. Third floor for new applicants. Drug Testing on the second floor.

I went to the third floor and took a general assistance application and a number from the front desk. I was number 92 and it was 8 o'clock in the morning. I took a seat by the window and began filling out the application while the babies slept in their stroller. The room was crowded. Crying babies, frisky toddlers, lots and lots of mothers. It reminded me of a monologue I heard once in acting school in my early teens. It started, "Ain't no daddies where I come from...just mad mothers." Inner city Philadelphia will do that to you.

In this place that smelled like spilled milk and broken lives, I was the statistic. The form I filled out read:

Marital Status:

Married _ Single_ Widowed _
*Divorced_ Separated_ Deserted_*

I wavered there among Single, Separated, and deserted. But I was never married because I refused Man's offer so I suppose separated would not apply, and Man did desert me with no money and two babies but his argument would be that I drove him away. Single made me out to be the bad guy when in fact I was the victim. I wasn't born pregnant. I didn't choose to do this alone. I didn't choose to have the babies in the first place. It was a lot placed upon me and I had little say in the matter. I was by myself because that's where Man and life left me, not because I was the Virgin Mary and woke up one day with child. I wrote in "I don't understand the question."

Employment and Other Cash Resources ____________________

Salary ____

Commisions ____________________________________

Cash on Hand ______________________________

*Savings*____________________________________

Annuities __________________________________

Worker's Compensation _______________________

Alimony/Child Support _______________________

Government Bonds ____________________________

Unemployment Benefits _______________________

Friends and Relatives ________________________

Other income _________________________________

I left everything blank and continued the form. It was 2 hours and 4 minutes before my number was called. My eight month olds were awake now ready to play. I followed the grey haired woman to a tiny office in the back. It was like I was next in the chow line at a prison cafeteria or a soup kitchen. Everyone gets the same treatment and no one even looks up to see what you look like. The woman motioned for me to have a seat and I handed over my paperwork. She was a fast typer, putting my information into the computer.

"You left all of your income sources blank. Would you like to apply for emergency food stamps?"

"Yes please," I said. "That would be helpful. I barely have enough money to get through the day."

"It takes 30 days to approve your application for cash assistance, but we can give you food stamps right away. That will allow you to eat. Everything else has to go through a background check. Drug testing is required before the state will give you any cash."

"30 days huh?"

"I see the children are under a year old. You'll be exempt from the mandatory job search program, WorkFirst, until they reach a year. But cash assistance isn't much. The most you'll get is $540."

"A week?"

"A month."

"My rent is $1200."

"Unless you get a job, you'll have to move. The city has some section 8 housing programs but the wait list is long. Do you have any family you can stay with?"

"I'm in school. I just have a couple of months left, and I don't have any family nearby. Even if I did, the shame I'll feel moving in with my parents with two babies may be enough to kill me. I'd almost rather be dead."

"The waitlist for housing does not take pride into account. That's a non factor."

"They probably never knew my mother."

The woman stopped typing and looked up at me for the first time since we sat down. "There is some childcare help available. That application process takes at least 45 days and you'll need to show proof of employment."

"Right now I don't have a job."

"You'll need to get one before they will even consider your application for childcare assistance."

"How am I supposed to go job searching with two babies on my hip? And even if I am able to secure a job, what do I do with my kids in the 45 days I'm waiting to get financial help? Childcare around here is $300 a week. Per kid. I can't even put gas in my car. Where am I gonna get that kind of money?"

"Have you applied for child support?"

"I thought I could do that today."

"You have to do that at the courthouse, about 5 miles up the road. Once you two go to court and a judge orders support, you can come back here for modifications. But you can't get cash assistance and child support. It's either or."

"Let me guess. In order for a judge to order contributions to daycare, my babies have to already be in daycare? Only I can't afford daycare until I get support."

"No one ever said life was fair."

Kiefer and Kye were my prized possessions and if I could, I would set them in glass in a high up place in my apartment. They were that accomplishment for me that said *fuck you* to all the times I needed love as a child and walked away without it. In my twins, I finally had someone to love, and someone to love me...times two.

When I was in fifth grade, my mom put a bad perm in my hair and I had to go to school with hair so short, I looked like a boy in a dress. The kids teased me, and even when my hair grew back, the teasing didn't stop. My mother was too busy to notice the tear stains on my face when I returned from school and my Daddy had an accent so thick the kids at school would barely understand what he was saying, much less heed his words to stop their bullying. So, I found solace in my pillow, my face buried deep in its crevices in the minutes and hours before I fell asleep each night. I could wring it out, it was so wet with my tears. My pillowcase. I could wring it out and season food, it was so salty.

I was watching a movie one day back then when I heard a child therapist say that children who experience emotional trauma often create a world inside a world. A fantasy life of some sort where everything is just as they wish it to be. It gives them an escape, a way to feel the pain less. I dreamt of life when I grew up. A world away from my current situation, and those mean kids at school. I dreamt of a fairytale wedding and a baby, my very own, that no one could take from me. My own children would love me unconditionally simply because I was their mommy.

Chapter Nineteen

There are all these moments when you think you won't survive. And then you survive.

Late September, 2008. A week after Luke and I redecorated my bedroom with our own nudity, my angelic voice, and the scent of sex, I saw him with the girl. Just one week after The Memorial Project Gala, and the infamous night Luke spent inside of me, I saw him at the coffee shop on the third floor in Macy's Department Store.

I recounted the latest happening to Dr. Hannah, this time over peppermint tea.

Sunday and I were in the city with the children shopping for a gift for Mommy's birthday. A new blouse maybe, or a picture frame. I pushed my double stroller cradling my two year olds past the coffee counter, Sunday in front of me going on about the latest fall colors.

"I'm fashion forward," she said glancing back. "Mommy is not but that's exactly why she needs our help. A warm orange sweater or jungle green blouse would look good on her skin tone. I'm sure we can find something before the day is done."

I adjusted my purse on my shoulder and saw that Kiefer

dropped his sippee cup to the floor. It rolled to the right and I chased it before it rolled out of my reach. "Wait up, Sunday," I called to her. But she didn't seem to hear me or to care. Sip cup in hand, I stood up and found myself facing a small round table in the back. Luke was sitting there deep in conversation with a woman whose curly brown hair was all I could see from my view. I gazed for a moment, and then turned before he would see me. I hurried off to grab the stroller and catch up to Sunday.

She was busy sifting through a rack of tops in the women's section. "I just don't know what the best size for her is these days. What do you think?"

I was numb, not because I had seen Luke with another woman, but because I had seen him with another woman just one week after that beautiful night he and I spent at the gala and today he looked really...happy. I was numb because I didn't have rights to confront him about it or get upset. He was a once-in-a-while-when-its-convenient kind of man. Not an everyday-shoulder-to-lean-on kind of man. And I was the stupid one for believing things had changed or would ever change.

"She's small but she's not that small," said Sunday.

What hurt so much was the fact that he gave me goosebumps when we were together. He made me feel like the world was coming together and we would be the center of it when the time was right. *Just be patient Kericho. Things will pick up speed. He'll let me in to his heart and his soul and in time he will commit. Just a few more months. Just one, two, three more months.*

“The medium might be too big around the shoulders. This blouse is supposed to be snug,” she continued.

I had to face facts. Luke was never and may never be my man. He may never be the father I want for Kiefer and Kye, or the husband I need to make me feel like my world is complete. In Luke, I had a wound that never healed since every time he came around he opened the sore and it bled all over again when he broke my heart.

"Let's get out of here," I said to Sunday. "Mommy wouldn't like anything in here."

The next night, we all gathered at Mommy and Daddy's house for a birthday soiree for Mommy. Her 50th. Sunday and I settled on a green Donna Karan blouse for my mother and had it gift wrapped. When we found out Daddy hadn't gotten around to buying a gift, we just added his name to the card.

"Bathday gifts. We neva geeve bathday gifts in my country." My Daddy and I were in the kitchen finishing dinner, waiting for Grace to finish napping before it was time to eat.

"So...you're saying you didn't get her a gift, again?"

"Maybe you can go and get something quickly. A parfume or something nice."

"Daddy it's much too late for that. Mommy's birthday comes on the same day every year and every year you manage to forget it. I reminded you. We reminded you to get a present."

"I did not forget. I went shopping and bought all of this food. We will eat. Why is that not enough?"

Grace never liked restaurants. "It's always so crowded and you have to wait for a table. I'd rather be home in my houseshoes," she would say. So...we cooked. We made stewed chicken with curry spices, dirty rice, fried bananas, collard greens, and ugali, a staple food of Kenya made by boiling cornmeal in water and adding a little salt for flavor. When Sunday and I were babies, Daddy used to break pieces of ugali off, roll it in his hands and make a little boat for gravy. "Nummy," I would say.

"In my country, we celebrate with food. Food and dancing and singing and laughing. Who cares about presents when we have each other. Family is the important thing."

I checked the chicken and then sat on a bar stool at the counter. "Hmmm. That makes sense. You're right. But this is America. I guess in Kenya, a good African meal would be enough. But when in Rome…"

"Ya motha loves my cooking." Daddy sprinkled the bananas

with cinnamon and brown sugar and turned them around in the skillet. The sweetness wafted up and filled my nose.

"So how did that happen? Tell me."

"When I met her, I showed her how to make chapati, and ugali and she learned quickly because its easy."

"Did she like it?"

"What is not to like?" He raised his hands.

I laughed. "So you cooked together a lot? Did you ever go out to eat?"

"We went out to eat all the time. Nice restaurants. Expensive. But then we married, and you guys came and the chance to eat out came less and less."

"Sometimes I wonder if Mommy really hates eating out, or if she just thinks she hates it because she never does it. I think if you surprised her with dinner reservations somewhere really nice, she would feel special. Like the most beautiful girl in the world."

Daddy leaned on the counter next to where I sat and folded his arms across his chest. "We have this beautiful house. We have beautiful children. The bills get paid. We eat everyday. That should make her feel special."

I paused a moment. "Try thinking like a woman sometimes. It's not about the obvious needs being met. It's about the way a man makes you feel."

"Feelings wither. Feelings change with the weather. Feelings don't pay the bills and keep a roof over your head. What do feelings really matta?"

"Do you love mommy?"

"Of course I do."

"You love her because you love her or you love her because a husband is supposed to love his wife?"

Silence.

"You want to know why I let Man walk away, Daddy? I let him leave and I didn't fight it because I never felt like he loved me. I never felt like he cared to find what makes me unique and cater to that. Man did what he was supposed to do and for that I respect him. He tried to keep the bills paid. He really did. He tried to be the man of the house and do all the things that men do, but it wasn't good enough for me. I could never see myself growing old with him."

"Kericho, you are just a child. You don't know whut you wunt."

"I do know what I want. It might change but I know what I want right now. I know what I don't want. I don't want to end up in a marriage where my husband stops caring about making me feel special. I watch you and Mommy. I watch the way you interact, like you got old secrets bottled up. You kiss each other every once in a while, but it's always just a peck. I never see you two get loose with each other. I never see you become your natural selves. Sometimes, it seems like she hates you. Sometimes she blows up over a dirty dish or socks left on the couch."

"That's just a part of being married."

"I think there is more. I think she carries this hurt from the past that she never got over. She looks at you with such scorn sometimes. She looks at you like she wishes she never got married."

"In life you have disagreements. Your mudda has hurt me too but I still take care of her. I take care of the marriage. I could have left after she killed our children. Two boys I could have had, and she took that away from me."

I always knew the abortions my mother had cut my father deep. I always knew because he brought it up whenever he could but she never did. She kept that part of her life a mystery from Sunday and me until Sunday got pregnant her senior year of high school and my mother told her an abortion is completely moral and the only way her life would remain unruined. Sunday came to me in my room that evening crying tears as big as snowballs.

"Mommy said I should get rid of it. She said she had two abortions and God gave her peace about it. God said it was alright."

I don't know if God spoke to Grace that day she decided to kill her unborn children. Maybe that was Grace talking to herself, something she did often because I would see her lips moving but nothing coming out. She'd replay an encounter or confrontation in her head of something that happened at work or should have happened, but didn't. I would watch her when I sat in the passenger seat of her white Cadillac sedan, her lips going a mile a minute, when she thought I wasn't paying attention. I was too scared to ask her who she was talking to. Most of the time I didn't care.

I was about to tell Daddy how people sometimes make mistakes. They sometimes do things they wish they hadn't but can't turn back the hands of time. Sometimes they do things and have regrets. And sometimes, they just do things. I was getting ready to tell Daddy that I know that must have hurt bad, but there is no sense dwelling on the past and maybe the best thing to do would be to talk about it. Maybe. But Mommy strolled into the kitchen, Sunday behind her and my little boy holding on to her pants leg.

"So what ya'll got cooking for me?"

Grace was in a good mood today.

We ate well. We didn't sit around the table like we used to way back in the day. Mommy and Daddy set up TV tables at the couch, Sunday and I kept our plates on our laps and we put the children at the kids table. We didn't talk about much of anything, our mouths stuffed with chicken and gravy, ugali, and all the other fixings. My mind wandered back and forth between what woman Luke might be inside of and whether or not I had enough money in my bank account to pay my rent next month AND buy train fare to get to and from work.

"So...looks like I went and got myself into another relationship," Sunday blurted when her plate was clean. She wiped her mouth neatly with her napkin and smiled wide.

"What? You didn't tell me." I was not amused.

"That's because I wanted to be certain this was real before I said anything. Ever since Nigel and I went out a few weeks ago, things have taken a turn." She got up and took her plate to the sink. "Ya know, we had a long talk the next night. He called and I told him I couldn't keep doing this. I couldn't keep dragging this thing out. I wanted something meaningful. Last night he told me he's considering moving to New York and he wants to make this an exclusive relationship." She poured herself a glass of wine and reclaimed her seat on the couch.

I looked at my mother, who was quietly chewing like a lady. Then at my father, who looked more confused than anything else. "Who is this Nigel?" he said.

"Daddy, Nigel is a long time crush of Sunday's. He's no good, Daddy. A wolf in sheep's clothes. Tell her no."

"A what?" The wine must be affecting Sunday's hearing.

"You heard me, Sunday. Nigel is a player, out for one thing. He probably only told you that so he can keep on f--" I stopped myself short because Mommy and Daddy and the children were here.

"Keep on what, Kericho? This is exactly why I didn't say anything to you. I knew you would have no faith in my relationship."

"Sunday, you're being stupid. I know you think you love him, but any man that takes five years to notice when he has a beautiful woman's attention is not worth your time."

"You don't believe people can change? Five years ago, he wasn't ready. And to be honest, neither was I. I was in a dead end marriage still trying to figure out who I was."

"You got it all figured out now?" She cut her eyes at me. "Mommy what do you have to say about this?"

My mother smiled. It was a smile that said I don't get involved in business that's not mine. She always was the type to think things she would almost never say except when all her harsh feelings added up and got to be too much to keep inside. Then Grace would blurt everything out all at once at the least convenient time and we would all just stare in shock. *So that's how she really feels?*

"Sunday, no," Daddy interjected. "What do you really know about this guy?"

"I know my feelings are strong. And right now, I want to see where this goes." Sunday sat back and sipped her wine. I got up, my plate still half full, walked to the trash can and started to dump its contents inside.

"Why are you throwing it?" Daddy yelled. I stopped and sat my plate on the counter.

"I'm just not very hungry I guess," I said turning to leave the room to find a hidden place to cry in.

"Kericho don't go. Sit." Sunday motioned to the empty seat next to her on the couch. I turned and slowly walked back to fill it. "Is this about me and Nigel or is this about something else?" "This is about you always going overboard. The pills when you were 16. Your pregnancy a year later. Your marriage. Guam. Now this. You're always leaving me." She squinted and put her glass down.

"Kericho. I'm not leaving you. I'm just you know, I'm looking for love just like the next girl."

"And when you find it where does that leave me?"

"Same place you are right now. In the center of my heart."

I sucked my teeth and looked down. I wanted to go. Bad. I wanted to get the hell out of there because I knew what I was really mad about was Luke and his lame excuse for a heart.

The phone rang and instead of us all jumping up to grab it, none of us did. It rolled over to the answering machine and then I heard my Auntie on the line. "Grace, it's Deena. Just calling to let you know that Daddy died. In his sleep a few hours ago. Charmaine found him. Call me back."

Mommy's eyes closed on the word "died" like she was taking

it all in. I gasped a little and then we were all silent.

"He was old. And weak. So it was expected," Grace finally said.

"But on your birthday? That's a lot to take in," said Sunday.

"Are you going to call her back?" Daddy came in.

"I will, Lemuel. I will."

"Who is Charmaine?"

"The day nurse we hired."

"What's going to happen to Grandmommy?" I said.

"I guess we have to figure that out now."

Luther was born the son of a sharecropper back in Arkansas in 1920.

"He watched the Candy boys take their turn with his mama. They'd come by sometimes after breakfast, sometimes when the sun was high in the sky, and sometimes in the dead of night. Well it didn't really much matter the time of day. They'd come by just about whenever they felt like it drunk on moonshine and call for her." This from my Great Aunt Sweetness.

She told me the story when we'd went to visit in '96. Grace, Sunday, Daddy, and I piled in the minivan we called Ola and drove up north to the motor city of Detroit. The morning after we got there, my period started when I was on the toilet in the only bathroom Granny and Grandpa had, and Great Aunt Sweetness was waiting outside the door telling me I better hurry up because she was an old lady with a bad bladder.

"Sweetness, I need a minute." With that, she pranced right in and saw the blood drops resting on the toilet seat.

"Oh we got to clean that up good, baby. Lemme git chu a napkin. I didn't know you was a woman already." She closed the door behind her and reached into the cabinet and pulled out a dusty box of sanitary napkins. "Yo Granny keeps these around for when the children come to visit. You know how, baby?"

"I think I can figure it out."

"Your grandpa was the first to show me. I was a gal, just nine years old when I got mine."

Sweetness didn't mind me. She wiped the toilet seat down, pulled her drawers over her knees and had a seat, her fat bottom spilling over the edges. I pressed the pad into my panties just like I had seen Sunday do and pulled my panties up under my nightgown. "Grandpa Luther showed you how to wear a pad? Your brother?"

"Who else was gon do it? Our mama wasn't no good after those Candy boys took her spirit. It wasn't long after that my own daddy took her life."

"Sweetness why did your daddy kill your mama?"

"That's what I'm telling you baby. She was already gone. Luther saw it more than I did. I was nothing but a little girl. I stayed in the house and cleaned the floors and made the lunches. Luther watched them Candy boys call for Mama whenever they wanted someone to jizz all up in. And Mama was a pretty thing. That mama of yours looks just like her. Bright skin and a curtain of hair that fell down her back and could wrap around her breasts." Sweetness was done her peeing but she still sat there reminiscing. I sat Indian style in the corner, my chin propped on my hand.

"Is that why the white boys raped her?"

"Maybe. I spose so. But Daddy couldn't do nothing. Back then in Arkansas, you don't stand up to no white boy and keep on livin'. So they would call for her and she would go and when she come back, those Candy boys had their palm prints all over her dress, all over her ass, and the smell of their jizz was all over her kiwi. Luther seen her come in one day with a slight smile on her face, and asked her 'Mama why you smiling?' Daddy looked at her and asked her the same thing. She said it wasn't no smile but Daddy beat it off her anyway." Sweetness rolled some toilet tissue up and dragged it between her legs before she pulled her drawers back over her bottom and returned to her seat on the toilet.

"That was the way it started to go." She continued. "Mama would fuck those Candy boys and then Daddy would beat her. Her mind went before I was seven years old. She'd sit in the corner, humming a tune for hours. I would call to her and it was like I wasn't even in the room. Well Daddy got tired of it one night. Tired of her humming, tired of the smell of the Candy boys' jizz, tired of the other cats callin' him a pussy for letting those boys fuck his woman in the first place. He told her to quit her humming. Luther said the same.

'Quit your hummin Mama, we tired of it.' he said. But she didn't. So Daddy stomped across those floorboards and wrapped his hands tight around her throat. He squeezed the life outta her and she didn't even put up a fight. Her eyes just got real big and then she and her hummin were no more."

I was lying in bed at Mommy and Daddy's house tonight, full on Birthday dinner thinking about how my mother must feel now. I felt like a kid again in my twin sized bed that I grew up sleeping in, the covers pulled up to my chin. Grandpa Luther was hard on his children. Almost beat one of his teenaged daughters to death years back when she disagreed with him on something Jimmy Carter said.

The oldest of my aunts, Auntie Mildred, left home early, eloped and had two babies before she was 20. Since then she's been divorced and married twice more, with a host of other children. Some of them without daddies. Auntie Robin married a Muslim, converted to Islam, and moved to Chicago. My mother was followed by the twins, my aunties, Kendall, and Kiss. They were living separate lives, one in Hawaii, with a husband and teenaged son, and the other a tomboy, an army officer or something like that. Never married, no kids. Last I heard, she was in Germany. She sent us a picture of her in uniform.

Then there was my Uncle Jamie. I often imagine what our talks would have been like. Auntie Deena was just a year younger than Jamie, and they were the closest. I know she felt the pain of his death the most and here she was, the one to bring us the news of yet another death. Overall, the girls have done well for themselves, but their hearts were never reconciled. Their grievances with their father never settled. I know because Auntie Mildred still referred to Grandpa as the devil and I always noticed the elephant in the room during those vacations we spent at Home.

"But Grandaddy was always nice to me for as long as I can remember," I said to my mother one day over lunch a few years ago.

"You grandkids get to see the good side of him. And that's great. But growing up, we weren't so lucky. He doesn't have the task of raising you, and maybe that's what makes it different for him."

"Do you think he loved his children?"

"I don't think he knew how to."

Even after Mildred left home, he never apologized. After Jamie died, he never said "I'm sorry." Never a word to show remorse. And today, he reached the end of his life. Well, it's much too late to mend wounds over tea now.

I shifted in my bed when I heard my cell phone vibrate. I looked at the display. Luke. What could he want with me? I let it go to voicemail.

With Luke I must be living a fantasy. Forever wanting what I can't have. Maybe it's time to let it go. To let him go and find my heart another home because if Luke doesn't even show any interest in my children, then he may never really want to be a part of my life. A real part...the part I want him most involved in. There are other men. Sunday told me men are like New York City trains, there's always another one coming, so there was no need in me stepping over people, and hurting myself to hold doors for one that was too damned crowded anyway. Luke was only 20 percent of what I wanted in a man. Hell, probably less than that, but boy was that small percentage tempting. We had a history. We had all these years, but perhaps "all these years" isn't enough...anymore. Two high beeps on my cell phone. Luke left a voicemail this time. The devil really knows how to tempt me. Waiting until morning to listen will take will power.

Sunday was a trip. She's "in a relationship." Whatever the hell that means. I hope that Nigel fella doesn't hurt her like her ex-husband did. Actually I hope he does, so she can realize men shouldn't come between us and in the end that's all he's really going to do. Maybe I'll talk some sense into her tomorrow.

I hear yelling downstairs. Could Kiefer or Kye be awake? No, that sounded like Grace. Mommy and Daddy's room is below mine. I thought they had been sleeping. I hear her again. Something about a woman.

"You should have told me you were married," she said. She was angry. I could hear the disdain in her voice. I couldn't hear Daddy's response. "No Lemuel. They liked you because they didn't know you. They didn't know all those deep dark secrets. The ones I was privy too. They didn't know that, did they?"

I climbed out of bed and tip toed to Sunday's room. I couldn't sleep anyway. I cracked the door. She didn't budge, fast asleep in bed. After I closed it quietly, I crept to the top of the staircase and saw my parent's light on under their bedroom door downstairs.

"I was a good husband. Your father knew that." I could hear Daddy now, but he was softer than Grace.

"My father wouldn't recognize good if it was standing right in front of him. And you were not good, unless by good you mean very, very bad."

Silence. Grace could cut deep when she wanted to.

"I put up with your mess for a long time. Well no more Lemuel. No more! I have to make me happy."

I sat down on the top step and pulled my t-shirt over my knees. I've heard this line before. When I was eleven or twelve,

Grace had threatened to leave Daddy. She took me and Sunday aside and told us she was going to save some money, find a place for us and we were getting out of there. When Daddy was pleasant, more often than not, I loved him. But when he was angry, I hated him, and that day I hated him. When I think of it now, I can't much remember why, but I wanted a change. I wanted to be a kid who had parents that loved each other and showed it. So I waited with anticipation for the day that Grace would tell us it was time to go. That day never came, and here I was a decade later hearing the same old song.

"I have to make me happy," she said again. For a moment I thought I heard her voice crack as if on the verge of tears. But I know better.

Chapter Twenty

If the road is easy, you're likely going the wrong way.

When I wake up, I see the red light flashing on my cell phone indicating that I have a voicemail. I sit up and glance at the clock. 11:43. It is Sunday morning and too late to get ready for church. Guess I have to miss it. Grandaddy's funeral was yesterday in Romulus, Michigan. I missed that too.

"Mommy, send the family my blessings. With work and Kiefer and Kye, I just can't make the time to fly out there. You understand right?" I had said to Grace three days ago. She understood. I call my voicemail and put in my password. Four messages. The first was from my Auntie Robin.

"Your mother told me you couldn't get away. I really wish you could have. It's not often we get the family together. It would have been nice to see you even considering the circumstances. Calling to say hello."

The second was from Sunday.

"Hey Babygirl. I'm flying back today. Mommy and Daddy are staying a

little longer to wrap things up. Lots to tell you. Call you when I touch down. It'll be late. Wait up."

The third was from my therapist, Dr. Hannah.

"Kericho, you missed your appointment last week. I want to make sure we are still on for Monday. Let's talk." I turn my nose up at that. The fourth message was from Man offering his condolences. *How did he know?*

I take a hot shower and get dressed. Kiefer and Kye are coming home today after the weekend with Man. I need to grocery shop for the week. At the store, I buy chicken nuggets, frozen mac & cheese, spaghetti noodles, sauce, mozzarella cheese, meatballs, some fresh spinach, lots of juice, milk, and baked beans. For me I got one porter house steak and for a moment it reminded me of Leonard the butcher. That seemed so long ago now.

At checkout, I saw Luke. He was walking towards my line in a tight red tee that showed off his body and some baggy jeans. He saw me too and came over to say hello. A kiss on the cheek.

"Kericho, nice surprise running into you."

I kept my composure. "Likewise. What are you doing here?"

"Getting some snacks for the guys. Football Sunday, you know. I'm having a get together at my place to watch the game."

I smiled.

"So listen, umm, I haven't heard from you," he said.

"You haven't called. How could you hear from me if you didn't bother to call?"

"Wait a minute. Number one, I did call. And number two, what your fingers all broken or something?"

"My grandfather died. His funeral was yesterday so I've had a lot on my mind."

"I'm sorry to hear. I didn't know."

"How could you?"

"Kericho, is everything okay? Did I do something?"

"No Luke. You never do anything."

"Is that supposed to mean something to me?"

"It can mean whatever you want it to mean?"

"Stop talking in circles."

It was my turn to load the groceries on the belt. "I'm sorry Luke. I guess I just don't know what you want me to say to you."

"For starters, you could be a little more enthusiastic about seeing me. It's always nice to run into you."

Run into me? Run into me!? Why does he have to run into me? Why can't he call me like a normal person and make plans for a date?

"Just a couple of weeks ago, I thought we had a really good time." He leans in closer and says in my ear, "I get hard just thinking about it."

"Luke, stop. Not here."

"What? I can't tell you how you make me feel?" I pick up the bundle of spinach and throw it on the belt. Then the cans of beans, then the steak. I turn to Luke.

"No you can't. I just have a lot of things on my mind and sex is not one of them."

"So talk to me." He crosses his arms.

"I can't. I can never talk to you, Luke. Not like how I want to."

"And why is that?"

I look at him blankly. *I saw you with the girl. And it cut me because even though we've never been an exclusive couple, I've always deep down wondered why. I've always wanted you to be mine and I'm selfish Luke. I'm selfish and jealous, and I can't keep letting you screw me whenever you want because when its all said and done, I always feel more lonely than I did before.* I thought these things but didn't dare let the words slip through my lips because Luke would never understand and I would end up embarrassed for having said them in the first place. Instead I said, "I really don't think this is the time or place to talk."

"Okay. So...come over tonight. After the game."

"I can't. The kids will be home. And plus it will be late, and you know what happens when I come over and its late."

"Call me sometime. We'll talk."

"Do you have a club card miss?" The checkout clerk was yelling to me as I watched Luke walk away. I turn, a little startled. "Yes...I...I do."

Sunday calls like she said she would. It was 11:30 at night and I had just slipped into my pink negligee, and put on my Best of Sade cd. I like to feel sexy even when I'm all alone. *Your Love is King* was playing when I hear the ring. I climb in bed with the phone.

"So...how was the funeral?"

"It was good...in a funeral sense," she said. "Deena cried, first because of Grandaddy, and then because they spelled her last name wrong on the program. She went and married that French guy and they spelled Phillippe like Philip and she was pretty upset."

I laugh. "That's not funny. It may seem petty, but that was her father, and she only has one, and he only dies once."

"They're reprinting programs. But more importantly, I got a chance to see our cousins Teddy and Carl after all this time, and Babygirl, when I say fine, I mean FINE!"

"They were looking good like that?"

"Both of them. Fine like I wish they weren't my blood cousins fine. All grown up, sexy, muscles, goatees, everything was beautiful. Auntie Mildred must have raised them on meat and potatoes. And single girl. They are single. "

"You talkin' like they're possibilities for us. That's incest woman. Our first cousins?!"

"Nothing wrong with dreaming."

"I hope you took pictures."

"I took a few."

"How's Mommy holding up?"

"You know Grace. Never show your emotion. Never let them really know how you feel. That's her motto right? I think she's ok. What's sad is that granddaddy caused a lot of hurt for everyone who knew him and he died before anything was resolved. All those tears never got a chance to dry. Maybe now they will."

"Maybe now he can reconcile things with Jamie in heaven."

"Babygirl, that ship has sailed. Plus, according to Mildred, and Robin, and Deena, and almost everybody else, Grandaddy didn't make it to heaven."

"You think he's in hell?"

"I'm not God and I don't have a heaven or a hell to put anybody in, but that's what they say."

"That's gotta hurt like hell. I don't care what anyone says. Even if he did beat and abuse his children physically and emotionally, that was still their Daddy. There has to be some feeling there knowing they will never see him again. I wonder if anyone has any regrets."

"Doesn't everyone always have regrets? It's a part of life."

"I think so. But sometimes the world thinks they have it all together. No one wants to apologize for anything. No one wants to believe they could've done anything differently. Mommy's come undone and she doesn't even realize it." Now *No Ordinary Love* was playing.

"You know I had a talk with her in Michigan. I told her if ever there was a time to tell her family how much they mean to her, it's now."

"And?"

"And, she didn't hear me. I mean she was listening but she didn't hear me. She said her sisters know what they mean to each other, they don't have to say it. I said 'mom, I wanna hear you say it. I wanna hear you say I love you. I wanna see a tear. I wanna see emotion. Some sign of life.'"

"I'm 24 years old and I've never seen that woman cry."

"It's amazing she doesn't get frostbite, she's so cold. You know what she said to me when I asked her why she can't say it? You know what she said?"

"What she say?"

"She said 'I wasn't raised that way.' The woman said she didn't grow up like that!"

"Typical. 1950's traditional households."

"Typical maybe, but that doesn't mean it's right. Her children are hurting. You and I are hurting. Her brother shot himself in the face. Half her family is fucked up. I took pills and ended up in a mental hospital at 16. Sixteen! And she still can't see past her own nose to tell that maybe her parents model for raising children wasn't the best there is out there."

"But you know what I realize though. It ain't even worth it. Trying to change mommy. Trying to get her to come around. In the end, it's only my wounds that get picked at because I keep giving myself hope that she'll change and when she never does, I'm left bruised all over again. It's not worth it."

"Nah. I disagree. It's always worth it for your family. I don't want to give up. We need counseling. I don't want twenty years to pass and one of us dies, or worse, all of us, and no one ever got a chance to say how they really feel. Who's that therapist of yours? Does she help families?"

"Dr. Hannah. I can ask her. She might be willing to see all of us. I have an appointment tomorrow. I'm a little scared though. Pissing Grace off is never fun and I don't want her to think we don't appreciate her. I don't want her to think we're ganging up on her."

"So we'll just say that. We'll say, Mommy, we appreciate you and we're not ganging up on you. Really this therapy wouldn't be to resolve issues just with her. But maybe I need to learn a thing or two about myself. And Daddy, you know him, he's the one always so busy trying to keep the peace. None of us really gave him a chance to talk about how he feels."

"I heard them arguing last week. The night of mommy's birthday. Something about secrets Daddy kept."

"That man has his skeletons. I never said he was perfect. But he's not bitter. I don't think bitterness gets anyone anywhere. He forgives and forgets and maybe he should throw an I'm sorry around here and there. I'm sure Mommy deserves it. But if he never does, she can't walk around carrying all that weight on her shoulders. It can't be good for her back and it damn sure can't be good for her soul."

Kiss of Life was on the tuner now. I closed my eyes and listened to Sade sing. *There must have been an angel by my side. Something heavenly led me to you. Look at the sky. It's the color of love.* Her voice makes me want to exhale. She makes me want to take all the turmoil Luke is to me, all the scars my mother left on me when she wasn't there when I needed her, when she didn't care how she made me feel, all my uncertainty towards Sunday and her newfound love life, my anger towards Man and his definition of love, my disappointments in myself, my fear of being a bad mother...I wanted to take all of that, exhale, and let it go with the wind. *You gave me the kiss of life, kiss of life.*

The singer made me believe if just for a moment, that someone so powerful could really sweep me off my feet, plant a kiss on my lips so enchanted, that he could breathe life back into me. That life I used to have before everything and everyone got in the way.

Chapter Twenty-One

I know that pain is the most important thing in the universe. Greater than survival, greater than love, greater even than the beauty it brings about. For without pain, there can be no pleasure. Without sadness, there can be no happiness. Without misery there can be no beauty. And without these, life is endless, hopeless, doomed and damned. Adult. You have become an adult. ~Harlan Ellison

"Do you have any regrets? Any remorse for what you did?"

"I think so. Some days I do. Other days, not so much."

It was warm for the first day of October. Autumn colors danced on the trees outside Dr. Hannah's office window. Today I was on time for my appointment. I gazed at the sky, a shade between peach and salmon. *Pretty,* I thought to myself.

Dr. Hannah always wanted to talk about the past. She said that understanding the past better would help me make sense of my present. But sometimes I think the past should be left there, to wither and die like an old widow. Remembering always made me shudder a little. But the two years that had passed since Man walked out was not long enough to forget. So I told her my story and it was just as if I was reliving the events of the past.

I was 22 again, coming home to eviction notices on my door every week that the rent wasn't paid since Man left. I had just a few more weeks of school and then I could focus on a job and getting out of there. I tried to buy time on rent until then.

One afternoon I ventured across the hall to meet the new family. I was curious. A woman answered the door, the one I saw carrying all those boxes up the steps. She was in her early forties and breathtakingly beautiful. Neat blonde dreadlocks pulled back into a ponytail, and skin the color of cinnamon sugar.

"Hi," I said cheerfully. "I live across the hall and I was just wondering...if you had a vacuum cleaner I could borrow. I'm doing some cleaning. Or trying to."

"Gosh...I don't. I'm sorry. We're still getting all settled ourselves."

"I understand. Well, I'm Kericho." I extended my hand and she graciously shook it.

"Glynda. Say is that a baby I hear you've got over there?"

"Yes. Two. Twin boys. Eight months."

"Wow. Well we love babies. My son and my daughter just went out for a movie, but they'll be back and you can meet them and believe me, we're happy to babysit for you anytime."

"Really? I'll keep that in mind."

Two days later I was knocking on her door again.

"Glynda, I have a class I take two days a week. Trying to finish school. And well, since me and the kid's father split up, I've been having a hell of a time finding someone to watch them while I go to class and so I was wondering if I could take you up on your offer. I can't pay you right now, because I don't have any money, but we can start a tab, and well--"

"Don't worry about it. I'm happy to. Bring them on over."

"Are you sure you don't mind?"

"Well I just said I was happy to. We're still getting settled here. Just moved up from New Orleans on a grant. I got family around the way. It's good to be close to family in a time like this when you're still figuring your next move."

"A time like this?"

"Katrina. You know the big storm that hit my city last year. It was really terrible. We lost everything. I mean everything. You wanna come in?"

We built a rapport, she and I, her teenage daughter Jordan, and son Atiba. She watched the babies when I went to class, when I job hunted, when I grocery shopped, and sometimes just to let me sleep. Her family was my help in a time of need.

One night, I got back from class late and Glynda was sitting on the floor with Kiefer wrapped in her arms, rocking back and forth. Just the glow of the kitchen light in the distance.

"Makeshift rocking chair?" I said.

She put her finger over her mouth telling me to keep it down. "He just went back to sleep. Seems to work," she whispered.

I joined her on the floor, kicked off my shoes and rested against the wall. "Thank you." She smiled. "For everything," I said.

"Child, you don't have to thank me. I love this." She looked at Kiefer. "I absolutely love this. Miss when mine were this small. Cherish it."

"I know. They grow up fast. Everyone keeps saying that."

"It's because it's true. You'll wake up one day and wonder where the time went. You'll wonder how the years passed without you knowing about it."

I pulled my knees close to my chest, hugged them and rested my head there. "Glynda tell me something? Tell me about Katrina. What was that like?" She looked up deep in thought.

"Katrina....was a lot like being with my ex-husband. I moaned like hell when I came and took the house when I left."

It took a moment for me to understand the joke. Then I chuckled softly. "Good one."

"It wasn't a joke. I'm so serious. You know people were warning us about the storm. Telling us to get our stuff, get our families, and leave before we saw the worst of it."

"No one took it seriously huh?"

She shifted Kiefer in her arms. "Oh it's not that they didn't take the warnings seriously. Moreso, they didn't have anywhere to go. Whole families born and raised in the area. Everything and everyone they had was right there. Not everyone has a rich uncle in California."

"But you could have left. You said you have a sister here in New York."

"Funny the way you never know what you have until you lose, or almost lose it. My sister and I hadn't spoken for a long time. We were close as kids but you know we kind of drifted apart. She's a lot older than me so it's always been more of a mother daughter relationship than anything else. I didn't want to be a burden. I married someone I shouldn't have, and she knew it. Then the divorce took a toll on me but I bounced back. Then there's the kids, and then Katrina comes. Kericho, it was bad. I don't think the media ever really showed anyone how bad it was."

"I was in Africa. I saw the pictures after the fact."

"You can't capture that level of devastation in a photograph. You had to be there. Not that I wish you were. Babies drowned. Children floating underwater, their bodies cold and lifeless. Maintenance workers using forklifts to carry the sick and disabled. Nurses forcing air into the lungs of unconscious folk.

People broke into boat yards, stealing boats to rescue their neighbors clinging to their roofs. Mechanics helped hot-wire any car that could be found to ferry people out of the city. The kids and I left just before the storm hit and checked into a hotel in the French Quarters. We took what we could but we couldn't take everything. We packed up our truck and went."

"Were you scared?"

"We didn't have time to be scared. We did what we had to do. On day 2, we were told that all sorts of resources, including the National Guard and scores of buses, were pouring into the city. But I never saw any of 'em. We decided we had to save ourselves. By day 4 our hotels had run out of fuel and water. Outside water levels began to rise and so did the street crime. The hotels turned us all out and locked their doors, telling us that the "officials" told us to report to the convention center to wait for more buses.

So everyone's frustrated. Everyone's hungry. People can't find their families. Cell phones don't work. We were all a mess, and folks were breaking into stores, robbing people, getting into fights just to survive. It wasn't until Day 5 that Bush landed and we were bused to San Antonio Texas. We had to apply for a FEMA grant and waited four months in Texas with nothing before we even got it."

"And then you came here?"

"I got a hold of my sister and told her we were okay. We had survived. She invited us up and its still been hard, but this grant money is what's keeping our heads above water now."

"Literally."

Now she smiled. "No pun intended."

I looked at Kiefer sleeping in her arms. He looked completely at peace. "You said babies drowned, huh? You think they felt it?"

Pretty soon I got a part time job waiting tables at a local diner. Glynda helped me as much as she could with the babies and when I finally got the call that I could pick up my child care vouchers, the relief felt better than holding in my pee all day and finally making it to a toilet.

At first didn't know where Man had gone off to. We had a court date coming up the next month to establish child support. I am supposed to bring paystubs for the last four weeks and receipts for all the babies' expenses. Man said he was staying with a friend a half hour down the turnpike. He comes to get the children every other Friday and returns them Sunday. When the kids are away I rest, like God on the seventh day.

Sunday I wake up to white light shining through my two-months-behind-on-rent apartment window. I lay there for a moment, and then for some reason, I don't know why, I get up, shower, and put on my purple dress. The belted one that just grazes my knees. I color my lips a soft shade of pink, and pull my hair up into a slick ponytail. Then I grab my bible from the nightstand and get in the car.

I know I am going to church but I don't know which one so I just drive. I drive through the neighborhood into New Jersey and then I get on Interstate 78 headed West. I pull a gospel cd out of my visor, pop it in the CD player, and turn the music up as loud as it can go. After the third song, I exit the freeway at a sign that says Morristown and make a left at the light. I follow the curve of the road, pass three traffic lights and then see a sign that points to Parker Memorial Baptist Church. The building doesn't look like a church. But I see men and women, boys and girls dressed in their Sunday best congregating at the entrance. A middle aged man with a bowtie is directing traffic and motions for me to park in a spot in front.

"Good morning beautiful," he says to me when I get out of the car. I smiled.

"Good morning."

Inside, everyone was filing up a red staircase that led to the sanctuary. I was right on time. I take a seat a few rows from the back. The choir sings a medley of songs. Some of them I have heard before. Others are brand new but I like what I hear. The choir director directs the congregation to hold hands and then she says a prayer of invocation. I close my eyes and pray with her. Sometimes, oftentimes, I listen to prayer. But this time I prayed along. When the woman finished praying, the man to my left squeezed my hand before letting it go. It was like he was comforting me without saying a word.

A man that looks like he could be the pastor steps to the podium and welcomes all the visitors. He asks us to stand and tells a handful of us to make ourselves at home. Then the band plays and the people come to greet me. One by one they shake my hand, give me hugs, kisses, pats on the back. This feels good because for the first time in a long time, the affection feels genuine. They all looked me in the eyes and smiled like I was family. When the greetings quiet down, a man on the piano starts to sing and his voice sounds like warm caramel. Fluid, and sweet. Deep, confident, but humble. It's intimate.

When the battle makes me weary
It seems that I've lost ground
It's so hard to hear your voice Lord,
With distractions all around.
I try to lift my hands
To give you praise.
But then a spirit of heaviness
Tries to shield your face

I listen. I sit there in the pew, childless for now, husbandless for now, motherless for now, and I listen. Somehow between what seemed like just yesterday and today, I lost my way. Grace took Sunday and me to church every Sunday when we were little. We learned about Noah, and Moses, and the prophets, the four gospels, and Jesus. We learned about Jesus and how he saved our souls that Friday on the cross and Grace always told us kids, "when I'm dead and gone, don't forget to pray. About every detail of your life. The big things and the small things. The sad things and the happy things." Well, Gracie, I forgot to pray. You told us all the time. You raised us on a healthy diet and prayer. You dressed us up in our Sunday best, patent leather shoes, and ribbons in our hair. You taught us bible verses and kept Sunday holy. No motown, no secular music, no hip hop on Sundays. You did all that, and I still forgot to pray.

Breathe into me oh Lord
A breath of life
So that my spirit will be whole
And my soul made right

When the preaching started, my face was soggy. I reached into my purse and dried it with a Kleenex. Now all my senses were open.

Days later, I counted my money in the break room at work. I made $40 today in tips, giving me a week's total of $256, half of which I would have to turn over to the daycare, my weekly fee that was left after the vouchers. What remained was barely enough to put gas in the car, buy diapers and soap and everything else food stamps didn't cover. I stopped at the pharmacy on my way home from work. Kye had an earache and his doctor prescribed liquid drops. I picked up some household items I needed. Deodorant, toilet tissue, a pack of diapers, lotion. “$42.80.” I could have hit her, the clerk said it so smug.

When I got home, the electricity was out. The company kindly left a note on my door telling me my bill was overdue as if I was not aware and $300 was needed before my service could be reinstated. *What if I don't have $300? "No one said life is easy"*, was their reply in my head.

I carried my sleeping babies inside and laid them in their cribs. Good thing I had a gas stove and the summer months meant longer days. When the house did get dark, I lit two candles and set them by my bedside. No better time than now to read. I kept my brown leather Bible tucked under my pillow. Tonight I opened it to Job.

I laid in bed the next morning with my hands clasped across my chest. Sunlight peeked into my bedroom window in between the blinds and I inhaled long and hard. The babies were not yet awake so I lay there appreciating the few quiet moments I would not have again for a while. No electricity meant no music, no cartoons for Kiefer and Kye, no hum of the microwave. Just me, them, and God.

It is a wonder the turn my life has taken in the time that has transpired between dancing in the sand with Beauty on the shores of Ghana...and now. I am a mother that cannot provide for her children. Man was irate. He'd say tell me what you need and I will get it for you because giving me money was out of the question, his question, only the electric company only accepted money, and how could I anticipate my baby's earache?

I wanted to cry, but the tears did not come. This time. Maybe my tear ducts were dry. Or maybe I had become desensitized to what would be pain to someone who could still feel. I was not sad. I was angry.

When I picked up my cell phone and dialed Grace, my fingers felt light on the keypad, like air. Yes my fingers felt as if they were not even attached to my own body, but like they worked on their own, a separate entity.

It rang four times before she answered, still only half awake.

"Mommy, I need some money."

"I don't have much to give you Kericho."

"Anything would help. My lights got cut off. My rent is a few months past due and I keep saying I'll have it soon but soon comes and I still don't have enough because I don't make enough."

"It's not my job to babysit you. You made your bed, Kericho. Now you have to lay in it. I'll send what I can."

Three days later, my car stopped running. The check engine light had been on for weeks, but I ignored it because it was better than reminding myself that I had another problem I could not fix. I was a half a mile from home with the babies in the backseat when it stalled. So I popped the trunk, pulled the stroller out, and I walked the rest of the way. A cigarette would be nice right now, and I don't even smoke.

At home, I pray to a God I am not certain can hear me but want to believe He can. I feed the babies by candlelight and hum a song I must have made up.

Glynda walked through my mind that night. I thought of her and Hurricane Katrina. How she lost everything. She and I really weren't that different. The evil that caused her pain was an act of God, a hurricane. Mine was my own stupid decisions, and a God that allowed me to make them.

On my last day of class, I didn't celebrate. There would be no graduation walk for me. No cap and gown. No photos. No commencement speech. I had more important matters on my plate. I finished my final, put my pencil down, and exhaled before I rushed out to catch the bus to pick up Kiefer and Kye. Days were less convenient having to fit my already busy life into a bus schedule. Today I had on jeans and a faded yellow t-shirt that fit me nicely. My nipples poked through the thin fabric. The bus was already crowded and the line to get on was long. Kiefer and Kye had to be picked up from daycare by 5pm and if I was late, even five minutes, I was charged ten dollars. That was ten dollars more than I had in my bank account or in my wallet. I filed in the line and inched closer to the folding door. I was halted just before I stepped onto the bus.

"That's all. Miss, you'll have to wait for the next one. I'm at my limit," the driver said.

"Oh please. Just one more won't hurt. I'm in a rush."

"There is another bus behind me. You won't wait ten minutes."

"I don't have ten minutes. I can squeeze in and stand."

He motioned for me to step up. "That'll be a dollar twenty."

I scrounged through my wallet and came up with 2 quarters, three dimes, a nickel, and four pennies.

"I'm a little low on cash, but I take this bus often. I can pay you the difference the next time."

"No handouts miss. It's a dollar twenty."

"I found another nickel," I said feeling around in my bag. "That makes eighty-five...ninety...ninety four cents. I'm really not short much. Please."

"Please step off the bus."

"I have to get my children from daycare. There is no one else to get them," I said calmly.

"Miss. You're holding up the bus."

"Just wait." Now my voice cracked. "You wait. I'm short twenty six cents. I have no one to get my children. Who is supposed to get my babies?"

"Please step off."

My eyes stung with water and my heart felt like pounding in my chest. "Sir?"

"I have twenty six cents for you," a woman said sitting to my left. I looked, still standing motionless on that first step, my jaw tight. "Here you go," she said reaching. "Twenty-six cents is what you need right? For God's sake, take it so we can get going."

I reached and let the cold coins fall into my hand. "Thank you. Thank you very much."

It came in the mail the next day addressed to Man almost like it was heaven sent. A credit card application from Discover. Now more than ever, It Pays to Discover. Those were the words written across the top of the invitation letter. I only needed enough to get the lights turned back on, bus fare for a month or so, until I could come up with enough money to get my car out of the impound and fixed. Now that I'm finished with school, I can do some real job searching and make some real money and live like a normal person.

I wrote his name on the line where it said Name and his social security number under SS# because my own credit was ruined. I didn't think much about anything when I filled out the form. Just that I was doing what I had to do and Man's feelings on the matter stopped being a factor when he stopped caring how we lived. I folded the application and licked the envelope when I was done. No postage necessary if mailed in the United States.

I walk past the produce, past the seafood, past the grocer's freezer to the back of the store, carrying the little red basket. It's the middle of the week, and nightfall is upon us. Glynda was watching the babies while I shopped. It was better this time of night. Always easier. The shiny new credit card came in a week with a $500 limit. I paid the electric bill first.

I strolled the aisles and reminded myself that with school out of the way, things would start to look up. The hour I spent last Monday at a temp agency could move my career forward.

"I want to work in the non-profit industry. It's work that feels good to the soul," I remember telling the interviewer. He was young. Just a few years older than I was. Asian. Handsome. "I know I need a higher degree to do the real work I'm passionate about, but I'd like to get my feet wet. Working on policies for low income populations. Prison reform. Drug rehabilitation. That's what I want to do." He filed my application away and said he would be in contact if any openings matched my qualifications. I hoped. And then I prayed.

A few cans of formula, some baby food, lunch meat for me to snack on throughout the week. Now for something special. I take a number at the butcher's counter, although there doesn't seem to be anyone else in line.

I spotted the porterhouse steaks in the window, already seasoned. Then like whodini, he appeared from beyond the door, and then stopped like it was him who saw a ghost.

I was silent. Just looked him in his eyes, not blinking, not moving. Then Leonard the butcher spoke remembering me with fondness.

"Kericho Jericho." A half smile.

"It's been three months. I thought you might have died or something," I said to him straight faced.

"I should be saying the same thing to you."

"You never called."

"I didn't think I needed to." He came closer and rested his arms on the glass in front of me. "I thought about you Kericho. I did. I wanted to call you, but you're in a relationship, whether you like it or not and I liked you too much to share you."

"Correction. I was in a relationship. You still should have called."

"I waited for you. I came to work every day hoping you might walk through the door and want a steak or something. But you never came."

"I found another grocer. After I didn't hear from you, I was afraid to see you. I was ashamed. I was hurt. I regretted everything, the whole night was a mistake, and for me avoiding you, made it less real."

"My music started to take off. One of my songs got featured in a movie. I made a killing." He smiled sarcastically. "So I took a break from this cutting meat thing to focus my attention. But then, you know, things slowed down. I still have bills so last week

I asked them if a brotha could come back to work."

"I guess they said yes."

"Of course they said yes. They know I'm the best meat cutter they got. So...here I am."

I opened my arms like the magicians do when they say voila. "Here you are."

We were quiet there for a minute, neither of us knowing exactly what to say next. I looked at his gloved hands, and remembered the way they felt on my body that night at his father's place.

"So what do you mean, 'was' in a relationship?"

"That ended a couple of months ago. We couldn't make it work. I'm not sure I wanted it to."

"So where does that leave you?"

"Alone."

"Alone?"

"Alone with two babies. And a lot of bills."

"When can I see you?"

I moved closer to the glass separating us and set my basket on the floor. Lee's eyes were a perfect shade of hazel. "What we had was absolute beauty. But beauty fades and for you and me it only lasted but a minute. I need more than beauty to fill my crevices."

"What does that mean, Kericho?"

"It means I'll take my steak now. I need to get going."

"I guess my timing is always wrong, huh?"

"Uh Uh. Your timing is just right. I needed to see you. Right now. Right here. I needed to see you to bring some closure to the gap you left open in my heart. You hurt me. But I forgive you."

"For that I'm sorry."

"Don't be. I needed to feel the pain. It hurt, but it hurt much less than everything else going on in my life." Leonard wrapped my steak with special care. He didn't weigh it but entered something in manually. "Are you doing me a favor?"

"It's the least I can do."

Chapter Twenty-Two

Everytime you are able to find some humor in a difficult situation, you win.

My meetings with Dr. Hannah had started to bother me. I was tired of rehashing old news, but she was certain it did me some good. I learned Daddy was sick when my parents flew back from my grandfather's funeral. Daddy was struggling to breathe and the pilot had to make an emergency landing in Pittsburgh. He was transported to the nearest hospital where they ran a bunch of tests, found an enlarged spleen, and diagnosed him with Myelofibrosis. They air lifted him to a hospital closer to home where his primary doctor told us he had already diagnosed him six years earlier and the prognosis from diagnosis to death is five years.

Daddy didn't tell us in order to avoid broaching the subject of death. When his doctor advised him to consider his family and make arrangements for his passing, Daddy told him his family was on an extended stay in Kenya and would not be returning for some time.

"We're not just going to let Daddy die," Sunday said to me at breakfast this morning. The food at Tillman's was always either overcooked or undercooked but we kept coming back for the young, but good looking waitstaff.

"What do you think we should do?" I asked her, fiddling with my cheddar cheese omelet.

"I'm going to call his doctor tomorrow and make an appointment for all of us to go in and have a consultation. We need to know what the options for treatment are."

"Can you imagine Daddy not being here anymore?" Sunday looked through me as if she was trying to summon the feeling, but was having trouble. "I can't. I think about him being a memory and it's a life I don't want to be a part of." I took a bite of French toast.

"Babygirl. I guess we all learn how to do some things by doing them. Learning to live without him is no different."

"Don't say such things."

"Death is inevitable."

"Maybe. Maybe it is. I know one day I have to die. Everybody dies. I just don't want to be there when it happens."

A cute waiter came over to refill our coffee. "Anything else I can get you two?" he said.

"We're okay for now," I said admiring.

"Unless you're on the menu," Sunday added. The waiter blushed a little before walking away.

"I need a man that looks like that, with a job on Wall Street, and a dick like Luke's." I said.

"You mean a dick like Nigel's."

"I wouldn't know."

"That's why I'm telling you."

"How are you two anyway?"

"We're good. You know we have a lot of fun together, but sometimes I wonder if he can really be a part of my life," Sunday said as I stuffed a forkful of egg in my mouth. "He doesn't believe in God."

"An atheist?"

"More so agnostic. An atheist says there is no God. Agnostic says there may be but we can never really be sure."

"Are you sure?"

"More than I am this coffee is lukewarm."

I smiled. "When my babies were born prematurely, the doctors came in to tell me the risks. They said they may have difficulty breathing, eating would be a challenge, and death was possible. You know I cried for a long time. I was so mad at God. Here I was in Africa having babies I didn't want in the first place. I begged God to take it away. My pregnancy, Man, my heartache, and he didn't. And then just when I fell in love with them, just when I got excited about being a mother, he goes and scares me with the possibility of losing...again."

"God works in mysterious ways."

"You know you have to define what you want in a man. Define it for you and then don't compromise on that. Accept Nigel the way he is, his beliefs and his non beliefs. Accept him or don't accept him. That you can do, but one thing you can't do is believe you can change him." I took a sip of my coffee. Sunday was right. It was lukewarm.

"You're right. Tell me why does love have to be so complicated?"

"Truth is, it's not. We just make it out to be. Be honest. With yourself. With Nigel, and with anyone else who comes into your life. I wasn't honest for a long time and maybe that's how I got so wound up with Luke. I want to let him go. I can't do this anymore."

"Do what babygirl?"

"Him. I can't do him anymore. Luke brought nothing good to my life. Not one good thing unless of course you say he made me see me better."

"What do you see?"

Another sip of coffee and I held it on my tongue before swallowing. Sunday's question was severe. *What do I see?* I see a little girl that's been holding on to a fantasy for far too long. A girl who loves hard and bruises easily. A girl who is much stronger than she ever might know because she's too afraid to find out. These things I thought but I said, "I see a girl that's been waiting for my knight in shining armor to appear on a white horse and all of my happiness is wrapped up in that very thing. And shouldn't be."

Christmas came faster this year than it does most years. Daddy's health had declined, his spleen grew, making his stomach poke out, but he shrunk everywhere else. His arms and legs started to look frail, like bones wrapped in mahogany skin. I pulled at it once when he was sleeping on the couch, one arm tucked under his head, the other hung loose over the edge. The skin around his wrist reminded me of chicken skin, wrinkly and supple. He stopped eating as much, just soup here, and yogurt there. He slept a lot, and visited the hospital weekly for blood transfusions.

One night, he couldn't hold his bowels in and defecated on the living room floor. We all thought it was the end after that. Sunday called and I drove straight to the hospital and found Daddy on a gurney in the emergency room, Grace seated on a chair at his feet.

"Daddy," I whispered, hugging him. "Are you going to die?"

"Not yet." He struggled with the words but I believed him.

After meeting with his doctor, we concluded there was not much more we could do for him. Intense chemotherapy would mean frequent stays in the hospital, tubes, hair loss, and no guarantee of recovery. Quality of life over length was what we chose. So we took him home. Sunday and I took turns a few nights a week making dinner. I got the boys after work and made the drive to Jersey. We didn't know if he would make it til Christmas so we made every night Christmas. We bought greeting cards just because. Decorated the tree six weeks early and played Nat King Cole's "Chestnuts Roasting" each night at dinnertime. I even heard Daddy humming it once while he ate.

Nigel came around more and more. Sunday worked up the balls to tell him how she really felt. "My faith is important to me and I need it to be for you too," was what she said. She brought him to her church on Sundays, read him scripture throughout the day, and prayed over him like he was an ailing child. He bent a little, considered her proposal, considered God and the Bible and if it was something he could "do." "I want to be here for you and your dad in this time," he told her. If that means me praying to your God, I'll do it. At that, Sunday celebrated. "Every little step counts," she said. "If you're trying, I'm staying!"

The thought of Daddy dying was still non existent. He was a part of my life, always there to pick up the phone when I called home and I couldn't imagine it any other way even when I tried. Yes he was thin. Yes he was sick, very sick. But dead? That could never be a reality in my lifetime. Trust your gut. Intuition is often right. That was a mantra I heard time and again. I always thought of it as God's answers to prayers. Whatever you felt in your gut was really God and all of his heavenly angels.

I was right because Daddy got better. The new medicine the doctor prescribed after the first two unsuccessful attempts decreased the size of his spleen. The cancer was in remission. He started eating more and gaining weight. He started laughing more and calling me on occasion to bring the kids to visit. On Friday nights, I stayed over. Once I got up early Saturday morning and found him in the kitchen on his feet. Making tea.

"Daddy. You're up," I said skeptical.

"Just making some tea."

"How are you feeling?"

"Today I feel okay."

Christmas Eve, Daddy came home with one of the biggest turkeys I ever did see. The next morning, Mommy and Sunday made all the fixings. Dirty rice, sweet potatoes with lots of cinnamon and butter, creamed corn, collard greens, cheddar biscuits that looked like the ones from Red Lobster but way better. I brought a couple of bottles of wine over and we feasted while the children played, Daddy at the head of the table, Grace at the other end, me and Sunday on opposite sides.

"Nigel is eating dinner with his family, but I invited him over later tonight so he's driving down. I want you all to meet him," Sunday started right after Daddy's prayer.

"Is he a good guy?" Daddy asked her.

"If he wasn't, would I be with him?"

"I hope not."

"Daddy he makes me happy.

"I want you to be with a man who can take care of you. With that, happiness comes."

"Be nice Daddy, and give him a chance."

There were two things about Nigel I knew. One of them, everyone could see, the other, only I and a few others were privy too. He was a tall skinny boy and he had a crooked penis. When he showed up in our livingroom that night, his penis was all I could think of. Sunday told me it was crooked and veered off to the side when he got an erection.

I could tell right away that Sunday didn't love him. The chemistry was absent. She wanted to love him but the connection was missing. I watched the uncomfortable way she sat next to him watching his every word, filling in where he said the wrong thing in front of my parents.

"He means he wants to try his hand at lots of different things," she said when he told them he had about 5 different jobs in as many years.

"His basic beliefs are the same," she said when he told us he grew up agnostic. She filled the awkward silences with details of their dates, how she knew he was the one, and when they see themselves getting married. I don't see them getting married at all. It was a very different story from what Sunday had told me weeks before. It's not that I don't like Nigel. It's that I don't like him for Sunday.

Grace served dessert, apple pie slices topped with vanilla bean ice cream. We ate on the couch.

"This pie is amazing Ms. Blu," he complimented my mother. I sneered.

"Oh thank you." She smiled a wide fake smile that was reserved for guests. "I used my mother's recipe. It's a secret recipe." It was a recipe from a cookbook she kept in the pantry. I decided to offer that information.

"Mommy, isn't the recipe in that old book you keep?"

"It is. So? It's my mother's cookbook, and its so old, I'm sure no one else has it." Her voice was thick with humor.

"Oh. Well you made it sound like it was an original recipe."

"Whoever's recipe it is, it is good," Nigel reiterated.

Sunday played with her pie, a nibble here and there.

"So how are you feeling, Mr. Blu? Sunday mentioned the cancer was in remission," Nigel said.

Daddy stretched. "Well... you know we are a strong family. I come from a very strong family. Our family name means that Gawd is with us."

"He sure is. And I can tell. It's good to know you will stay with us to one day see some grandkids."

"He has four," I interjected.

"He means see more grandkids," Sunday said. "Nigel and I want to have kids of our own one day."

"You're just going to be one big breeding machine I bet."

"I think Sunday and I would make beautiful children."

"Sunday has already made beautiful children. Have you forgotten?"

"How could I forget. Her daughters are gorgeous. And spitting images of her."

"No I actually think the youngest looks just like her father."

"Kericho." Sunday seemed unhappy. "Her father is not a factor right now."

"Is that so?"

Sunday got up. "Can I talk to you outside. The porch." She didn't wait for answer, just started walking briskly towards the door.

I was reluctant but obliged. I got to the porch. She slapped me. I held my cheek in the place that was struck. "What is wrong with you?" I blurted.

"What is wrong with you? You're rude. You're embarrassing, and it's really pathetic."

"Sunday you're crazy. I love you! I love you and that's why I'm trying to look out for you. You're blind."

"You're jealous."

"Of what? Of him?" I motioned to the screen door. "Please. I wouldn't want him if he was handed to me wrapped in gold. You're settling and I know you know it."

"We're done. Got it? You will always be my sister but we don't have to be friends." She scooted past me and marched back inside.

Now I had no one.

Chapter Twenty-Three

Love understands the loudness of life and the quietness of death

I suppose Sunday and I fell from grace a little at a time. It didn't begin that night on the porch, but perhaps a year earlier, I told Dr. Hannah. November 2007. Two months had passed since I saw Leonard again that night in the grocery store. I got my first child support payment on a Tuesday. Six hundred dollars deposited directly into my checking account. The Asian at the temp agency called me on Wednesday and informed me of a temporary job opening at The Memorial Project.

"It's a four month assignment, and its not exactly what you were looking for, but it's a good opportunity to get your foot in the door. The organization charged with designing and building the memorial and museum at Ground Zero needs some administrative help in their fundraising department. They're offering $18 per hour to start and--"

"I'll take it," I said before he could finish. "If the job is 9 to 5 and I can be home in time to get my babies, I'll take it!"

My first day, I wore the most professional looking outfit in my closet. Grey slacks, and a button down black blouse. It was a thirty story black building with huge windows and lots of security. The office was quaint, twenty floors up, and a pretty girl with hazel eyes sat at the reception desk. She told me to have a seat while she telephoned the appropriate contact. Five minutes later, Carol Blaney greeted me with a smile but no eye contact. She introduced me to others in the development department. Anna was a big woman, with a plain face. I decided right away she was a lesbian. Laurie was petit, blonde, and a mother of twins, just like me. Blake was Carol's right hand woman. Smart, business oriented, funny, and single. Marco was tall and dark but not very handsome. I was younger than everyone there by at least ten years. I was also of a darker complexion, and living week to week, but when I got my first paycheck, I decided I would fit right in.

Life became easier, and the days brighter. I slept better, smiled more, and danced often. With my babies in the kitchen while dinner was cooking. By myself, in the mornings, getting ready for work, using my hairbrush as my microphone. At night, after the twins were asleep, in my bedroom with a glass of wine and Ella in the cd player.

Some nights Glynda came by with Jordan and Atiba and we watched movies under a blanket with a bowl of popcorn. Mostly horror films about serial murderers or demon possessed towns. It's what made me feel safe when I compared my life to those in the movies.

I thought about Sunday and her girls. I prayed a lot. I prayed for Sunday and my babies and my finances and my relationship with Grace. But most of the time I prayed for comfort. Sometimes tears would come and sometimes they didn't but when they did, I didn't fight it. I simply let them run down my face and hit my pillow because somehow it felt like toxins leaving my body, and I felt a whole lot better.

I made church friends. They weren't people I would have

drinks with on Saturday night, but they were people that cared about me. They asked me how I was doing and listened for the answer. Sometimes they would secretly hand me a twenty or a fifty dollar bill for no reason at all and I graciously accepted. They didn't seem to care much that I was a 22 year old mother of twins with no husband to brag about, but only that I could find a welcoming space to plant a seed of faith. There was one guy. Tobias. He joined the church the same time I did. I remembered him from our New Member's class when he sat next to me one Sunday. He was older. I saw the grey at his temples. And he looked worn. As if once upon a time he was shiny and new but the years had taken a toll and he had been worn and washed several times over. The pastor had told us to greet each other with a warm welcome and say "God loves you and so do I." I turned in his direction, but he beat me to it.

On the twins' first birthday, I had a party at my place. Daddy came with Sunday and the girls. Ms. W. from church was an older lady with greying but pretty hair. She stopped by with toys for the kids and a batch of cornbread. One of the kids daycare teacher's came over with her toddler and we ate and sang and celebrated together. Man asked me days before if I had plans for their birthday.

"I don't think we should see each other. You can't handle it," I said.

Man was bitter that I was moving on with my life and it showed in the way he got angry over the smallest offenses. Once I was in the middle of changing Kye when he came to pick them up for the weekend. He yelled I should have them ready when he gets there. Another time, Kiefer fell ill, on a weekend visit with Man and he complained I was not caring for them properly. But I was convinced this was Man's way of fleshing out his frustrations that I didn't care to be with him and I was much happier on my own.

I was ironing one evening for work the next day when I heard the knock at the front door. I opened it and saw the two police men standing there, their hands on their hips, and faces empty.

Chapter Twenty-Four

I heard Oprah once say there are no mistakes. Everything leads you back to where you're supposed to be.

"We have a warrant here for your arrest." The officer said it reluctantly and for that I was grateful. My heart sped up and I pulled my robe tighter around my chest. He held out a piece of paper. "You're being charged with credit card fraud. I gotta take you in."

Time stopped there in that moment and I looked through the officer that was speaking like he was a halogram. He was tall and stocky and his accomplice a bit shorter and quiet through this whole ordeal. I could hear the hum of the television behind me, and even the sound of my babies breathing in their nursery. I gasped on the inside when I realized I was caught. *How did I get caught?*

Lifetimes passed before I spoke, and even then my voice was uneven and I struggled to push the words off my tongue and between my teeth. "I...I...uh." I took a breath and started again. "I have two...t...two babies sleeping in the back." My mother told us a long time ago that Sunday was abnormally shy when she was a child. So shy she was sent to a special school for children with disabilities. When Sunday cried she sounded like a kitten, and when she spoke, her voice was barely audible. I was a seven year old Sunday here in this moment, ordering myself to speak louder, but disobeying vehemently. My gaze met the officer's eyes and he looked down at me with empathy.

"Do you have a friend or family that can keep them?" A head shake no. "Do you have any priors? Any previous arrests?" Another headshake. "Then this shouldn't take long. You can be home within a couple of hours if they let you go on your own recognizance."

"I...I've got no one nearby."

"The kids' father? He's the one that filed the complaint. Where is he? Can we call him up?"

My legs were going numb. I stumbled backwards and took a seat on the couch. The officer caught the door before it slammed shut and followed me inside. *He's the one who filed the complaint.* I was stuck there on that. Stuck on the idea really that the man who loved me, said it over and over again, that man, would do me in. Love. That four letter word much more complicated than any college calculus class. Imaginary numbers made more sense than love. Love wasn't tangible, it wasn't visible, it wasn't audible. Love is everything and nothing really at all. Love is in the eye of the beholder. It's all relative. Everything is relative. It's about perspective, perception, permission. Permission to come inside, to wait until someone decides to rip their heart from their chest. Couldn't he have done it when my heart was still made of 42 carat solid gold. Beautiful and hard. *I love you Kericho. I love you so much it hurts.* That's what he said. "Y...yes. I can call him," I finally said. Love sucks. Love got me arrested on a Monday night when I was alone with my baby boys.

The police car ride to the precinct was long. It may have been the longest car ride I've ever taken. Officer Ridley, the short one, stayed behind with the babies and waited for Man to arrive and I was handcuffed outside and seated in the back of the SUV. My heart had dropped and was somewhere lodged between my stomach and spleen. I was sick.

My vision was a blur. I watched the shadows of the trees glide by in the blue grey color of dusk. I watched the back of the officer's head partially covered under his hat. I watched the curve of my thighs wrapped in faded blue jeans. I watched but mostly I listened. Man's voice was a throbbing sound in my head boasting of victory. And what of Grace? She would berate me for yet another disappointment I've added to the roster. She pointed her slender index finger at my chest and reiterated how small I had become. Yes her voice was clear. She pursed her lips and shook her head.

But I was planning to pay the credit card. Just a few more weeks and I would pay the card off and close the account. Now it was too late.

And what of Daddy? He would be disappointed in me along with Grace, but with him, he would be more worried than angry. Yes, Daddy was soft and gentle. I'm sure Daddy will understand.

But what of Kiefer and Kye? Will they understand? Will they understand my desperation? *Mommy had to do it. Mommy had to find a way to take care of you.*

I didn't cry. I didn't think to. I simply sat upright and was still.

"How old are your sons?" I remember the officer saying.

"They just turned 1."

"Twins?"

"Yeah." A pause. "Twins."

"That's a blessing."

I was photographed, fingerprinted and thrown into a cell with brick walls painted an eggshell white. There was a cot in the corner, a square table, and four fold away chairs along the wall. I took a seat in one of them and waited. I waited for the seasons to change, for the earth to rotate completely around the sun. I waited for God to send me a savior, the second coming of Christ. I waited for Grace to tell me she loves me, for a kind word, for a hug. I waited for an orgasm, that feeling I had really only experienced with my own two fingers. I waited for relief. I waited for the door to open and the big black guard on the other side of it to call my name. *"Kericho Blu."* I would get up and go to him and he would say, *"Its time to go home."*

They called my name two hours later. My eyelids were heavy and I was suddenly thirsty. The guard led me out of the cell and down a corridor to a slightly ajar window facing an office. A woman with red hair met me at the window shuffling papers. She spoke at me and not to me.

"You're being charged with credit card fraud and forgery, a felony. Your bail is set at $3,000. You can pay a bond of 10 percent."

The last time I checked I had 31 dollars in my bank account. I was livid. "But I have no priors. The officer told me I would be let out on my own recognizance!"

She didn't look up. "Bail is set based on the severity of the crime. This is a felony. You can choose to spend the night here tonight and speak to the judge via satellite in the morning. He may lower the bail or he could raise it. That's all." She closed the window.

Wasn't I supposed to get a phone call?

I didn't sleep much the rest of the night. At some point the guard brought me and my cellmates an orange jumpsuit and we took turns changing in the bathroom. I befriended a woman named Robin. No last name. She was a little older than me but not by much and her hair reminded me of Halle Berry's, short and sweet. She was arrested for shoplifting. She stole expensive razors from the grocery store to sell them on the street and get money for her babies.

We sat together in a hallway for the length of a Nick at Nite marathon waiting to be transported to another cell. The kind for long term guests. I considered the wait was because they had to prepare our room. Radical hospitality.

I did get my phonecall. I called Man. He didn't answer. So I left a voicemail in between short breaths and quiet sobs. "Would you call my job, please. Tell them I won't be in tomorrow. Tell them I had a family emergency."

When we were escorted to our suite, a cell we shared with 6 other women, I laid on my assigned cot and closed my eyes. The night was riddled with haze, a mixture of a lot of things. Never quite asleep and never quite awake. There were tears and thoughts of tears. Anger, sadness, doubt. The bunk above me formed a fog around my bed, and the shadows in the dark reminded me of demons from hell, walking the earth seeking who they may devour.

I thought of Kye and Kiefer and my heart was crushed under the pressure of my despair. When the morning came, I felt as though I hadn't slept at all.

They brought us breakfast in bed. Toast, an egglike substance, and the boxed juices you get in grade school. I shoveled it down my throat. "*You have to eat babygirl*," I told myself pretending I was Sunday.

"Why are you crying sweetie?" a tall skinny girl said. I must have been crying without realizing it.

"I'm in jail. I got two little babies to care for. That's something to cry about."

"Ain't nothing you can do about it. Right now, ain't nothing you can do about it but smile and know that in the end, everything is gonna be alright. So if it's not alright at the moment...that just mean it ain't the end."

She was happy, that girl. Or carefree. Maybe she's been in jail so many times, this was just another walk in the park for her, but whatever it was, I envied her. I envied her attitude, the way she was so light, so unworried, unfettered.

By noon, a few of us were lined up and taken to a room to talk to the public defender. I stood there next to Robin, back against the wall, my hands chained in front of me. Two guards marched the men prisoners past us and around a corner. I saw Robin smile and wave at one of them.

"You hangin in there babe," he shouted as he stumbled by.

"Trying to, she responded. The guard in front of us admonished her.

"There's no talking," he said.

"That's my husband," she argued.

"So what?"

She sucked her teeth quietly and I looked slightly at her to my left.

"How'd you both manage to get in here?" I asked her.

She swallowed. "Just trying to make ends meet. We got a couple kids at home. That's a couple mouths to feed. A couple backs to clothe. A couple bills to pay. We thought we do this one time. One last time and make enough to get through this month."

A nodded. "And you got caught?"

"It is what it is. I just wish the kids didn't have to see their parents go to jail. They didn't really have shit to do with anything. You know, they just being kids and shit." She licked her lips, leaned back against the wall and closed her eyes. She was beautiful, this Robin. Her face smooth like fresh churned butter, lips small and pursed, a nose chiseled in a factory.

None of us are safe I guess. We all have to fight our own battle, we all get dealt a hand none of us are really pleased with. But still, she had a man toiling with her. Mine was the one who put me here.

Kids, your Daddy sent your mommy to jail when you guys were one year old, I imagined telling the children when they were older. *Never be that cruel. Never give your lady back what she dishes out. Cus us girls, you know we make mistakes. Us girls, we can be cruel. We can dish it out good. But don't return the sentiment. Because us girls, we have hearts too. Hearts that break real bad, and most times don't ever get put back together. You know it might seem we get mended up just fine, but the cracks are still there. Even if they're hairline cracks, they're still there and they burn. We hold the hurt in and it destroys us. It destroys our relationship with the man who did us in and we can't ever get things back right because we remember what he did and how he made us feel, and how he made us hurt and kept calling it love. Kids don't be that way to the women in your life. Love unconditionally. Love when they don't love you. Love when it's hard, because I promise she'll remember you for it and in the long run, she'll know it was real.*

I met with a short stocky gentleman with blotchy skin. Mr. Kilmichael was his name. We sat in silence for a few minutes, him behind his desk, me at the side, before he spoke.

"You have a job?"

"Yes."

"You don't have any prior offenses. I'll do all the talking when we go in front of the judge. I think it should work out in your favor."

More waiting. And then I stood in line to speak to the district judge through a tv screen. I couldn't make out his face since he didn't look up from his paperwork. But he was white. Nicely groomed. And young considering the full head of dark hair.

"Legal aid is suggesting we release you on personal recognizance," the judge started. " This matter is a serious offence. Forgery. Credit card fraud. How can I make sure you will return for trial?"

Mr. Kilmichael stood at my side, his hands clasped behind his back. "Your honor, the defendant has no prior record and a full time job to attend to."

"I understand but I'm not sure I'm comfortable without a bail being paid."

I interjected with a raised hand. "Your honor may I speak."

"Sshh." That was Mr. KilMichael.

"I'd like to speak." I was loud so the judge could hear me. He nodded. "Your honor, I have a full time job, and two 1 year olds to look after. I've never seen *the inside of a jail* in my life until now. The credit card in question belongs to my children's father. We *lived* together. I want nothing more than to return to court and settle this matter."

The judge looked up. His face was soft. "Ok."

I was released 3 hours later with my belongings and a cab voucher. Home smelled like heaven.

The next two months were a constant stomach pain. I woke up in the middle of the night sweating from my brow and out of breath, but the dream I could not remember. February 18th 2008. I grew to hate that day with every passing moment. It was the day I was to return to court and face the judge's wrath for my sins. My crime against humanity.

Casper Brown was an attractive gentleman. He was bald in a good way and distinguished looking. I found him in the yellow pages and I went to visit his office on a Friday morning before work. It was quaint, and cozy, and yellow on the outside. I saw a red Jaguar convertible parked in the driveway. *Nice,* I thought. Inside an older woman greeted me and told me to have a seat. Mr. Brown will be right out. I looked at the auto magazines on the table. I saw BusinessWeek, Time, and some legal pamphlets.

This is a shot in the dark. It dawned on me. What if he hates me? What if he tells me I deserve whatever is coming to me? What if he's worse than Grace?

I closed my eyes and thought of Mrs. W. and all the good folks from Parker Memorial. What would they think of me now? Surely I have disappointed them most of all. "*Look*" they would say. *"The birds of the air and the fish of the sea do not have a refrigerator. They don't store up food for tomorrow and yet God still provides for them. If he can supply food for the birds and the fish, surely, he can take care of you."*

But they were liars. My lights got cut off. And but for the $138 I got per month in food stamps, my cupboards would be bare like Old Mother Hubbard in the nursery rhyme. God didn't provide.

The woman told me I could follow her and she led me to an office in the back. Casper was finishing a phone call when she motioned for me to have a seat and then left the room.

He clasped his hands together on his desk and looked me in my eyes.

"What can I do you for, peach pie?" he said in a southern drawl.

My eyes started to water at that.

I told.

By the time I was finished, he had handed me the box of tissues.

"I like you," he said. "And I know you don't have a lot of money. I'm going to charge you $500. And you can make payments. I'll do my best to get this in front of a female prosecutor. He owes you $4,000 in back child support, and he's whinin about a $300 credit card bill. This looks good for us. Real good."

Five hundred dollars wasn't too bad. It was five hundred more than I had but it wasn't too bad.

"Ok." I said. "I get paid next Friday."

"I want you to keep your head up," he said standing. "This is not a death sentence. Never think of it as such."

"Sound advice." It was advice to live by.

That night I rocked the babies to sleep and watched reruns of The Cosby Show. I wondered if they had a life that only happened on TV. The doctor husband, the lawyer wife, five children and a happy home in Brooklyn. I would never have that. Mine was only half a life and even if I found my knight in shining armor, Kiefer and Kye could only be half his.

I attended church every Sunday and put on a smile that lied

to everyone. I pretended for those 3 hours that I wasn't a felon awaiting my sentence. The babies started fussing one morning during service and I took them outside to the corridor, found a seat far enough away from the sanctuary and rocked them gently. I heard the toilet flush just inside the men's bathroom and a few moments later, Tobias emerged in a red tie, one of two colors acceptable for the man who wants to be taken seriously. This time I spoke first.

"Hi. Tobias right?"

"Yes." He was solemn. Easy in his walk. "How are you?" He stopped beside me and leaned against the wall, both hands nestled in his pocket.

"Doing well. My baby boys were fussing so you know, I just came out here."

He bit his bottom lip. "How was your week?"

"It's been ok. I'm dealing with a court issue so just a little anxious about that." I don't know why I shared.

"Everything ok?"

"I'm sure it will be."

"Let me know if there is anything I can do."

I nodded. "You should get back into service."

"I'm not missing anything. I needed to stretch my legs anyway. I was nodding."

"Not enough sleep last night? You should stop staying out too late Saturday nights and turn in earlier."

"I'm not staying out late at all. I have a curfew. I'm home and in bed by 9pm everyday."

Tobias had to be at least 45 years old. I squinted at that. Was it sarcasm?

He continued, "I'm in a program that the church supports. I thought you knew. The mission."

"The mission?"

Another bite of the lip. "Right it's a program for some of us trying to get back on our feet."

That didn't offer me much information other than that he was off his feet and he was trying to get back on. Maybe I should enroll too. "Aren't we all? And in that case, you let me know if there's anything I can do to help."

He nodded. "How old are your son's?"

"One. Twins."

"I see that. That must be a blessing."

"Some days. Other days its just overwhelming. You have any kids?"

"Nah I don't have no kids. I always wanted a little girl. Just never happened."

"It's not too late."

"I gotta find a special lady first."

"She'll come along I'm sure. At the right time."

He ignored that. Curled his lips together. "How do you like the church?"

"Very much. I like it very much. I grew up in the church so it's kind of like me returning to the faith of my childhood."

"I don't think you can return to the faith of your childhood, unless you suffered some coma that lasted years or decades. Your faith as an adulthood is hopefully far removed from your faith at age 5."

I squinted. "I don't follow."

"Don't worry. It's not important."

He lingered. "Well nice talking to you Tobias." I stood up clutching the now calm twins. "I'm going to head back inside." He nodded…and then watched me walk away.

Sunday had come to visit two days before my court date. She brought her girls and they played in the bedroom while she and I sat at the kitchen counter peeling sweet potatoes for dinner. We hadn't spoken since the night I was arrested. At least nothing more than a facebook comment or a "hey, miss you babygirl."

She heard about my pending court case through the grapevine. Man had seen my mother at church and mentioned something about how she better watch out for that daughter of hers. Said I was a con and a thief and I was going to pay for my mistakes. Then my mother told Sunday, she couldn't trust me with money and recounted a time she caught me stealing from her purse when I was younger.

When Sunday first called me to get the news straight from the horse's mouth, I didn't want to talk about it. I felt the judgment in her voice and so resorted to telling her I had it under control and it wasn't something I wanted to discuss.

"How's the job going?" she asked after a bout of silence now at the kitchen counter.

"It's going. Been three months. The assignment was for a four month term. I'm hoping they extend it. You know, maybe hire me full time."

"You saving any money?... In case things go south."

I hesitated. "Trying to. But you know if it ain't one thing, it's another. Had to come up with five hundred for this lawyer, ya know?"

Now she hesitated. "I didn't want to say anything before, but I feel like I should now. That was stupid what you did. How could you think you would get away with that?"

I shot her a look. "Please don't."

"No Kericho. I have to. Mommy said you did the same thing to her before. Stole a credit card just so you could buy stuff. It's called having respect for people's property."

"You don't even know the whole story."

"And now you're complaining about life being tough. Well *you* made it tough. *You* stole that card. *You* charged it. *You* got caught. That was all *you*. So now you gotta lie down in the bed you made."

My eyes welled up, but I fought blinking.

She continued, this time pointing the potato peeler at me. "I hope you learned a lesson. How could you be so stupid? And then to get arrested. To go to jail when you have those two babies to take care of. Be an adult. Kericho. Jesus, use your head."

"You weren't in my shoes."

"No, you wanted a new pair of shoes. Admit this was about greed. Greed and--"

"This was about needing to survive," I blurted. "This was about making a way for me to eat. So don't talk to me about my motives. Don't talk to me about what I was going through. You weren't there. Just like Grace. Just like our momma."

She sucked her teeth. Then she picked up the potato and kept on peeling.

Chapter Twenty-Five

"The old law of an eye for an eye leaves the whole world blind." MLK

I started working Monday and Wednesday nights at Dream House. It was a nonprofit organization dedicated to bettering the lives of former prisoners reentering society. Dream House was built on four principles. Housing, Healthcare, Education, Employment. Those were the four entities they believed everyone needed to make it in today's world. I tutored students working to get their GED in the Next Step program, their education department.

A Google search for organizations that served the underprivileged, a community of beautiful people I always thought were misunderstood, brought back 193 results. Dream House covered the first page. Prisoners weren't born evil. Society made them that way. They were really just desperate people whose circumstances somehow got the best of them. Just like me.

Casper Brown managed to knock my penalty for the credit card fraud down to a slap on the wrist. Forty hours of community service at an organization of my choice and my record would be wiped clean. But putting in two hours every Monday and Wednesday evening after my day at The Memorial Project meant asking Glynda to babysit. She said she was happy to do it. After that, I started calling her Glynda, The Good Witch and I remembered the words of the women from Parker Memorial. *God always provides.*

The class teacher, Mrs. Donahue was a short pudgy woman with dark hair. She always wore one of those fanny packs around her waist even when she was at the blackboard instructing the adult students when to use “their” and “there”, “who's” and “whose”. My first day, she assigned the class a 200 word paper on a sport of their choice. We spent the second hour of class time getting started.

Mrs. Donahue introduced me as Kericho, her trusty teacher aide that she was more than ecstatic to have in class.

"Kericho recently graduated from NYU. She's here to help you all dot your I's and cross your t's, so don't be shy. She's such a smart girl."

I walked around from desk to desk sitting with the students, mostly men, ranging in age from 18 to 48. Palmer was one of the gentlemen somewhere in the middle. He had written one line when I walked by his desk.

"I like baseball. It's a sport I realy realy likes."

"You look like you're doing a good job, so far," I said. "Only thing is you spelled "really" wrong. You need two l's. And no s at the end of "like."

"Thanks," he said. "I can't seem to figure out what else I should say."

I pulled up a chair. "Well, let's see. Why don't we make an outline? That's the way I like to do it. Maybe you will too." I tore a page out of his notebook. "Write down a few questions you think your reader might have. Then answer those questions, a paragraph for each one. Once you've answered all the questions, you know you have a good essay, and you'll reach the 200 word mark before you even know it."

"What kind of questions you think I should write down?"

"Hmm. Well you start by saying you like baseball. If you weren't writing and you and I were just having a conversation, I might ask you, why do you like baseball."

"So should I write 'why do I like baseball?'"

"Go for it."

As he was writing, I continued. "You know I don't know much about baseball. I know there's a bat, and there's a ball, but after that, I don't really know how to play. So why don't you answer that next. How to play baseball." I tried not to sound condescending. Palmer was at least 10 years my senior. He wrote it down. "Let's see. Maybe next you can write about the last time you went to a baseball game."

"Oh I ain't neva been to no real game before. But I got a son and he used to play in the little league."

That made me smile. "How sweet. How old is your son?"

"He's gotta be 11 now. Haven't seen him in a while. About four years."

My smile waned. "Oh. I'm sorry."

"I went away for a little while and me and his momma were having problems. I didn't want my son seeing me in jail so I told her not to bring him. When I finally made it home last year, I just couldn't find her. Heard around town that she moved to Florida somewhere. Can you believe that? Moved to Florida with my son."

I was quiet for a moment. "I'm really sorry to hear that. But at least you can write about the last time you watched your son play baseball. That's gotta be a good memory."

"It is."

"So there ya go. You've got your five paragraphs. Intro. Why you like baseball. How to play baseball. Memory of your son's game. Conclusion."

"I already have the first sentence. What should the second sentence be?"

"Palmer. You don't have to make it more complicated than it has to be. Pretend you're just having a conversation with me. Kind of like you just did. Only this time write it down. You say you really like baseball. Why?"

"Baseball is a game of skill. That's why I like it. You don't have to be big. You ain't gotta be strong, but you gotta have skill."

"Write it down."

He was stumped.

I laughed, then guided his pencil to the paper. "Palmer. Write down exactly what you said to me. It's that easy."

He doubted. Then he said, "Ok," and he did.

On Tuesday, Mrs. Blaney called me into her office to ask me if I wanted a job. A full time job working for The Memorial Project and not that temp agency. I tried to seem like I wasn't ecstatic so I remained composed, my hands folded in my lap.

"I'd love that."

"We can start you off at 42,000." She paused. "It may go up."

Mrs. Blaney didn't think $42,000 a year was a lot of money, but she didn't know it was the most money I had ever made in my life. She didn't know I would have been happy with 35.

"I'll take it," I said. It wasn't until later that night when I was filling out pension plan papers that I realized I should have held out for more. At least put up an argument.

The folks at work took me out for a celebratory lunch and then gifted me with a fancy candy jar full of jolly ranchers. I snacked on them daily and they lasted exactly one week. I kept the glass jar with red trim on my desk for old times sake. Now that I was a permanent employee, I had bigger responsibilities. I had to setup and execute grants from initial application to completion. Anna was my direct supervisor under Mrs. Blaney.

I sat with her in training the first two days.

"Government grants are tedious and require a lot of attention to detail," she started. "You should keep a spreadsheet and list all the pieces you need to have completed. Then you can keep track and check them off one by one."

Anna wasn't feminine. She wasn't necessarily masculine either. She was just plain. It would be amazing to see what a little ruby red lips and a higher heel could do for her.

Once I caught her checking her personal email on her computer when I approached her desk. She jumped, startled by my sudden appearance and clicked the X in the upper right corner.

She thought I was Mrs. Blaney. I ignored what I had seen. "Can we go over this form together Anna. I'm getting the hang of it, but this one is a little tricky."

"Pull up a chair."

I grabbed one with wheels from the empty cubicle next to her. "This is asking for the top salaries of executives here. Where would I get that information?"

"Oh thats all reported on our tax forms. We're a 501c3 organization so we're required to report salaries plus fringe."

"Fringe?"

"Benefits. Health insurance, life insurance, pension contributions. Let me send you the folder. You can access previous tax filings on our share drive. I'll give you the passcode but it's confidential."

"Thanks Anna. So I just input that info right in these boxes?"

"That's right. Why don't you get it all filled out and I can review it just to make sure all our i's are dotted and our t's crossed."

Back at my desk, I opened her email and pulled up last year's budget, projected and actual.

Scott Riley, the President and CEO made $340,000 last year. Mooney, the CFO made $310,000. Jim Pinzon, the COO,

$240,000. Carol Blaney was fourth on the list at $200,000. I wondered where I fell in the pecking order.

Anna invited me to have lunch with her that Friday. "There's a place down the street that serves the best burgers south of Times Square."

"I didn't know you were a burger kind of girl." Anna was big boned, not fat. She usually brought her lunch from home. Neatly packed soup or sandwich made with only organic foods.

"I try not to eat too much red meat, but its Friday. We can splurge on Friday."

We ordered two blue burgers. A half pound burger topped blue cheese, bacon, and dill mayo. And sweet potato fries.

"What's going on with Blake and Lori?" I asked her before I swallowed the first bite.

"What do you mean?"

"I just see the way they interact. They're friendly but not friendly. Blake seems a little passive aggressive."

"You think so?"

"Like the other day for instance, Lori walked into the meeting a minute late and Blake made some comment about her skirt being too short for the workplace. She was joking but still, in a way it felt like she wasn't."

"Don't mind those two. They're jealous of each other." She ate a sweet potato fry.

"Why? I mean what do they have to be jealous of?"

She laughed and I saw the remnants of the fry. "Lori's got the family, the American dream. She has a husband, a daughter, and they just closed on a house. Blake wants that. She's in her mid thirties and still single. She wants the husband and even though she doesn't admit it, I think she wants the kids too."

I sipped my water taking it all in. "And Blake? Why would Lori be jealous of a woman who wants what *she* has?"

"Blake and Carol are close."

"You mean Mrs. Blaney?"

"Um hum. Blake is her right hand woman. You know Carol used to own her own business before she came here. Blake was her assistant and I guess they worked so well together that she brought her with her when she got the Development Director position."

"And Lori is jealous of that?"

"Lori is jealous that she is not the one on top."

I was only halfway through my burger. "And what about you?"

"Me, I sit back and watch it all happen."

I didn't like this. Gossiping like school children about our colleagues. According to Anna's logic, I should be jealous of both of them. I had neither the family, nor the status. I was just trying to pay all of my bills this month.

I traded in my 10 year old Civic for a three year old Nissan and I bought new car seats for Kiefer and Kye so they could ride in style. They were always too good for the used ones I bought on Craigslist.

The extra rush of energy I got from my new sense of security subsided after a month.

All the men at Dream House hit on me. All of them. Once in the middle of simple algebra, Deshawn wrote his number down on scrap paper and passed it to me across the desk. "Me and a few friends are going out to Coney Island this weekend. You should come," he whispered. After a quick no thanks, I tried to return to the algebra. I was unsuccessful. "Why not Kay Kay?" *Kay Kay?*

"I don't think that would be a very good idea. Plus I'm busy this weekend."

"Why isn't it a good idea? I think it's a great idea. And what chu got to do this weekend?"

"Deshawn, this place has a strict policy against mixing business with pleasure. This is work for me."

"But Ms. Donahue said you not even gettin' paid for this here. You just do it outta the goodness of your heart. So if that's the case, this ain't really work."

"Just because I don't get paid, doesn't mean its not work. And I told you, I'm busy anyway so lets finish this math."

"Busy with what? What does Miss Kay Kay do in her spare time?"

"I have two little boys I gotta look after."

"Two little boys?"

"My sons."

"You got kids Kay Kay!? Well damn now I really wanna get to know you. Fact that you got kids means you put out." He laughed one of those I-was-just-kidding laughs, but I didn't find it very funny.

Another time, an older guy, I called him Mr. Sims, told me I had a nice smile and a nice face and a nice ass. He said he didn't mean to be disrespectful and hoped I didn't take offense.

I said, "It's okay Mr. Sims," and then I went in the bathroom and cried.

Dr. Kelly, my physician gave me a depo shot for birth control. I lost 6 pounds in the first 4 weeks after the shot. I thought my frail frame would ward off the boys, but by the time I was finished my bid at Dream House, all 40 hours, I weighed in below 100 pounds and the guys were all still ravenous.

On my last day, I told Mrs. Donahue and the class that it wasn't really my last day. I said I had a ton of fun with the class and I would be back once Dream House had a paid position available. By summer of 2008, my life had become a roller coaster of sorts. Up some days, down others.

Credit cards, and jail, and my life with Man was behind me. I had healthy twin toddlers, a job, and a home. But with my new life, came bigger bills and more responsibility. I hadn't had sex since Leonard the butcher and I was aching something terrible.

I reunited with Luke via the internet. A network where everyone could connect with former friends, or flings. I logged on one day and his face appeared like a long lost love on my computer screen.

"Luke," I said out loud to no one in particular.

We met for coffee at a Starbucks after work and I was convinced after that meeting that he would be my husband. He has always been the only one I felt like I belonged with.

PART III

Chapter Twenty-Six

When I'm lying in my bed, I think about life and I think about death and neither one particularly appeals to me.

"How many sexual partners have you had?"

"Too many to take that question seriously."

"We can get out paper and pencil"

"Why?"

"Why not?"

It is January 2009. Dr. Hannah had somehow convinced me to continue my sessions after I adamantly resisted. Just one more I kept saying. Despite the men hitting on me, Dream House had been a kind of recreational activity for me and now that that was gone my life had been dwindled down to work and kids. Kids and work. Even the occasional sex with Luke was never fulfilling.

Daddy was doing better. Sunday was happy with Nigel and had cut me out of her personal space with imaginary scissors. Boredom for me took over after that infamous Christmas night.

"Why do you want to force me to remember?"

"Maybe that's not the point of the exercise."

"Well maybe you should cut the bullshit and tell me what the fucking point is."

She was silent. Dr. Hannah never responded to my cursing.

I looked down at my hands. I always picked at my cuticles when I was uncomfortable. After a decade of silence, I began, "I almost let this boy named Justin fuck me when I was 15. He went as far as putting the condom on his little hard penis, and pressing it up against me. But I was scared I guess. Got up and ran out of there like a bat outta hell." I laughed quietly. "My mother called me a slut. Can you believe that? I was a virgin and she said I was a slut. In some ways that made me want to do it more. Less than a month later, I got my next opportunity. I guess I just wanted to prove to myself that I could do it. I could be a big girl. His name was Kirkland. Kid I knew from school. He took my virginity right there on the cafeteria counter. No candles. No wooing. Just a lot of heavy breathing and some blood. He didn't even know I was a virgin until after the fact."

Dr. Hannah raised an eyebrow but didn't speak so I continued. "There was a whole big thing after. He had a girlfriend and she found out and I felt terrible, but really what I wanted was to do it again. We never did. The second time was a guy named Omar. I had a crush on him but he treated me bad. I mean bad. I snuck out the house one night and went to a party he invited me to. Took me in a bedroom and screwed my brains out. Then he left me to get dressed and another guy came in. A friend of his. I guess he wanted some too. I never want my sons to be that way ya know. Using women the way you use toilet paper. I wouldn't treat a dog like that."

"What happened with the friend?"

I kept her waiting a few moments. "I said no. I said no and they threw me out of the house at midnight. No ride home. No goodbye." I fought the tears I felt swelling. "Then there was Aaron. I let him have me a few times. Then Antoine. Then a guy named Bryant. I snuck him into my parent's house and got caught halfway through. That was the last time I would have sex for a while."

"Why the change of heart?"

"I had had enough. I told myself before I gave away my virginity, I said, I'm only going to do it once. Just to see what it feels like. Just to say I had done something. But I got carried away. Five guys in less than five months. My dad caught me in my room with Bryant. He must have heard us upstairs. I just remember being humiliated. Not because of the boy, but because now Daddy knew what I had been doing. He knew I had sex. A few days later I heard Bryant at school talking to some kid about me and making fun of my dad's accent. Bryant. The one I let into my home. The one I let fuck me, feel my insides, kiss my nipples. He would do that to me."

"So you stopped having sex?"

"I stopped for about a year. Then I gave Charles head in his bedroom one evening while his mother was making dinner. I thought he was different." I smirked. "I made him chase me for two months before I said yes to the junior prom. Told him this was no love thing. Wasn't looking for a relationship. The prom and that was it. Then I was hanging out at his house after school and somehow his dick ended up in my mouth." I sighed. "Whats worse, is that a month later, I let his cousin Travis take me to a cheap motel and screw me."

"That's seven."

"Who's counting?" She was silent. I continued. "Senior year of high school I laid low. But I fucked one of my best friends, Micah, in my Honda Civic the night I graduated. I grew up with him. That night we were both celebrating adulthood. Freshman year of college, I met Luke. A month, maybe two before I was in his bed. On winter break, I came home, and reunited with a dude I had been crushing on since high school days. Stephon. I think I mighta fell in love with Stephon. We got some liquor and a hotel room one night to watch the basketball game. I don't remember what happened next. I just know I let him taste me that night and when I felt him, it was like heaven. Now that I think of it, Stephon was the first time sex felt good to me. I mean really good. So there was this pattern with me through the first two years of college. Luke fucked me at school. Stephon fucked me at home. And I loved them both. Equally."

"And then?

"And then....there were some dates. There were some one night stands. Two Stevens. Two Brandons, a Kris, with a K. And then Man."

"16?"

"Give or take. There was Gerald. I think of him as the one who got away. I left out Leonard. Leonard the Butcher, I cheated on Man with him. That was before I found Luke again and decided--"

"Decided what?"

"I decided I wanted to be with Luke. Like for real. I wanted to be in a relationship and be faithful and get married and have babies. He was the one I was doing it with but--"

"But what?"

"But now I'm not so sure. I'm not sure he wants that. I'm not even sure I want it anymore." I shifted in my chair and fiddled with my fingers. "Ever since we reconnected, it's like he's there but he's not there. He was my date for a gala my job did. We always have a great time when we're together but I realized I'm the only one trying to build a relationship here."

"Have you talked to him about it?"

I gave her a blank stare. "Some things aren't meant for talking about. I have to let him go. I have to cleanse myself from that part of my life. He can only keep hurting me if I let him. Do you think I'm a whore Dr. Hannah?"

"What do you think?"

"No. I think no. Now what do you think?"

"Why does it matter what I think?"

"Maybe I'm making conversation. It doesn't matter, but I'm curious. Fuck." I took a breath and felt my heart speed up. Dr. Hannah was pulling her voodoo shit again. That mind control reverse psychology stuff. I started to speak and realized I was crying. "Ya know--" I pulled a piece of skin from my thumb and I saw a spot of blood form. I tried again. "Ya know, all my life, I've kind of been a fuck up. Slept with a whole bunch of guys and now I have this rap sheet I can't get rid of. My mother called me a slut at 15. The woman who fucking birthed me said that I was a slut. That's the worst thing you can say to someone. And then, at 21, I found myself pregnant in Africa. Fucking Africa. And I couldn't even carry my own babies to term. Man left because he couldn't put up with my shit. I cheated on him with Leonard the mother fucking butcher and even he fucked me and never called again. I ended up in jail for credit card fraud and my own sister couldn't even look at me straight after that. And here I am at 24, thinking *'hey maybe I'm finally getting my shit together'*, but no. Even Luke doesn't take me seriously."

I couldn't look at her so I focused on my bleeding cuticle. "I've never done one thing right my whole life. That takes skill Dr. Hannah."

"So what are you going to do about that? Huh?" She met my tone. "You want to spend your whole life feeling sorry for yourself. You want me to have pity? Huh? You want the world to have pity on you? Would that make you feel better?"

"No one's saying –"

"You want to give up? You want to die?"

" –that I'm looking for pity. I never said that." My voice was rising.

"You want to crawl up in a hole? You want to disappear? You want--"

"Sometimes I do. Sometimes I do Dr. Hannah." I didn't fight the tears anymore. I talked over her. "Don't pretend you know anything about me. You don't know shit about me."

"Kericho. Take some responsibility! You say you messed up a lot. So what. Ok. Now what? What are you going to do? Make a decision. Take some responsibility for your life!"

"Fuck you. I did! I took responsibility and you don't know what that feels like. You're not me. You're not in my shoes. You don't know what it's like to be afraid to go to sleep because sleep is where dreams lurk. Fucking nightmares."

"Kericho--"

"No you wait. You don't know what it's like to dream of killing your children. To dream of killing yourself so often that dreams and reality blend together and sometimes you're dreaming and sometimes you're just thinking. You don't know what that's like okay. To not know the difference between a thought and a dream because both scare you half to death. To spend nights in bed counting the number of ways to do it. A knife, a gun, the car. That one is recurring. One day, I'll just drive the car off a fucking bridge, I swear I will. And I don't want to. But I swear I'll do it because somehow ending my life and my children's is the better option."

I sniffled. She was quiet.

"You don't know what it's like to feel like you're screaming at the top of your lungs and no one can hear you and it's better that way because if they did, hell would break loose. If they heard me, my children wouldn't be my children anymore. They'd all say I was crazy and take away the one thing I have left that is holding me together. Motherhood." I sat back in my chair and watched her watch me. "I want drugs Dr. Hannah."

"What do you want?"

"I want something that will make it go away."

"You never told me about the dreams."

"I was scared to. That's not the kind of thing you want people to know."

"Suicide?"

"I hate having those thoughts Dr. Hannah. I hate feeling like this. I need help and I don't know where to get it. If I don't get help, I don't know what's going to happen and if I do, everyone will think I'm crazy. Damned if I don't, damned if I do."

"You can't throw drugs at every problem."

"I need something." I pleaded with her. "This is not working. Nothing else is working." I looked up at her like a child does its mother when he's in need. "Please."

"Should I be worried about you? Should I be worried about those boys?"

A laugh on my part. "I thought these sessions were confidential."

"Kericho, I care about you. I care about what happens to you."

"Confidential until shit gets real." I got up and grabbed my purse.

"Kericho, don't just leave."

"I believe we're over time Dr. Hannah. And I gotta pee." The door closed on Dr. Hannah and just like that, it was done. I walked away leaving the past behind me. I didn't look back lest I be changed into a pillar of salt.

Chapter Twenty-Seven

Everything heals.

Glynda knocked on my door on the first day of spring to tell me she was moving back to New Orleans.

"Well come in," I said. "I just put my two year olds down for the night. You want a cup of coffee. I got some brewing. Whipped cream."

"Girl, I don't know how you do it. Coffee? I'd be up all night." She had a seat on my couch.

"Where's the clan?" I asked.

"Who Jordan and Atiba? Those kids are out being teenagers. It's Friday. I thought I'd let them."

"Hey, it's some alone time for you," I yelled from behind the fridge door. "Last chance. Coffee? Tea? A snack?"

"I just ate some leftovers. I'm fine."

"Suit yourself." I squirted whipped cream all over the top of my mug just like they do at Starbucks and sat down next to her. "So you're leaving huh? Well I'm gonna miss you."

"This is see you later. Not goodbye."

"When are you going?"

"We leave next week. We already got a flight outta here. An uncle of mine has us staying with him until we get ourselves settled. Ya know, its home."

"Well I'm happy for you. I really am." I sipped. "Part of me almost wants to come with you."

"You're always welcome. But you belong here."

I smiled. "Glynda...lately I'm not sure where I belong. I'm paddling, but I ain't moving. I don't know if I'm existing, or living. Kinda feel like I'm living day to day waiting to die."

"Babygirl! You got those two little boys. Those two precious little boys. You got a roof over your head, food to eat. You're good."

"You sounded like my sister. My sister and my Daddy."

"How's he doing? You don't talk about him much."

"I talk about him all the time. In my head. He's doing okay. He's strong. Stronger than I knew anyone could be. This cancer thing is going to blow over. I can feel it."

"That must be a good feeling to have."

"What do you think, Glynda?"

"What do I think about what?"

"What do you think happens when you die?"

"They say heaven's got pearly gates and streets of pure gold."

"Is that where you're going?"

"I sure do hope so."

"You think God puts you back together again. Like Humpty Dumpty sat on a wall."

She raised an eyebrow.

"See. I've got this theory. Life breaks us. We come all wrapped up like a ball of yarn and life unravels us. I haven't been able to figure out how to put myself back together."

"Girl all you need is some pie."

"Pie?"

"Apple. Peach, cherry, mince meat. Take your pick. That's

what my grandmother used to say. Pie cures everything."

I laughed. And sipped. "I wish it did."

"It does. If you believe."

I sat back and slumped. "I believed for a long time in a lot of things. I used to believe my mama was going to change. Used to think one day I'd come home and check my voicemail, and she'd be on there crying and everything. Telling me how sorry she is for never being there for me. She was always here in the physical and I love her for that. But she was never where I needed her most. Right here." I made a circle around my heart. "Never really made me feel like her love was unconditional."

"Oh come on baby. You gotta stop waiting on somebody else to make you happy."

"So what should I do?"

"Be happy! That's what you should do."

"That's what I'm trying to do. But you know, maybe I don't know what happiness feels like. How will I know when I get there if I ain't never been there before?"

"You telling me you've never been happy? In your whole life?"

My eyes welled up while I thought back to my days as a kid, playing barbies with Sunday, picking berries in the woods with Daddy. "Maybe when Daddy would come home from work and my sister and I would run to meet him at the door. He'd lift us up high over his head so we could touch the ceiling with our fingertips." I smiled. "Yeah, I was happy then."

"That's your problem. You're looking for euphoria. Some out of body experience that you expect to last your whole life. That's not happiness. Happiness starts here and here." She pointed to her head and then her heart. "See honey, you gotta first think it. Every action begins with the thought. Decide to be happy. Decide to be content no matter what life throws your way because it's gonna throw some daggers sometimes. But make a decision to be happy. Aren't you tired of being sad all the time anyway?"

"I really am. I really am tired of it."

"So then stop."

"Its not that easy."

"It sure is. Girl you just make it complicated. What do you like about you? What do you really really love?"

"I'm sure I can think of a few things."

"I'm sure you can think of many. Let's go." She held up a finger.

"You mean now?"

"I mean right now. List them. Number one?"

"I'm shy."

She didn't let down.

"People tell me all the time I'm such a pretty girl."

"No No No. This is not about other people. This is about you sweetheart. What do you like about you? Not what anybody else likes."

"I don't want to sound arrogant."

"Why not? It's okay to be an arrogant bitch sometimes. Here I'll go first. I'm fabulous. I'm fucking forty one and fabulous. Don't look a day over 35. My breasts still sit up like melons. My skin is like whipped butter. I like the way my profile looks when I pull my locs up tight. And I still make men drool when they get a taste of my kitty kat. I've been raising my kids for the last ten years alone, and I did a damn good job. Honor students. Both of them. Jordan's on her way to college next year. I'm a friend. I'm a genuine friend to the people in my life. I try to be loyal and I'm not saying I don't fuck up sometimes. I'm also human but I try. I can make cheesecake that melts in your mouth. Once upon a time I used to sing and I bet if I tried again, I could still do it beautifully. I've worked hard, and its paid off. I'm proud of me."

I grinned wide. "I like your list."

"That's the thing. It's *my* list." She quieted down, took my empty mug from me and set it on the coffee table. "Now tell me yours."

"Well." I wasn't looking at Glynda. I was looking past her, seeing my life spread out like a storyboard on the eggshell painted wall behind her. "I'm smart. I'm intelligent. Grace didn't think I could do it because I was a rebellious teen but I got into NYU. I think my essay was what did it. I'm a good writer. One day I'll be a great writer. I like my ambition. I went to Africa for a year and met some of the most beautiful people I've seen in my life. I've got drive. Sometimes I get stuck but I always somehow hold on to hope that it won't always be this way." I paused and smiled. "When I got pregnant with Kiefer and Kye, I decided I would let my obstacle be my testimony, not my excuse. And I am a great mother. I love my sons to death. I bent over backwards so many times for those little boys and they're only two. But they keep me sane. They keep me present. I'm pretty. I don't like my hands and I don't like my chin, but--"

"Uh uh...we're only talking about things you like."

"Ok. I'm cute damnit. I like the way my eyes roll up at the corners like a china doll. I like my small frame. I'm petit and I dig that. I know how to dress. My hair is always in place despite what curveballs the day throws me. I was born in July. The middle of the summer. I like that. Something sexy about that. I get bored sometimes, but I like that too, because it means I'm built for greatness. Mundane tasks don't suit me well. I'm a mother, a lover, a woman, a writer, respectively."

She applauded. I laughed. "Good job. Honey child if that ain't enough to make you happy, I don't know what is. You don't have everything, but look at what you do have." She looked around. "Damnit look at what you do have."

"You're right. I got you."

"You got me," She nodded.

"What was it like? Raising Jordan and Atiba all by yourself?"

"Their Daddy stayed in their life for a little while after we split. And now that we're finished talking about things we like about ourselves, I can tell you the things I don't. I don't know if I will ever stop feeling like I pushed him away. You know I was so bent on doing things my way. So stuck on believing I was always right. I mean I was right a lot of the time but had to be one or two times I was wrong."

I looked away.

"The kids were six and four when we divorced. He hated me because of the child support. I hated him because he wasn't paying. He'd stay away for weeks at a time and then show up out of the blue on a Tuesday wanting to see the kids. I told him they needed stability in their lives. That he should stick around or go. He chose to go."

"You can't blame yourself for that. That was his choice. Nobody can say anything to make me leave my children."

"Men are wired differently. With women, our children come first, pride second. With men, their pride comes first, children second. Or third or fourth. I hurt that man's pride. It was no big deal to me then. Even now, it’s not him I care about. It's my children. If there was something I could have done different for them to have their father in their lives, well if I could go back in time, I would."

I touched Glynda's hand with mine, stroked the veins just beginning to bubble through the skin. She was like me. My mirror image. Man was still around. He still picked up the children like clockwork every other Friday, but he was a stranger to me. We barely spoke. Not even a "hello" on those encounters, not even eye contact. Just a text message saying he was outside and then I walked the children out to him and turned around to go back indoors. The distance between us was growing and in a way it brought peace. The less we spoke the less room we had to argue, but the tension was still strong. It was a certain unavoidable discomfort that made my heart beat faster every time I saw him. If he felt the same, would he one day decide it was too much to bear?

Daddy, my heart and soul was my saving grace growing up. Where would I be without him? And my children, my pride and joy held my heart in theirs. If nothing more, I want them to be loved by as many and as much as possible.

"We all make mistakes Glynda. Don't we? It's how you learn how to live." She covered my hand with hers making a sandwich.

"I guess it is Kericho. I guess it is."

Chapter Twenty-Eight

The soul always knows what to do to heal itself. The challenge is to silence the mind.

Esi was a creature of beauty. She walked around broke everyday with a million dollar check in her pocket, and slept with men in hopes of finding that which she already possessed. She was looking for purpose in between bed sheets. Silly girl didn't know she would never find it there. I felt for her.

Spring of 2009 was quiet. Glynda was gone and the apartment across the hall was now an empty vessel. Some days when I heard noise outside my door, I thought she'd come back, realized she forgot that she was the only friend I had left and decided to stay after all. But when I opened the apartment door, I only saw an empty hallway that reminded me of what used to be.

Dr. Hannah was a thing of the past. Her therapy sessions were out of style and the past was dealt with as much as it could be. I hated her the first few weeks after we stopped. She was a waste of my time that made me feel worse about myself, not better. But the dreams subsided and then completely stopped and when I thought of it on Sundays, she didn't seem so bad.

Sundays were my favorite day of the week. The twins and I went to church these mornings. Came home and took our Sunday nap. I put the boys to bed and then strip completely naked. I climb in bed, pull the covers to my chin and slide my fingers in the moisture between my legs. After I finish, I lay there, watching the breeze outside my shadeless window and go into my head. These times, I ponder Dr. Hannah, and Esi, and the three G's. Gerald, Glynda, and Grace.

Gerald was in my life but for a season, and now he seemed like merely a figment of my imagination. I remembered our dance at Afrodisiac, the gentle way he rocked me in his arms, the brush of his lips on my cheek. Gerald represented the anticipation of happiness. He was what I looked forward to, what I hoped for. The romance that pervades the very idea of Gerald was and is the essence of love. He was the blueprint, my knight in shining armor. He was and is what my Uncle Jamie represented in the photo. My quintessential mate, my soul reincarnated. Gerald and Jamie were long lost loves.

And Grace. The woman who bore me. Her womb was my home before I came into this one. She housed my body, but bruised my soul. I wonder if she'd known what I would become, would she still have wanted me. I don't know if I have ever talked to my mother. Yes we have spoken, but I don't know if we have ever spoken on a level that broke the barrier that stands like the Great Wall of China between us. I talk but she never hears. I replay childhood memories. Her washing dishes at the kitchen sink. I approach, a girl of maybe seven...or eight. "Do you love me, Mommy?" I'd say curious. "What do you think?" she replied. Even in my prodding, the words never breached her lips. I was doomed searching for hope in my mother.

But I had a second mother in my rebirth. Yes that is how I think of it now. The truth is Dr. Hannah is next to Jesus in the hierarchy of saviors. Dr. Hannah was my mirror. I answered her but she only asked me the questions that I wanted so badly to ask myself. In a sense, she saved my life. I'd had suicidal thoughts but never called them that out loud. I never spoke of the issues in my head to another soul and in her I made them real. It has been six months since I've seen Dr. Hannah. I want to call her to say hello. We didn't leave things on a good note. I reach for my cell phone but I can't find her number. I must have deleted it, I tell myself.

A google search on my laptop returns the African American Psychologists Association website and the same picture I'd seen this time last year. The friendly woman with short neat dread locks. I dialed the office number listed and got a voicemail telling me the office was closed but to leave a detailed message and someone would get back to me. Nothing is open on Sundays.

"*This is a message for Dr. Hannah. My name is Kericho Blu. I was a client of hers and I was calling...I guess I was calling to thank her for saving my life.*" I hang up. I lay back onto my pillow and drift to sleep in the shadow of the sunbeam peering through my window.

There was a coffee stand outside my office building that sold dollar coffee in recycled paper cups. Monday morning, when the sun was high in the sky, on the first day of summer, I cut in front of a gentleman in a brown jumpsuit, Corbett scrawled across the front pocket.

"Sorry," I apologized. "I'm in a rush."

"No need. Woman as beautiful as you are deserves to be first."

I half smiled. Then a second look. Tobias. The guy from church. He was the color of my coffee. 1 cream.

"Hello again" he continued.

"Hi Tobias. What are you doing here? I haven't seen you downtown before." I handed the clerk four quarters in exchange for my coffee, and then took in the sun rays. "It's a beautiful day."

"It is. And you look just like sunshine. Matter of fact, I can't tell the difference between you and the sun." I smiled even though

I thought he was trying too hard. "I'm on location for a job." He pointed to a construction site in the distance. "Where do you work?"

I gestured to my building. "I haven't seen you at Parker Memorial. You disappear or something?"

"I go here and there. Early service." A beat. "Have breakfast with me."

"Didn't you hear me? I'm late for work."

"So? Spend the day with me instead. I'll pay you for today."

He was clever. I squinted. "Nice of you. I have to run."

I am always conscious of the way my butt moves when I walk. Men are watching, their perverted eyes always inclined to settle there to investigate the way my hips sway, the stride of my step, and the bounce of my flesh sitting round and neat atop my slender legs. He was sweet to ask me to breakfast, but I had bigger fish to fry. And Tobias would not be considered the type of man you invest time in. A gentle conversation, an ear on a lonely night maybe, another Man at best. But I wouldn't make the mistake of getting close to Tobias and one day waking up impregnated with his seed. That wouldn't happen to me again.

Today the office smelled like donuts. It was the quintessential smell of a New York office that signaled a morning meeting or a pile of emails awaiting me at my desk, or both. Anna met me at my cubicle before I could unload.

"Get settled, and then let's talk," she said. "This year's gala will be our biggest yet. Carol wants to raise 10 million."

I sighed. "I have a new list of prospects. Worked on it all last week. Amex has a new CEO. Get this, his sister was made a widow after 9/11. I think we can consider Amex a brand new anchor sponsor."

"I like the way you're thinking." Anna leaned against the wall, coffee mug in hand. I sat.

"What's this I smell?" I referenced the donuts.

"Oh donuts. Blake brought in a warm batch. New shop

opened across the street. They look pretty good. Get one."

"I don't mind if I do."

"Here, I'm up. I'll grab you one. Boot up the computer." I did and the first pop up I saw was an outlook message alerting me that today was Luke's birthday. I must have put the recurring day in my schedule last year. I watched it for a moment, the rectangle box obstructing my screen. I hadn't seen Luke in months. Not since the grocery store run in. Not since I let him go. If I had things my way, I would have erased him from my memory, no erased him from my very past, my own vivid history that painted a picture with strokes of heartbreak and ill luck. Luke was another "almost love" that did nothing but sour my appetite for the stuff. Yuck. My face turned up at the screen, my eyes still glued to that box. It was his birthday, another anniversary of the year he was born and a reminder of another year I had gone without a solution to him. The Luke problem. It was almost like that thorn Paul speaks of in the scriptures. A nagging hurt, a pain dug so deep it constantly chokes you but never kills you. I hated him. I hated what he did to me. He made me fall and didn't stand to catch me.

Amy returned with my donut to see me staring at the screen. "You seeing a ghost, lady?"

I turned. "No. No, no ghost. Just realizing today is an old friend's birthday. Remember Luke? My date for last year's gala."

"I do remember him. He was good looking. What happened to you and him?"

"Well we were never really dating. We were...just friends. Just...you know...acquaintances."

The next day, I got flowers at work. A dozen pink and white roses with a hint of baby breath. The card read:

They need lots of Sunshine

Thinking of you,

Tobias

917.234.2400

I was impressed so I stored his number in my phone. But I didn't call and probably wouldn't. The flowers were nice though and made me feel if just for a moment like I mattered.

Wednesday is the day my life changes. I come to work this morning in black pantyhose, a green knee length skirt and a sleeveless blouse. I eat yogurt for breakfast, the kind with fruit on the bottom and granola on top. It rains today, at times it pours. Work is a blur. Some paperwork, some emails. A staff meeting. I scarf down three tacos for lunch. The daycare calls a quarter after three. Kye is sick.

"I have to run Carol. I'll finish this memo tonight."

My phone vibrates again on my way out the door. Whoever it is must wait. Kye is smiling when I arrived. A hug. A kiss. I strap the twins in the car and pick up my dry cleaning on the way home. There is something on the news about the impending presidential election. A black guy named Barack Obama has a good shot. A car crash. Some kids drowned. I warm up some fish for dinner. Mashed potatoes and mac and cheese. The kids clean their plates. After their bath, I read a story. Hansel and Gretel. They are asleep before it is over.

My muscles ache so I start my bath water. I put on some music, Whitney Houston, and light a candle. I undress. Then I remember the call I missed. It was from Dr. Hannah's office. She returned my call. She left a message. I sit on the edge of my bed. I listen.

The woman speaking does not sound like Dr. Hannah. Her voice is much deeper. She has an accent, Caribbean.

"Hello. This message is for Kericho. Dr. Stephanie Hannah returning your call. Unfortunately, I think you may have called me in error. Have we met? You mentioned you were a patient of mine however I don't recollect treating anyone by your name. I'm sorry for the confusion. Perhaps it was another Dr. Hannah..."

This lady is not the Dr. Hannah I remember. I check the number. I replay the message. Again. And again. My hands went numb. *How could she not remember me?*

I drop the phone against my cold mattress. *Did I have the wrong Dr. Hannah? Where was the right one? Who was this Caribbean lady?*

Suddenly I felt cold. My nipples hardened and I sat motionless, nude, in the still of the room. I notice the bathtub is overflowing, but I do not budge. My heart races. I feel faint. My phone rings loudly and I am startled. Sunday's number flashes across the screen. I answer.

"Sunday"

"Hey Baby girl. Are you okay? You sound strange."

"I need help. Please come."

When I was a little girl, Sunday and I used to play paper house. It was like playing dollhouse, only on a flat surface with sheets of white paper. We glued the paper together at the edges and laid the house out on the floor. Then we went through Grace's old magazines and catalogues and cut out people, furniture, dogs and cats and put them in the house.

We imagined that they were a family and everything was perfect. When we got older, we grew out of it, but I spent the rest of my life trying to get back to that perfection, imagining life as I wished it would be. But now I know the struggle is in vain. We all live here in a place between consciousness and unconsciousness. We straddle the road between first making a wish and the wish coming true. The doubt, the uncertainties, the longing for something better is a part of the human experience. I just wish someone would have told me sooner.

Aren't we all just finding a way to cope? Defense mechanisms for the masses are the way out. We can't find a way out of this world alive, so we create one. We purpose a world within the confines of our own minds and experience life within that world. We convince ourselves that our perception of things is in fact the way it is, that all we see, is all there is. If we didn't, we'd be shattered beyond repair, our souls thrown to the dogs to devour. We'd be pressed and broken under the weight of the world, and the weight of the many trials it has to offer. We would become the vase on my grandmother's kitchen table, only remnants of what used to be. The content of things undone.

Sunday came over the night I had a nervous breakdown and found me lying naked facedown in the puddle of water that had taken over my bedroom. She called to me and I answered in a cataleptic state. When the ambulance arrived to take me away, Sunday covered me in a robe and packed the sleeping babies in her car to follow close behind. They tested my system for drugs, and then a cat scan on my brain. I went in and out of consciousness and heard doctors and nurses mumbling and shuffling around my bed. A feeding tube. A catheter. I woke up two days later in my own bed to the smell of bacon and sunlight.

The hardwood floor was cold on my bare feet. Someone had dressed me in a pair of grey sweats I hadn't worn since my pregnancy days. Sunday was at the stove.

"Hi." I said.

At that she turned abruptly.

"Where are the babies?" I asked her.

"You're out of bed."

"What happened to me?

"A lot."

"Where are the babies?"

"Mommy has them. She is taking care of them so I can take care of you. We didn't think they should see you this way."

I sauntered to the kitchen table and sat. "What time is it?"

"11."

I paused. Squinted at the brightness of the room. "Tell me."

Sunday turned the stove off and sat next to me. "Can I get you a glass of juice? Some tea?"

"Something has happened to Dr. Hannah, hasn't it?"

"Kericho, you kept mentioning Dr. Hannah in the hospital. You kept saying she would make it better and we had to find her. I told the doctors that I thought that was your therapist, so they tried to locate her. They did."

"Did they find the right one?"

"There is only one Kericho, on the entire east coast. She said you were never a patient of hers but had left her a strange voicemail a few days ago."

This again. I started to cry. "I saw Dr. Hannah every week, every Monday at 5:30. For almost a year!"

"Kericho."

"She works in a brownstone. Her office has a big oak desk and cream color leather couches."

"Kericho no."

I jumped from my chair and slammed my fists down. "I can show you!"

Sunday sat quietly, pity or sadness covered her. "Then show me," she said.

The drive to Dr. Hannah's office was quiet. No radio. Sunday didn't want to disturb me, so the silence was only broken with my occasional, "turn here" and "go straight at the light."

When we pulled up to the brownstone, it was closed. The second floor window had been busted in and no one was inside.

"Come on. Let's go inside," I said and hopped out. I found the lock broken when I tried the knob and I didn't find that strange. Sunday followed behind me. The floorboards were broken, paint chipped on the walls. The exposed brick was dirty. Someone had abandoned the place. They wanted me to look like I was crazy.

"Kericho. The doctor said sometimes when people go through things. You know traumatic experiences, they sometimes make things up in their head. It's a way to cope with the stress."

I turned to look at her.

"You told me you were seeing a therapist and I thought that was great. You talked about her like you two had some really intimate conversations. But no one else was there except you."

"There was a-- a receptionist. She sat...over there." I pointed to the back corner.

"What was her name?"

I shrunk back and then whispered, "I don't remember."

"I was so worried about you. When I found you there in that bedroom. I didn't know what happened. And then Dr. Hannah, the real Dr. Hannah, said it could be a sign of hallucinations, a mild form of schizophrenia."

I felt tears welling, stumbled backwards and had a seat against the wall. "How could I make that up? How could I make all of that up?"

"You needed someone to talk to. I'm so sorry I wasn't there for you. You just needed to sort some things out and I'm so proud of you because you found a way to do it."

"I found Dr. Hannah's picture on the internet. She looked so nice. I called her. I did."

"I'm sure you meant to Babygirl. Poor thing, you were so busy with work, and the kids. You just probably never got around to it. I talked to your physician. Dr. Kelly says it's a good idea that you start seeing someone. For real this time. She has a few names she can recommend."

"I told her everything. I told her about Man and Grace. I told her all about Luke and all of the other men that have hurt me. I told her about you Sunday. She has a lot of patients. I'm sure she just doesn't remember."

Sunday came to me and dropped her purse down beside me. We sat on the floor with our knees up, shoulder to shoulder. "Maybe. Maybe she did forget. What else did you tell her, Babygirl?"

I tilted my head back. "I told her how much I loved my sister. That you were my best friend. We handled Grace together. I told her about Africa. Esi and Gerald and Bella and Justice. I told her things went awry after I had the babies. And I told her about all of the fighting. Man hated me. And the credit card. And the jail time, and court. I told her about Luke and all of the men who took advantage of my vulnerability. She told me I had to be a better me. I had to stop being comfortable in my insecurities. She made the dreams stop."

"What dreams?"

"I used to have really bad dreams. Dreams I couldn't tell anyone about. I only told Dr. Hannah. And when I did, they stopped."

"She sounds like she's good at what she does."

"She really is. Only you don't know it until it's all over."

The initial thought that one may be losing her mind is enough to make her go ahead and do it. The manic depressants, the bipolars, the schizophrenics are only ok so long as they take their daily meds, a conscious effort, one that requires the patient to know she's on meds, and well, the knowledge of that alone is no comfort in a hopeless place. I often wondered if there is some way to tube feed the medication to a crazy person, while they sleep. This way they get better without ever knowing they were crazy in the first place. Depression stems from hopelessness. Confirmation that you're a certified lunatic that will have to take pills for the rest of your life simply to exist in this world without destroying yourself only adds fuel to the fire. Maybe dying is the better option.

I can't say I was ever completely hopeless. I found God in between the pages of despair and that one question became increasingly loud in my mind, in the room, any given room that I was in, and infiltrated the walls of my heart. It was an open ended question that never completed itself, it simply begged "What if?" What if things change? Sarah was an old woman when she gave birth to Isaac. What if God is working it out for my good? I never wanted to see the twins in pain when they got their annual shots, but they needed them so they wouldn't get sicker. What if I'm dreaming? The song says life is but a dream, the real living only begins on the other side of eternity. The what if was enough. The what if kept me warm on cold nights, it soothed me like a baby's bottle, it comforted me like the very hand of the Almighty was stroking my hair, massaging my temples. The what if carried over into an "It is so." The next morning after those bouts of depression was always better. The question became an answer and I could live again in some kind of certainty even if the certainty was only that I was uncertain.

A month later, when Grace and Sunday trusted me, they sent the twins home. I was well rested, and despite Sunday's encouraging a first run at therapy, I resisted going into therapy again. "I've been there, done that," I would say. "I'm cured so there is no need."

Yet how do you trust your senses again when they fail you? I questioned the existence of others in my life. Glynda, Leonard the Butcher, even Kiefer and Kye before photos confirmed for me their tangibility. In the attic of my mind, I accepted the flaws in my argument. Despite my memories of our sessions, the smell of the office, the feel of the leather against my often sweaty palms, the pristine oak desk, the yellow notepad Dr. Hannah used, my reality was false. But although it was happening within the confines of my own head, how should that mean it was any less real? It was false to others, but true to me. Dr. Hannah would forever be an integral part of my life, a nugget of influence that put me back together again. I had a need that was left unfilled, and in my creation of Dr. Hannah, I filled it.

Grace called twice. Daddy called often. He called to say hello. He called to ask how I was doing. He called to ask me if I had taken my medication.

"You ave to do the doctors orders specifically," he said. "If you don't it might appen again."

Daddy didn't know I had refused further tests and so I wasn't prescribed any medication. I don't want to live like that, a slave to six pills a day. I lied to Daddy to keep the peace. Perhaps no different from his lies to us a year before.

"Daddy?" I asked him that day on the phone. "Can I ask you something?"

"Sure you can"

"Do you love me?"

"Of course I do. You are my daughter?"

"Of course you do what?"

"Heh?"

"Of course you do what?" I repeated slower this time.

"I lav yu."

I laid in my bed that morning with the phone to my ear and remembered a similar scene three years ago in a hospital bed in Accra. I told my mother I was pregnant and waited for words that never came. Maybe I should have told Daddy. Perhaps the subsequent recourse of my life would have gone differently had I spoke to Daddy that night in that hospital bed. Perhaps I would not have given my body to Gerald, a body already overused and worn down. Perhaps I would not have treated Man the way I did hoping to find some unconditional love in him even in the times I pushed him away. Perhaps I would not have run to Leonard or back to Luke. I wonder if my life trajectory would have taken a different path if Daddy told me he loved me that night when I needed to hear those words the most.

"Thank you Daddy," I managed through welling tears. "I love you too. Very much. Very very much."

I dreaded a return to work. The crew sent Get Well Soon cards and flowers. It's unclear as to whether they actually knew what the problem was. They knew I was dealing with "personal stuff." Anna called with news that another bouquet of roses arrived from Tobias. They were white, a symbol of death. Something had died in me. The last morsel of sanity. The card read:

To the lady in a rush. Stop sometime to smell the roses.

From Tobias

My birthday fell on a Saturday this year. Sunday called me in the morning to tell me that Nigel fellow had proposed, and that I should be happy for her. I forced a smile and a congratulations.

"I need you to be my Maid of Honor," she said.

"I can't wait." I lied.

For my birthday, I made cornish hens, sweet potato casserole, smothered greenbeans and strawberry cornbread. The twins and I ate in front of the TV, and after they fell asleep, I had a glass of wine. I chose the bottle because it was pretty. A royal blue label trimmed in metallic silver. When I finished the last swallow, I glanced at the clock. Just 9:30. Much too early to turn in on a Saturday night. I wanted to talk to someone. Not Sunday. She didn't have time for me anymore. Not Glynda. She was miles away. My hormones were ablaze, my sense of touch was extra sensitive. I wanted to feel sexy. I wanted to talk to a man.

I stared at the entry in my phone for a full minute. I hoped I wouldn't look silly. When I heard it ringing, I didn't know what I would say but imagined the words would come. It had been over a month since I had seen Tobias that sunny morning at the coffee stand. Since then, I had taken a break from church services, I had had a nervous breakdown, spent two days hospitalized and had been certified a lunatic. I should spare him. It rang four times before he answered. His voice was exactly what I needed to hear. It was deep and rustic. He sounded just like hot chocolate in the middle of a storm. It soothed me, invigorated me. My panties moistened. My nerves jumped.

"Hello. Is this Tobias?"

"Speaking."

"Tobias, this is...Kericho. I wanted to thank you for the flowers. They're beautiful."

A pause. "Kericho! Yes, I remember. Sunshine."

I smiled loudly. "That's right."

"You sure take your time getting in touch."

"I had quite a few things going on. I apologize. I certainly didn't want to be rude."

"No offense taken. What do you do lady?"

"For work?"

“For life.”

“I'm in Development for The Memorial Project. 9/11."

"That's noble work. You like it?"

"I used to. It depends which day you ask me. It's not really that noble." I twisted my hair between my fingers.

He laughed. "Why do you say that?"

"I don't know. I guess in the beginning I wanted to put my soul into something that would make a difference. But most people at these nonprofits don't want to be there and if they do, it's for all the wrong reasons. Every industry is nothing but a competition. No different in nonprofit. It's a competition among organizations to see who can charge the most per plate at their annual benefit."

"I see. But you're in it for the right reason. That counts for something right. It's people like you who change the world."

He thought too much of me. "And what do people like you do? Besides stay home on a Saturday night?" Some humor maybe.

"Ahh. Jokes. I'm home because I'm tired. Long week. I worked fourteen hours yesterday. Got in late. I'm in construction. I work on a lot of city projects. Old building renovations. I'd love to go into architecture"

"Creative."

"I am. I love art. All kinds. You know it takes a certain level of imagination to be able to create something from nothing." "I once heard that all artists are deeply troubled. Writers, great musicians, photographers... architects."

"Maybe. Maybe that's true. I know I ain't really never been normal."

"Nobody's normal. We're all kind of fighting our own battles. Ya know. That's something I've found to be true."

"I know but I'm not talkin 'bout that kind of normal. I just mean I never did normal things."

"Tobias, none of us are normal."

"No, I mean you become an adult, you get married, buy a house, have some kids. That's normal."

I laughed. "I guess. I guess you could say that. But I mean if that's the formula, then I ain't normal either."

"Alright so what do you think about unnormal people going out to lunch next Sunday?"

"Two abnormal people?" I corrected him. "I don't know about that."

"What's not to know?"

I hesitated. "Tobias."

"Yes."

"That sounds nice. But—look I don't want to waste your time."

"Then I guess that means we should have lunch as soon as possible."

Starting over always felt like defeat. There was Man. There was Leonard. There was Luke. Yet the new thing always brought with it hope, for my greatest joy is having something to look forward to. The hope of tomorrow is a kiss on the verge of love, darkness on the verge of light, misery on the verge of happiness, hell on the verge of heaven.

I wonder sometimes why God dealt me this hand. I mean, there are some people, really smart people, who grow up, go to school, finish that and then go to school some more. Then they meet a man who touches them on the inside the way they've always wanted to be touched. Then they have a dream wedding and buy a dream house and have some dream kids. Maybe that's what Tobias meant by normal. I been chasing that but now-a-days it feels like chasing the wind, chasing something that's just not meant for me.

God, quite literally, might be the cruelest man I know. Worse than the worst kind of man, I mean, a mortal man. All the boys who hurt me, the ones that took my innocence and ran off holding it out in front of them like you taunt a baby with a toy, those boys were only doing what was in their nature to do. They couldn't help it if they were wired to be selfish and treat women like fleshy clumps of breasts, ass, and pussy. They were born in sin, destined to be bullshitters. But God? They say before anything was anything, there was God. There he was in all his glory sitting on a throne dolling out who gets what and how much they get and in what fashion and for how long. He did that. God designed me to yearn for love and joy, and respect, and comfort, and a human touch, one that wouldn't hurt me or neglect me, or make me feel less than or misunderstood. God put that in me. He made me want it so bad that I can't breathe or eat or sleep or even get along in this life without driving myself insane unless I have it. He did all that and then decided not to give me anything that he designed me to want. No, need. He made a decision that he wasn't going to fulfill my needs. And it would be one thing if he couldn't do anything about it. But the man is God. He's fucking God! And that's a mighty cruel God to do a thing like that.

So I accepted Tobias' offer because I've gotta find some way to pass the hours.

I took myself shopping, bought a knee-length dress and a new lipstick. Purple Haze. Modest but sexy. By the following Sunday, I was ready, dressed, oiled, hair pulled back tight. I would tell him the truth. When he asked, for the first time in my life, I would tell the truth.

Lunch was at a quaint pizzeria, Red Tomato. Some bread and a bottle of wine for the table. And a pizza.

"So tell me about yourself?" I opened after the first bite.

"What do you want to know?"

"What brought you to Parker Memorial? The new members class. We joined around the same time."

He took a bite of pizza. Chewed. Swallowed. "I was in the Mission. It's a rehab for recovering drug and alcohol addicts." He paused for my reaction. I gave him none. "I'm from Harlem. Grew up between there and my dad's place in Long Island. My mother was an addict. My father was abusive. My brother died of AIDs. My sister died of cancer. I woke up one morning and it was just me, four white walls, and a crack pipe. So I had to ask myself what was I doing for the rest of my life."

"So you checked into The Mission?"

He nodded. "Parker Memorial supports The Mission along with some other churches in the area. But you know I didn't just get introduced to church at The Mission."

We both sipped our wine. "No? You grew up in the church?"

He swallowed hard. And then he said to his plate. "I'm a preacher."

At this my eyes widened. "Yeah? I wouldn't have guessed. What kind of preacher?"

"A crackhead preacher."

A nervous smile.

“You have a pretty name. Kericho. You know I forgot your name. That day at the coffee stand. I couldn’t remember it. I was afraid to ask. So I just called you sunshine.”

“Is that what that was about? I thought you wanted me to feel special.”

“I do want you to feel special. You should feel special. You are special.” Typical guy statement. “I was new to the church. And you know Christians don’t always act like Christ. You were friendly. You spoke when no one else did.”

“No sense in not speaking. We’re all there to make friends. Fellowship. Learn how to be better individuals.” I chewed silently.

"Tell me about your kids. What are their names?"

"Kiefer and Kye."

"Kiefer? That's different."

"Ever hear of Kiefer Sutherland? The actor."

"No."

"I heard the name and liked it."

He nodded. “You want any more?"

"What kids? I guess so. I don't know. Not for a while. I've had a tough couple of years. If I do it again, I want to do it right."

"You have any help?"

"The kids' dad is still involved. My family helps when they can. But I'm not an easy person to help. I like to do things my way."

"Hey I'm the same way. Working on finding a balance though. Everybody needs help. Classic smart man's mistake is thinking no one's smarter than him. It's all about perspective. Didn’t you tell me no matter where you are in life, everyone is fighting their own battle?"

"What battle are you fighting?"

He finished his first slice and reached for another. "I spent a long time hurting a lot of people. The way I grew up, you assumed the worst in people, not the best, so you know I always learned to have my guard up. Always put myself first. Tried to protect me...and in doing that, I sabotaged a lot of relationships. Didn't speak to my father for like twenty years. He died in '97. I was just beginning to see if I could put that back together."

"Twenty years is a long time. Why?"

He sighed. "Umm." Chewed. "When I was a kid, I played football. Almost got a scholarship to play in college down in Florida. My parents were going through some things. Found out my Daddy was running around on my mother. They ended up separating and I was angry and I blamed him. Only I took it out on some kid on the field over something stupid. Got in a fist fight, broke his nose. All this in front of a recruiter. Lost my scholarship. At the time, it felt like I lost everything."

"And you blamed your dad?"

"I just felt like he was never the kind of father I wished I had. My parents split. They were never married. I graduated high school and stayed home. Called myself taking care of my mother. She died two years after I finished high school. Then I spent years working a bunch of dead end jobs going nowhere fast."

"Sounds like the story of my life..." I took another bite.

He chewed. Swallowed.

"Kericho, do you believe in God?"

"I do." I smiled with a mouthful. "You know that."

"Then you already know that God can turn things around fast as soon as you make a decision to trust him."
"Is that what happened for you?"

"I'm hard headed. God opened a ton of doors. I just never walked through any of em. I guess The Mission was a step in the right direction. I was tired of living that way."

"Good for you. So how did things end with you and your dad?"

His third slice. "I reached out to him a few times. Never exactly had the opportunity to have the kind of conversation I wanted to have."

"Me and my mom are going through something similar. I let

her down when I got pregnant. I let her down when I didn't get married. I just wanted her to be proud of something, ya know."

"Well I think you have a beautiful spirit. Don't let anyone take that away. Not even your mother."

"A beautiful spirit?" I blushed. "How can you tell?"

"I'm nervous sitting here with you. I don't get nervous. Where I'm from, you have to be a power player to stay in the game. Everyone thinks their tough and everyone carries a pistol but I stay calm. My hand is always steady. But you? You have my palms sweating."

I laughed. "What!"

"You do. Believe it. Feel." He showed me his left palm. It was moist."

"Nice to know I have that effect."

After lunch, we walked for an hour. Him on the outside, me on the inside, my palm tucked inside his. He made me feel safe. I watched his stride, shorter than it could have been. He was careful to accommodate me.

"Three options," he started when the conversation winded down. "I know a good place where we can get some sweets. They have great ice cream. We could do that. A friend of mine is a musician. Used to play backup for Prince. He's doing his own set tonight at The Bluenote. Nice little scene in there. Or...if you want to party, we can go downtown later tonight. The Fat Black Pussycat is always fun. Good music. A lot of energy in there."

"A preacher at The Fat Black Pussycat?"

"Why not?"

"I don't know. I'm a little tired. You know I have work in the morning."

"Don't tell me you're ready to call it a day. Give me one more hour. Whatever we do, I'm gonna make sure you get home safe."

"I like The Bluenote. Your friend play the sax?"

He stopped mid stride. "Does he?"

It was dark. Almost a midnight blue inside that place. The air was cool. We sat at the corner of the bar in the back, me on a stool in front, nestled between his legs. He wrapped his arm around me to maneuver between stroking my waist and resting it on my thigh. I let him. I sipped another glass of red wine just as the friend's set was starting. He was a skinny dude, butter brown with messy dreadlocks, blowing on the saxophone so hard, I could feel it in my bones. Music so smooth I wanted to lay in it.

A few more sips of wine and then it happened. I closed my eyes, rested my head on Tobias' chest, and if just for this moment, right now, everything was perfect. I didn't think of Man. I didn't think of Leonard the Butcher, or Gerald, or Luke. I didn't think of Dr. Hannah, what was and what wasn't. Right now, I only thought of Tobias, felt his lungs expanding, his hand on my thigh. I felt him. And everything was right in the world.

The next morning, I woke up with a headache from the wine and a smile on my face that quickly turned upside down.

Chapter Twenty-Nine

Tomorrow…death comes.

"He's not all there Baby Girl. It's like he's got amnesia or something. I found him in his room sitting on the floor in a pile of poop. He smelled like urine." Sunday's voice was cracking on the other line. She was crying. "Something...something's wrong."

When Daddy first got sick, I used to close my eyes tight and imagine life without him. It never seemed real. It was almost like when Sunday and I would play paperhouse when we were small. It was a make believe world where everything was as we believed it ought to be. A piece of the puzzle was always missing when I tried to pretend there was no more Daddy. We'd speak of him in the past tense. *Remember how Daddy loved to sing. Remember those songs, those African songs. And the food. He made Mommy cook ugali every night. And remember the games he played, and his favorite robe, and those red pajamas.*

The idea of Daddy being dead was foreign and awkward as if the very thought didn't belong in my mind. It didn't fit nicely with the other thoughts. It didn't stick. It is inevitable that we all must die and yet we never really think of death. None of us. We never consider death. We never allow it to settle in our minds. It's always a fleeting thought. We believe yes, we must die, but certainly not today, and probably not tomorrow and this goes on until we dismiss the thought altogether. Dying is something other people do.

My father, in his sixties, or late fifties, we never have been sure, is expected to live forever. If you get sick, you take medicine. If the medicine doesn't work, you take more medicine. Sometimes you have to be aggressive, surgery, or radiation, or, God forbid, remove a limb, but die? Dying is never an option.

Sunday was always the emotional one, making mountains out of molehills. Her weeping was an overreaction since Daddy was having a bad day and soon he will be better and we will all wonder what a waste all of those tears were.

"Well let me talk to him," I said to her. "Are you with him now." I sat up in bed, wiped the sleep from my eyes.

"We're here at the house waiting on an ambulance. Daddy's sitting here with me. He's awfully quiet."

"Put him on the phone." I cleared my throat and sat up straight on the edge of my bed.

When Daddy spoke, he was like a ghost. A zombie from Night of the Living Dead. "Alo," he said slowly.

"Daddy. What's going on Daddy?"

Silence.

"Daddy why are you worrying Sunday? Are you okay?"

"I am okay. Just tired."

"Daddy who am I? Who are you talking to?"

"I know you. I know it is you Kericho."

I smiled, remembering the way he picked me up when I was a kid, over his head to reach the ceiling. I remembered the dance recital that he almost missed. I remembered our conversations about Grace. About love. I remembered meeting him in the airport. Me, post-pregnancy pushing a stroller with two babies, meeting his gaze...wondering what would come next. "Kericho

Blu," he had said. It was recognition and acknowledgment. "I know you Kericho."

"Daddy. Cooperate with the doctors. I'm coming down and I'll see you soon."

"Okay. See you soon."

"I love you very much. Very much Daddy."

"And you too."

I drove down to the hospital in silence, just the wind rapidly beating against my face and my heart pounding out of my chest.

Daddy died that night. When I got to the hospital, he was sleeping. But this was a different kind of sleep. He reminded me of sleeping beauty and her hundred year nap. Not even a kiss on his lips could wake him.

Brain hemorrhaging in the left ventricle rendered Daddy unresponsive. Surgery was the only option and really wasn't an option at all since Daddy was too old and his condition had deteriorated immensely.

The doctor's response was grave. "He won't survive surgery. I'd be surprised if you could find a doctor who would even attempt it."

So instead Daddy was transported to hospice, a floor that reeked of disease. It was where the hospital sent people to die. On that day, me and Sunday and Grace came together and prayed around his bed in a half circle for the angels to come down from heaven and move mountains. We ordered pizza and sat in that room eating around Daddy, our centerpiece.

"You think he'll wake up?" I had said watching his eyes for movement. His mouth drooped on the right side, his chin moist with saliva. "It's like his eyes are glued shut."

"I have some things I still need to discuss with your father. Financial arrangements. I don't know where he wants to be buried," Grace said.

Sunday shot her a dirty look. "What?" You can't be serious."

"We haven't discussed the arrangements," Grace defended

herself.

"Mommy. There's a good chance Daddy won't wake up. Did you really think this was something that could wait until the last minute? Doctors say this is the end. He said people in his condition rarely ever wake up."

When I was in high school, my English teacher assigned us a project. We had to write an essay comparing our perception of ourselves with others' perception of us. I started with my family and asked them to name my top five weaknesses. Grace told me I don't worry enough. I never met anyone who encouraged me to worry more. But there in that hospital room, I could see that Grace was the one not taking the situation as seriously as me and Sunday would have liked.

"I have to get home. Take some meat out for dinner," she continued.

"Mommy. Fuck the meat. Daddy could die any minute. Do you even care?"

Grace got up and dusted off her pants. "I'll be right back."

When we could no longer hear her footsteps in the hallway, I reached across Daddy and took Sunday's hand in mine. "You know people have different ways of dealing with death."

She sucked her teeth. "Yeah. Guess they do. Don't mean I have to like it."

"Daddy spent his life fighting with that woman. Maybe better he spend his last moments without her." Sunday looked up at me and then at Daddy, still Sleeping Beauty. "You remember any good times? When was the last time they kissed and meant it?"

She smiled. "I wish I could remember."

The sun set outside his bay window. We said another prayer. This time we didn't ask God to move any mountains. Daddy was the lucky one. Death is not the end. It's only transition. He was entering a life much better than the one we had to endure. The prayer was for me and Sunday. The mountain may be there to stay but we needed strength to climb.

"What do you think heaven's like Baby girl?"

"Remember those apple pie milkshakes we had when you were sick?"

"Those shakes were so good. They were the best thing about that crazy house. They were better than sex."

"An eternal orgasm. A lifetime supply of apple pie milkshakes. That's what heaven's like."

Sunday started crying again. "I can't imagine what life will be without Daddy."

"Don't cry. Just think. What if he pulls through this thing? Wakes up, gets back to health. Five years from now, we'll be saying 'remember that time we thought Daddy was dying." I said it for me. But it made Sunday smile through the tears.

Maybe God heard me because Daddy's breathing quickened. His eyelids fluttered, and Sunday and I looked intently.

"Daddy," she called.

He struggled but I saw the white of his eyes peak through his wrinkled skin and my heart jumped. This was my moment. "Daddy, we love you," I said his hand held tight in mine. "We love you and you gave us a great life. Don't forget that." I knew it was the end. I don't know how but it was the way he watched us but didn't speak. His mouth never left that awkward position, drooped to one side. He heard. He understood. He gave us this moment to say goodbye.

Sunday sobbed and held his other hand like a sandwich in hers. "We love you so much Daddy. And everything is going to be okay now. This is not goodbye. It's see you later." Daddy tried. I could see he tried to stay awake. Not for him, but for us. He wanted us not to be sad.

Cheer up, I heard him say on the inside. *Cheer up*. And then he was gone. He closed his eyes to slumber and exhaled deeply. One time. Two times. That's it. The last breath left his body like an eternal rest. Peace at last. Apple pie milkshakes.

We stayed there that way for a long time. Clasping Daddy's

hands. Sunday on one side, I on the other. I sat back in my chair, a single tear streaming down my cheek, and then finally, "Let's call Mommy."

The days after were an array of feelings. I stayed at Mommy and Daddy's house for a week up until the funeral. Anna and Mrs. Blaney said I should take as much time as I needed. Man kept the twins. I was a mess. Caskets come in all colors. Shades of blue, to green, to silvers and golds.

"Daddy wouldn't want us to spend a lot of money," I told Grace through tears and a shaken voice. We settled on a metallic pewter with silver trim. Tobias called twice and all voicemails and text messages went unanswered.

The door bell rung consistently. Ladies from Grace's church brought over sandwiches and cakes, pies and fruit baskets. Neighbors had flowers delivered. Daddy's family came just to sit and talk, and laugh. We stayed up late talking about Daddy and reminiscing on old times. His brother flew in from Kenya with a whole tin full of chapati.

One night, we sat in the living room, Sunday, Grace, and I, along with uncles and cousins on my father's side, drinking rum punch and telling jokes.

"Daddy used to sing us songs when we were little in Luo," Sunday said. "Funny thing is, I still remember the words, but I had no clue what he was saying. Yandere. Uchengawitiyandere." She sang. I smiled. Then the group laughed out loud.

"That sounded like you were speaking some other language. That's not Luo," my auntie said. She corrected her.

"I have an idea," I said. "I'm delivering a speech at Daddy's funeral. I want to say something in Luo to start. You know to welcome everyone. Daddy would like that."

"I think that' s a very good idea."

"I need your help with the translation."

My cousin Eric with the thick mustache spoke up. "Send meh whaat you wud like to say. I can translate."

That night I found an old card I had gotten Daddy for Father's Day. The poem inside was a perfect reflection of my feelings right now. I jotted down the words in an email and sent to Eric to translate for me.

Tobias texted the next morning. "Miss your face. Is everything ok?"

I wrote back this time. "Hey. I don't mean to be distant. My father passed a few days ago. I'm out of town for a while."

A quick response. "So sorry to hear that Kericho. I know we don't know each other well, but if there is anything at all I can do, please let me know."

The funeral was on a Saturday. Pastor John, Man's Daddy, delivered the eulogy. Kiefer and Kye's father's father eulogized their mother's father. I spotted Man way in the back. When I got up to speak, nothing else in the world mattered than that moment right there. My knees shook. My hands quivered, but I got through it. The tears came later.

When I got back home with the twins, my house was as I left it but it seemed like a million years had passed. Daddy was dead, but life goes on. Flowers were waiting for me on my desk at work. This time, they were from Anna and the crew. The card simply read, "We're here."

I made an attempt to be normal again. I stayed busy. Idle moments gave way to sadness, so I worked late, mainly sitting and not really working, played with the children and went to church for Sunday service, Wednesday service, and extracurricular activities. I was driving home late one night when Tobias called. I let it go to voicemail.

Sunday stopped by two weeks after Daddy died to show me a catalog of headstones. We sat perusing at the kitchen counter.

"Which one do you like Babygirl?"

"I guess any is fine. I just want to get past this."

"You and me both. Nigel and I want to get started on the wedding planning. I still need to find a dress, and a venue. Just so much to do."

I shot her a look. "You're still going through with it?"

"Why wouldn't I go through with it?"

I looked back down at the catalog. "I guess I just thought with everything that's happened, you might put that on hold for now."

"Kericho, the last thing we need to do is put our lives on hold. I mean until when? Daddy's dead. For good. I want to put this behind me and move on. That's what Daddy would want."

"Sure. You know best."

"I thought you were happy for me."

"Hey look. Whatever."

"You're not, are you?" She smirked. "I knew it. What's it going to take for you to show some humility?"

"What are you talking about?"

"Everything is not always about you."

"Look Sunday. You've been married before. You should be happy someone cares enough to tell you you're making a mistake."

"Fuck you."

"Get out. I don't need this."

"What about the headstone?"

"Whatever you and Mommy decide is fine with me."

That night I sat in my room looking through old photo albums. Daddy really was a beautiful soul. Most beautiful person I've ever met. His smile bared a thousand teeth, white like elephant ivory set against his dark skin. And he was happy. Not because everything was perfect in his life but because he lived in the moment. He had a family, a home, and food everyday. What more could a man ask for? I found a picture of Daddy with Kiefer and Kye when they were babes. He was sitting on the couch in an undershirt, one twin in each arm. I took it out and taped it to my mirror. I want the kids to always remember.

The phone startled me. Tobias. I breathed deeply before I answered. "Hello?"

"Hi." He said and then waited.

"Hey."

"Sunshine. I was afraid I may have lost you forever. How you feelin?"

This time his voice sounded like Columbian coffee, dark, rich, and smooth. "No. It's not a bad time. You know I just have a lot on my plate. My father passed and I feel like I'm starting from scratch putting my life back together. Again."

"That's a big task Kericho. You need some help?"

"I have to sort some things out. I don't want to put you in the middle of anything."

"I want to see you again. That may sound selfish considering what you're going through. But I want to be here for you."

"You don't even know me."

"Exactly. That's what I want to work on. I like what I do know. I can tell there's a lot more to you, a whole lot of stuff under the surface."

"You know...you are selfish. You just can't have what you want when you want it."

"Ok. But with all due respect...you are too."

I settled back on my bed and drew my knees to my chest.

"Why are you running away Kericho? Do you want me to leave you alone?"

I was silent. I didn't know what I wanted. I didn't want to get hurt once he realized how much of a mess I was.

"If you really want me to leave you alone. If that's what you want. Say it. And I will."

I said I would tell the truth. "Tobias. I like you. My dad died a couple of weeks ago. My sister and I had a big fight today. So I don't know where to start with you."

"You want to tell me about your Dad? You could start there."

A half smile. He was Dr. Hannah. Only he was real. "They

called it a brain hemorrhage. He's been fighting cancer for a couple of years now. My sister called me the morning after our date." I told. I told him about the day I met Daddy in the airport. His last days at the hospital. The funeral. I told it all. And I wasn't afraid. And he listened.

Chapter Thirty

Are we here? Or are we not here?

The first time Tobias invited me over was on a Sunday. After church, he said he would make the twins and me lunch. His apartment wasn't much. Its best asset was the bay window that overlooked the outskirts of the city. He caught me gazing and came to me. Put his arm around my shoulders.

"You see that? The brick building over there with the cross?"

"Yeah. Is that a church?"

"Was a church. That was my project."

"You built that?"

"It was an old Apostolic church in the eighties. Takes up nearly a block. There was a fire that burned the building partially and it was vacant for over a decade. We dug it out, renovated it, and turned the whole thing into luxury condos."

"Sounds a little eerie."

"Why do you say that? It's like living somewhere that's already blessed by God."

"Well when you put it like that....."

"We could go over and see it if you want to."

"Maybe later. I'm enjoying your place. It's nice."

"Well I cleaned for company. Trust me its not always like this. Don't be alarmed if you come over unannounced."

"I wouldn't do that."

"You don't believe in surprises?"

I spotted a painting on the far wall. Malcolm X. One of those cheap portraits you get from the street vendors in Harlem. I'd seen the image before but this time his gaze held me captivated. "Malcolm," I said. "He somehow adds character to your home." I turned to walk towards it but Tobias pulled me back. He pulled me in close and before I could pull away, he kissed me. He held me firmly, and moved his tongue inside my mouth. I kissed back and my heart sped up. The temperature in the room rose 20 degrees by the time we pulled away. I caught my breath staring at him.

"You're great, Kericho." His gaze was hypnotizing. I wrestled to look away. Embarrassed. He saw my discomfort and changed the subject. "You hungry?"

A pause. Then peering back into his eyes, "I could eat."

For lunch he grilled fish, while I snacked on cherries. He had one of those heavy coffee table books resting on the corner table. I looked closer and saw it was biblical commentary on the book of John. I ran my finger along the engraved golden letters on the cover before I opened it to see the inscription. *"To Tobias. From Zora. 97' 98' 99'… and still going strong."* It read.

We ate in peace at a corner table. Wooden. Worn. The chair cushions were still covered in plastic. I watched his hands, carefully bringing the fork to his mouth. He tasted the food for a moment before chewing and swallowing. On some bites he even closed his eyes, those deep set wide eyes. His nose was pronounced but not too big or small, a perfect centerpiece for his face. A strong jawline, characteristic of a man of great honor. A face fit for a magazine cover. Gritty. Hard but soft at the same time. Maybe he was 49. I always hesitated to ask. It never seemed like the right time.

This was our fourth date. The second was supposed to be dinner and a movie. But it was a long dinner. Between the wait for a table and my long winded stories, we missed the movie and ended up calling it a night. He called twenty minutes after he took me home and rode off in the taxi once I was safe inside.

"I miss you already," was his opener. "I feel like talking some more." That night we watched the sunrise together. Me in my bedroom, him in his. We talked about many things but I was careful to leave out the bit about my bout with insanity. He told me smugly that he lost his virginity when he was 8 to his sixteen-year-old babysitter. I told him he was raped and that's not something to be proud of. He joked he may need to seek counseling. Counseling. That was a sore spot for me. To tell him I had gone through counseling or not. Most days I still wasn't sure.

Our third date was a housewarming party for one of his coworkers. I wore a modest knee length black dress with lace detail. He told me I looked heavenly and introduced me to his colleagues as his "lady." There were several men and their wives, all upwards of age 40. The men were gentlemen. The women stared at me. We snacked on beers and homemade chicken wings, courtesy of the lady of the house.

Halfway through my second beer, I got clumsy and dropped it, splashing drops on Tobias. He chuckled softly, asked if I was drunk and suggested it was time to go. In the cab, he remembered he was still hungry so we went to Pop Burger to fill our bellies.

"This is so good," He said in between bites. "And that's huge coming from me. I don't eat much red meat. Bad for the heart."

"I could never give up burgers and bacon."

"You shouldn't say that. God never intended for us to eat meat."

I raised an eyebrow.

"The Garden of Eden has a lot to say about God's original intent. My old Pastor...you should meet him. He's one of the best.

I never heard a church get into the Bible as deep as he does. We study Hebrew translations, original context. All that stuff."

"If I told you church saved my life that would be an understatement."

"Did church save your life, or did God save your life?"

"I'd say a lot of both. I wasn't doing well for a long time Tobias. I was a new mom. I was struggling. Things didn't go as planned."

"Whose life really does? I wonder Kericho, are we here, or are we not here?"

Another eyebrow raise.

"It's like when you read a book or watch a movie. Are the characters real…or fake?"

"I guess they're kinda both. They're fake cus its just a movie. They're all just following a script. But the screenwriter had to base his material on something. He had to have some inspiration ya know. So the characters are real to him. Real in his head."

"Ah ha. Real in his head." He sipped his soda, eyes glazed with thought. "It all starts with a thought. Thoughts give birth to reality. This burger I'm eating? Somebody thought about this burger. Then they put it together. That dress you have on, as good as it looks on you, somebody had to think about that. This chair I'm sitting in, the shoes on my feet, the walls that are holding this whole building together…somebody had to think about it first." A pause. But he wasn't finished. "And God did the same thing." Now a laugh. "He said 'let there be light', and there was light. He had to think about it first. He thought about Adam. He thought about Eve. And then they were."

I stopped chewing.

"So, these characters you say, exist in the head," he continued. "We only really exist in God's head. We're just a part of his imagination. Our lives are just a part of the story. A script…that God wrote."

Wisdom…from an old man.

He walked me all the way home that night. It was warm, the moonlight was bright. I wanted a kiss on the lips. He teased me with one on the cheek. I thought of Daddy and whether he would approve. I think he would. I think he would but one could never be sure. Just three months without him and the wound was still fresh. I wondered if Tobias was merely a band aid, some pacifier, a remedy for the symptoms of heartbreak. Or was he the real thing. One could never be sure.

I haven't spoken to Sunday in weeks. My anger subsided but the fear didn't. I lost three souls this year. The three people who completed me were long gone. And Sunday, the greatest of them all. *I should call her,* I remember thinking that night. I imagined the conversation the way I wanted it.

"Sunday, I miss you."

"Miss you too Babygirl."

"Sorry about that stuff I said about you and Nigel."

"Ain't no thang. What's new with you?"

"I met a new guy. His name is Tobias."

"You like him?"

"He's sweet. We go on dates. Real dates."

Oh but the way we imagine things is never as they actually are or turn out to be. Now we are back at Tobias' dining table, after a morning at church.

"Do you like the food?" he asked me after a few minutes.

"You're a good cook."

He smiled to himself. He was thinking of something.

“Is something funny?” I asked.

“No it’s just that…that’s what they used to tell me back when I was cooking crack. I used to free base. Heat the cocaine until it turned into a rock. Then put it in the glass and light up.”

“What was that like?”

“What was it like? It was the best feeling I’ve ever had in my life and it was nothing I would ever wish on anyone.”

“What did it feel like?”

"Hmm. Like sex. That moment when the climax is coming. It's on it's way and you couldn't stop it if your life depended on it. The moment when you can think of nothing else except the orgasm, the taste of ecstasy in your mouth, the smell of intoxication in the air. Yeah, it's better than that. It's better than sex." He forked another mouthful into his mouth. "And you know I was a functioning drug addict. Still working, still living. Still looking good."

"So why'd you stop? I mean if everything was working out so well for you. What made you stop? What made you want to stop?"

"Well everything looked good on the outside but you know inside I was dying. I was spending all my money on drugs, I couldn't get ahead in life. Relationships with women never lasted."

I thought of the inscription in the book. Zora. Had he forgotten her? Who was she?

"Why'd you do it if it was such a miserable life?"

"You know I asked myself the same thing for a long time. It was the time. Everyone was dabbling in the unknown. After I started, I used to tell myself I could stop anytime I wanted to. And I would. I'd stop sometimes for months at a time but I would always eventually go back and I couldn't understand why. Not until I went to The Mission."

"How long were you doing drugs for?"

He paused, his breath caught in his throat. "What do you mean how long?"

"I mean how long?"

He swallowed and admitted, "A long time. You know The Mission taught me it was a disease. I had to understand that first. I had to understand it wasn't something I could beat on my own. I needed help, a decision, some dedication, and a whole lot of prayer. I graduated the program with a whole new outlook on life."

"Are you afraid you might go back?"

He chuckled. "Yeah right. I'm not going back. I'm done. I've been delivered. And when God finished that thing, he finished it."

"I'm really proud of you. I'm sure it wasn't easy. What made you tell me? That's gotta take courage."

He nodded. "I told myself if I was going to beat this thing, I had to be honest with myself and everyone I talked to. I couldn't run from it anymore. I couldn't run from the truth. I was tired of that."

"Hey can I ask you something." He nodded. "You know how the pastor today was talking about forgiveness. Letting go of the past. What exactly do you think that means?"

He scratched his nose. "Well. I guess it means to stop thinking about the past hoping one day it will change. It won't.

"Have you forgiven your father?"

"I believe I have."

I gazed out the bay window once again and then back at Tobias. "What about me? Could you forgive me?"

Chapter Thirty-One

"I don't want to be married just to be married. I can't think of anything lonelier than spending the rest of my life with someone I can't talk to, or worse, someone I can't be silent with."

Daddy was making tea late at night. He wore the same red pajamas that I remember so well and I startled him when I came into the kitchen.

"What are you doing up Daddy?"

"I can't sleep."

"Make me a cup too." He did and we sat at the table like old friends sipping our hot tea, and talking about old times. "Remember the berries Daddy. Blueberries, blackberries, strawberries. You took Sunday and me for long walks in the summertime when the sun was high and the air was muggy. Remember we'd wear our pink flip flops and you in your sandals. Mommy would coat us good with bug spray but it never really worked because we still came back with a thousand mosquito bites. Just scratching all night long. But we came back with berries too. Bags full of colorful berries. And Mommy said they were the poison kind. No good for eating, but we picked them anyway. We picked them just to see how many bags we could fill. Remember Daddy?"

"I remembah."

"I wonder what happened to those berries. They'd go away every winter, the shrubs would wither, and the snow would fall. Each spring the berries came back to life until one spring they didn't. Just shrubs and weeds. No more berries. What happened to those berries Daddy?"

"Kericho Blu. They died. The berries died. All things come to an end."

"No. I don't believe that Daddy. They're still alive. We just can't see them anymore. We lost our vision Daddy." I stared off and sipped the tea still steaming. "We lost our vision."

When I woke, I couldn't move at first. Just the still of the night and, the moonlight shining through my shadeless window and the white ceiling staring down at me. Then I glanced at the clock. Just before dawn. It read 4:51. Then I started crying. It was a silent cry. Tears wet my face, and then my pillow. They were both happy and sad tears. Happy because I got to visit with Daddy. Sad because the visit wasn't nearly long enough.

I squirmed in bed and felt the hard muscle of a man next to me. *Where am I?*

My own bed. My own sheets. My own bedroom. Tobias was fast asleep on his back, shirtless, his arm raised above his head, his mouth a perfect O. I noticed the strands of greying hair on his chest, his physique still fit, skin smooth like Nutella.

I remembered now. The twins were with Man this weekend. Tobias came over with a pumpkin and we spent all night decorating it and the apartment with Halloween streamers and lights to the tunes of Michael Jackson's Thriller album. We finished a bottle of cheap Chianti and talked about good things until our eyelids got heavy.

"I should go," he said a quarter to midnight.

"You can stay," I said.

So he carried me to my bedroom, and with my t shirt still on, gave me the best massage I ever had by candlelight with sweet almond oil from the kitchen. I fell asleep with his fingers nestled deep in the tissues that had finally begun to relax.

I climbed out of bed now, thirsty, and went to the kitchen halfway hoping to see Daddy there making tea. But it was empty, just a lone bottle of wine and two empty glasses lay resting on the kitchen table. A reminder of the emptiness I now felt, remembering Daddy, remembering the berries, remembering all the men who had left me and all the times I tried so hard to replace them. I opened the fridge, scanned it a minute before settling on a can of soda, and then reclaimed my seat at the kitchen table.

Tobias could be the one. Or he could be my preparation for the one. Or he could be another mistake. I read an article in Redbook about a lady who made her boyfriend sign a contract never to hurt her. The contract didn't work because in the end, he turned out to be another heartbreak, only this one hurting worse than all the rest because she expected it to be different. It is true Tobias is pretty cool, but I shouldn't get my hopes up. If we get married, who will walk me down the aisle? Who will give me away? It's just not fair. Daddy never got to see me happy, really happy. He never got to see the man who is good to me, and loves the outside and the inside. He would never get to see my happily ever after.

I closed my eyes, trying to imagine his face. His skin, his thick lips, his tiny eyes with a blue ring around his pupil. I squeezed my eyelids shut and begged for a picture, an image of his face staring back at me. And then there it was. I could see him. I could see him in his glory days, before the sickness, and the weight loss and the thinning hair. I could see him and he was beautiful.

Footsteps in the hallway approached me. I saw their shadow, light from the rising sun shining through the window. Tobias took a seat in the chair next to me. He looked into the whites of my eyes and he could tell.

"Is there anything I can do?" he asked me.

I smiled. "I just miss him so much," I said through the tears that had started again.

He leaned over and wrapped his arms around my shoulders.

"Daddy's gone. Sunday's gone. I have no one now."

He kissed my cheek and then rested his forehead on my face. What was this? An attempt at sex? An attempt to comfort. Genuine empathy? Or Pity? What was his purpose in my life? Why had he come? Was he worthy of witnessing tears for my father?

"You have me."

Maybe he was right. Maybe I did. Maybe I did.

"I love you, Zora," he said with his eyes closed, his face still pressed into mine.

Or maybe I didn't.

The day I got fired I wore pink shoes. They were flats with a little bow atop a pointed toe. I wanted to be comfortable. Mrs. Blaney called me into her office midday and I found Blake, her right hand woman already sitting there.

"Kericho we have to let you go." Mrs. Blaney didn't waste any time once she sat down behind her desk. "I think you're great, it's just that we have some budget cuts and we have less work. People just aren't spending the money the way they did last year"

I wasn't sure what to say. So she continued.

"You've been slacking."

"I've been working hard," I chimed in.

"You've been working just enough. You skipped the gala this year."

"My father just died."

"And I'm sorry to hear that. I am. But we're running a business here."

"I thought this was a charity."

"Everything is business."

I sat in silence forbidding tears to form. I really needed this job. Just 10 months ago, we were celebrating my permanent employment here."

"If we have to let someone go, that person's gotta be you."

She was right. My heart wasn't in it. My mind was all over the place. A nervous breakdown. Then two months later, I lost my father. And now I lost my job. I wanted to run away.

"Listen, we're giving you three months severance pay. So you'll get your regular salary. I'm happy to help you look for a new job. You just let me know what I can do."

I took a breath and licked my lips. "Ok," I said asking to be excused.

They ordered me a car to help me get my medium sized box full of desk stuff to my apartment. Some photos of Kiefer and Kye, a couple of notepads, the empty glass candy jar and the front page of the New York Times that I had hanging in my cubicle. Obama. Yes we can.

The car ride home was a familiar one. I remembered it coming home from the hospital in Ghana after learning I was pregnant. I remembered it in the back of the police car after they arrested me for credit card fraud. And now the feeling was the same. *What am I going to do now?*

I called Tobias when I was home. He asked if he should come by. I said yes. I just wanted to be held. When he did get there later that night, he brought toy foam footballs for the twins and a box of chocolates for me.

"So now you want me to be unemployed and fat?" I said when I let him in.

"You could never be fat. No reason you shouldn't eat like a

fat girl at a time like this though."

We sat on my couch and I laid my head in his lap.

"You want to talk about it?" He asked me.

"Not really."

"So what do you want to do?"

"Anything else."

And he stroked my hair. And he told me I was a gem. And we laughed about stupid things we did in our past. And we made the night beautiful.

The summer extended deep into Autumn. The leaves hung onto the trees well past Thanksgiving. Tobias came over to my place to celebrate Turkey Day and we cooked together for us and the twins. He was gentle with them at first, handling them like you would a newborn baby although they were 3 years old now.

We ate at the table, Ella Fitzgerald crooning softly in the background. When Tobias and I got together we always played the greats. Ella, Duke, Billie, Sarah, and Nina. Sometimes when we were in the mood, we even threw on Marvin Gaye, the Temptations, and Ms. Ross. He'd sing along. He knew every word. He told me I had an old soul. I told him I was glad he liked it. And he did. I could tell by the subtle way he looked at me when I talked about my love of the arts, the history of jazz, or the way a picture can tell a story. He hung on every word and cocked his head slightly to the side the same way a dog does when he tries to make out what you're saying. When I'd ask him what he thought, he scratched his nose, and repeated the last thing I said in different words.

In the days before Thanksgiving, Tobias was easy with me. The first time things got heated, he had returned me home after an evening out. It was dark, the neighborhood was asleep. He grabbed my chin in his fingertips and kissed me like he had before right there in my doorway, but this time he didn't stop. He kept kissing me, sliding his tongue in and out my mouth and whispered, "Let me have you." It felt good but I stopped him cold, leaned back against the slightly ajar door, and put my hand on his chest nudging a little.

"I don't want this," I whispered. I was finished making the same mistakes.

"I don't want you to do anything you don't want to do."

I looked at the floor, and then the world behind him, anywhere but in his eyes. "The last time you stayed was a mistake. I just think we need to have a conversation before we do anything I'll regret."

"So let's have a conversation."

"Right now?"

"Right now."

The air was still warm, just a nighttime breeze floated by every few moments and a car or two whizzed down the street. I released the pressure on his chest and let my arms fall limp at my side. He stood in front of me, arms folded behind him waiting for me to speak. An invitation for him to come inside would only be a recipe for disaster.

"I made a decision Tobias. I want to be in a relationship before I sleep with you. And I'm not even sure that a relationship is what I'm ready for right now."

"I want you, Kericho."

"What does that mean?"

"It means I want to be with you. I'm ready to be with you."

"That's not a decision we can make right now."

"Why not? I already made it."

"Well you're not the only one that makes decisions here. And besides, it's a quarter to midnight and we've both had a glass of wine or two."

"So you're saying you want to sleep on it? Perfect let's go inside...we can sleep on it." I stared. He smiled. It didn't move me. He backed up. "I'm sorry Kericho. That was stupid." He scratched his nose. "I'll call you tomorrow." And with that, he walked off, didn't hail a cab, just walked due south. Didn't look back and I watched him there in the doorway until I couldn't see him anymore.

He didn't bring up the subject again for a while. Just said that he wanted to be present with me. To enjoy the moment whatever that moment entailed. We started seeing each other almost daily. He said he just wanted to be around me and I enjoyed him immensely. He would call after he got off work and offer to bring over a pizza, or to take the boys out to the park, or to sit with me and watch a movie, or to just sit with me.

My car broke down. The dealer wanted $900 to fix it, so Tobias offered to drive me to church Sunday mornings. We were together a great deal almost like a family. One Sunday I woke up with heavy cramps on bloodstained sheets. "My period came on," I told him. "I'm not feeling too good." So he picked the boys up and took them off my hands for the day.

"Get some rest. Let me know if there's anything else I can do." He reported that a lady at church asked about his wife. "Where is she today?" she had inquired.

"My wife?"

"The young lady I always see you with. Pretty petite thing."

"Oh she's not my wife. But she is a beauty. She's under the weather today."

Some days every couple of weeks or so, Tobias would disappear. His explanation was always vague but I didn't push. It was better that way. "I have to go upstate." Or "I have a job to do. I need to pick up some money."

It never bothered me too much until the afternoon we were at his place watching a marathon of I Love Lucy and his phone rang. He ignored it and it rang again. This time he excused himself, took the phone into the bathroom, locked the door, and stayed there for an entire episode trying to keep his voice down. When he emerged, he told me it was important, and it was work, but everything was taken care of. I remembered the commentary on John, the inscription, and Zora.

By the time the holidays approached, the weather had cooled, and Tobias suggested we spend Thanksgiving together. Yes it was him who suggested it after I complained that my sister Sunday and I had drifted and it had gotten so far off that I forgot how to say I'm sorry. "Where would I even start?" I told Tobias on the phone one night.

"Listen don't make the mistake I did with my father. Don't abandon the whole idea of making up just because it's hard."

Sunday calls. She calls to update me on Grace, or the wedding plans. But never to talk. Never to really just talk the way we used to, and laugh until our sides split. "We're going to do it New Year's Eve, just like Mommy and Daddy," she said the last time. "It'll be small. You, Grace, Auntie Deena, Auntie Mildred, the twins, a few folks from Nigel's family. We reserved space on a boat for the night. A cruise ship around the Hudson."

"Sounds beautiful Sunday," I remember saying and meaning it.

"It will be. Thank you. Talk to you soon" she said before hanging up. But she wouldn't.

Today, after we finished dinner, Tobias watched the football game with the twins. I loaded the dishwasher and then joined them on the couch.

"Oh I forgot to tell you," he started at halftime. "I'm going to see an old cousin of mine. Johanna. She's upstate. I'm driving up week after next. I want you and the boys to come with me."

I hesitated. Afraid to say yes. Afraid to say no. It wasn't exactly a question. It was a statement. Tobias did that often. Asked questions with statements. “You want me to meet your family?”

“Don’t you want to?”

“I guess so. I mean I don’t know. Do you think they’ll like me?”

"Why wouldn't they? Listen, it'll just be Johanna, her daughter, a couple of her cousins on the other side of the family. I don't stay too close with them. I never had much of a reason to hang out before, but I want them to know what I found?"

"What you found?"

"I found a woman I fell in love with. And I want them to know about it."

I winced.

"Stop calculating everything." He scolded.

"Excuse me?"

"That's what you do. You stay up in your head, calculating everything, weighing the pros and cons, deciding how far you want to go and not go."

"Well what's wrong with being careful?"

"Nothing until being careful has you missing out on stuff."

I turned away. He was trying to wear me down. I've been here before.

"Kericho. I love you. I do."

"You don't know that," I said still looking away.

"I do know that. Right now I know that. Most of the problems in this world stem from two causes. Some people act without thinking, and maybe I'm guilty of that. But most people do too much thinking without ever acting, and that's your problem."

"I don't have a problem."

"Oh, you don't have a problem? You have no problems?"

"Maybe I'm just not ready to meet your cousin."

"Well when are you going to be ready?"

"When I get ready!" I shot back. The twins looked on. Tobias stood up.

"Ok," he said. He got his coat from the closet. "You have my number. You call me when you're good and ready."

"Why are you overreacting?"

He mumbled something under his breath.

"What?" I said.

"A year Kericho. It's been a year."

"It's been three months. But why are you counting anyway?"

"I met you a year ago. That day at church. The new members class. I knew then that I wanted you to be my wife. I don't need years to know what I want. I see you do."

"Please." I sucked my teeth.

"Please what? I don't have time for games. I'm too old for that."

"I bet." I said.

He stared. His eyes cutting me like a double edged sword. "Right. That's what it is. Why didn't I think of that earlier? I'm just an old man. The guy to drive you around and buy you dinner, but not the guy you could ever take seriously."

He was unbelievable. To accuse me of using him.

"Not anymore. I've been waiting for you to be comfortable, but be straight up with me. Am I waiting in vain?"

"What is that supposed to mean?"

"I mean are you ever going to come around? Are you ever going to stop being so damn afraid?"

"Get out. This is not something I want to talk about in front of my kids."

"Oh in front of *your* kids, huh?" Now it was his turn to suck his teeth. Then he went for Kiefer. I reacted.

"Don't touch my baby," I said pulling the boy close to me.

He leaned in and planted a kiss on his forehead. Then a kiss for Kye. "Good bye." He went to the door, put his hand on the knob and began to turn it. I couldn't let him get away that easy, thinking this was my fault, thinking he had done no wrong.

"Who's Zora?" I said nice and loud.

He stopped. "What?"

He heard me so I didn't repeat.

"Don't flip this?" he said.

"Flip what? I just want an explanation."

"What are you talking about?"

"What am I talking about? I'm talking about the woman who wrote you a fucking love letter in your Bible book. I'm talking about the times you're MIA with no explanation. I'm talking about the long quiet phonecalls you make locked in the bathroom. I'm talking about you calling me her name every other day. That's what I'm talking about." I was angry now. "You love me? Please? Maybe you love her. Or maybe you don't know what love is. Maybe you're a fucking liar who—"

"Listen, you don't know what the hell you're talking about."

"—wouldn't even know love if it knocked on his door. You think I'm young. You think I'm naïve. And that's fine, but don't walk around here like you're blameless. Like you're so perfect—"

"Kericho, stop!"

"Mommy, bad word," Kiefer said.

"Mommy yelling," followed Kye covering his ears.

"You're right. We shouldn't talk about this in front of the kids," said Tobias.

And just like the others, he was gone.

Chapter Thirty-Two

"Love never dies a natural death. It dies because we don't know how to replenish its source. It dies of blindness and errors and betrayals. It dies of illness and wounds. It dies of weariness, of withering, of tarnishings." Anais Nin

His touch was one I couldn't deny. Tobias touched me on the inside in a place that had never been stroked before. How did I feel such uncertainty yet certainty at the same time? I was certain that he loved me. Certain of that. Certain also that I loved him. Or did I? Maybe my love for him was simply an extension of my selfishness. I cared about his wellbeing because I didn't want to be lonely. I didn't want to be without someone to lay my head on anymore.

I don't know if I know how to truly care, to truly love someone from an unselfish place. I often wonder if anyone does. We love the ones who love us back. We love until we hurt irreparably. Or until that someone leaves. That was the way Man loved me. He loved me until I left. And that's the worst kind of love you can give someone. It's a love with a period at the end and I could never rest in that. But Tobias was different. Perhaps Tobias loved me because he gave up the search for someone else and likewise those were my sentiments. I settled. I was tired. The search was a weary one, looking here, looking there, and never being filled or satisfied in the way I needed most. I needed a love that transcended time and space, that moved with me and through me, a love with no period. A love that didn't even understand itself. Yeah. A love that was incomprehensible, that moved mountains and uprooted trees. A love that broke barriers, and healed broken bodies, mended broken souls. I was looking for God. A love that emanated from God himself. *He made man in his own image, in the image of God, he created him.* God created Tobias and filled him with his characteristics, his well meaning attributes, his forgiving heart, his kind of love…and I found him. I found the man in the Garden of Eden. I was certain of it. Now I just had to figure out how to be his Eve.

I must face head-on the what ifs. I must look them in the face, right into the white's of their eyes and dismiss them like you would a servant whose services are no longer needed. I calculate too much. That was exactly what he said. Do I analyze far more than is needed? No… Surely I don't. I think with my heart that has been bruised often and easily. So much so that calluses have begun to form, only able to be softened through consistent and repeated rubbing away with epsom salt, warm water, and a pumice stone.

My battle is in me, gnawing on that which I love, gnawing until that love leaves me. A strange dichotomy that finds no solution nor a reason. It's a defense mechanism that keeps me in need. Keeps me lonely. Keeps me in solitude so that I can continue to look forward to something better, a something that never comes and has come all along.

The following week passes in solitude, Tobias distant and

silent. I checked job boards daily and resolved to send at least 3 applications out per day. Daddy's birthday is December 7th, the day of completion. Sunday called me and suggested we visit Daddy's grave to pay our respects.

It is cold today but the sun is out. I chose a pale pink turtle neck sweater and covered it in a hooded coat. Sunday beeped the horn when she came to pick me up. I hadn't seen her in months. I slid into the passenger seat next to her. She looked well, her face bright with happiness.

"Hey Babygirl."

It's been way too long since I heard those words together. I was unsure how to respond. I mostly just felt like crying. I smiled and we rode in silence to the place where Daddy was resting. When we arrived at the grassy knoll, Sunday got out first. I followed behind her making no haste, almost afraid at what I might see on Daddy's plot of land, where we had laid him to rest five months prior.

It crept up slowly but when it arrived it was overwhelming. The sadness. The loss. The empty vessel. I once heard that no one can make you feel sad unless you have sadness in you. Well I must have sadness in me, somewhere lodged between my spine and my right lung, adding pressure to my heart, obstructing my capacity to breathe, to stand upright, and to love unconditionally.

I broke the silence. "When you look back over your life, have you been mostly happy or mostly sad?" I asked Sunday, standing to her right.

She looked over, thoughtful. "Hmm. Mostly happy," she answered. "Cus you know you gotta add in childhood."

"Yeah. I've been mostly sad. I've been sad consistently since the fifth grade. I mean there have been happy days, but generally I've been sad."

"Really?"

"Really. I don't know how to get the sadness out. I wish there were some way to pass it like you would a kidney stone or some urinary tract infection that I could simply flush out with enough vitamins and h20. It's just stuck there unmoving, unbudging. Some days life tricks me into believing the sadness isn't there anymore. Like when I have a really good day at work or I get a bonus or somebody tells me they love me and for that brief moment I actually believe them. Days like that, I feel good and the sadness wears a mask. It wears happiness' mask and silly me, I fall for it every time. But the sadness reappears sometimes heavier than it was before, heavier than it ever was in my life and I think the sadness is getting bigger. It's growing like a tumor, taking over my body and mind, infiltrating my thoughts and making me cry blood. Like the way Jesus sweated blood right before his crucifixion, I cry blood stained tears that remind me that the sadness is here to stay."

Sunday gazed at Daddy's plot. "Just decide to be happy," she said. "That's what all the self-help books say. Decide how you will react to every situation. Decide how to feel about it."

At that I chuckled. "I wish anyone who ever said that would have their insides ripped from their chests, and feel the pain like a woman given a c-section without anesthesia. Then I'll be there to tell them to decide how to feel about the situation." I bent to kneel on the grass and stroked the blades where Daddy lay. "You know between the three of us Sunday, Daddy lucked out. I believe he got the best deal. Cus it hurts. Knowing this is my life. This is my lot and there is no escaping because the funny thing about this world, there's no way out alive. It's either suck it up or die a dishonorable death, me strapped to the driver's seat of my car while I speed off a bridge and into the abyss."

Sunday knelt beside me. "Don't talk like that Babygirl."

"How long would it take for them to officially deem it a suicide? The whispers behind my back would haunt me even in death. 'How could she,' they would all say. 'I never realized Kericho wasn't well.'"

"But don't they say suicide is the unforgiveable sin? The

other side of the door would just be more hell."

I smirked. "Right. Right. So the better outcome is to somehow get into a car accident that wasn't self-inflicted. Some carjacking on the side of the road that ended in my face getting blown off. In this way, I could escape without suffering the wicked judgments of others. I could escape the sadness."

"Maybe you're missing the point. Who says you're supposed to escape? Maybe there's a method. You know a reason, some lesson you've gotta learn. Maybe your life isn't for you. Maybe it's for someone else. Maybe it's for me."

I glanced over at her and in that moment I remembered the girl who had a rose for a belly button. The girl that kept me sane throughout my childhood, the one who even in anger, gave me solace. What would I do without her? I mean really how would I live? Who would I talk to about Daddy, or Mommy, or all the boys that hurt? Who would hug me when I'm down or laugh with me when I'm up?

We sat there on our knees for a long time, gazing, thinking, feeling.

"I miss you Sunday," I said some time later. "Right now I miss you."

"I'm right here," she said.

"I know. And I miss you just the same. You think God would ever be so cruel as to take you away from me like he did Daddy?"

"I ain't going nowhere no time soon. I promise. But you know when I do, decades from now, that would be God doing you a favor."

I raised an eyebrow.

"You gotta learn to be ok even if it's just you. I love you Baby, but I'm not your savior. It's like when Daddy used to throw us in the pool when we were little. He threw us in and stood back waiting for us to swim. Waiting for us to figure out what we were going to do. And it wasn't until we had nothing else, no other options, that we kicked our feet and floated all by ourselves."

"I can't swim by myself Sunday. Everybody leaves. Everybody always leaves me. I don't know how to swim all by myself. And why should I have to?" My breath quickened, tears welling.

"There's always somebody. If I leave… if I have to go, there will be somebody else, another one to pick up the slack, but in a new and completely different way. You just gotta recognize her when she comes. Maybe you have to recognize him when he comes…"

Tobias. I imagined his face. His soft brow, his poised jaw, his smooth lips.

"I don't know if I can do that."

"You can. I did. So you can."

"Is Nigel that person for you?"

"I'm sure he is. It took us both some time to see it. But I'm certain he is. Everyone's love story is different."

"I'm going to miss you."

"I'm right here. Our relationship may change. Our relationship has changed, but Babygirl anything that isn't changing is dead."

I chewed that for a long while. Anything that isn't changing is dead.

Chapter Thirty-Three

"For the living know that they will die, but the dead know nothing, they have no further reward, and even their name is forgotten." Ecclesiastes 9:5

The children were gone for the weekend. I stayed at the library job searching until after nine even though today is a Friday. I wanted to think, to feel the cool air, to breathe it, like it was new life, so I took the long walk home through the park instead of hopping the train. I walked, assuredly and briskly through the night air. The day had come to a close and stillness and shadows of stillness were upon me. I remembered my mother's words growing up. Desolate areas are where evil lurks. But I didn't feel unsafe tonight, instead just the opposite. I felt comforted by the presence of God. *In quiet and rest, thou shalt be saved.*

Around the empty basketball court, through the blocks of trees, down the trodden path I walked, my hands tucked neatly in my pockets, my head upright, eyes forward. Night time held a multitude of mysteries that were only uncovered when you listened hard and now, right now, my ears are perked listening for the heartbeat of God, whether in an owl's hoot or the cars whizzing by on the distant road. I was aware. I was alert. I could see. I could see in the way Tobias could see when he smoked reefer. No. It was better than that. I could see the world for what it really was. What a beautiful place it was when one stripped away its infirmities, its flaws, its blemishes, its damages that tarnished an otherwise perfect garden. I didn't see the world as it was the way Adam and Eve saw the Garden after The Fall. I saw it as it should have been, before The Fall.

A noise. Almost like a baby's whimper. I was not alone.

When I inclined my ear, the sound was more fully manifest. It was a girl. She sat on a bench to my right, her cell phone to her ear, crying. Her belly was full. I continued to walk by but slowed. Her image intrigued me. She was young, 20, maybe 21 years old. Her hair was pulled neatly in a bun, her sweater covered her protruding stomach, her skin pale, almost transparent. The caller on the line, perhaps a boyfriend. Boys have an uncanny ability to make us girls cry like children. It could be her mother or her father. No one has the power to cut like kin. She sobbed, sniffles making her sparse words inaudible. Muffled at best.

"I can't," I heard her say. More sniffles. "— doesn't mean anything. I believed—and—not fair."

That was me there on that bench, a young 21-year-old girl, pregnant and defeated, on the brink of life and death at precisely the same time. I was drawn to her. I inched closer and found a bench opposite hers facing the other direction. I sat. I listened.

"This is a lot for me. I gave up a lot," she managed through her tears. "What did you give up? What did you sacrifice?"

She was hurt, bruised on the inside, almost like she wanted and needed validation. She wanted her struggle recognized and validated. Yes, she wanted to matter, to feel important, honored like she had climbed Mt. Everest or done some other insurmountable task that could have cost her her life and she wanted a Nobel Peace Prize, or an award of Merit, or something to show for it. It was a feeling all too familiar. I am the victim.

Not you. I am the one hurting. I am the one compromised. Me. Not you.

I imagined myself walking over to her, putting a gentle hand on her shoulder, and shushing her. "It'll pass," I'd tell her. "All the hurt will hurt less one day. Cry, but know it won't be forever. Life is but a dream." The words sat with me instead in my own heart and in my own being. I wasn't alone. There were other Kerichos, other me's in the world, fighting my battle, struggling with my demons, and there in that moment, my story mattered. My story was validated and it was better than any award of merit I could receive publicly. It mattered most because I had endured the feat and lived to tell the story.

When I stood up from the bench, I didn't continue in the direction I was going, but I turned back around, sprinted out of the park to the main road and hailed a cab uptown. I threw a twenty at the driver and rushed out, scurried up the stone steps and rung the bell for Tobias' walk up apartment. 202. I waited. No answer. I rung again. And again. No answer. I looked at my cell. The battery was dead. Where is he? I heard carolers in the distance singing Hark the Herald. I caught my breath. *Upstate. His cousin. Wasn't this the week he said he was going?* I sighed. Then I cried. I needed him like I had never needed anyone before. I don't know why. But I did. I had missed it. I had missed my opportunity to love and be loved, to feel and be felt. I had gotten in my own way and warded off the very thing that could comfort me.

I am so in love with Tobias that I am convinced that no one in the world is as lucky as me. Convinced that somehow God saw it fit to bless me at this time and in this way…in such a way that he has never blessed anyone else ever, and brought a man into my life that fits me so perfectly. A man that has found his way into my mind and my heart and infiltrates my soul, understands my thought processes and I'm sure that when we finally make love, he will fit inside me so perfectly, so precisely, like my insides were in fact made for his body part, my lips made for his, my tongue made to someday be intertwined with his, my heart made to beat alongside his in a rhythm that both speeds up and slows down time, stops it really in its tracks.

By now the cab had pulled off. So I walked. The city was ablaze with Christmas lights. I took in the sites, walking down to the end of his street and then I hung a left, walked downtown. I didn't know where to. I was much too far to walk all the way home. Or was I? The air was cold but it felt good against my sweat soaked skin, my heart just now returning to its normal speed. I walked six blocks and then a left, four more blocks, and then a right. I gazed up and found myself in front of the Abyssinian church turned into condos. The cross was enormous. *A place already blessed by God.* I stopped briefly. Remembered. The day at his house, his kiss, the cherries, the fish. Him. Then as I turned to continue my journey, to find a train, or a cab, or something, I heard it.

"Kericho?"

The sound of my own name startled me. My first inclination was to run. But how did they know my name? I turned in the direction of the church. He spoke again.

"Kericho, I'm over here." He rose from the church steps. Began to approach. I squinted. I didn't see before. The grey jacket, his ebony skin, those deep eyes, it all blended into the night air.

Tobias faced me, reached and put his hand on my cheek to see if I was real. "What are you doing here?"

My face was moist from my tears, my eyes puffy and swollen. "I—…" My voice cracked. Then I hugged him. I stood on my tippy toes and wrapped my arms around his neck and hugged him hard and tight. He hugged me back. He squeezed me between his biceps, pressed his hands into my waist, stroked my back, kissed my neck. The embrace was good, and pure, and needed. "I came to see you," I finally said when we relaxed. "I love you. I'm sorry. I'm so sorry."

I saw. His face was moist too. His eyes swollen, his nose

tinted a slight pink. He grabbed my cheeks between his palms, kissed me slow, sucking my lips, tasting my nectar, showing me love. "I missed you so much," he said.

"Upstate. You said you'd be gone this weekend."

"I didn't go. I couldn't go. You have me all messed up. I feel empty. I've felt empty ever since Thanksgiving. Since I left you that day. Kericho, I think about you all the time. Every morning, every night, and all the hours in between. I need you. I don't want anybody else. I came out here to think, to talk to God. Have my burning bush experience, a real encounter. And just now, I know you're supposed to be in my life. You're supposed to be my wife."

I took that last statement in. "And here I am," I smiled.

"Kindred spirits think alike."

"Like magic. Strange coincidence."

"I don't believe in coincidences. I believe in God."

He was real. In the flesh, standing in front of me, my knight. I was in awe of God and how he worked this very moment out in this way.

"Come home with me. Spend the night with me." He motioned for my hand and I offered it. We walked back to his house, arm in arm. Nature inclined its ear to us. The atmosphere shifted in our direction. I saw a city bus pass by and I remembered standing on the step waiting to board, a few dimes and nickels short on fare. I remembered the night I spent in jail, the mental breakdown, the inadequacies that plagued my existence until now and I knew I wouldn't have to feel like that anymore.

Tobias' apartment was chilly.

"Sit tight, I'll put the heat on," he said when we were both inside and then disappeared down the corridor. I went to the bay window and gazed back at the church we had come from, the cross still lit bright. It hypnotized me for a moment, holding me, speaking to me. Somehow it was security that everything was going to be okay, that Daddy was in heaven, that Sunday was just fine, and that Grace really did say all of the things I wanted her to say to me in her heart, and that was enough.

The commentary still sat on the end table, untouched. The gift from Zora.

A hand on my shoulder. "Let me take your coat," Tobias said lifting it off of me. "Get comfortable." I obliged and found a seat on the couch. He disappeared with the coat and then returned to sit next to me, leaning over, his elbows on his knees, hands clasped together. He breathed in and out deeply, and then took my hand in his. "She's a friend."

I was silent. Who was? Zora?

"I saw you looking at the book."

"Oh –you don't have to d—…"

"Yes I do. I've been wanting to tell you. I just didn't know how it would sound. Zora and I used to be a couple. Years ago, many years ago. I had stopped using for a while and I got hooked up with a church upstate. They had me doing speaking engagements in the prisons up there, you know just giving my testimony, telling my story. I met this young lady, Zora O'Shea in the ministry, and we fell in love." He paused for my reaction. I listened for the rest.

"I wanted to marry her. I thought we were going to get married. But I bought her a ring and she didn't like it. She gave it back, told me something about it wasn't the right time. Another year or two went by and things started changing. I started using again. She started seeing someone else, and then one day she called me and said she don't want to be with me no more. She say she love someone else. She say she was pregnant by some other cat. I was hurt real bad. But I let her go. A couple months later she tells me she lost the baby and days after she found her guy cheating, sleeping with some girl from the neighborhood and they broke up. Less than a year after that, she got diagnosed with MS and she got real sick. So I had to be there for her."

I swallowed. It was a mouthful.

"That's all it is. Zora's a friend. I go with her to her doctor appointments. I sit with her sometimes. She's in the final stages so I feel like I need to be in her corner."

"Are you still in love with her?"

"No. No. I'm in love with you."

I wanted to believe him. I needed to for my own sanity. "You call me her name sometimes."

"She was a big part of my life for a long time. But I promise you the error is due to my head, not an indication of where my heart is. The brain works by repetition."

"Can I meet her?"

"We can do whatever you want to do."

I sat back. Took a breath. "Tobias, I'm trying to let go. I'm trying to do something different but I don't know if I know how. You know my mother, she hated my father. She resented him for the duration of their marriage, right up until he died. Maybe she still does. I think I just try so hard to not be her, to not repeat her mistakes. I wish I could've had a happy mother. I wish she could have had a husband who lit up her life, made her smile every day, told her she was beautiful and meant it. I feel for her, you know, because my dad wasn't that way. I long for those things. I think every woman does whether she admits it or not. And you know, I just been searching, I been looking, and no one gives me that feeling. That feeling of absolute certainty. That feeling of connecting with someone at their core and knowing them intimately, without sex. No one until you, and I don't know why."

He stroked my hand. "That means a lot. I feel the same way Kericho. I know you but I wanna know you more. I want to meet your family if you'll let me. I want to know where you come from, what drives you, what hurts you." He looked up at me and stroked my cheek. "What makes you smile."

It felt right. Whether it was or wasn't is not the issue. Maya Angelou was the one who said folks may not always remember exactly what you did or exactly what was said, but years removed what remains in the mind, is how you made them feel. Well

Tobias made me feel loved, and wanted in a non-sexual way. I ain't never had that before, never. And well, that felt right.

Chapter Thirty-Four

It never rains forever.

Christmas came on a Wednesday. The night before came the season's first snow that painted the tree branches and lawns a bright white. Tobias and I made the two hour drive down to see Grace, Sunday, Nigel, and the girls, my twins nestled in the backseat.

The year and my severance pay were coming to an end. I stretched my money wide and far, and attempted to save a little for the uncertain future. Tobias said he would be here for me but still I worried. One income hasn't been enough for a family of four in decades. He helped with Christmas gifts for the boys. A football, some toys, and some new clothes.

This morning in the car we listened to Eartha Kitt, the Jackson 5 and all those Christmas tunes from the sixties and seventies. He held my hand in silence. I laid my head on the seat, gazed out the window, and watched God.

I thought about Cinderella, Snow White, all the great fairy tale legends. They were frauds. They made me believe a happily ever after existed in that fashion and in that form. The truth is it does exist, but not on this side of life. This side of life is a journey of ups and downs…good times and bad times but the heart's memory erases the bad and magnifies the good, a coping mechanism to endure the pains of the past. Who came up with those story lines anyway? The girl with all the problems finally gets rescued by her prince. I believed in that for a long time. I went into every relationship expecting a savior. I wanted my man to be my knight in shining armor who had finally come to take me away from anything and everyone that had previously been the source of my misery even if that someone was myself. I waited expectantly for any sign that he was not the one, that he couldn't in fact live up to all I intended for him to be and that was my queue to move on. I was looking for an infallible love in fallible people, expecting a god in human form, an expectancy that can only ever bring disappointment.

Man could've been the one. Leonard the butcher too. It was a sad case of the wrong place and wrong time in my own life for me to let go of the life I planned so as to have the life that was waiting for me. I'm ready now. I believe I'm ready. If I could, I'd tell them I'm sorry. If they'll receive it, I'll call Man, and Lee, and Luke, and all the others and tell them I'm not mad. It was me, not them. It was me all along.

Mommy's house smelled like holiday everything. Turkey and sweet potatoes, dressing, holiday ham, and grocery store apple pecan pie. The kids played, the men watched sports, us girls we reminisced. Sunday was pregnant with happiness. That Nigel kid did it I guess. She and I set the table, crystal glasses, silver trimmed plates, all on top of a winter white table cloth.

"I'm happy for you Sunday," I said setting the last glass down. "You look amazing and if Nigel makes you feel that way, I love him for it."

"I know you must know the feeling. I see that same light in your face." We smiled. "We do everything together. I thought you already knew that. Do I hear wedding bells in the future?"

"I don't know. I like him. He helps me in more ways than I could ever help myself. You think he's too old for me?"

"I think he's perfect for you. I don't believe in the idea of soul mates. Not anymore. Love at first sight is fiction."

"No? Why so cynical? That's not you, Sunday."

"Well listen, I'm beginning to believe that a very few times in your life, if you're lucky, you might meet someone who is exactly right for you, not because he's perfect or because you are, but your combined flaws are arranged in some unique way that allow the both of you to hinge together."

"Like puzzle pieces?"

"Just like puzzle pieces."

"I like that."

After dinner we exchanged gifts and then sat around playing Monopoly and eating store bought desserts. Grace was a little lazy this year but none of us cared. She seemed to take a liking to Tobias or maybe she had become indifferent to my choices in men. In any case, she alerted him quickly when I landed on his property and I had to fork over a hundred bucks for Boardwalk.

"Why are you taking sides?" I accused her.

"I'm not, but I can't let you get away with that," she spat back.

Nigel is subdued, Sunday's smallest one resting against his arm, her thumb tucked tightly in her mouth. She likes him. Maybe she even loves him. Sunday jokes that she is the best player of us all. Maybe she is because two and a half hours later, she won the game by a landslide.

The men and Sunday clean the kitchen, wipe down the counters, then Sunday and Nigel say their good nights and packed the little girls up to go on home.

Tobias and I sit with Grace, hot coffee mugs in hand.

"This was nice Mom. Thanks," I went out on a limb to say.

She was sarcastic in her reply, never quite being the type to take a sincere moment for what it was. "It better be nice, all this slaving I did for ya'll."

"Slaving? We had store bought pie." I kept it light.

"Yeah and? If you didn't know, you couldn't tell the difference."

Tobias chimed in. "I thought everything was great."

"Thank you," the lady said. "Someone knows how to appreciate fine dining."

"Best Christmas I had in a long time. I see where your daughter gets her charm."

"Your family wasn't sad to miss you this year?" Grace asked Tobias.

"No No. My parents passed over a decade ago. I had a brother and sister that died too. So… you know, it's just me."

"Oh I'm sorry," said Grace.

"Don't be. I'm a strong believer in heaven. I don't believe in death. I believe it only gets better from here."

Grace nodded. "Sounds good to me."

"I wish I could've met your husband. Your daughter says she has lots of good memories."

"Well," I chimed in. "Good and bad but my heart remembers the good. Dismisses the bad."

"Don't we all," said Tobias. "And you?" Tobias wasn't sure how to address my mother. "You have a big family?"

"Five sisters. My mother is in Michigan. My father passed last year."

"That's gotta take a toll. Your father and your husband in such a short period of time."

"She had a brother too," I offered. "An uncle I never met. He died years ago."

"Wow. I'm really sorry. How did he die?"

My mother gave a solemn smile. "He shot himself."

That brought on silence. Tobias didn't expect that. I'm not sure why I never mentioned it. "Wow," he finally said. "Well you know we all got our demons."

Demons? Was Tobias suggesting it was a demon that killed my mother's baby brother? In that case was it a demon that trolled my dreams for so long? Was it a demon that ignited my hatred for men or for myself or for everyone in the world it seemed? If it was, that soothed my worries. It's not me. It's the demon inside of me.

"He was a good kid. But I don't think about him as much these days. You have to move on. You have to live life," Grace said.

We finished our coffee. By now the twins had fallen asleep on the floor in awkward positions in the playroom. I gathered them up, bundled them in their coats and we said goodbye. I hugged Grace a second longer than I should have or would have if this were an earlier time. "I love you Mom." I wanted it to sound natural. She said it back.

The night air was brisk, the ground still covered with untouched snow. A full moon sat high in the sky and it reminded me that we were all still here, alive and well, Tobias and Mommy, and Sunday and Nigel, and the children. My family. We had our problems, our unspoken as well as spoken issues. It was the family I was appointed, the one that made me and raised me and molded me, sometimes hurt me, but more than that shaped me. An unraveling of sorts...a coming undone. That is precisely the way I remember it.

However, there are virtues that have been added unto me. Patience. Humility. Acquiring still the skill of selflessness. Could it be that instead of coming apart, it is quite the contrary? A coming together that could only be accomplished through experience. It was Shakespeare who reminded us all that experience is by industry achieved and perfected through the swift course of time.

We settled in the car, Kiefer and Kye strapped in. Tobias started the engine and fuddled with the radio dial.

"Tobias?"

"Yeah babe," he said, still fuddling.

"Inside, you said we all have our demons."

"What's that?" he says not looking up.

"You were talking about my uncle. You said we all have our demons. What did you mean by that?"

He grabbed his pockets. "Oh shoot, I forgot my house keys. Can you grab them? I think I left them on your mothers dining table."

"Sure. We wouldn't want to leave those." I climbed out and rushed back to the front door, still unlocked.

The house was quiet, the day's visitors now gone. It was almost too quiet. I peeked into the living room and saw my mother had left her place on the couch. The keys were where Tobias had promised they'd be, resting neatly on a clean dining table. I grabbed them and started to rush back out into the cold. *Maybe one last goodbye for Mommy.*

I found her in her bedroom, kneeling beside her bed, the nightstand drawer open before her. She was holding something. A watch it looked like, one of those antique watches, golden, and worn. She didn't hear me come in and I felt almost awkward standing in the doorway. She just stared almost entranced, the whole of her fully occupied with what was inside the glass face.

I decided to speak. "Mommy, you ok?"

She jerked. Then she met my eyes. Silent. Her eyes were moist. *But Grace doesn't cry.* Then a whispered, "I could have done something but I just sat there."

She was caught there, not five feet between us, kneeling holding that watch, unflinching.

"What?" I said.

"He was a baby. He was only seven years old and he beat him so bad, you could see flesh. I heard him screaming. I heard him beg him to stop and I just sat there holding this watch." At that, she threw it hard against the wall and fell back against the bed.

"Mommy, who are you talking about?"

She dared to blink, forbidding tears to emerge.

"Mommy?"

"Jamie. Luther."

"Granddaddy?"

"He gave me that watch a long time ago. It was one of the good days. He gave me that watch and told me don't waste time. Never waste your time because it's something none of us, not one of us can ever get back." She didn't look at me, she looked at the wall, or rather through it, at the place where the watch fell. "I wasted my time Kericho. I had time to stop Luther. I had time to save Jamie. That day or the next day, or the day after. I could've told him how much I loved him. I should've told him how much I cared. But I didn't. I just kept staring at that watch. I kept looking at time and not using it. Because loving never did anything. I loved and where did that leave me? Where did that leave Jamie? Your father? Where does that ever leave any of us? I don't want to go back there. Onward, never backwards. That's all we can do. Maybe I could've loved harder or different. Maybe I could've loved stronger."

She blinked and that's when I saw it. A single tear escaped her tear duct and flowed down her cheek. I went to her. I sat beside her against the bed and I remembered Sunday sitting with me in Dr. Hannah's vacant office. I remembered my mother in earlier times. Picture day at school. Sleeping under her desk. The letter she wrote to The Jersey Journal. The trip to McDonald's for my eighth birthday. The late nights she stayed up helping with homework. The early mornings driving me to school to make the teacher's office hour when she couldn't help anymore. I remembered the pension money she used for summer school. The way she fell in love with Kiefer and Kye. The days she spent slaving in the kitchen for Thanksgiving, and Christmas, and Easter, and just about every other day of the year. I remembered how much my mother showed me she loved me and without touching her, I said. "You loved me just fine, Mommy. You loved me just fine."

Epilogue

Our mistakes as children become our triumphs in adulthood.

Tobias took the day off Monday, the day before Sunday's wedding. I had so much to do. My hair, my nails. I still needed to make a last minute trip to the mall for sparkly shoes. He called me in the morning and said he would bring over breakfast and then stay with the kids so I could run my errands. I woke up to a quiet house, the children still fast asleep. The snow outside was just beginning to melt away showing the tips of brownish green grass underneath. I showered, the hot droplets of water beating against my skin. I felt new and rightfully so. A new year was upon us. 2010. It would be a good year because I said so. I stepped out of the shower and wrapped myself in a grey towel, tossing my hair up in a messy ponytail. I slathered my lips with a bright shade of purple lipstick. Heroine it was called. I wanted to be pretty today. My phone rang. Tobias was early.

"Hello," I said.

"Hey Beautiful, I'm outside. Buzz me up. It's freezing." I hit the buzzer against the wall and unlock my apartment door. Then I rush to dress before Tobias makes it up the 3 flights of stairs. The towel now on the floor, I reach for a pair of panties in my drawer when the phone sounds again. I answer quickly.

"I hit the buzzer! Did you miss it?"

Silence.

"Hello?"

"Miss Blu? Is this Kericho Blu?"

"Uhh yes." I fixed my voice. "This is she."

"Kericho, great to get you on the phone. I have to tell you I wasn't sure I would, this being the middle of the holiday week. But we're in a tight situation."

It was a man…a black man if my ears served me well. His voice was deep and dignified, not one I've heard before. He continued.

"You and I haven't had the pleasure of meeting. My name is Steven Jones. I'm the Communications Director here at Dream House. I understand you volunteered here with us earlier this year with the Next Step Program."

"Yes. Yes I did." *What did he want with me?*

"Well maybe you can help me. I had one of my associates leave suddenly last week. We're right in the middle of a campaign. I have press releases to get out, write-ups to do, The New York Times wants to run a feature on the latest discovery from our research series. I'm looking to hire my associate's replacement as soon as possible and I haven't got time to waste. You came highly recommended from Ms. Donahue. I don't know what your current work situation is but could I interest you in the position here with our Communications Team?"

Was this a joke? Nothing good ever happens to me. Certainly not offers like this. Someone must have told him I was out of work, my severance pay was ending and all I had left was my faith and a lot of prayer.

"Miss Blu?"

"I'm—I'm here. I'm sorry I'm just speechless. This sounds like an excellent opportunity. I'm so happy you thought of me."

Did he know my volunteer work was in place of a prison bid? Did he know I was mandated to do it because of a credit card I fraudulently applied for? Did he know how much I cried that night in jail, the money I glued together for the lawyer? Did he know about my shaking knees that morning in court, when the judge handed down my sentence? Did he know I was a criminal? Did he know I was mentally insane and had a breakdown in this very room months earlier, my cell phone in hand? It was precisely in this manner—my phone against my cheek, nude.

Nude. I was still naked. I looked up to see Tobias standing in my doorway, two paper coffee cups in his hands. In shock. He had never seen me this way, my breasts hanging suspended in the air, hair drawn up, purple lipstick on my lips, my skin still a bit moist from the shower. Tobias had never seen me naked.

"I'm happy this is good news for you. I know this is extremely short notice, but if I can get you to come in just after the New Year. Say Thursday, we can meet and chat a bit. Really an informal interview. You've already come highly recommended. We just need to go over the details. If it works out, how soon could you start?"

"Um… I could start soon. I could start right away." Tobias lifted his eyebrow, overhearing my words, still standing in the doorway. Why didn't I cover up? My eyes stayed on his. I was motionless.

"That's great to hear, Miss Blu. Listen I'll shoot you my details over e-mail, and we'll plan to meet Thursday at 9?"

"Perfect."

"Hey listen, Miss Blu?"

"Yes?"

"Happy New Year."

"Oh it already is!"

No sooner did I hang up the phone, did Tobias rush to me, setting the cups down on my dresser. He held my waist between his palms. Stroked my hips. Peered into my eyes. "You got a job?" he whispered.

I was unsure how to respond. Should I rush him out? Feign embarrassment and reach for the towel? It was a bit too late for that. I was happy he was here. "I guess I did," I whispered. "I mean I think—I think I did."

He looked at my lips wanting to kiss them, wanting to taste my goodness but hesitant to ruin the color. Instead he kissed my chin, then my neck. "I want you Kericho," he said.

Tobias was here. I was in love. A new job at Dream House. Was this the moment I was waiting for, the relief I told Dr. Hannah I was waiting on so long ago? Had my life come full circle? The Universe, or God, or the vibrations in the air were screaming at the top of their lungs, screaming to me that dreams do come true. God does answer prayer. Heaven does have ears. Everything is connected. Our past, our present, our future. Our mistakes as children become our triumphs in adulthood. Our quirkiness, our shyness, our inabilities, become what makes us unique. God, the almighty God, the one who created us from nothing wrote the stories of our lives before we took our first breath. The idea is not to fight the journey, but to lean into it.

I let him lay me down. I caressed his head and enjoyed his kisses. For a moment I thought about the coffee getting cold on the dresser, the children sleeping in the next room, my vow to wait for something real. Then I closed my eyes, and let him love me.

The wedding was full of laughter, and joy, and apple pie milkshakes. We gathered on a boat on the Hudson River and watched Sunday walk down the aisle to After 7's "I Swear".

The children played, the music blared. I sat finishing my last bite of cookie dough vanilla wedding cake. I thought I should feel empty, like I had lost something. My best friend Sunday was entering a new chapter of her life and I couldn't go with her. I thought that should make me sad and it did once upon a time. Not now. Now I was content. Surprisingly, I was ok. I watched her. I watched the way her teeth glowed when she laughed, her head tilting slightly to the right, her eyes revealing her secret. It was a secret that deep down, right now, she was happy. There is no telling how long the happiness will last. But in this moment, she's enjoying bliss. I can only hope for her that this bliss lasts forever. My Sunday. The chocolate baby born with a rose for a belly button. The young at heart, and strong in spirit creature created by God. She was in Nigel's hands now.

I got up to use the toilet and on my way back, I was caught off guard. The water outside looked like pure glass. It was calm, motionless, serene, a page out of a picture book. The sight drew me and I ventured out onto the deck, gathering my gold embroidered dress around my ankles. The air was brisk. It bit me with the first step but I continued out shutting the doors behind me and peered over the ledge leaving the laughter and merriment inside.

Surely there is something mysterious about the waters, a holding place for possibilities. Jesus walked on water and the way its surface looked to me now, perhaps I can too. The water is pregnant with life beneath its a surface, fish and sea creatures live there concealed from the naked eye. Only faith uncovers their proof. Isn't the verse in the Bible? *Now faith is substance of things hoped for, evidence of things unseen.* The fisherman extends his rod into the waters with faith that there are fish there and those fish may bite, and he may have dinner. The water, now a shiny glass like substance held hope there. My life and future was under the water if I could just have faith enough to believe it. The sea was upon me. The choice to step into it was not mine to make. Despair would mean sinking. Faith would mean walking upon the waters, trusting with no borders. Trusting and believing that the places the water would take me could only be good, an edifying of my spirit man, a molding into useful content.

Tobias found me outside looking over the railing, watching God.

"It's cold out here. You ok?"

"I wanted to get some fresh air. Cold is ok sometimes."

"Take my jacket," he said draping it over my shoulders. "Can I ask you something?"

I nodded.

"What do you think about us."

I smiled. "Shhh… look."

"Look at what?"

I held my arms up. "Look at this. Look at the water. Look at the moon. Look at God. Isn't it amazing Tobias?"

He laughed. "I love you Kericho." I took that in and watched his lips form the words.

"I gotta tell you something," I said finally.

He met my gaze in anticipation. I hesitated but pushed myself. "Last summer, you know after you sent me the flowers?"

"Yeah. I remember."

"I went through something—I was going through something. I haven't really figured out how to tell you."

He reached for my hand, interested now. "What is it, baby?"

"After I had the twins and I broke up with Man, I wasn't doing too well. I lost a lot of weight, I had all these thoughts of suicide. You said to my mom that that's nothing but the demons inside us."

"We all have demons, baby."

"Just listen. Please." I took a deep breath. "I started sort of seeing someone. A therapist. Her name was Dr. Hannah and I saw her for 7 months and we talked about a lot of things and she helped me get past a lot of the hurt from my past. I saw her every Monday for an hour." Another deep breath.

"Last summer, after you sent me the flowers. I—I found out she wasn't real. That it was all in my head. I had a mental breakdown. Schizophrenia." Tobias was quiet.

"Listen Tobias, I don't expect you to know how to react, I know—"

"Baby. Baby." He pulled me close. "Calm down."

"—it's hard to take in and I'm trying to be honest with you."

"It's ok. Why did you feel like you couldn't tell me that?"

"Cus sometimes I still get scared. Sometimes I wonder if you're real. I find myself asking Sunday if she can see you because I worry. You know I worry that maybe you're just a figment of my imagination… a way to feel—to feel—I don't know to feel good."

"I make you feel good?"

"Too good to be true."

He hugged me tight. "What are you afraid of?"

"I used to be afraid of losing…again. Not anymore. Just now I realized I'm not afraid of that anymore."

And I wasn't. I yearned for new experiences, risks that only lead to strength, love that only led to more love. I took it in. The water, Tobias, his scent, the sharp air, the faint sound of music floating outside… I took it in, and it was beautiful.

Acknowledgements

It's been a long time coming and finally my baby was born. I have to thank all of the people in my life who have helped this process whether knowingly or not. The Bible says all things work together for our good so even the bad relationships I've had, the ones who have seemingly hurt me, have enabled me to come alive in ways I otherwise would not have. They were strategically placed in my life for my growth.

Mommy, you have been a wonderful mother, human, flawed, but absolutely wonderful. Thank you for encouraging my writing and taking the time to read my stuff. God has used you in miraculous ways to grow me up. You have a heart that never stops pumping and I admire you for that. Daddy, you know how they say you don't know what you've got until its gone. They were talking about you. I miss you dearly and I thought about you and cried about you often while writing this book. I'll hold the book close to my heart when I go to bed and hopefully I can pass you a copy when you visit me in my dreams. Rest in paradise and I'll see you soon.

Tilina, you are my Sunday Rose and I love you. You never told me anything I ever wrote was bad and that's why I couldn't trust you to edit my work. But ya know, we need more people like you in the world… those that only see the good.

Chris, thank you. If it weren't for you I would never have seen the gravity of my fall from God. Alan, you were the first man I ever loved and the one whom sets the blueprint for that feeling that I know is possible. Dell, you believed in me more than I believed in myself. Thank you for your encouragement.

Lindsay, what a beautiful cover. Talent girl. Thank you for putting on my glasses and seeing my vision.

To Elena, thank you for being a part of my story.

To Chrissy and Miah, you are the reason I am still here, alive and well, and moving forward. You were the seed that gave birth to this story and I love you madly. I am far from being a perfect mother, but I can point you to the One who is perfect and will perfectly use everything in your life to draw you closer to Him. Thank you for your patience with me, your "crew kisses" and your inspiration. You are my sunshine.

To Christ be the glory. I can look back over my years and see His hand in everything. He has held me up, rocked me when I was weary, and loved me when I needed him most. We come undone, but God puts all things back together again. I'm just a beggar willing to tell another beggar where I found the bread.

www.ingramcontent.com/pod-product-compliance
Lightning Source LLC
Chambersburg PA
CBHW030820310726
48980CB00006B/572/J
9780578187280